THE ACCIDENTAL POPE

ST. MARTIN'S PRESS 𝄢 NEW YORK

THE ACCIDENTAL POPE

RAYMOND FLYNN AND ROBIN MOORE

THE ACCIDENTAL POPE. Copyright © 2000 by Raymond Flynn and Robin Moore. All rights reserved. Printed in the United States of America. No part of this book may be used or reproduced in any manner whatsoever without written permission except in the case of brief quotations embodied in critical articles or reviews. For information, address St. Martin's Press, 175 Fifth Avenue, New York, N.Y. 10010.

www.stmartins.com

Book design by Victoria Kuskowski

Library of Congress Cataloging-in-Publication Data

Flynn, Raymond.
    The accidental pope / Raymond Flynn and Robin Moore. —
1st ed.   p.   cm.
    ISBN 0-312-26801-7
    1. Catholic Church—Clergy—Fiction.   2. Ex-priests, Catholic—
Fiction.   3. Popes—Election—Fiction.   4. Cape Cod (Mass.)—
Fiction.   5. Vatican City—Fiction.   6. Fishers—Fiction.
I. Moore, Robin.   II. Title.

PS3556.L897 A66 2000
813'.54—dc21   00-031763

10 9 8 7 6 5 4 3 2

AUTHORS' NOTE

If the following story at first seems implausible, the authors refer you to the original. Sometimes history has a way of repeating itself.

LUKE 5

One day as Jesus was preaching on the shore of the Sea of Galilee, great crowds pressed in on him to listen to the word of God. He noticed two empty boats at the water's edge, for the fishermen had left them and were washing their nets. Stepping into one of the boats Jesus asked Simon, its owner, to push it out into the water. So he sat in the boat and taught the crowds from there.

When he had finished speaking he said to Simon, "Now go out where it is deeper and let down your nets, and you will catch many fish."

"Master," Simon replied, "we worked hard all last night and didn't catch a thing but if you say so we will go out again. And this time their nets were so full they began to tear. A shout for help brought their partners in the other boat and soon both boats were filled with fish and on the verge of sinking.

When Simon Peter realized what had happened he fell on his knees before Jesus and said, "Oh, Lord, please leave me—I'm too much of a sinner to be around you." For he was awestruck by the size of their catch, as were the others with him. His partners, James and John, the sons of Zebedee, were also amazed.

Jesus replied to Simon, "Don't be afraid! From now on you'll be fishing for people!" And as soon as they landed they left everything and followed Jesus.

Later Jesus addressed the fisherman, Matthew 16:18.

"And I say also unto thee, That thou art Peter, and upon this rock I will build my church; and the gates of hell shall not prevail against it."

And so Peter, the married fisherman, became the first leader or pope of the Catholic Church.

THE CONCLAVE 1

At the turn of the third millennium, in the year 2000, the college of cardinals in Rome, following the funeral of the pope and Novemdiales, in this case a fifteen-day period of mourning and reflection, convened to elect a new pope.

The soft drizzle of rain settling on the cobblestones in front of the magnificent, recently renovated Basilica of St. Peter's reflected the somber mood that had fallen over the city, and indeed much of the world, with the passing of this pope. Despite the weather, eighty thousand people had gathered in front of St. Peter's for the opening of the conclave, literally meaning, "locked in with a key." The crowd had been growing since dawn to wish the princes of the Church Godspeed, to pray with them, and to witness the spectacle of the cardinals, each one in his splendid robes, arriving one by one for the serious business of electing the next successor to St. Peter.

Seated with the diplomatic corps inside the basilica, a masterpiece of the Italian Renaissance under the dome of Michelangelo, Edward Kirby, United States ambassador to the Vatican, took in the colorful proceedings, his wife, Catherine, at his side. Except for daughter Maureen, the Kirby children were all back at school or at their jobs in their father's native Chicago, where he had been mayor until the president had offered him this irresistibly prestigious diplomatic post.

When the news of the pope's death had reached the State Department, they had pushed Kirby to give them the inside track on just who the next pope would be. The question was impossible to answer. When pressed, Ed laughingly replied, "Look, my father's not mayor here. I can't rig the election and guarantee who the winner will be." It was an obvious reference to the old "ward boss" Chicago days of big-city politics where "vote early and often" was the common greeting of politicians and their constituencies.

Kirby was a zealous jogger whose clear eyes, lean face, trim stature, and universally respected work ethic belied an undeserved reputation in the hostile Chicago press for excessive consumption of wine and beer. He had been devastated at the death of Pope John Paul II, whom he profoundly admired. His relationship with the pope had been close and personal. He was cordial with every one of the cardinals likely to be Supreme

Pontiff. With the possible exception of two or three, none of them inspired him to want to stay on in his Vatican assignment. But Kirby recognized himself as the man most qualified to conduct business between the world's most powerful political figure, the president of the United States, and the planet's most important moral voice, the pope.

When he was mayor of Chicago, he was regarded as the champion of working families, and also a fighter for economic justice and human rights in Northern Ireland, South Africa, and, for that matter, many areas of the world. He was an active member of Opus Dei (God's Work), a disciplined, conservative, and often mysterious organization within the Catholic Church, of which the deceased pontiff had been a staunch supporter. Nevertheless, it was an organization the U.S. government considered at the very least secretive, at the worst sinister.

Ed had known Pope John Paul II for several years before he ascended to the pontificate. While mayor, Ed was a strong supporter of Solidarity, the outlawed labor movement in Poland, and an ardent opponent of Soviet Communism. Born in a mostly Polish neighborhood of his city, Ed knew Polish culture and traditions well. In this same neighborhood he had first met the then–archbishop of Krakow, later Pope John Paul II, at the Church of Our Lady of Czestochowa. Ed Kirby had been termed the "Lech Walesa of American politics" by respected newspaper columnist Peter Lucas because of his populist, pro-working-family image.

When Kirby's oldest son had become clinically depressed, shortly after his father's appointment to the Vatican, it was the Holy Father who privately offered support, prayers, and comfort. He even offered to help pay the family's astronomical hospital bills. Kathy Kirby told a close friend, "If it weren't for the kind words of support from the Holy Father, Ed probably would have gone into depression himself." At the onset of his son's illness, he had been under great pressure because of unfounded accusations of campaign irregularities, assertions leaked for political reasons to ever-hostile reporters by reckless state prosecutors.

With all these considerations and memories, the present ambassador could not see himself, nor did he want to become, attached to yet another pontiff.

To the astonishment of the spectators, as the princes of the Church left St. Peter's Basilica where they had celebrated Mass and were on their way to the Sistine Chapel to elect a new pope, the rain stopped and the Italian sun came out. The crowd and diplomatic guests smiled and nodded at this sign from above that would ensure God's blessing.

Brian Cardinal Comiskey of Ireland, a relatively young prince of the

Church at age fifty-five, tall, athletic, with reddish hair and a youthful face, was one of several members of the college of cardinals publicly mentioned to succeed to the throne of St. Peter. He had been elevated to primate of all Ireland and archbishop of Armagh by the late pope because of his achievements and courage in helping bring a degree of moderation to Ireland's troubles between Catholics and Protestants. He was an early advocate of the Good Friday Peace Accord and spoke out often for the power-sharing government of Catholics and Protestants in Northern Ireland.

Ambassador Kirby, watching the parade of cardinals in their red robes and sashes and tri-cornered red birettas on their heads, resolved that should Brian (against all odds) be chosen, he would consider asking the president to reappoint him to the Vatican post. After the presidential election the White House, realizing that it was weakest with the Catholic vote, had sent Kirby to the Vatican. Ed caught Brian's eye as the cardinal walked by, and the two men smiled and nodded familiarly to each other.

The most logical choice of successor to St. Peter's throne, however, was the *carmelengo,* or chairman of the conclave, Eugenio Cardinal Robitelli, Vatican secretary of state under the deceased pope. Scion of a noble Roman family, the tall and ascetic cardinal with flashing black eyes emanated the aura of a medieval city-state prince and reminded some historians of the noble Borgias.

Augustine Cardinal Motupu, the most prominent African serving the Church throughout much of the "Dark Continent," represented the liberal wing of the college of cardinals; some even called it the left wing. Motupu was a leader respected throughout Africa and by people of all persuasions. His forceful personality, wide smile, and inclination to question many of the established traditions of Rome with apparent impunity promoted wide speculation by the media, as well as within the Church hierarchy, that many traditional Church leaders had been fearful of him. It seemed certain that the six black cardinals would back his election to the papacy, and many European cardinals spoke highly of him because of his evident sincerity. Ed Kirby's eyes narrowed as the short and rotund Pasquale Cardinal Monassari passed by, smiling and in animated chatter with the others. Known as "Patsy" to his intimates among a following of New York, Chicago, and Roman penumbral financial speculators, Monassari enjoyed powerful support as a result of the control he exercised over the Institute for Religious Works, better known as the Vatican Bank.

Patsy had been close to a previous custodian of the financial institution, suspected by Scotland Yard agents of what appeared to be a friendly association with questionable business characters connected to smuggling cocaine into London via Sicily and North Africa. These two Italian business confederates were later found to be using counterfeit bonds engraved by international Mafia craftsmen to secure a large loan from the bank.

From his Chicago contacts and the persistent street rumors, Ed Kirby believed it was only a matter of time before Cardinal Monassari and his underworld acquaintances would be implicated in another such scam.

Ladbrokes, the London betting consortium, gave the highest chances for election to Robitelli. Emma, the affable owner and waitress at the small restaurant Osteria dell'Aquila, in Trastevere, also predicted that based on what she heard in her popular restaurant, which was frequented by many Vatican officials, Robitelli was a sure winner. Vatican observers often said, "If you want to know what's going on in the Church, talk to Emma. She knows everything."

The unique circumstance of this conclave, made much of by the record number of journalists covering the Vatican, was a single statistic no one had overlooked. There were 120 members of the college of cardinals under eighty years of age and thus eligible to vote, the precise number stipulated by Pope Paul VI in his 1975 Romano Pontifici Eligendo (The Election of the Roman Pontiff). Expert observers sensed a quick decision.

The one voice most popular on the TV shows was that of Father Ron Farrell. An American, he was a sociologist by bent and skilled at getting to the bottom-line feelings of ordinary people. He was a frequent self-appointed Vatican spokesperson and envoy to the four corners of the world. Farrell was good copy; he could discuss people, analyze situations, and describe the religious controversies behind them, and, in the words of a famous baseball announcer, "He comes across as exciting and immediate as the seventh game of the World Series."

"History is being made! A moral battle for the soul of the Catholic Church is going on behind these walls," Farrell announced to the TV audience, pointing to the Vatican, where as he put it, "the world's most exclusive men's club—the college of cardinals—is meeting behind locked doors within the Sistine Chapel. Soon the princes of the Church will elect the two hundred and sixty-fifth pontiff in the Catholic Church's two-thousand-year history, after Jesus Christ himself named St. Peter to be his vicar, his rock on earth, and commanded him to build his Church." Farrell knew what the media wanted to hear, and he was always ready to accommodate, particularly since the exposure shamelessly promoted his racy, Church-based novels.

Perhaps it was unfair for a member of the curia, the Vatican bureaucracy, to call him a shameful self-promoter. It was obvious that many envied his friendship with the press. "He's good copy and gives us red meat," said a CNN spokesperson.

Perhaps the only absolute fact to emerge out of the guessing game played by the media and churchmen alike was the conclusion drawn by the highly respected CBS anchorman Don Mather. After seemingly endless interviews and discussions he concluded, "We really have no idea what will happen and what surprises may be sprung at that conclave, once the doors are closed and those men of God take on the awesome responsibility of electing the leader of the Roman Catholic Church throughout the world. As for front runners, you go in a front runner, you come out a cardinal."

History would prove him more right than he could ever have imagined.

THE FISHERMAN 2

"Dad, come quick," Meghan Kelly shouted excitedly in the direction of the boat dock. "Uncle Brian is on TV. Hurry!" It was six A.M. in the fishing village of Buzzards Bay, Massachusetts, twelve noon on the last day of September in Rome, where most networks were telecasting worldwide the opening of the conclave. The Kelly family was up early to watch the proceedings at the Vatican.

Bill Kelly headed up the long wharf where his fishing trawler was moored. Briskly he mounted the steps up the hill to the home he had, with his own hands, transformed from a Cape Cod cottage into a spreading colonial-style house. Room by room, he had expanded it as his family grew—until a tragic illness took his wife, Mary, from them. As he walked through the front door, his oldest daughter, Colleen, called out, "Look, Dad. There they are all entering the conclave." Her voice took on a slightly scornful edge. "Don't they look just grand in their beautiful colored robes!"

"Hey, Colleen," Roger shouted as his finger touched the TV screen, "there's Uncle Brian near the middle of the bunch. Isn't that him, Dad?"

Bill smiled reminiscently and strode toward the sofa in front of the television set. "Yes, that's him. I'd recognize that ugly mug anywhere."

"Dad," Meghan, the second youngest of his four children, retorted, "Uncle Brian is not ugly. He's a handsome Irishman." Then, after a pause, "Just like you."

As Bill flopped down on the sofa next to Colleen, who seemed bored with the pageantry being telecast from Rome, Meghan squeezed in between them. Roger returned from his side of the TV set to sit on the arm of the sofa by his dad. Colleen turned to scold him. "Roger, get off. You'll break it."

Bill reached an arm out and wrapped it around his young son. "We'll buy your sister a new one if it breaks."

"I was Roger's age when Mom picked it out at Jordan's Furniture." As Colleen turned back to the TV, the picture was focused in on Father Farrell describing the scene via CBS. "There go the cardinals in all their splendor. Soon the doors will be closed behind them and sealed until a new pope is elected. All are focused on one issue: Whom will they choose to fill the shoes of St. Peter as pope? Only time will tell."

"Dad," Meghan interrupted, "could Uncle Brian ever be elected pope? That would be unreal!"

Bill smiled. "He'd make an excellent one, but that's not likely. Probably be another Italian."

"That's not fair. They always seem to win."

"I don't think we should call it winning. Being pope is a lonely, exacting job. He has to do what's best for a majority of the billion Catholics in the world. But I guess the reason for Italian popes is because there are more Italian cardinals than any others." Bill contemplated his statement. Then, "Sometimes an outsider does get elected. They've come up with at least one surprise over the last four centuries. Consider—"

Meghan interrupted her father. "If Brian got elected, could we go to see him?"

"Of course, love. We'd let the two trawlers sit here and rust while we fly off to Italy."

"But he was your classmate at the seminary," Roger argued.

"We all love him," Meghan exclaimed. "I'll bet if he got elected he'd ask us to his coronation."

"Maybe," Bill laughed. "But I'd tell him 'Send the plane tickets with the invitation.' Anyhow," he sighed resolutely, "he hasn't got a ghost of a chance, according to all that Farrell has been telling us on TV. It seems the strong favorite is Cardinal Robitelli, Vatican secretary of state. Brian is young for a cardinal and that would go against his being considered, I'm sure. And he's from Ireland."

"What do popes do all day, Dad?" Roger asked.

"I guess they meet lots of people who come to visit them so as to check up on what's going on in the thousands of Churches in the world." Bill ruffled his son's hair. "Get ready for school."

"Dad, we want to watch Uncle Brian," the boy replied.

"The Vatican news is almost over, boy! Brian is locked tight in the conclave and can't get out till they elect a new pope. So get ready to have breakfast. You too, Meghan."

As the two teens went to their rooms, Bill turned to Colleen, who was trying hard to replace her mother as the woman of the house. "Hey, young lady, do you have a big school day ahead?"

"College, Dad," Colleen corrected her father. "Second year at the community, remember?" Bill nodded. "Dad, have you and Ryan got your nets fixed yet?"

"They'll do for the next fishing trip. I have more darn repair knots in the net than original ones!" He smiled at his daughter. "How about some breakfast?"

She stood up. "Breakfast will be ready by seven o'clock. Waffles, bacon, and in honor of the Vatican, cappuccino!"

"Wow! To what do I owe all this special service?"

"Well, you're still a close friend of God through Uncle Cardinal Brian." Colleen gestured toward the TV set. "So I have to be nice to you—just in case there really is a God in heaven." She had taken to obliquely criticizing dependence on religious faith.

Bill repressed the slight frown that threatened his face. He and the children had all been devastated by Mary Kelly's death from cancer three years earlier and it had affected them in different ways. Colleen had been particularly close to her mother, and the loss had instilled in her a deep sense of desertion by God. Since the funeral she had stopped going to Mass, and Bill never pressed her on the matter.

Colleen left the room for the kitchen. "Bring it in here," he called after her. "I'll watch a bit of the TV special on the conclave just to see if Brian is in any of it." She soon returned with a tray and placed it in his lap, then sat down beside him.

"Thanks, Colleen. Looks delicious." He began to devour it.

"Will you stop for lunch in town?" she asked.

"Nah, too much repair work to do. Remember, I'm leaving at six-thirty tonight. We've got to be out on the banks at sunrise tomorrow or the fish will swim away."

"But you've got to eat! We want you to stay healthy—so us kids can keep taking all your money."

"Sure you do. So I'm thirty thousand in debt right now."

"Don't worry, Dad." She smiled encouragingly. "You'll make it. You always do. And just think, Ryan will handle the captain's job in a year. Won't you be proud of him then? Imagine, my brother, only twenty-one years old and captain of his own boat! Incidentally, I heard Captain Charlie is sick and can't go out on this trip. Did you find someone?"

Bill looked at her sheepishly. "Yes, as a matter of fact, I did. Meant to tell you. His name is Ryan!"

"Dad, you didn't! You said yourself he needs time to season. He's barely three years out of high school."

"Times are tough, Colleen. One less captain's pay will help us considerably, and I think Ryan will do OK. I noticed last trip that I shouted at him very seldom. I was reminded of the time I asked my dad when I would get to captain a boat and he said, 'when I have to shout at you half as much as I do now—I'll think about it.' "

Bill nodded and smiled at his reminiscence. "It's true Ryan is just twenty-one, but my God, he's six foot four, weighs two hundred twenty-five pounds, and could wrestle a lion."

"I guess he takes after his father," Colleen laughed.

"In any case, I did tell our mate, Manny, to keep an eye on him. We'll be back in three or four days with a boatload."

"Mom said you didn't make captain until you were thirty-eight."

"Ten years trying to be a good priest didn't help make a seaman of me."

"Hey, look, Dad!" Colleen exclaimed. "There's Uncle Brian on TV again!"

"Yes, yes," Bill replied. "That's an old repeat from after the funeral. They must be running out of new material."

"You were close, weren't you? Mom always said he was your closest friend at the seminary."

"Yes, we were buddies, you could say. Had a lot of fun together."

She caught the glow in his eyes as he spoke. "Dad, do you miss being a priest? Are you sorry you have four kids on your hands?"

He looked back with a steady gaze. "No, I wouldn't trade my years with your mom and you kids for anything." He paused thoughtfully. "Naturally, there are some feelings of guilt for going back on a commitment, but I know Christ has washed away my failure in his own blood. If I have a faraway look, it is directed at Brian. Imagine...a cardinal of the Church! He could do anything." Bill paused, suddenly remembering how talk of religion could upset his daughter. He laughed. "Except hit an inside curve ball."

"What do you mean?"

"Just that. I was in my sophomore year when he came out for the baseball team." Bill stared at the cardinal answering questions on the TV screen. "He was good at anything when he put his mind to it. He'd never played baseball in Ireland, just soccer, and we didn't have a soccer team. But he worked hard and finally became a dandy second baseman and pretty good with the bat, but he always had trouble with the curve!"

Bill glanced at Colleen and chuckled at her look of relief now that he was away from the subject of religion. "I reminded him of that when he was made bishop...just to keep him humble!"

Colleen laughed. "That's sweet. He owes you one."

"I never thought of it that way. How are your college classes coming?"

"I have a makeup exam today on Renaissance art. Missed it last week. We had a birthday party for Roger, remember? Where's Ryan?"

"Good lad. Already on the boat."

Bill finished his breakfast and walked across the living room to look out the window at the fisherman's cove below his home. His thoughts wandered once again to seminary days and to Brian. He had always been impressed with Brian's resolve. It had inspired him after his original enthusiasm at hearing God's call to the priesthood weakened, whereas Brian's only intensified. Bill's father had accepted his son's announcement that he was joining the priesthood with little joy. He had been counting on Bill to join him in the fishing business. However, the more the elder Kelly visited his son in the atmosphere of the seminary, the greater his understanding of Bill's spiritual aspirations grew.

Brian Comiskey often spent his vacations and holidays with the Kellys and soon became one of the family. After their ordinations, Brian was sent to Rome for advanced study, and, following completion of his doctoral thesis, he was assigned to the Pontifical Institute for Justice and Peace, an important Vatican agency dealing with various worldwide humanitarian concerns of the Church. After completing his first four-year tour, Brian wanted out of the Vatican and out of Rome. He petitioned for and was assigned to a parish and a part-time professorship at Maynooth University in Ireland.

Bill Kelly had found himself teaching at a prestigious parochial high school in San Francisco but got bored and was transferred to various parishes in the Boston area. He found them interesting enough but far from the challenge he had set for himself as a missionary in some developing nation. High-strung and energetic, Bill felt increasingly frustrated and unfulfilled by the unending routines of the parishes.

In the fifth year Bill was assigned to an old Irish pastor in a predominantly Portuguese immigrant community on Cape Cod. Although a big tourist area in the summer, it was quiet the rest of the year. Here he was near his family, yet kept routinely busy in his parish, where he built a playground for immigrant children and learned to speak Portuguese. Then, as fate would have it, his old pastor sent to Ireland for a niece to act as his housekeeper.

Mary was then a lovely colleen of eighteen. For three years the youthful priest and vivacious Irish lass, together on almost a daily basis, struggled to resist their natural, almost fierce attraction to each other. But when Bill finally, impulsively swept her into his arms and kissed her, he was crushed by his own weakness and confused by the sheer power of his emotional upheaval. He drove to see his superiors in Boston, finally asking for their assistance in releasing him from his vows so he could get married. The shock to the family when he told them he was departing the priesthood was almost as devastating as when he had told them he was entering it.

He asked Mary if she would consider marrying him when he received his dispensation. Overjoyed, Mary repeated the thrilling proposal to her uncle. Being a priest of the old school, he was affronted and immediately sent her packing back to Ireland. A letter in which her uncle painted an evil picture of the situation, far worse than the innocent facts warranted, prefaced Mary's arrival at home. Mary was not welcomed with open arms. Lost and adrift, she wrote to Bill for help. The day Bill received the letter, he called his old classmate, Brian.

Soon he learned how close the two men still were despite the separation of time and distance. Brian, already a monsignor, found Mary a job in one of his parish schools and kept Bill informed of her activities.

After a year and a half of waiting, Bill's dispensation finally arrived and he flew to Ireland to bring Mary home to Cape Cod. They went somewhat fearfully to the pastor at the local church on the Cape. He too was older and Bill feared the worst. But when the priest told them that they could plan a wedding in two months, their fears were turned to tears of joy. "A certain priest friend of yours named Brian Comiskey has been in touch with me," their pastor mentioned. "He will be coming over here to perform the wedding ceremony. Let him know the date."

That thoughtfulness and care sealed the bond between the two men forever. Brian later came to baptize three of their four children. He regularly spent a week's vacation with them during the summer months. With Mary Kelly's death especially, Uncle Brian completed the Kelly family circle. But even Brian had been unable to reason with the grieving Colleen, who refused to believe that if there really was a just God in heaven her mother would have died and left them.

Bill turned from the window to go down to the docks. It was the last week of September. He could hardly help wondering what his famous friend was doing inside Vatican City. Undoubtedly, Brian was deep in prayer as he prepared to help select the new leader of the Roman Catholic Church.

CAPPELLA SISTINA 3

While the outside world was kept informed by constant repeats of past TV interviews and stories, the little world behind the conclave doors began to take on its own special character. The official mourning and reflection period over, a sense of excitement tinged with anxiety prevailed as the cardinals filed into specially prepared chambers to begin the process of electing a new pope. The magnificent Sistine Chapel had been meticulously swept for bugs or other electronic devices by two highly trained and trustworthy security technicians.

But even before the Sistine officials had put their security experts to work, two days in advance of the conclave, the cardinals were obliged to swear a solemn oath. Under pain of excommunication, they were forbidden to ever discuss the balloting "either by signs, word, or writings or in any other manner." The cardinals also had to promise and swear "not to use devices designed in any way for taking pictures." It was apparent that Pope Paul VI, who laid down these rules, and Pope John Paul II, who affirmed them, were well acquainted with the foibles and proclivities of the princes of the Roman Catholic Church.

Every cardinal was an individual with his own distinct ideas. Yet together they possessed an esprit de corps similar to that of any body dedicating itself to a distinct purpose. All confessed to one faith and shared one common bond. All believed to the depths of their souls that divine guidance would shape the outcome of their deliberations, come what might, and that they were, each one, chosen specifically by God to select his next representative on earth.

Thus, for these princes of the Church, an intense animation emanated from the very gathering itself. Each was acutely aware that the world outside was awaiting the outcome of this conclave. They were aware also that their decision would have a profound effect not only on the Catholic Church but also on the entire sectarian and even secular world. Their growing apprehension was born of the knowledge that many divisions existed among them. Much time, reflection, and compromising lay ahead before any final decision could be reached. Also, much active politicking.

Although the *carmelengo*, who as the chamberlain of the Holy Roman Church was in charge of the proceedings and was not supposed to be a candidate for the papacy, Robitelli had apparently convinced the deceased pope to appoint him to the position just prior to his death. Thus he was both ruler of the conclave and contender for the election, a position that almost guaranteed him succession to the throne of St. Peter.

Cardinal Robitelli had informed the other assembled cardinals that he would open the first session of voting at three in the afternoon, and precisely at that hour the *carmelengo* struck his gavel on the table before him. He looked out over this group of equals with what seemed a friendly smile. "*Benvenuto al Vaticano.* Dear brothers, you are certainly aware of why we are here. The Holy Spirit will be our guide; therefore, we have nothing to fear. Put yourselves at ease and we will begin the preliminary process of electing three scrutineers, counters and tabulators of the votes," he explained in three languages to ensure that all the cardinals understood the procedure. "And then we go to the first vote."

This brought appreciative chuckles from the assemblage. A raised hand from the African, Augustine Motupu, brought a slight frown of annoyance to Robitelli's brow. Rules of procedure did not permit interruptions; the African was surely aware of this.

"Cardinal Motupu, I see your hand is raised. Is there a problem?"

The black cardinal rose to his feet and cleared his throat nervously. "No, Your Eminence. That is, I don't perceive it as a problem. I just had an idea and would like to address this illustrious group for a moment if I may."

"This is highly irregular, Cardinal Motupu. You received a copy of the rules for this election several days ago."

"Yes, yes, Your Eminence, I read them through. It is in regard to those rules that I wish to speak."

The *carmelengo* was caught so off guard by the statement that he failed to reply immediately to Motupu. The pause was taken as a sign of consent by the African cardinal. "Dear brothers, as you know, I have on occasion in the past requested that the Holy Father review this method of election and perhaps give consideration to an election by acclamation, which has been done in the Church before." A gasp of astonishment, almost a hissing sound, was audible. "I would like—"

The sharp banging of the gavel rang out. Robitelli was now fully recovered and showed marked signs of irritation.

"Dear brother," he interrupted testily, "we are aware of your opinions of concern expressed to our late pope. We are aware also that nothing resulted from them. We must and will proceed according to the process laid down by Pope Paul VI in the year of Our Lord 1975. As *carmelengo* I have both the duty and the authority to run this conclave in that manner. We will commence voting until we have a two-thirds-plus-one majority. With the tragic death of our brother in South America we now have one hundred nineteen voting cardinals. Thus the number of votes necessary to elect a pope is eighty." He nodded to Motupu. "When our new pope is elected, you may take your proposition up with him."

The silence in the room suddenly lay on the gathering like a shroud. Cardinal Motupu felt stripped naked in front of all. Robitelli immediately realized he had allowed impatience to color his demeanor and tried to smooth it over. "I'm sorry if I spoke overly quickly, dear brother. It's merely that...as you can see...this *carmelengo* posture is new to me. I feel I must follow the rules exactly as laid down. Perhaps we can entertain your ideas again afterward, when we have finished the election. There are many ways to elect a pope, as we are all aware from our history. Right now, however, we have a proven method, and we will abide by it until this particular election is over."

Cardinal Motupu slowly seated himself in silence. Robitelli was back in control.

"Let us first elect the three scrutineers." He suggested three cardinals who were immediately elected unanimously. The next order of business was the introduction of the handful of staff allowed to be in the conclave with the voting cardinals. The dean of the college of cardinals was presented, followed by three masters of ceremonies, a clerical assistant to the dean, and two physicians. All had subscribed to the oath of secrecy that each cardinal had solemnly taken.

"This afternoon we will take the first vote of this conclave," Robitelli announced. "Tomorrow morning we will take the second and third. In the afternoon we will cast our fourth and fifth ballots. Each day we will take four votes. If at the end of three days we have not elected a pope we will take a day of prayer and reflection and start again. If at the end of thirty ballots we still have not elected a pope, a simple majority will carry the day."

Robitelli could hardly restrain a smile, knowing that he could almost certainly command a simple majority of the cardinals eligible to vote. "After the ballot is cast this afternoon, we will return to the Domus Sanctae Marthae. In this new hotel within the walls of the Vatican, for the first time in the history of the Church the cardinals will enjoy comfortable rooms with showers and soft beds. If any cardinal is sick during the conclave, his vote can be taken from his room."

Within minutes Robitelli's organizational skills brought everyone in focus and the first vote was taken. Every cardinal had studied the rules of procedure. On a rectangular piece of paper with the words *Eligo in Summum Pontificem* (I choose as Supreme Pontiff) at the top, each voter wrote the name of his choice in disguised handwriting.

The paper was folded twice, and one by one the electors approached the altar. Holding his ballot above a large silver receptacle, each one proclaimed aloud, "I call as my witness Christ the Lord who will be my judge, that my vote is given to the one who before God I think should be elected."

It was well over an hour before the 119 electors present had all cast ballots and returned to their armchairs. The votes were counted by the three cardinal scrutineers, and the choice on each ballot was read aloud to the voters. One of the masters of ceremonies then collected the ballots and burned them, sending the first stream of chemically induced black smoke up the chimney of the Sistine Chapel. The outside world was thus notified that the voting for the next pope was under way.

As expected, the ceremonial first round of balloting brought forth the usual "honorable mention" votes, singling out elderly cardinals with a few votes each in recognition for their contributions to Vatican and Church affairs. As a cardinal's name was read from the ballot by a scrutineer, he smiled politely and tipped his tri-cornered biretta. Friendly back patting followed the first round of voting and the cardinals, some still suffering from jet lag, gratefully adjourned for supper.

Officially given an evening of prayer and contemplation alone, some used the time lining up votes in closed-door strategy meetings. It would be more accurate to say they began the many clandestine exploratory conferences the moment it was known the pope was dead. These prelates were sincere and willingly swore allegiance to the Holy Father, once elected. They were also practical men ready to do everything in their power to propel and manipulate their own best choice upward toward that uniquely high office.

The next morning at ten, the *carmelengo* needed only a short, friendly address to refocus the group and call for the second mandate. In this polling the cardinals listened intently. Each name was announced by the scrutineer as a ballot was taken from its gleaming repository on the altar. This round of voting produced the names of several cardinals, one of whom would almost surely be elected eventually.

Cardinal Robitelli captured the most, with forty. The Jesuit Scholar from Milan, Cardinal Martini, received twenty-one votes. Cardinal Comiskey of Ireland received fourteen votes, and the African Cardinal Motupu found himself in the pack with a surprising fifteen votes. The German cardinal, Hans Willeman, caught the fancy of eight cardinals; the cardinal from Brazil picking up fifteen votes on this first serious round; and Pasquale "Patsy" Cardinal Monassari garnered six votes in recognition of his financial power with the Vatican Bank.

Since none of the names from the actual first voting appeared on the new list, it was evident now that the honorary vote had served its gratuitous purpose. Accolades had been awarded and gratefully received, and now the real votes were emerging and were posted on a large board. Each cardinal could start judging realistically the chances of his preferred candidate getting elected when the final ballots were cast. There was plenty of time now for thinking, planning, speculating...sometimes out loud. The black smoke curling above the chimney of the Sistine Chapel after each vote made for more and more media attention and intense reviewing of earlier predictions.

The third vote at the end of the morning session confirmed the fact that much deep thinking and politicking had taken place. Only four names now realistically remained. Robitelli with forty-two votes, Motupu with seventeen votes, the cardinal from Milan improved to thirty votes, and Comiskey moved ahead to twenty-two votes with Cardinal Monassari trailing with eight. A curious pattern seemed to be forming that nobody could understand.

Oddly enough, the early afternoon vote yielded the exact same number of votes for the same candidates. Perhaps, the *carmelengo* suggested, a rest period would effect some change? The five o'clock vote confirmed the fact that more than tea and pastries had been digested. Four names now remained in the running, with forty-three for Cardinal Robitelli. Motupu, Comiskey, and Martini almost evenly divided the rest of the votes. Monassari registered an embarrassing single vote.

It seemed certain to all that things were at last progressing. The Holy Spirit and the political process were both at work. Perhaps tomorrow they would finish and they could leave their ornate prison. But the ten A.M. vote was a surprise to many, yielding the same three-way split as on the previous night, with Robitelli only one vote in the lead.

Suppertime had proved helpful during the first two days. Hopefully, it would affect the eight P.M. vote called by the *carmelengo* as well. It did not. The same three cardinals remained the only viable candidates. An obviously concerned Robitelli rose to announce that, as prescribed by the rules, he would adjourn the conclave the next day to celebrate the Mass of the Holy Spirit and then the cardinals would spend the day in quiet meditation, praying for divine guidance.

Outside, Father Farrell was happily, ubiquitously engaged in various TV appearances, explaining to his global audience the significance of the periodic puffs of black smoke in a concise, clear review of the intricacies of the conclave process. His commentary added little to the understanding of the procedure secretly taking place inside, however. But it was obvious that some more or less profound disagreement was festering within the college.

The day of prayer finally over, Cardinal Robitelli observed a greater expression of calm in the faces of the assembled cardinals. He was aware that other meetings had taken place among the three factions. Indeed, he had actually participated in several meetings with his supporters. "God helps him who helps himself," the *carmelengo* firmly believed. But despite the secret (and proscribed) conferences, his expectations were shattered when the morning vote was taken. Robitelli remained the leader, but fell short of the necessary two-thirds-plus-one vote to ascend to the papacy. Comiskey and Motupu were second and third respectively. Nothing had changed.

The *carmelengo* mentally shook his head in disbelief. It was as though the Holy Spirit was attempting to communicate something new and different to the conclave and its leader. What was God trying to tell the assembled cardinals?

"Brothers," he pleaded, "we must move forward. God's work in the world must proceed. The bark of Peter is without a captain. A ship without a captain is a doomed vessel! Please consider our situation and resolve to put aside personal considerations for the sake of the Church. This is why we were called here."

By the sixth day of voting the pall of a crippling depression hung heavily over the conclave. Not one vote had changed. The morning of the seventh day yielded the same results. While no contact outside the conclave could be made, it was more than obvious to all the cardinals that a great deal of anxiety was rising out there regarding the future stability of the Church throughout the world.

At the evening voting session Robitelli noticed a longer moment of prayer as each cardinal knelt before the silver receptacle, casting his vote. His heart lightened as the counters processed the ballots and marked them up on the board. Out of the corner of his wary eye Robitelli had seen Cushman of Boston surreptitiously lean toward the superannuated cardinal next to him, one indeed who was on the borderline of being declared a nonvoting member of the college. The American had scribbled a name on his neighbor's ballot. The *carmelengo*, hoping that this bit of assistance might signify an end to the deadlock, said nothing. But the alert scrutineer, comparing the ballots of Cushman and the somnolent old cleric from Spain, cleared his throat and challenged the American. "Dear brother from across the Atlantic, did you not assist your fellow cardinal in casting his vote?"

Cardinal Cushman grinned sheepishly and nodded forthrightly. "Yes, I confess I assisted our dear brother from Barcelona in the casting of his vote. I wasn't born and brought up in South Boston for nothing." The conclave broke up in laughter. Cushman, the colorful Boston Irishman, was a popular figure within the college of cardinals.

Robitelli realized he must adopt a new strategy if he were to put an end to the crisis. "Brothers," he once more addressed the gathered princes of the Church, "despite my efforts to move this conclave to a conclusion, it must be obvious to all that we are getting nowhere. Therefore, I will bend the rules and ask for some suggestions from the floor." The *carmelengo* sat down and waited to see if this new course would have any effect.

After a two-minute silence that seemed an eternity to most, Comiskey of Ireland rose from his red velvet armchair and raised his hand to be recognized. Robitelli nodded. "Please speak, dear brother."

Cardinal Comiskey cleared his throat and began. "We are all, it seems, in something of a no-win situation. Allow me to agree with the *carmelengo* that we need to interrupt these proceedings and get back on course. I feel some embarrassment speaking to you as a newer, younger member of this esteemed assemblage. But seeing the same sense of frustration reflected in your faces as I feel within myself, I would like to request that my name be withdrawn from consideration to assume the papacy post."

Shouts of "No!" rang out from the group—or at least from his supporters. Cardinal Comiskey raised his hand, motioning for silence. "Thank you for your kindness, dear brothers, but the point I have to make is that this quandary in which we find ourselves reminds me of a similar situation I confronted some ten years ago. Perhaps we can draw a lesson from my experience. May I proceed?"

Murmurs of encouragement sounded from around the chamber. The cardinal nodded and continued. "A few years ago I was visiting a dear friend named Bill Kelly while vacationing on Cape Cod in America. Bill and I had gone to the seminary together in the United States. It was not unusual for Irish novices to be sent to seminaries in America, particularly in Boston, once an Irish enclave. And indeed most of the leadership of the

American Catholic Church for years was Irish-born or first-generation Irish. That's changing, I know, but that's the way it was at the time."

Cardinal Petrocelli of Philadelphia could not restrain a laugh. "We've now had Italian mayors in New York, Boston, San Francisco, and Philadelphia."

Comiskey grinned and bowed his head. The informality that was pervading these somber proceedings, including bringing in the comments of other cardinals, suited the parable he was about to tell the conclave.

"Six of us priests were on a one-day fishing trip at sea with our friend and classmate, now a skilled fishing captain, who stood at the stern of his boat like Peter guiding his bark on the Sea of Galilee. We had a successful trip, each of us catching our share of fish, until a sudden squall came up and, despite Bill's efforts, we were blown onto a large rock just beneath the surface. Our craft began to take on water.

"Bill Kelly quickly turned his boat towards shore and shouted for all of us vacationing priests to start bailing. As we manned the buckets and scoops, trying to bail water out of the boat faster than it was coming through the rent in its hull, one of us priests jokingly, but nervously, demanded, 'When ever did we decide that Bill was captain and the rest of us were crew?'

"We began to show our concern, and Bill called out as he struggled with the tiller, 'Why are you fearful? Still no faith?' He paused. 'Mark four, forty.'" Cardinal Comiskey glanced around the conclave of cardinals, most of them older than he, and determined they were paying attention to his story. "Bill spoke to us sharply as he held the boat on course. 'Gentlemen,' he responded to our chiding, 'may I remind you that if you do not bail like hell there won't be any need for a captain, since there won't be any boat afloat. Follow me, then, and I will keep you fishers of men!'"

Peals of relieved and sudden laughter rippled through the recently renovated Sistine Chapel. Cardinal Comiskey's parable was a welcome diversion, a sudden relaxation from the constant pressures of voting. The laughter died down and the younger cardinal turned serious. "Following Bill Kelly's orders we finally made it to shore and beached the leaking boat. Bill jumped ashore. As captain, he drew us priests in a circle. All of us stood holding hands as he thanked God and Our Lady of Good Voyage for our deliverance and indeed the salvation of our own lives." Once again Cardinal Comiskey paused, savoring the rapt attention of his Vatican peers. "I am harboring the same concern that Bill Kelly, in a symbolic way, expressed to us priests on that day. Our mission, our only duty, is to ensure the preservation of Peter's bark. Above all else, the Church itself has to stay afloat and on course. That's why I ask that my name be withdrawn."

Cardinal Comiskey fixed on one cardinal after another with an explicit glance. "We all, dear brothers, must realize that although our beloved Savior has promised to be with us till the end of time, he has left us responsible for determining who his representative here will be." The Irish cardinal had prowled about the chamber as he delivered his brief but moving homily, and he now walked back and took his seat amid enthusiastic applause. His fellow cardinals were obviously deeply impressed by the passion and sincerity of this newer member of their assemblage who had displayed such wisdom beyond his years.

The sharp crack of the gavel, as Robitelli rose with a smile on his lean face, silenced the approving undertones. "Your point appears to be more than well taken, Cardinal Comiskey." Then, to the entire council, "We must, dear brothers, display greater concern for the fact that we are responsible for the bark of Peter. And though we may cling to sharp differences over who may be the right choice, let us consider that, as Cardinal Comiskey's friend Bill Kelly aptly put it, there won't be a captain if the boat sinks. So please pray and search your hearts as we prepare for our next balloting tomorrow morning. Sleep well and let the Holy Spirit inspire and direct your dreams." He rapped his gavel and winked at a close associate as they turned to leave the chamber. He felt his tact had carried the evening, that he had done his duty as *carmelengo*, and that perhaps by the next morning, finally, he would be duly elected pope.

By seven-thirty the following morning, all members of the conclave had finished their light breakfast of sweet cornetta rolls, fruit, and cappuccino, and celebrated Mass either individually or in small groups. As they filed into the Sistine Chapel for the morning balloting, Robitelli studied their faces, trying to read their thoughts. He was not the only cardinal playing mind games. Other brains had been spinning all night in the same manner. The scarcely concealed undercurrent was apparent. *You change your views to agree with mine and everything will work out according to God's ordinance.*

Robitelli, remembering previous conclaves, quickly grasped the undertone pervading the room that morning. He sighed to himself as he sat down to prepare for the vote, and he prayed and expected that today would be the last day of the conclave, wondering if Comiskey's little story yesterday had made a lasting impression. It had occurred to him in a dream—or perhaps a vision that came to him in the middle of the night—that in any case he had an opportunity to make an impact on the entire assembly, one that might make them reconsider their positions and allow the Holy Spirit to do his work.

This must have been an inspiration sent to me from the Holy Spirit himself, Robitelli thought, knowing he could never have conceived of it on his own. *I'll cast my symbolic vote for Comiskey's fishing captain, Kelly! One vote only, but it will shock everyone so severely that they will be forced to recall that story and make more serious efforts to shift their positions.*

Everyone noticed the strange smile playing across Robitelli's lips as he called for the morning vote. Brian Comiskey read it as a smirk and thought to himself, *I can't believe it, he's laughing at my story about Bill Kelly! Well, I'll show him! I'll cast my vote for Bill and shake up the place! A perfect protest vote, and then we can move on to a more serious ballot.*

Cardinal Motupu also read the smile and thought about it. The other cardinals studied it also, drawing their own conclusions as to what was going on in Robitelli's mind and what they could or should do to counter his "scheme." All of them had relived Comiskey's parable of Bill Kelly during the night.

Each cardinal approached the altar, folded his ballot in two, and repeated the election proclamation as he cast it into the magnificent silver collection receptacle.

An ineffable sense of calm settled over the group. The wry smile originally detected on Robitelli's face appeared on the countenances of many more cardinals. All sat down and watched while the vote scrutineers moved the receptacle to the designated area before the *carmelengo* and began counting again. Most leaned forward to watch the chief vote counter, Cardinal Laventu, unfold the first ballot as he walked toward the posting board. Suddenly he stopped in his tracks and paused, a shocked expression on his face. He cleared his throat and glanced at the *carmelengo*, then at the other cardinals. Finally he reached for the marker and announced as he wrote, "One vote for...Bill Kelly!" A pause, then laughter burst from the assembly as the faces of many displayed revelry in the vote!

Cardinal Laventu was handed a second ballot. He stared at it in disbelief, raised his marker, and put a second slash mark beside the name of Bill Kelly. More laughter pealed forth. When six more ballots had been opened and chalked up to Bill Kelly, the merriment became more subdued. As the counting continued, some mumbling among the cardinals began to mix with the laughter and smiles. Cardinal Robitelli's name was on the board, also Cardinal Motupu's, and, despite his withdrawal, Cardinal Comiskey's. But the weight of the votes still drifted to the first name on the board. When the counting was completed, a nervous hush descended over the group as they surveyed their handiwork. Bill Kelly: eighty-one votes; Cardinal Robitelli: thirty votes; Cardinal Motupu: five votes; and the remaining three to Comiskey despite his resignation from contention.

Even Robitelli could not avoid laughing with the others as they all sat staring at the election results. Finally he stood up and called for order. "Dear brothers, I'm very glad that what we do in this chamber is confidential." He smiled. "It does warm my heart to see that so many of you were thinking, just as I was when I cast my ballot, that yours would be the only vote for Mr. Kelly." He received a short round of appreciative applause for his forthright confession. "Well, we've certainly had our change of pace," he went on. "Now we must get back to serious business and move this conclave to completion. We shall have another round of voting."

The voice that cut through the voting chamber was calm, firm, and deep. "Brothers, we have a pope." The depth of Cardinal Motupu's words and tone hit the assembled cardinals like a thunderbolt. The startled faces of the assembly turned toward him.

The *carmelengo* rose to confront the black cardinal with an icy stare. "What do you mean, Your Eminence?" Cardinal Robitelli shouted.

"I mean, dear brother"—Motupu returned the frigid glare—"exactly what I said. There is no need for another vote. We have just now elected a pope!"

ONE LESS WITCH DOCTOR 4

The frost in the *carmelengo*'s eyes turned to an ominous glow as the heat of anger rose within him. He recognized with horror the ploy Cardinal Motupu was imposing on the assemblage. It made his stomach churn with pain as he heard the words he should have anticipated flow from the black cardinal.

"Did you not at the beginning of this gathering, Your Excellency, remind me most sternly that we were to follow the rules of the procedure laid down by Pope Paul VI? Those rules state that a two-thirds majority, plus one, elects the new pope. William Kelly received the necessary votes. He is the pope."

"Are you insane?" the *carmelengo* returned. "We can all see that what happened here was a mistake made by many of us in a supreme moment of levity, a stupid joke."

"It may have been a joke, dear brother," Motupu replied, "but if rules are rules, then it was God's own joke! We are his representatives. We have made his choice! The Church is Christ's creation, not ours."

The *carmelengo*'s face was flushed as he recognized the firmness of purpose chiseled on the dark features of Cardinal Motupu. He knew there would be no backing down now. He had seen that expression once before on this man's face when, as Vatican secretary of state, Robitelli had been sent by the pope to visit the newly elected cardinal in Africa, a member of the Ibo tribe. That visit flashed through the *carmelengo*'s mind now as he stood nervously trying to collect his wits in defense of his stand. He felt the late pope had made Motupu a cardinal only to satisfy the clamor of the growing and already large and powerful African branch of the Church that had long been insisting on representation in the college of cardinals.

Motupu was but fifty years old and, in the minds of many in Rome, totally unfit for such a lofty position. But the pope had buckled under the people's pressure and selected Motupu as one reflecting African feelings and traditions. Motupu was a powerful advocate of tribal customs ranging from prescribing herbal medicine to pounding tom-toms in church and wearing tribal robes at Mass in place of the standard vestments. He had also been an unyielding proponent of more democratic and less hidebound ways to elect popes and had made public statements to that effect without permission. It was at that point that the pope had sent Cardinal Robitelli to try to persuade the new cardinal to take a more guarded approach and to discuss such weighty concerns with Rome before going public on any issue. It was important for Motupu to understand the big picture, not just local, isolated issues. His provincialism was attributed to lack of experience in the traditions of the Church and his rather limited background in theology and international politics...at least as far as Rome was concerned.

When Cardinal Robitelli had finally sat down to talk to the African prelate, he was jolted by the large picture that hung on the wall behind Motupu's desk—Michael Jordan of the Chicago Bulls slam-dunking a basketball. He also had a photo of his nephew, who played basketball for Wake Forest University in North Carolina. The Vatican secretary of state had smiled bleakly at the recently elevated cardinal and commented, "Most of us usually hang a picture of Our Savior or of the Holy Father behind our desks, dear brother. May I ask why you have that picture hanging there?"

"I love to witness God in his handiwork," Motupu had replied. And thus began a long history of flawed communications.

The *carmelengo*'s thoughts were abruptly snapped back to reality by the brilliant Cardinal Willeman, who was among the older cardinals in the conclave. "Dear brothers, I feel I must put an end to this whole issue. It seems you have all forgotten some of your Church history. If I may remind you, in both the eleventh and twelfth centuries, when the papacy was going through its most difficult times, the Church passed some laws that are still in effect today. A layperson cannot be elected to the papacy! That is that!" Quietly, smugly, he seated himself.

The *carmelengo* breathed a sigh of relief and quickly reiterated the German cardinal's dictum. "Why, yes, yes. Now I do recall that." He turned slightly toward Cardinal Motupu and continued. "There, you see, my dear brother, how it was all a joke to us. But we all do appreciate your concern for the rules of order."

The black cardinal could not miss the coldness in this left-handed admonition as he sank back into his chair. The *carmelengo* continued. "Now, dear brothers, if there is no further concern, we will adjourn."

"Your Eminence, please!"

The *carmelengo* looked up to see Cardinal Comiskey standing in his place. "I'm afraid we do have a slight problem here."

"What do you mean?" the *carmelengo* retorted.

Cardinal Comiskey blushed slightly and cleared his throat. "Well, you see...Bill Kelly is a priest. I mean..." The cardinal stuttered, searching for the right words. "He was ordained with me. A few years later he just went the way some of our brothers have done and continue to do. He applied to the Church for a dispensation to become a layman, then left the Church to get married. But, as is pronounced at our ordination, '*Tu es sacredos in aeternum,*' 'You are a brother for eternity,' meaning once a priest always a priest. In fact, his lovely wife, Mary, passed away several years ago from cancer. She suffered and fought it so gallantly."

Dead silence greeted the cardinal's assertion. Then Cardinal Motupu again took to his feet. "We must therefore offer the papacy to Mr. Kelly. I will not vote again until that is done. It is my belief that God has already made his choice through us. Besides, any one of us can reinstate him as a priest by canon law, as I read it."

Just as he thought this awkward matter had been settled, the *carmelengo* felt circumstances getting out of hand again. His anger suddenly rose again as he felt this black upstart was seeking only to humiliate him by insisting on such an outlandish procedure. At the same time, deep inside himself he realized that he had laid the foundation for the problem by his own need to keep control of the proceedings and do everything by the rules laid down by Vatican II. He felt his stomach tightening with his own guilt and anger. He must control his ire, he knew, and might have succeeded had he not continued to behold the smoldering eyes of his African adversary. Never had he been confronted with such a hostile stare.

Cardinal Robitelli felt his years of training, discipline, and prayer dissipate in the face of the unrelenting defiance that emanated from Motupu's countenance and bearing. "Well," the *carmelengo* heard himself spewing forth, "I guess we can get along with one less witch doctor's vote...." He tried to halt the words that had escaped his quivering lips, but it was too late. Five other black cardinals in the conclave rose almost as one. Robitelli realized, as he stood before these six black princes of the Church, that he had permanently lost control. There was no rule or regulation to cover this horrible situation. His legs suddenly went weak. Even the anger that had seized him evaporated. He collapsed into his chair, head down. Silence settled on the group. It was an eerie spectacle. Some cardinals sat staring into space. Others were fingering rosary beads or reaching for the crosses they wore, heads lowered, eyes closed. The six black cardinals continued to stand at attention, eyes fixed on the chastened *carmelengo*. A perplexed Cardinal Comiskey slowly rose from his seat and walked over to stand in front of his friend Cardinal Moputu.

"Dear brother," the Irish cardinal began, "I realize by the letter of the law that you are right, but I humbly beseech you to reconsider and back down from your position."

Cardinal Motupu turned slightly to look into the eyes of the other five black cardinals who stood with him. A look passed between them that could be understood only by those who were a part of their culture. In mere seconds Motupu had read the "high fives" in the eyes of his brothers. He turned his eyes back to his friend, Cardinal Comiskey. "Sorry, my friend. It has been our experience that 'spear chuckers' who back down tend to end up in bondage a second time!"

The young cardinal winced as he lowered his eyes. "I understand," he muttered.

"No, you don't," was the gentle reply.

Best to leave that one alone, Comiskey thought.

At that point, Hans Cardinal Willeman stood and asked to speak. No objection was offered. "Dear brothers, may I offer some advice? We seem to have opened our mouths and put our collective foot in it. However, there is no problem we face that cannot be resolved if we all agree to sit here and work it out together. Can we do that? In the name of our beloved Savior, whom we all wish to serve? If anyone is opposed to working it out, raise your hand and speak."

No one moved. "Good," the German cardinal said. "It is still early in the day. Let us solve our problem forthwith."

The Church had been through many problems as thorny as this in its long history and had risen to the occasion. Some of the solutions had risen to the sublime. Some sank to the ridiculous. Perhaps this one would come down somewhere in between: sublimely ridiculous, or vice versa.

THE SOLUTION 5

To the surprise of the assembly, Robitelli, trying desperately to regain his credibility, suggested that the proceedings had taken a bizarre turn and a new effort was required to get the conclave back on a normal course. Perhaps another cardinal should be appointed temporarily as *carmelengo*. Robitelli suggested that his loyal supporter, Cardinal Willeman, be chosen. The notion was greeted with subdued yeas and nods. There was no doubt the German cardinal was loved, or at least respected, by all. When he opened the meeting it was evident that Willeman had done more than merely pray.

"Dear brothers," Cardinal Willeman began, "I have made some notes for discussion, most of which, I think, can be carried out by a simple raising of hands. There is no doubt that many of us voted for Mr. Kelly as a gesture to reinforce Cardinal Comiskey's excellent point. Now, how many of you believed that a layperson could not be elected to the chair of Peter?" Forty-one hands were raised. Cardinal Willeman nodded. "Then we can conclude that there was no intention of electing a pope by a majority of the people in this room. We are also aware that the first vote we took in this conclave was a straw vote based on long tradition. We voted not for a pope but rather to show our deep respect for years of service on the part of certain of our older colleagues."

Willeman paused to let the statement have an effect, then continued. "Now, we have learned from Cardinal Comiskey that the man we voted for was once an active priest. Therefore, it seems evident that according to the rules of the conclave, he was officially elected pope, and unless someone can prove otherwise, he has to be offered the Chair of Peter."

The cardinal of Great Britain raised his hand to speak. "I can't understand, Your Eminence, why this should be so if, as you say, so many of us voted without an intention of electing the man—someone we don't even know, or wish to consider—as pope."

Cardinal Willeman smiled along with the rest of the assembly. "That is an interesting point, dear brother, but may I point out that many of us assembled here who have been part of past conclaves have voted for someone without any intention of electing him pope...only to move votes away from someone else. That goes on all the time. Even when we do elect a pope, I'm sure you will agree, many cardinals are not inwardly happy with the outcome. So we have no rule to fall back on against or for the argument that we did not mean that the person we voted for should become pope!"

After a moment Cardinal Mederios of Portugal raised his hand and at the chairman's nod stood up to speak. "This may be a little premature, but before we make a decision on this issue, we should find out just who Bill Kelly is. Perhaps Cardinal Comiskey could tell us something about him?"

A round of applause and laughter supported this suggestion. Comiskey rose again to face the conclave. "I guess I owe all of you that much, but I'll be very brief. Bill and I went through seminary together, and he was ordained with me. I was sent home to Ireland to teach at the university after studying for a time in Rome and serving here at Justice and Peace. Bill taught at a parochial school for boys in California and later he was sent back to a small parish in Massachusetts."

Comiskey paused, his eyes fixing on Cardinal Mederios. "It will interest the cardinal from Portugal to know that Father Bill Kelly went to great effort to learn the Portuguese language and conduct year-round activities for the young Portuguese immigrant children in the parishes of southeastern Massachusetts and Cape Cod. As has happened to other priests, he fell in love and asked to be laicized. He returned to his family home on Cape Cod to work with his father on their fishing boats and has been happy in that trade for twenty-odd years. After he received his dispensation from Rome he married an Irish girl named Mary, who, as I said, has since passed on. They have four children..." He paused momentarily and then added, "Oh, yes, to answer an implicit question none of you have asked, I think that if he was to be informed that he had been elected pope, he would laugh his guts out and tell us all to go jump in the Tiber River."

Cardinal Comiskey looked about the group. "He is a devout Catholic, but Church matters of this scale would either intimidate him or strike him as a big joke...as foolish as our big joke here. Any more questions?"

Cardinal Mederios thanked him after the mumbling and puzzled laughter had died down. As silence enshrouded the group again, Cardinal Willeman moved the meeting forward. "Well, as I see it, brothers, we have dug our own grave. If, as the *carmelengo* pointed out and we all knew from the first day, we have, by the rules, elected a legitimate pope, then we must inform him of it even though he will no doubt laugh at us and forever wonder what really goes on in a papal conclave."

A visibly shaken Cardinal Robitelli stood up, asking to be recognized.

"Brothers, do you have any idea what will be said—what the consequences will be—if we send someone out of here without any indication to the watching world about what has happened? It would immediately be perceived that we had elected someone outside the conclave, as has happened on rare occasions in our past history. Or perhaps there is a question about the background of the new pope. The press will have a feeding frenzy!"

Robitelli turned abruptly to confront Motupu. "Please, dear brother, for the sake of the Church, please reconsider your position and withdraw your demand."

Cardinal Motupu pushed himself out of his seat and looked around. "I openly confess, dear brothers, that, as many of you may suspect, I reacted out of anger at being so blatantly chastised when this conclave began. I apologize herewith to Cardinal Robitelli for my actions. But having heard all the arguments presented so far by Cardinal Willeman, I am confident in another reason for my position. I have always felt that our hierarchy is apt to get entrapped in rules and tradition, frequently to the point of losing sight of our duty to lead Christ's flock with love and not doctrine. So I cannot conscientiously withdraw from the position, which to me is right. Who of us is to say that, though we call this Bill Kelly affair our ill-conceived joke, it is not the call of God to bring a new dimension into our near-moribund Church, an attitude more like Peter and his bark?"

Motupu's demeanor was not challenging now that he had expressed himself; indeed, the African cardinal seemed to be trying to conciliate. "If you decide at the very least not to confront Bill Kelly with the result of our vote, I will accept your group opinion and never do or say anything about the subject again. But I won't vote unless the offer is made. One less vote cannot make a difference." He gave Cardinal Robitelli a reproving glance. "I will accept anyone else this conclave may choose...other than myself. I withdraw my name from consideration. That is final."

Silence again settled over the group as Cardinal Motupu seated himself. It now seemed evident to many that Cardinal Robitelli would be elected. Willeman stood to try to define the position in which the conclave found itself. "Thank you, Cardinal Motupu, for your open and sincere statements. I am certain we all respect your opinion." He looked around the seated assemblage. "I suppose, then, dear brothers, what I need to determine is whether any of the rest of you share Cardinal Motupu's persuasion."

After a short pause the five other black cardinals stood up. Then other cardinals from Europe and all the American cardinals took to their feet. Soon thirty cardinals were standing, and others looked indecisive.

"Well, dear brothers," Cardinal Willeman said, taking charge, "it seems the next issue to be determined is how we will proceed to communicate with Mr. Kelly as soon as possible and get back to our conclave after he has refused. Only then we can get on with the business of electing a pope."

Tension ebbed and flowed as, without waiting to be asked, the cardinals broke into small groups, discussing ways to solve the problem. Unanimously, the conclave agreed that since Cardinal Comiskey knew Mr. Kelly personally and indeed had been the source of the impasse, he must be the one to go out on their behalf and deal with it. Since a second three-day period of voting had ended, the conclave was due another day of retreat, and no voting would take place tomorrow in any case.

Australia's Cardinal Keating now took over. "With efficient travel plans Cardinal Comiskey can see Bill Kelly in America and be back in two days," he said.

Cardinal Cushman nodded. "I will call my Boston diocese from the emergency phone here and have Bishop William Murray meet Cardinal Comiskey at Boston's Logan Airport, to take him to my residence. I will instruct Murray to ask no questions and keep this entire mission a secret. He will drive our brother to Fall River, where Bishop Sean Patrick will arrange for him to get to Kelly on Cape Cod."

Brian Comiskey nodded gratefully. "I appreciate your making all these arrangements, Your Eminence."

Cardinal Cushman glanced at his watch. "If you are to make Alitalia at two o'clock, you had best be on your way. With the six-hour time difference, you should be in Boston by three-thirty this afternoon."

Robitelli snapped back to his takeover mode. He strode to the emergency phone, picked it up, and had Monsignor Cippolini, administrator of the Sistine Chapel, on the line.

"Your Eminence, do you need medical services?" came the wary tone.

"I need for you to listen carefully and do exactly as I say. Do you understand?"

"Yes, yes, Your Excellency," Cippolini replied.

"We have found it necessary," the cardinal continued, "to have one of our number leave the conclave to obtain important information necessary to proceed with this election. Discuss this with no one. Call the Vatican travel office for a round-trip ticket to Boston on the afternoon flight today for Cardinal Comiskey, and have Tony bring a car around to the emergency side door. Cardinal Comiskey will be coming out shortly. Everything must be kept completely confidential. Do you understand?"

"Of course, Your Excellency. Immediately." Cardinal Patsy Monassari stood up and addressed Brian Comiskey. "Not to worry about the cost. I will see that all your expenses are taken care of by the Vatican Bank."

Inwardly Brian grinned at the overt manner in which Patsy had reminded the college of cardinals of his ultimate financial power.

✠ ✠ ✠

Within a short time of leaving the conclave, Comiskey had returned to his room in the Vatican hotel, at Piazza Santa Marta, changed to the black suit and Roman collar of a parish priest, then decided to call his friend, Ambassador Kirby. Brian was well aware of the unexpected problems that could arise along the way in the course of this mission. Also he had an uneasy feeling about Kelly, a resolute man known to follow his own judgment above that of any other man or, when he was a priest, any other cleric. Comiskey called Kirby's private number at the residence, and Kathy Kirby told him that her husband was out jogging.

"Please, Kathy, I must speak to him."

"The conclave?" Kathy began.

"I'll call back in half an hour. Please try to get word to him out there on those paths."

✠ ✠ ✠

Tony, the deceased pope's favorite personal driver, was standing at the back door when Brian, carrying an overnight satchel, emerged from the newly constructed St. Martha Hotel inside the Vatican, built at the close of the millennium especially to house the cardinals during conclaves. Tony shut the door, then took his seat behind the wheel and started the engine of the sleek black Mercedes.

"The airport in half an hour, Your Eminence. There's the Santa Anna Gate ahead and we're on our way out."

Passing the Vatican City post office and shopping market on the left, they drove by two alert Swiss guards who recognized Tony and the car and waved them through. They took the turn at Via di Porta Angelica.

Loitering across the street from the Santa Anna Gate in front of the souvenir and pizza shop were two members of the regular Vatican press corps, Victor Simon of Associated Press and the Reuters correspondent, Mario Pullella. Also there, ever looking to make media contacts, was Father Farrell, giving the two veteran reporters the benefit of his informed opinions and hoping to get his name mentioned and even a plug for his latest novel on Catholic Church intrigue.

"The seventh day," the AP man remarked. "Has it ever happened that a conclave was so stalled?"

"Oh, yes. The college has been known to be locked in for twelve days. Let's see, that was in fifteen hundred and—"

"Hey!" the Reuters reporter exclaimed. "Isn't that a Vatican car?"

Tony was waved through at this moment.

"It is," Farrell responded. "Considering nothing is moving, it's strange to see a motor pool Mercedes coming out."

"There's a guy wearing the collar in the backseat," the AP writer observed.

Farrell stared into the backseat of the vehicle. "My God! It's Comiskey. What's he doing outside?"

"I don't know," the Reuters man replied. "But there's a story here for sure!"

The AP man was already reaching for a roll of lire as he ran to a parked taxi. "Deloce, fifty thousand lire if you don't lose that Vatican Mercedes," Simon shouted, pulling open the door and climbing in. Before he could shut it, Pullella and Farrell had crowded in beside him.

"Hey! This is my cab!"

"Ours," his Reuters colleague contradicted.

AP was already furiously dialing his cell phone. "Give me Elizabeth Redmond."

The AP bureau chief came on the line immediately and her reporter breathlessly described what was happening. "Any idea where?" Redmond asked.

"We're past Circo Massimo, *l'ambasciata,* and now on the Appian Way. He seems to be leading us onto the *autostrada.* Maybe the airport. Something's up. We've got Farrell with us. I'll put him on. Maybe you can get a quote."

Farrell took the cell phone authoritatively in hand and barked into it, "A cardinal leaving the conclave is unheard of. There may be some kind of schism there."

The AP man grabbed his phone back.

"Simon, how did you get onto this?" the bureau chief asked.

"Something had to be happening after seven days, so I waited at the Santa Anna Gate to see what."

"Good show. I'll put it over the wire."

The Reuters reporter was already gathering quotes from Farrell to build up his story when it finally materialized.

"We're definitely heading for Leonardo da Vinci, that's right, *Fiumicino* airport," the AP man called to his bureau chief.

"Cardinal Brian Comiskey of Ireland has left for the airport. Something big."

"Stay with it all the way. Climb on the plane with him."

"I don't have much money, but I got a credit card and my passport."

"Hang in there!" Elizabeth Redmond urged.

At the airport, Tony pulled the Mercedes up to the curb and the door was immediately opened by an official-looking man in a pin-striped suit. "Buongiorno. Come sta? Eminenza, I'm Umberto Alessi, Alitalia's vice president in charge of business operations. Follow me, Eminence. I have your ticket."

"*Bene, grazie,* Umberto. I've got to make a phone call."

Before Brian could say another word, the two reporters had leaped from their cab and were chasing after him, calling out questions. Umberto Alessi spirited Brian away from this would-be curbside interrogation and led the way past security to Alitalia's *sala d'aspetto*, a private briefing room that was only used for government officials from the Republic of Italy upon arrival back in Rome before being questioned by the press. AP and Reuters followed the cardinal's every move while frantically trying to find out where he was going.

KIRBY'S CALL 6

It was later in the morning than usual for Ambassador Ed Kirby to start his daily seven-mile-plus jog. At ten A.M. in beat-up running shoes and exercise togs, he left his residence at the top of the Gianicolo Hill, the highest hill in the city and perhaps the most beautiful location in all Rome. Gianicolo was not one of the original seven hills. It was situated outside Rome when the seven were originally fortified. Across the street stood the American Academy, a residence founded by J.P. Morgan, where visiting scholars and writers could live gratis. Ernest Hemingway was one of the many American writers so graced. Close by was Villa Pamphilli, with its seven and a half miles of paths, water fountains, formal gardens, bocci courts, ponds, soccer fields, and Roman statuary. One roadway had been named for Martin Luther King, Jr.

The ambassador was always impressed by the magnificence of the park and how beautifully it was maintained by the city and respected by the amazingly large number of people who used it every day. It was a very different picture than was apt to be found in most American city parks.

While Kirby jogged ahead, a security car with three Italian secret service agents slid onto the road behind him, apparently to follow.

Along with most Catholics throughout the world, Kirby wondered what was going on at the conclave. He looked down the hill, taking in the Vatican on his right and its Sistine Chapel, where for days the cardinals had been trying to elect their new pope.

Rome was spread out below him. He could see St. Peter's Square, where hundreds of tourists were gathered in anticipation of sighting the column of white smoke. When at last it emerged from within the chapel, those in the square would be part of history. They could say they had been present when the new pope was at last elected.

Kirby had seen many dramatic ceremonies at the Vatican. The beatification of the first Gypsy saint had brought over a hundred thousand Gypsies from around the world and the magnificent Easter Sunday Mass, with nearly one million pilgrims on hand.

As he jogged the path running parallel to Via Aurelia, one of the longest streets in Italy beginning at St. Peter's Square, his eyes searched for the Pacelli estate, home of the family of Pius XII. When Kirby had first arrived in Rome, the U.S. embassy was located there. Anytime he wanted to meet with top Vatican officials, diplomats, or world figures he could be sure they would show up because they so loved the atmosphere and the historic surroundings of the place. A staffer for the king of Spain had even called one day to ask if King Juan Carlos could stop by the embassy to see the home of Pope Pius XII after his meeting with Pope John Paul II was concluded.

The State Department, however, had little concept of how important the place was. In a shortsighted economic cutback, Foggy Bottom had let the lease lapse and moved the embassy to a smaller, less prestigious building farther away from the Vatican itself. It was an example of the State Department's political insensitivity, which elicited amazement within Church circles and the rest of the diplomatic community. Now Ambassador Kirby did most of his official entertaining and much of his State Department business at the comfortable and more easily accessible Villa Richardson.

The ambassador was always susceptible to the constant innuendos aimed at him by career State Department employees who resented the politically appointed. The career types felt that appointees didn't really understand the business or deserve their more prestigious positions. With the Congress in Washington cutting deeply into the State Department budget and fourteen new U.S. embassies opening in the wake of the Soviet Union split-up into independent republics, this placed further pressure on politically appointed ambassadors. The careerists resented political appointees taking jobs away from them—that was how they perceived it, at any rate.

Ed had run three or four miles when he noticed a reflection on the road in front of him from the flashing blue lights on the roof of the security car following behind. He turned and saw the driver, Fabio, waving to him. Stopping, he let the car come alongside him.

"Mrs. Kirby just notified us you had an urgent phone call," Fabio announced. "Whoever it was will call back soon."

The only other calls he had received like that were two from the president and one from the Holy Father. The ambassador flashed a glance at the Vatican, laid out below the hill. No smoke rising from the Sistine Chapel. His first thought had been that the conclave had elected a pope and he was being notified. It must be the president. *He probably wants to know what's going on,* Ed surmised.

Kirby jumped into the backseat beside Giovanni, an Italian secret service agent, and in a few moments they passed through the front entrance of Villa Richardson. Kathy was waiting and gave him a glass of water and a reassuring smile in reply to his anxious look.

"Brian will be calling you in a few more minutes. He's on his way to the airport!"

"What!" Ed exclaimed. "What's going on? I didn't see any white smoke coming from the chapel."

Kathy shrugged. "He'll call you when he gets to the airport."

Ed walked down the hall, entered his office, and slumped, confused, into a chair. He glanced up at the only photograph on his office wall. Given to him by the homeless people at the Pine Street Inn in Chicago, it was called "Christ in the Breadline." The homeless in the photograph were waiting in the breadline, and the image of Christ was in the throng. Mario Cuomo, former governor of New York, was one of the very few people who had looked at the picture (which had hung in his city hall office for years) and recognized Christ in the crowd of hungry homeless. It represented a political ideology that had been an important part of his personal and political life. Thoughts raced through his mind, mostly incoherent surmise at the absolute inconsistency of a call coming from Brian Comiskey while the conclave was still in session. And going to the airport!

Ed snatched the telephone before its first ring died out.

"Ed, I have to go to Boston. I'm leaving shortly." Brian said urgently. "I need your help. I trust you, as someone with the best interests of the Church at heart and having the political savvy. But it has to be absolutely confidential. Not even the White House."

"You called the right man, Brian. What's going on?"

"I can't tell you much now. What goes on in the conclave is secret. I can say I need your help. I need you to take the first plane to Boston tomorrow and guide me through what might become a very delicate situation."

"I understand, I think," Ed replied.

Brian went on breathlessly, "A couple of media people have followed me to the airport and are asking questions."

"What can I do, Brian?" Kirby asked.

"Be in Boston while I am on this mission. It will be helpful."

Kirby glanced at his watch. "I can get out on Alitalia's new morning flight and be there before noon tomorrow Boston time."

"It may be nothing, but if things work out unexpectedly, as an uneasy hunch tells me is possible, I will need your help. You can reach me through Bishop Murray at the Archdiocese of Boston. Here is his telephone number. Don't worry about personal expenses. The Vatican Bank will cover it." There was a pause and Ed heard the cardinal's muffled protests as an assertive reporter sought to question him.

"Brian, I'll call the bishop when I get in and let him know how to reach me. I'll be standing by for your call. I'm in enough trouble with State now, so another quick disappearance isn't going to make it much worse. The president will support me. He's not the problem."

"Thanks, Ed. Now, let me shake these news hounds off my tail and get on the plane. I'll be OK."

Ed hung up and returned Catherine's questioning gaze.

"What's Brian up to? He's going to the States," she stated. "What does he want you to do?"

"Something very strange is going on."

"What did I hear you say about going back tomorrow?" Kathy probed.

"Brian needs my help. That's all I know. Make sure tonight when the governor of California comes to dinner that we don't let it slip out that I'm flying to the States tomorrow." He paused, remembering an important item. "By the way, make sure to call Bill Fugazy in New York, and let him know that we're taking care of his friends. He wanted to get them into the Sistine Chapel for a tour. But tell him"—Ed smiled wryly—"somebody else is using it. Set them up with a tour of the catacombs."

"Don't you have to get State Department approval before leaving your post?" Catherine clucked her tongue. "Remember the fuss when you flew into New York for the Governor Al Smith Dinner? And how about the time you boycotted the reception for the queen of England and met with the leader of Sinn Féin?" She reproved him with a smile.

"Stop bringing up old stories." He grinned ruefully. "But there's no politics involved in this mission. Something is afoot in Boston, and Brian needs my help. Maybe they are going out of the conclave and a bishop in the U.S. is being considered." Ed grinned at his wife. "Or maybe some 'question' on one of the cardinals likely to be chosen has turned up. I know what the media can and will do when they think they have something on a prominent person, whether it be in politics, business, or religion. Think what the media would do with something juicy on the future pope! A hatchet job!"

"Ed," Catherine grumbled, "how can you even suggest such a blasphemous thing?"

"Patrick is on his way up to the residence," Ed said. The young man from Chicago whom Kirby had handpicked as his confidential assistant strode into the room. Patrick O'Hearn had no State Department aspirations and Ed had needed presidential influence to have his bright, young, loyal, former city hall aide hired to work for him at the embassy. "You'll have to cover for me for a couple, maybe three days while I make a quick confidential trip to Boston," he said to Patrick.

Patrick groaned facetiously. "Your deputy chief of mission will have a field day when he discovers you're off post again without permission. He'll call Washington immediately. They love to make life difficult for you political appointees, and they hate to have extra work while they're writing their book or looking for their next promotion or job."

"Just do your best to take care of things while I'm away. You and the DCM will have to handle the cable traffic."

Ed started out of his office. "I'll spend the rest of the day down at the embassy and try to give them the impression that everything is normal. If any press calls come in, you can say that the ambassador and the U.S. government have no comment to make regarding the conclave and Holy See policy. I know damn well that State would prevent me from traveling home if they knew about this mission—no matter how crucial to the Church or anyone else."

╺╁╸ ╺╁╸ ╺╁╸

Cardinal Comiskey left the private waiting room at the airport whence he had called Kirby. His worst fears were coming true. Cameras were everywhere. How had they gotten there so fast?

"Your Eminence, please!" the shouts went up. "Where are you going?"

"Why did you leave the conclave?"

"What's going on?"

Thank God he had considered a worst-case scenario and called Ambassador Kirby. He stopped and raised his hand. Amazingly the shouts of the reporters lapsed into silence almost immediately.

"I'm sorry," the cardinal began. "Our conclave is still going on. I am just being sent to obtain some information needed by the college of cardinals. I am forbidden to discuss anything further. As you know, all our work in the conclave is secret. I realize you have your job to do, but I have mine too. And my work for the conclave has to remain secret. I'll be back in Rome in a few days and fully expect the conclave will elect a new pope."

Questions were hurled at him as he walked to the gate. He answered none, and soon, followed by the press, he entered the gate to catch the Alitalia afternoon flight to Boston. Several reporters tried to buy tickets on the flight. But Pullella and Simon got the last two cancellations.

Brian Cardinal Comiskey was on his way to America at last. He sat by the window in first class, looking out at the boarding area. He smiled and shook his head. He could see Father Farrell in the midst of a knot of cameras and reporters, presiding as though he were the pope himself.

FEED MY SHEEP 7

At the moment Brian Comiskey left the conclave, it was eleven-thirty in the morning in Rome and five-thirty A.M. on Georges Bank off the rugged New England coast. Ryan Kelly went into the captain's compartment of their ninety-foot fishing trawler, *Mary One,* to wake up his father. They had fished for four days on the bank and after one more day they would be heading back to port.

Ryan stared at his father in disbelief. Bill Kelly's face seemed to be glowing in the lifting darkness of dawn. Ryan marveled at the exultation on his father's features. "Hey, Dad, what were you dreaming about? You look like you've seen Moses and Elijah on the mountain."

"I'm happy to note that you remember your Gospel studies," Bill replied dryly.

"Seriously, Dad, our catch has been good, but not that good."

"Just a funny dream. Get the crew moving. I'll be in the wheelhouse in fifteen minutes. We'll drag one more day and head home tonight."

All day the dragger crew dropped and hauled in the bottom-scraping nets, adding to the catch they would deliver to the New Bedford market by dawn the next morning. Manny, the faithful first mate for twenty years with Bill, and before Bill with his father, kept a curious eye on his boss. Bill Kelly indeed seemed transformed—different, at least—from the stoic former-priest-turned-fishing-captain. His countenance seemed to glow with some new but very palpable inner presence.

It was after supper and the ship was on automatic pilot now for New Bedford. Ryan came up to the wheelhouse to sit for a while with his father and Manny. As he entered he caught half a sentence that included his name. Bill turned to his son and smiled. "Come on in, Ryan. Sit down and you can hear the answer to the question I just put to Manny." Then, to his first mate: "Well, Manny, what do you say? Don't kid me. Is this guy ready to move up a notch or not?"

Manny glanced at Ryan with a friendly smile and wink. Then he turned back and, true to the captain's expectation, the mate's smile vanished as he paused to frame his response.

"Being captain can be a nightmare as well as a thrill. I've watched Ryan develop. He knows every job on this tub. Of course, there is no way someone can be trained to handle captain when problems rise up among the men...or the weather...or in an accident. Then it's more instinct than skill. It's all in how someone uses the new authority. There's a fine line between being one of the guys and giving orders that will be instantly obeyed." Manny sighed and his expression lightened. "That's really about all I can say."

Ryan eagerly joined in the conversation. "Wow! Dad, do you mean you might make me captain sometime? Of which boat? This one? The *Mary One?*"

"Maybe sooner than you think," Bill said thoughtfully. "Don't you have the watch?"

Ryan nodded and stepped out onto the deck, making his way forward to relieve the crewman watching for other boats in these waters. Manny's eyes followed him. "One thing I didn't say, but yes, Ryan has the right attitude. He'll make a first-rate captain." Then, after a long pause, a grin crossed his face.

"What's so funny?"

"Your son. He said when he woke you up this morning you looked like you'd had a happy dream, and he hoped it was about his mother." He refocused on Bill's face. "You know, you do look like the happy fisherman right now. The rest of us have noticed it all day, a sort of glow and a light step on the deck."

Bill's face took on a sober, serious expression as he looked at his mate and longtime friend. "Manny, I never asked about religious ideas, but I know you are a Catholic like me."

"I'm not an ex-priest," Manny said.

"Once a priest always a priest," Bill murmured. Then, "Manny, could I bounce something off your brain?"

"Sure. Can't say I'm much of a Catholic, though. Mostly I go to Mass because my wife drags me there. But I have faith in God. Out here you need it. What's on your mind?"

"Well, now, don't laugh at me, Manny, but do you believe in visions, prophecies, apparitions, Our Lady of Fatima? Stuff like that?"

"Yeah. I guess so. I just accept what the priest says in Church. I sure don't have any background like you to be able to argue about it. Are you telling me you had a vision?"

"Yes. I don't really know, but I feel warm all over. I think, well, something like that happened early this morning. Yes. It's so weird when I think about it, it gives me the shivers. It also exhilarated me from the time Ryan woke me up."

"Yeah, he mentioned your look this morning. Like I said, he hoped it was his mother you were dreaming about. God, Bill, did you see the Blessed Virgin or something?"

"Maybe Our Lady of Fatima was there, Manny. I felt like I was in a fog, but I could clearly see her and hear her. I seemed to be seeing myself standing alone with a mist around me. Then I heard this voice: 'Peter, do you love me more than these others?' I looked around, startled, and suddenly I said, 'Yes, Lord, you know I do.'" Bill seemed surprised by his own explanation. "'Feed my sheep, William,' I heard. Then I cried, 'What do you mean? Who are you?' And I heard a soft whisper. 'He's coming for you.'"

Bill paused, searching his mate's face. "That's it, Manny. I could dismiss the dream part as just a dream. Our Lady of Fatima has been on my mind since the Vatican released the third prophecy earlier this year. I know that quote of Jesus to Peter—it was sung at my ordination at the Cathedral of the Holy Cross in Boston. But God! I was wide awake when I heard the whisper. I saw the clock, five o'clock. It was almost time to get up, but I felt totally wiped out so I thought I'd try to grab a few more winks. Then Ryan shook me awake and I noticed the clock again. It had only been five minutes. But I felt like I was on top of the world. I was so rested, so elated...I can't explain it."

"God, Bill. It sure would scare the hell out of me...especially that 'He's coming for you.' What does that mean? Is that all?"

Bill shook his head. "I thought at first it was something I ate. The cold crab cakes. But later...er..."

"What happened later? For God's sake, tell me, Bill. Tell me," Manny implored.

"In a few minutes I fell back to sleep and I saw the vision of Our Lady of Fatima. She told me about the many challenges to the Church and the world. I don't know, Manny, I just don't want to talk about it anymore." Bill pressed the rosary beads in his pocket and, deciding not to reveal anything more to Manny, merely said, "Thanks for listening to me."

IRISH BREAD WITH CARAWAY SEEDS 8

Victor Simon of AP and Mario Pullella of Reuters jumped onto the Alitalia flight to Boston at the last minute and made one more attempt to question Cardinal Comiskey. He politely reiterated that he was on conclave business, which had to remain secret. Again, he assured the two veteran reporters that he would be gone only a few days and, upon his return, the conclave would elect a new pope. Brian had been bumped up to first class earlier by the head flight attendant, Lucia, who gave instructions to the rest of the crew that His Eminence was not to be disturbed. Comiskey was so tired he didn't touch his food and immediately fell asleep.

The Alitalia flight approached its three-thirty P.M. landing at Boston's Logan International Airport on time. The call from Rome by Cardinal Cushman had been acted upon at once by Bishop Murray at the Boston Archdiocese. The instructions were explicit. "Brian Cardinal Comiskey will be arriving on Alitalia at three-thirty P.M. You are to meet him there. Don't ask any questions. Don't inform anybody where you are going. Take him back to the chancery at Lake Street, where he will stay overnight. Then make arrangements to transport him and meet with Bishop Sean Patrick McCarrick at Fall River early the next morning. Keep everything as tightly confidential as possible."

Only an hour after the call from Cardinal Cushman, CNN telephoned to confirm the story that Cardinal Comiskey was on his way to Boston after an unheard-of absence from the conclave. Bishop Murray was smart, alert, perceptive, and well connected, all reasons for his rapid advance upward within the Church hierarchy. Turning on WBZ, the all-news radio station in Boston, he heard in minutes that Comiskey was on his way to Boston to collect information needed at the conclave. Bishop Bill Murray reacted immediately to the fast-spreading news as all the media began ringing the chancery.

Bill Murray called his friend Benny Tauro, the Italian-born, totally Americanized public relations director at the Massachusetts Port Authority. Benny had already heard that Cardinal Comiskey was aboard the Alitalia flight and had been about to telephone Murray when the call came in from the chancery.

"Yeah, Bill." Benny did not waste time with titles. "I've already got security standing by. The VIP room will be cleared if you need it. The Irish around here can hardly wait to see the cardinal from Ireland! What's his mission?"

"Don't know, Benny. Now look, I'll be at Logan to meet him. Help me get him off the plane, and you escort him through customs. Please ask the state police to allow my driver to park his car outside the baggage exit. I suspect there will be a lot of press waiting for him outside customs."

"Do you want a press room or the VIP lounge cleared for any media meeting?"

"No. What I heard from Rome is, he will be as brief as possible with the reporters. We'll get in the car and go to the cardinal's residence on Commonwealth Avenue and Lake Street, in Brighton. Some of the press will follow us and there may even be reporters on the plane trying to tail him. Let's just get him into my car as fast as possible."

"You got it, Bill."

"Thanks. See you about three o'clock, then, Benny."

An anxious Bill Murray and his young priest driver arrived at Logan International Airport in advance of the flight and was dismayed at the crowd of photographers, TV cameras, and reporters already waiting for Cardinal Comiskey. State Trooper Jim Harrington and his partner, Steve Long, were standing outside by their patrol car at the curb, just outside the baggage carousel where passengers would pick up their luggage and carry it through customs prior to getting outside. Bishop Murray thoughtfully fingered the silver cross that hung around his neck, setting off the severe black suit and silk vest that reached to his collar. Benny Tauro was waiting and took his arm. "We can sit in my office until the flight makes its final approach, then go out to meet him as he comes up the inner ramp."

A large photo of Benny and Pope John Paul II hung prominently on the wall. The photo had been taken at the airport when the Holy Father made his first visit to the United States as pope. Benny and Bishop Murray left the sanctuary of Benny's office to meet the cardinal's plane. The press were milling around. Reporters recognized Bishop Murray from the archdiocese and began bombarding him with questions. The smiling, friendly bishop replied like a mantra, "I'm as anxious as you to hear what Cardinal Comiskey has to say. I have no specifics as to why he is coming here to Boston."

"Isn't it absolutely forbidden for a cardinal-elector to leave the conclave before a new pope is chosen?" a reporter respectfully shouted.

"I don't know what it's about, Danny," the bishop replied to a reporter he knew from WBZ-TV. It was Murray's job to represent the cardinal in his absence and handle critical and complex public relations situations.

"Aw, come on, Bishop," another reporter wheedled. "What did the Vatican tell you when it called? Was it Cardinal Cushman from inside the walls?"

"I couldn't say. Like all of you I was asked to come here and meet the cardinal."

Adroitly, Bill Murray and Benny Tauro verbally jostled with the press a few more moments, then left the area outside customs to meet the plane as it was preparing to unload passengers. Cardinal Comiskey was the first to walk through the gate, carrying his only luggage, an overnight satchel. Bishop Murray, Benny Tauro, and Trooper Harrington introduced themselves and led him to customs, ahead of the planeload of people arriving from Rome.

In moments, Cardinal Comiskey cleared customs and found himself surrounded by the media. In reply to the torrent of questions about the conclave and amid snapping flashbulbs, he politely explained to the press that he was on official business. "As all of you well know, I am not permitted to talk about my assignment, and I hope you will all respect that. I'm sorry I can't be more specific but I do expect to be on my way back to Rome very shortly. When I arrive I expect the conclave will move forward rapidly toward electing a pope. There is really nothing to be concerned about. This is a matter of routine and protocol. I am carrying out an official function. Let me repeat that I expect we shall have a new pope very shortly after my return to Rome." *And*, he thought, *it will be Eugenio Cardinal Robitelli unless God really does make his own choice and perform the needed miracle.*

"Are you staying at Lake Street?"

"Is it about finances? Vatican Bank?"

The cardinal walked to the waiting car and gratefully slid into the backseat of the sedan. Bishop Murray stepped in beside him. "I'm afraid, Your Eminence, that when we reach the sanctuary of the chancery, the press will be outside, hoping for some scraps of information. I can understand the speculative frenzy gripping the newsrooms of not only Boston but the nation, and even the world," he observed. "I have asked Father Peter Conroy, editor of *The Pilot*, our organ here, to assist with the media. He will be there when we arrive."

"I can only say this mission was not to be avoided," Comiskey replied. "I'd personally rather be in Ireland. I've so much work to do, and the All Ireland Football championship is being played in Dublin this coming weekend. Nobody wants this conclave to end more than me."

It had been some years since Comiskey had visited the chancery of the Boston Archdiocese. The same old trolley tracks, still in frequent use, ran down the middle of Commonwealth Avenue. Approaching Lake Street, across the tracks as they left Boston behind them, he could see Boston College, where he had studied in what was now the Tip O'Neill Library.

They crossed the trolley tracks before Lake Street, drove down Commonwealth Avenue, and took a right turn into the driveway of the chancery, which wound around the back of the cardinal's imposing residence. As the car stopped at the entrance, Bishop Murray stepped out, carrying Brian's bag.

"By the way," Brian said, "I'd like to make a personal phone call to an old friend of mine who was ordained with me and is now a fisherman on Cape Cod."

"I'll take you to your room. You can make any calls from there. I think our lines are secure, but you never know for sure in this day and age of surveillance," Murray said as the pair walked past the large paintings of the former archbishops of Boston hanging on the wall.

"I'll be careful what I say, Bill." Brian and Bill Murray were already on a first-name basis. "And I'd best let Bishop Sean Patrick know he can expect a visit from me tomorrow morning."

"He'll be delighted. Fall River is one of the best and most diverse working-class dioceses in this state." Murray was careful not to betray his curiosity regarding the cardinal's mission.

"Sean Patrick. Yes, a wise and kind man," Brian observed as he followed Bill past the offices and up the stairs to the bedrooms.

"Shall I plan an early supper? You must be tired, and you'll want to catch some sleep." Brian's bedroom faced Commonwealth Avenue. Bill pointed to the window. "You may have noticed, the press is gathering across the street. I don't know what news they think they'll discover. Father Conroy is there talking to them. We've asked them to stay on the other side of the tracks. They've asked for somebody to do live interviews. I told Peter to do them, even though he doesn't have anything to say. He told me that he felt like he was back at St. John's Seminary taking his canonical examination before ordination."

"I know the feeling." Brian smiled, recalling his days at the seminary with his dear friend Billy Kelly.

From the moment he had left Rome, Brian had been aware of the fatal weakness in his plan to accept Bill Kelly's refusal and return within forty-eight hours. Bill was a fisherman, a hands-on captain of his small family fleet. Brian remembered that Bill went out to Georges Bank for four to six days at a time and might well be at sea when he arrived. Of course Bill Kelly would come in from the bank if one of his children radioed him to do so, but every ship at sea listened to the radio traffic and it could cause a problem if one of his children identified the reason for calling Captain Bill in to shore. Brian unpacked his satchel, drew out his address book, and, breathing deeply, put the call in to the house in Buzzards Bay he knew so well.

To his delight, Meghan answered the phone. She let out a shriek and gasped, "Wow, is it really you, Uncle Brian? I heard on the radio you were in Boston. What happened?"

"I can't tell you why, but as long as Church business brings me nearby, I thought I might try to get down and see my Cape Cod family. Maybe have some lobster stew and apple pie like your mother used to make?"

"Uncle Brian, we'd be thrilled. Colleen makes lobster stew almost as good as Mom's. Dad is at sea, but he expects to be at the dock in the morning. I'll call him on the radio."

"No, don't do that, Meghan! The media are all over me. I don't want them disturbing you. As long as your father is coming in, not a hint. Understand? I have a lot of reading to do tonight. Besides, I may not be able to come down there after all." Brian crossed himself at the lie but it was for the Church, he rationalized.

"I understand, Uncle Brian. You're a busy man. Mum's the word."

"Hopefully tomorrow, then, Meghan. God bless."

A weary Cardinal Comiskey descended the regal stairs to be met by Bishop Murray and a young priest, Father Charlie Burke, assigned to drive him to Fall River the next day.

Father Peter Conroy came in from talking to the media gathered across Commonwealth Avenue. "I never saw such a circus," he remarked. "It's worse than the nanny thing or the O.J. fiasco. Let's look at the news." He walked into the library and turned on the television set. Immediately, they were looking at the front of the chancery televised from across the street. The commentator was intoning that Cardinal Comiskey of Ireland had arrived less than an hour before. Then on the screen the picture switched to Rome, St. Peter's Square.

"And now, Rome. Father Farrell is giving his own expert view of the situation. It's after eleven o'clock P.M. there, and the world is focused on Rome and Boston."

Father Farrell talked for several minutes, summing up what had happened and speculating on the purpose of the cardinal's unorthodox "breakout" and his flight to Boston. Then the picture switched to the scene outside the library windows, where a gathering crowd of press and television awaited developments.

The Sisters of St. Joan of Arc, French-Canadian nuns living on the fourth floor of the chancery residence, brought in tea, sandwiches, slices of Irish bread, and a stick of butter. Hungrily, Brian buttered the bread and started to chew it. "Irish bread! I don't get as good in Ireland as I do in Boston. You have the best Irish bread going," he complimented the sisters. "And it's not even made by an Irishwoman; it's made by French-Canadian sisters." Brian sipped the tea and buttered a second slice of bread.

"Caraway seeds make the Irish bread," the cardinal continued, ignoring the excitement across the street and on the news. "You either like caraway seeds or you don't like caraway seeds. I remember my dear father complaining about the caraway seeds when my mother put them in," Brian laughed. "Father complained because the seeds got caught between his gums and false teeth. The little seeds would stick in there and he had a terrible time getting them out. But my mother made the bread the way us children liked it."

Bishop Murray, the two priests, and the attending nuns marveled at how completely Cardinal Comiskey was able to ignore the worldwide commotion of which he was the central figure. It was all Bill Murray could do to restrain himself from hinting at a leading question. Father Conroy said that he, as editor of *The Pilot,* the oldest Catholic newspaper in America, was sitting in the middle of the biggest story breaking in the world. "The only editor in the world so close to the story, yet he knows no more than the throngs of newsmen standing there across Commonwealth Avenue," Peter grumbled.

"Peter, Peter," Bishop Murray reproved him, "you must remember that you are a priest first and a newspaper editor second."

"Why didn't you think of that when I wanted to stay in my nice hometown parish, St. Ann's in Readville?"

Brian enjoyed the jousting between Bill and Peter. "Someday this situation will be clear and simple." He finished eating his sandwich. Inwardly he doubted that this would ever be the case.

Cardinal Comiskey and Bishop Murray talked and watched the expanded television coverage of the event occurring just beyond the library windows and in Rome. Finally, exhausted, Brian went up to his room, read his breviary, and soon was asleep. Twice he awoke during the night and peered out the window at the trucks with dishes pointed skyward as reporters, police, radios, and public address systems crackled. By this time, several hundred curious bystanders had also joined the all-night vigil.

At five-thirty the next morning Brian showered and went downstairs to the chapel, where he celebrated Mass with Father Conroy for the five nuns. At the conclusion, Brian led the small gathering in a song to Our Lady as they had never heard it sung before. Brian had a more than serviceable Irish tenor voice and they were quite delighted. They had never heard even their own cardinal sing it so euphoniously.

The nuns swiftly prepared a hearty breakfast of scrambled eggs, toast, and a pot of tea. Bill Murray joined Brian. Father Conroy left the chancery and made several visits to the press corps, giving them such trivia as he could: Cardinal Comiskey had pronounced Irish bread made in Boston superior to the same fare in Ireland, and "How much he enjoys being back in his home away from home, Boston."

"Cardinal Comiskey," Conroy said, when he returned from addressing the restless reporters, "it would be a gracious gesture if you could talk very briefly to the press. I promised them that if they would let you alone, you would meet with them for a few minutes. I can set up a microphone and lectern out back behind the chancery and invite them to walk across Commonwealth Avenue to our side. They would be happy with that. They say that they have to file stories and their bosses are shouting at them. After you have spoken to them, Father Charlie Burke can drive you out of the chancery grounds onto Commonwealth Avenue, down to the turnpike, and on to the Southeast Expressway, and you'll be off for Fall River. Is that OK?"

Then he gave Cardinal Comiskey a conspiratorial grin. "They all have their cars parked across Commonwealth Avenue in the Boston College parking lot. It will take them at least ten minutes to walk back across the trolley tracks, get their vehicles, and drive back across again. By that time you will be on the turnpike and they'll never know which way you went."

"Good thinking, Peter," Brian complimented the editor-priest. "Let's get them all over here and I'll think of something to say before our escape."

The chancery staff quickly set up the lectern in front of the statue of the Blessed Mother. A master microphone was installed into which the press could plug their own personal mikes. Father Conroy went across to the press camp and invited them all to come over across the street to the chancery grounds. There Cardinal Comiskey would talk to them.

At eight A.M. just in time for the final segment of the morning news broadcasts, the chancery back lawn was crowded with over a hundred members of the various news media. Cameras were recording this event with worldwide repercussions. It was obvious to everyone that something most unusual was afoot in the process of electing the next leader of the one billion Catholics throughout the world.

As Brian Comiskey appeared before the cameras and press, he thought unenthusiastically about his situation. Back at the Vatican the other cardinals were protected from this international around-the-clock live coverage. The foremost decision they had to make was probably whether to have red or white wine with lunch. He was thankful that, according to Meghan Kelly, Bill would not be docking until midmorning and would thus miss the television coverage of Brian's arrival in Boston. As Brian took his place in front of the statue of the Blessed Mother, he was suddenly acutely aware of the impact his leaving the conclave had had on the world. None of the cardinals, except perhaps Robitelli, had realized what shock waves would traverse the globe after the mention that one obscure Irish cardinal had left for a quick trip to Boston.

For the first time real apprehension gripped him as he looked out over the swelling throng. He offered up a silent prayer and mentally crossed himself as he faced the world alone, personally representing the entire sacred hierarchy of the Catholic Church. Perhaps humility and pretending an aura of insignificance would carry the moment, projecting an image of routine and calm on the cardinal's visit.

"For me it is always a blessing to return here to Boston," he began. "I have a special love for this city, where everyone welcomed me so warmly after I left Ireland as a very young man and came here to study at St. John's Seminary. And I want to thank the people of the United States for their prayers and expressions of sadness on the passing of our beloved Pope John Paul II. The pope often talked of his love for America and about his special memories here. He lectured at Harvard and attended socials at the Polish American Club in South Boston, and, while archbishop of Krakow, even received a plaque from the Veterans of the Kosciusko Post"—Brian glanced about at the faces of the reporters arrayed in front of him and smiled—"along with a heavy dose of indigestion from the undercooked kielbasa." This last drew a reluctant chuckle from impatient reporters who had stood outdoors in the cold waiting all night.

"He often spoke of his first visit to the United States as pope, right here in Boston. He had just left Ireland, but the rain that greeted him made the constant drizzle of my country feel like a warm and beautiful spring day."

"What's going on in Rome?" a reporter shouted.

"What are you doing in Boston?" another added.

Yes, Brian thought, there was no way he was going to con this dedicated group of news hounds. "Look, I—I'm on a special assignment. I have instructions that I can't discuss at this moment. I will be in the area for only a short time, and when I have completed the conclave's business, perhaps tonight, certainly by tomorrow, I will return to Rome and we will choose a new pope."

"An American pope?" someone shouted.

"Are you looking for something red hot on a specific cardinal?" shot out of the throng, probably from an anti-Catholic writer. Brian recalled from his study of Church history that the *Boston Globe* had the reputation of being anti-Catholic and anti-Irish even in this most Irish Catholic city. He instantly remembered a documented report by noted Church historian Monsignor John Tracy Ellis, from the Catholic University of America, in which the scholar called the *Boston Globe* "the most anti-Catholic newspaper in the United States."

"Come on over to our morgue at the *Globe*. Maybe you'll find what you're looking for in our files," a second Yankee reporter, H. M. S. Duckwell ("Poppy," as he was called by his classmates at Exeter Academy), added. Brian had been prepared for barbed questions from Poppy because Father Peter Conroy had told him how to recognize the skinny reporter by his large bow tie and wide suspenders that carried his wrinkled pants up almost to his chest.

Before he could form a suitable reply another question was shot forth. "Where are you going now, Cardinal Comiskey?"

"Again, I'm not at liberty to reveal any details," Brian answered lamely. "In a short time, your questions will be answered, this will all be behind us, and we'll elect a new pope."

Father Charlie Burke drove up behind the assorted reporters and opened the front door to the car. Cardinal Comiskey wished the gathered press a good day, slipped into the sedan, closed the door behind him, and they were abruptly on their way. Long before the reporters could run back across the wide avenue bisected down the middle by busy trolley tracks, get into their vehicles, and pursue their ecclesiastical prey, the cardinal's automobile had driven up Commonwealth Avenue and headed into Newton, where they backtracked and picked up the Massachusetts Turnpike into downtown Boston, then entered the Southeast Expressway on their way to Fall River.

Father Charlie Burke knew that he was to deliver Cardinal Comiskey to Bishop Sean Patrick at his Fall River residence. After some minutes of silence Brian said, "I'm sure you were given instructions not to ask any questions, but how did the Red Sox fare this year?"

After listening to a dissertation on why the Red Sox had once again failed to win the pennant or even go into the playoffs, Brian asked who was conducting the Boston Pops Orchestra. "I used to love going over to hear Arthur Fiedler conduct, and then John Williams."

It was a one-hour drive to Fall River, and Brian mostly prayed silently, but kept an uneasy vigil for helicopters, the paparazzi, and other media. So far, so good. Father Burke speculated that in the newsrooms in Boston, editors and bureau chiefs were putting out calls to everyone they knew in the surrounding area to be on the outlook for a black Chrysler with the license plate numbers some of the reporters were alert enough to mark down as the car sped away from the chancery.

The cardinal and the young priest talked about Bishop Sean Patrick and his history as a kind and caring priest who had organized soup kitchens and homeless shelters for the night people of Washington, D.C., and then around the Port Authority in New York City, where in the Franciscan church there he had established a home for abused and runaway children.

It was a beautiful, early October morning when they arrived in Fall River. To Brian's relief, the bishop's residence seemed devoid of reporters and cameras.

As they pulled into the wide circular driveway of Bishop Sean Patrick's residence, a priest came out the front door of the large old colonial house to greet them. "Good morning, Your Eminence. I'm Father Raphael. The bishop is expecting you."

"Thank you, Father." Brian slid out of the front seat.

"Do you want me to wait for you, Brian?" Father Burke asked.

"Please do, Charlie. You must be hungry by now. Let's see if our brothers here can find you a piece of bread."

Father Raphael was quick to reply. "Most certainly, Your Eminence. The bishop wanted me to ask you if you would like to have tea with us. I'll chat with Father Burke while you meet with the bishop."

Inside the residence Cardinal Comiskey was immediately shown into the bishop's office. Bishop Sean Patrick (his last name, McCarrick, was seldom used), a bearded man with thinning white hair, was one of the most active and respected bishops in the country. A welcoming smile illuminated his face and Brian sensed an aura of complete kindness and love of his fellow man about the venerable cleric.

Bishop Sean Patrick extended his hand, grasping the cardinal's with a firm handshake. "So good of you to visit our humble abode, Your Eminence. From what we have been seeing on the television all this morning, it's nice to see you without a pack of reporters at your back."

Cardinal Comiskey laughed. "Please, Sean, you've known me since I was ordained at the seminary and used to visit here on Cape Cod. And before I forget, let me extend my warmest wishes this day of the feast of St. Francis of Assisi, the special day of your Franciscan order."

"Why, thank you, Brian. You have a good memory. And how are the renovations going in the wake of the damage to the Church of St. Francis in Assisi?" They chatted about the earthquake that had caused extreme damage to the historic Church in Italy.

"And a beautiful fourth day of October you are enjoying," Brian concluded. "I regret that time is of the essence."

"I understand, Brian. I am trying to restrain my curiosity."

"Well, I can't tell you much. The conclave matters are all secret. I can only say that since I am down here, I'd like to drive over to Buzzards Bay and see my old friend Bill Kelly."

"Yes." The bishop clucked his tongue. "I remember him when he was an assistant parish pastor in this diocese. He did wonderful work with the Portuguese immigrant children; spoke the language, arranged camps for them. We excused him from his vows, as I recall, and he married a very pretty Irish girl. That was an interesting time. Her uncle was the parish priest of St. Anthony of Portugal Church, a poor parish in the mostly fishing town. Didn't like his niece and his assistant prelate having a relationship." He chuckled. "Billy Kelly is the head of the Southern New England Fishing Council. He's a good family man and good to his workers, and he still cares for the Portuguese children."

"I agree wholeheartedly. Sean, as you know, Bill's wife—Mary was her name—succumbed to cancer some time ago."

"Yes, I believe that I heard that. How terrible for such a wonderful family."

"I'd like to see him as long as I'm in the area. He is one of my best friends and I feel like his family is my family."

The bishop was too kind, and wise, to remark that it seemed odd that a cardinal coming out of the conclave to elect the next pope would have time to see an old friend from the seminary. Instead he said, "I can have you driven to Buzzards Bay, or"—he paused—"why don't I drive you down myself? We can talk on the way. Or we can remain silent." He gave Brian an owlish look.

"I think I'd be better off going alone. I might just have lunch with Bill and his children and try to get the late-afternoon flight back to Rome. If you can arrange for me to rent a car—"

"Nonsense. You can use mine. Give Bill Kelly my warmest wishes." He cocked an eyebrow. "Anything else I should know now?"

"The U.S. ambassador to the Vatican will be arriving within the next few hours in Boston. He doesn't know what my mission is, but he may be a part of it. He will call Bishop Murray, who will direct him to call you as a means of locating me. You can tell Ambassador Ed Kirby anything you know of my plans and whereabouts. It is possible that events will not proceed the way I am trying to steer them according to the conclave's instructions. I am beginning to think that God, the Holy Spirit, whatever, is taking things into His own hands, and as I see it my mission is do God's will, according to his call. Ambassador Kirby will be an integral part of doing God's work as He moves in mysterious ways His wonders to perform."

Bishop Sean Patrick smiled. "Your Eminence, thoroughly confused though I am, I will carry out whatever wishes you express to me."

"Good. Then I'll head for Buzzards Bay and contact you regarding my plans after I have seen my old friends, the Kellys. Your place is just a last stop on my visit to America, and it is solely designed to keep people wondering what I'm doing and where I'm going. You'll be hounded by the media. They'll want to know if you've been elected pope or have an idea of who has." Brian smiled. "You haven't. The conclave isn't over yet. Are you with me so far?"

"If 'nowhere' is with you, Brian, I'm right on track." He laughed. "Anything else I can do for you? Let me know if you want one of the priests to drive you to Buzzards Bay," the bishop offered.

"No. I don't want to turn a simple visit into a major media event by heading out of here with you or one of the priests. I need to keep them guessing. Call me at Bill Kelly's house when you hear from Ed Kirby and I'll tell you my plans. I will probably fly out of Boston tonight. And if I know that family, I'll be stuffed with lobster stew and apple pie shortly after noon."

"In that case, Brian, here are the keys to my car, a used but reliable wreck. If a policeman stops you on the way, tell him to call me!"

"Oh, oddly enough, I do have a valid Massachusetts driver's license. I've spent several summer vacations with the Kellys. I love to drive around the Cape and see the sights."

"It's settled then, Brian. Let's get you on your way so you can get to that lobster lunch."

Brian thanked everyone for their kindness, including Father Charlie, as the bishop led his guest into the garage and opened the car door. Bishop Sean Patrick handed Brian a small wallet-size picture of St. Francis with the prayer for peace on the reverse side. With a few directions and instructions, the cardinal understood the instrument panel, backed the car out of the garage onto the pavement, and headed to the Cape.

As Brian left Main Street in Fall River, he turned on the CD player to listen to some of the music that Sean liked. The selection that came on was the song "Nabucco" from the opera *Aida* by Giuseppe Verdi, which Brian had once heard magnificently performed at the world-renowned La Scala opera house in Milan with Ed and Kathy Kirby and Carlo Maria Martini, the archbishop of Milan.

"OH MY GOD! SO IT'S TRUE!" 9

As he drove toward Cape Cod on this clear October day, Brian mentally rehearsed his mission: namely, to obtain Bill Kelly's unequivocal refusal to take advantage of a mistake, an insane joke gone awry. A grim smile crossed his face as he considered the field day the press would have with this. The stern visage of the *carmelengo* reminding him of the secrecy required burned in his brain. He must tell Bill Kelly how this accident had happened and persuade him to take the information with him to his grave! Was it realistic to think that anyone could keep such a secret?

Brian thought back to an earlier visit to the warm and modest Cape Cod home years ago when he had been made a bishop. The Kellys had staged an elaborate clambake for him and his priest friends from the area, including the now Bishop Sean Patrick. Brian had stayed on a few extra days to catch up with the family news. He had delighted in how the children were growing up, how they were doing in school, all the things you talk about with close family. He truly felt he was "Uncle Brian" and that everyone accepted him that way.

Most of all he recalled the belly laugh from Bill as he watched him hand Roger, then age three, back to his mother and look down at the wet spot on his neatly pressed clerical trousers. "Well, Your Excellency," Bill had roared, "you have been officially baptized for your new position. How many bishops can say that?"

As a cardinal he was grateful to God that he had enjoyed close friends like the Kellys. They kept him mindful of the ordinary man and the many problems with which he must contend. Yet at times he was painfully aware that as a celibate he would never know life fully, just as the common people—Bill excepted—could never understand the priestly vocation either. Still, he was happy to be serving God in his chosen manner and was at peace with himself. He knew beyond question he could trust Bill Kelly with the knowledge of what had happened at the conclave, and that this matter would never be revealed.

Brian's heartbeat quickened as he caught sight of the bay and the Kelly residence on a small knoll just above the inlet and docks. Soon he was swinging into the wide driveway and parked next to Bill's Chevrolet pickup truck. He walked up the steps to the house, and the front door opened slowly.

"Uncle Brian." Colleen's voice was friendly, yet there was an air of coolness about her he had never experienced in the Kelly family before. "Meghan said you called last night. You really did come. Dad landed a couple of hours ago."

"You didn't tell him I might drop by, did you, Colleen?"

"No, Uncle Brian."

"Does he know I'm in the country?"

"I didn't tell him, and they don't listen to the news out there at sea. Dad reads poetry and books."

"Where is he now?"

"By the boat inspecting the nets. Like I said, they just got in."

God's timing, Brian thought. He gazed out the large bay window that gave him a clear view of the waterfront below. He saw Bill bending over his nets, busy as usual. "Where are the kids, Colleen?"

"Still in school. Ryan is off to see his friends."

"Hey, Colleen, why don't you fix up some of that lobster stew your mom used to make while I go down and surprise the old boy?"

"Wonderful, Uncle Brian! You'll cheer him up. His mind seems occupied with something he won't explain. Very quiet he's been since he landed. Not like Dad," Colleen mused. "Of course it wasn't a great trip; the fish are scarce out there. And always the bills coming in. But usually he goofs off and has a few beers with his crew at the Second Bristol Café or the Portuguese Club in New Bedford before coming back home."

"I'll see you in a bit." Brian stepped out the screen door and descended the steps. He smiled as he caught sight of his friend at the edge of the dock, half dreading Bill's reaction to the bizarre tidings he was about to spill. The story could be met with boisterous laughter as, cardinal or not, he was pitched into the ocean. They were that close.

I might as well get it over with.

The day was gorgeous, a slight wind driving ripples in the water and the bright autumn sun at its zenith.

As Brian approached the boat, Bill was kneeling, unraveling the fishing net. He became aware of footsteps and turned to see who was coming. His jaw fell open. He looked stunned. The net he'd been holding dropped to the deck. "Oh, my God! So it's true!" he gasped, reeling backward.

The words brought home Brian's perception of his mission in a lightning flash. He realized intuitively that calling Ed Kirby before leaving Rome had been an act of divine guidance. Abruptly he was no longer Brian but Brian Cardinal Comiskey, standing there. "What do you mean, 'so it's true'?" he demanded, eyes locked into Bill's, searching for the explanation.

Bill turned away from the cardinal's questioning stare, nervously recovering his net.

"Bill." The cardinal's voice was compelling. "Look at me. What did you say?"

Bill straightened up, forced a smile, and then threw his hand out to be shaken. "I don't know. Nothing, Brian. It's just so great, such a surprise to see you again."

"Bill." The cardinal's voice was sharp. "Of course, it's great. But what did you mean by 'so it's true'?"

Timidly and almost apologetically, Bill sat down on the boat's gunwale and looked up into his friend's anxious eyes. "Just some funny, stupid thoughts I had. Not important."

"I want to hear your funny, stupid thoughts, Bill." Then, sternly, "Tell me. That's why I'm here."

It was apparent the cardinal was not going to back off. Bill sighed. "Well, now, Brian, don't laugh at me. I suppose it's just because I know you and saw you on TV going into the conclave. I teased the kids that maybe, because you were my old buddy, you would cast one vote for me! We laughed about it. But the thought just wouldn't leave my mind. Then out on the bank yesterday morning just before sunrise—dear God, it scares me just to think of it."

"Think out loud, Billy Boy. I want to hear it all...everything!"

"Well, things are a bit tough out on the bank—less fish, more work, and less money. God knows Colleen is doing her best to keep the family together and still get her college education. She is doing well at both, but with Mary's death she has lost faith in God, the Church—in everything but our little family."

Bill was silent a few moments until Brian shuffled impatiently toward him on the dock. "I was really wiped out after a hard day's work. But I wanted to discuss something with my first mate, Manny, one of the great Portuguese fishermen. He's always been there for me in the worst of times. I wanted to get his feelings about making Ryan the captain while I took the good-paying desk job offered me at the Southern New England Fishermen's Association."

Bill rubbed his eyes as though clearing his vision or pushing weariness from them. "Ryan was all excited, of course, but I told him to get some sleep. He was pulling the late watch and he had to get me up at five A.M. sharp." He sighed and looked up at the cardinal, dressed in his simple black suit with Roman collar like any other parish priest.

"Keep on, Bill," Brian said in a steadying tone.

"I went down to my bunk and literally collapsed. Now comes the weird part, Brian. I'm not sure whether I slept or not, but somehow my tired old brain reminded me I hadn't said my Rosary." He paused and half smiled at his friend. "Is that just a pattern we get into by habit? I was thinking of Colleen at that moment, how to restore her faith in God."

Again Bill was silent for a few seconds. Then he continued more forcefully. "I pushed my old bones out of the bunk and on my knees started to say my Rosary. I was so tired I could hardly concentrate on what I was saying. Then I was suddenly aware of a soft light in back of me towards the cabin door."

Bill was silent in his recollection of the moment. Then, slowly, he continued. "I turned and...oh God, Brian! I saw the Blessed Virgin standing there. She was so beautiful...so radiant. The image of her appearance at Fatima. I felt the hairs on the back of my neck rise as she communicated with me. I don't know just how, but I understood her perfectly.

" 'Be at peace, my child,' she made me understand. 'My son has sent me to tell you how deeply he is saddened over the divisions in his Church. He is also heavyhearted at the mistreatment of his Father's chosen people, Israel. These things must cease! Like the first Peter who denied Jesus and suffered with sorrow until his death, you also will have to suffer. But in your weakness God will be able to show forth his strength. The chastisements I spoke of before will be upon the people, and the assault against clergy, Christians, and all people must end. Just trust him, my child. His messenger will come for you tomorrow.' "

Bill looked up helplessly at Brian from the deck of his fishing trawler. "Then she disappeared, and it was dark in the cabin. The rest is so shrouded I can't understand it. I just know that I opened my tired eyes and looked at the clock. It said four fifty-five. Ryan would be calling me in another five minutes. My head fell back on the pillow. I was almost in tears. Then I noticed my rosary lying on the floor beside my bunk. I tried to reach for it but my body was like lead. Then, suddenly, there she was again. She just smiled at me and reached for the beads. I felt them drop into my hand. Then I heard her say, 'Sleep, child.' That's all there was, Brian.

"The next thing I knew I heard Ryan saying, 'Rise and shine, Dad.'

Then he went on to exclaim something like I had a happy look on my face and must have been having a lovely dream. I flew out of the bunk, feeling like I could have wrestled with Moby Dick and won. 'Get the crew moving, boy! I'll be in the wheelhouse in five minutes. Bring me coffee and a doughnut.' "

Bill shrugged. "If I were Portuguese I would say it was Our Lady of Fatima who came to me. The message was substantially the same, but I will always think of the apparition as Our Lady of the Georges Bank, with a new message for a new generation. End of the story, Cardinal. Am I crazy or what? Will I be fishing for the souls of people in Rome or cod and haddock back on the bank?"

The cardinal shook his head in absolute mystification. Finally he said, "Bill, you haven't even a vague clue as what you would be getting into. Your story only makes me more confused than ever. Who can say where the truth lies?"

A half smile came over the fisherman's face as he stared into the cardinal's eyes. He slowly reached into his pocket, then paused. "Brian...tell me, do you remember what gift we gave to each other the day we were ordained?"

The cardinal, a puzzled look on his face, thought a few moments. Then, "Yes, yes, of course." He smiled reminiscently. "Almost like twins we gave the same gift. A pair of rosaries we made ourselves. But what's the point?"

"Can I see yours, Brian?"

"Well, not really, Bill. I used them so much and so hard they were pretty well worn by the time my mom died. So"—he grinned ruefully—"I traded mine for the nice new set the undertaker had put around her hands for the wake. I hope you'll forgive me."

In one quick, fluid motion Bill withdrew his hand from his pocket, rosary beads in his fingers. "Catch these, Brian." He tossed them at the surprised cardinal, who was skillful enough to snatch them in flight.

Brian looked closely at them. "Nice, Bill. They look brand-new. Did yours wear out too?"

"No, Brian...or maybe I should say yes. Those are the ones you gave me on graduation day. Like yours, mine saw a lot of use. I even had some string on them to hold them together." He gave the cardinal an owlish look. "I think the Blessed Virgin repaired them—almost—when she handed them back to me."

Brian searched the countenance of his oldest friend in the world.

"Come on, Bill. These can't be." He stared down at the string of shining, new silver beads in his hand. "They do look like the ones I made for you," he allowed.

"Well, pal, feel the metal joiner that separates the five decades. Go ahead, rub it!"

Brian began to rub the heavy silver medallion with its two wings reaching up to join the string of silver beads into a necklace from which dangled a string of five beads suspending the cross. "My God. The thing is bent. A little sharp edge here. Glory be! I remember now. You stupidly used it to tighten the screw on my bedroom door handle as we were packing to leave the seminary."

Bill Kelly raised his hands as though in supplication. "Right on! You got it, pal! Do you think this suddenly-like-new string of silver beads represents a little extra support from the Virgin for us weak souls who may be a little short on faith?"

Brian reached into his pocket and tossed his own beads to Bill. "I think I will need to borrow yours for a while, Billy. I'm going to need all the support I can get when I walk into that conclave again."

"You may indeed, Brian. I started thinking I had been called back to serve again. It was an epiphany. You know—I was getting another chance to keep my vows and my children, too. This is what Our Lady of the Bank said to me!"

"Dear God, I can't believe this! My God!" His legs shaking, Brian sat on the boat's gunwale next to Bill. "I don't know how to say this." He fumbled for the right words. "I left the conclave on a secret and delicate mission."

"I don't get the news at sea. I hope it's straightened out."

"Well, five minutes ago I thought..." He shrugged. "Now I don't know what to think."

"Brian, you're losing me."

"Well, old buddy, I seem to be experiencing the same confusion you are, so I may as well say it right out." He paused as though for inner guidance. "I was sent here to tell you, Bill Kelly, that by some accident or mix-up, the conclave of the college of cardinals has elected you the next pope!"

"What? Brian, I would say stop mocking me, only..." He paused and looked helplessly at his old and dear friend.

"Only?" Brian prompted.

Bill stood up, agitated. "As I said, this fisherman, Bill Kelly, experienced a revelation so incredible as to make him feel that he had gone mad." He stared into Brian's eyes. "So aberrant...such an epiphany... and at sea, too."

"Bill," Brian interrupted, also rising, "this has to be for your ears alone. You must never breathe a word of it...ever. In the conclave we got into...a 'factional feud' is the best way I can describe it." For a second Brian broke down and held his head. "I happened to mention your name in a stupid allegorical joke I made in an effort to make the point that everyone had to give more thought to what we were there to actually accomplish. By some foolish...mistake"—he cocked an eye at Bill—"the majority of the cardinals put your name on our last vote as a means of confirming what I was trying to say: 'If we don't bail out our dinghy together, it's going to sink.' Like Ben Franklin said during the Revolution, 'If we don't all hang together, we'll hang separately.'"

Brian and Bill looked at each other questioningly. Brian continued after hitting his temples with the palms of both hands, the rosary still in his right. "Now we had a problem. One of us needed to come to let you know that by the Vatican II rules you accidentally yet legally were elected pope. It wouldn't be so if you were an ordinary layman. But you are also an ordained priest. So it was official. We had to tell you that." He paused and shrugged. "I know it sounds crazy, and believe me, I wish to God it was all some strange joke, but it's not. You got elected pope! All we are asking now is that you quite simply tell me you decline. That you promise never to tell anyone. I'll go back to Rome and we will address the business of electing the real pope." Brian abruptly stood up. "So let's try to forget the whole thing and I can go back to Rome."

From his seat on the side of the boat, Bill looked up at his best friend in all the world. "I just don't know what to think, Brian. In one way it seems so simple. But on the other hand, maybe I have to consider my vision, what it means! Maybe God was sending me his tidings about how I have to serve. I hardly know!"

"Good God, Bill. Are you crazy? A dream? A vision? You said yourself you may have dreamed what you did because you saw me on TV going into the conclave and made some kind of connection in your subconscious mind. That's not a vision! You probably thought you saw Our Lady of Fatima because the revelation of her third prophecy was on the news not long ago."

Bill Kelly stood up beside Brian. "See, you're not sure, are you? It's easy to say 'God spoke' if someone has a vision of the Blessed Mother and then miracles happen to confirm it. Like Our Lady of Fatima and the sun dancing in the sky."

Bill paused, as though reliving the sequence. "She spoke to me and told me of the challenges that the Church and society face. Now, when it comes to plain old dreams, the Church gets nervous, doesn't it? Yet think of all the dreams we claim were sent from God after the fact. I'm not saying I'm any kind of scriptural scholar, but remember, I went through seminary with you and learned something there. And I didn't stop reading when I came here. Heck, I read a book on every fishing trip, not to mention what I read at home. Learning about God's history with man has always been my favorite subject. I may be a bit odd in my own ideas about the Scriptures, but by God, they are my thoughts! No one else's."

Brian realized he had touched some personal nerve deep within his friend he'd never encountered before. "Bill," he began after a moment's contemplation, "I don't know how to reply. As you obviously noticed, I was somewhat taken aback hearing your first words to me. The notion of a direct communication from God hit me at that moment. So let's examine it all and see what we have. Tell me how you really, honestly, view all this."

Thoughtfully, Bill put one foot in front of the other and walked along the deck toward the bow of the fishing trawler. He paused to look out at the waves gently rolling in on the tide. Then, startled, his eyes fell on the shrine, the "grotto" his dear friend and Portuguese first mate for many years, Rogerio Oliveri, had built on the side of the dock to honor Our Lady of Fatima. It was the ordinary statue displayed in most Portuguese-American homes. It had been there for years before Rogerio was lost at sea after he bought his own boat. The flowers, placed there by Portuguese fishermen, were wilted, but would soon be replaced. Until this moment Bill had ignored them. He thought now of the third prophecy for the beginning of the third millennium, recently revealed to the world outside the Vatican...something about the attempted assassination in 1981 of John Paul II and how it may symbolize an attack on the Church with drastic changes in the world. After a few thoughtful moments, he turned from the grotto and walked back to his friend.

"Look," he began, "you've always been my closest friend in the world. You know that. You're the only one who ever accepted me, and Mary, as we were. I guess I'll never get over the fact that I am a priest who failed to measure up to my vows."

Bill looked across the dock and up at the sturdy, cozy home he had built. "Certainly I know God loves and forgives me. But the loss of Mary changed me—and it changed the kids. It makes me wonder, is that all there is to it? I keep asking myself, is God finished with me because of some interpretation of Church law? Or will he show me a new way to minister unto others? I believe, you see, the Church was founded by Christ and we must obey His teachings and rules. It's just that...I guess I'm confused because I so want to serve Him."

Bill took several deep breaths of fresh air to get hold of himself. "So much has changed in the Church. A great deal, as we both know, is not new. It's merely going back to the way it was in the early centuries."

He remained quiet for several moments until Brian prompted him with a question. "What is your message for me to take back to Rome, Bill?"

Tears welled again in Bill's eyes and drifted down his weatherworn cheeks. "Cardinal Comiskey, you may tell your colleagues in the conclave that I accept your inspired vote. I feel that's what it all means. God help us and continue to guide us in all that happens from now on."

The cardinal struggled to hold back tears himself. "Are you aware of what you are telling me? Do you have any idea what will happen to you if you accept? I can't even conceive of the cardinals accepting you. You have no idea of the explosive effect starting at the Vatican and spreading throughout the world were I to go back and tell them this. Are you sure you don't want to think about it? Discuss it more? I could give you some appalling stories about the inside workings of the Vatican and the back-stabbing that goes on among"—his voice wrung out sarcastically—"these men of God. John Paul I, for instance, died in 1978, just thirty-three days after his election. A lot of people don't believe it was from natural causes, but autopsies of deceased popes are forbidden. You haven't a clue what you'd be getting into. It's a huge institution and it has more than its share of enemies. You surely read about all this Vatican Bank stuff and Nazi gold! That's why Pope John Paul II's historic pilgrimage to the Holy Land was so important for us in building on the positive relations between Christians and Jews. A challenge and an opportunity. The chair of St. Peter must be filled by a person of hope and experience."

"Wow!" Bill exclaimed. "This is certainly going to be an interesting venture!" His grin reappeared. He was in control again. "It's like that curve ball I taught you to hit, ol' buddy. Just step into the sucker and swing." They both laughed, almost desperately, recalling carefree days at the seminary.

From above, shattering their mood, they heard Colleen's shrill voice calling. "Uncle Brian, a phone call for you." Her voice was unemotional. "Someone is saying Bishop Sean Patrick needs to talk to you."

"Ask him to hold on." Then, "I guess, Bill, we need to talk…a lot… later." He smiled benevolently. "Your Holiness."

"Cut the holiness stuff. You better see what the bishop wants."

Brian followed Bill up the steps to the house. Colleen was unimpressed. "The bishop is waiting on the line."

Brian nodded, walked to the telephone, and picked it up. "Yes, Sean," they heard him say. "Harborside Hyatt Hotel?" Brian listened. "I'll call him, and please don't go away from your phone until you hear back from me."

He hung up and turned to Bill and Colleen. "A friend of mine called. He's in Boston." A serious look came over the cardinal's face. "Have you got another telephone I can use?" He glanced at his watch. One-thirty in the afternoon. Ambassador Kirby was right on time, Brian thought, thankful for his earlier premonition that he might need Ed in Boston.

"Sure. The children's phone is out back," Bill said.

"When will the kids be home from school?" Brian asked.

"In half an hour or less," Colleen answered.

"How about Ryan?"

"I guess I know where to reach him," Colleen said.

"Get him here as quick as you can," Brian commanded.

"Sure, Uncle Brian." Colleen was aware that something very unusual was in the wind. "I'll call Ryan from here. Take the other line out back." Colleen picked up the telephone and dialed a number.

Brian gave Bill a serious, almost severe look. "You want to brief Colleen before the others get here? Meanwhile I'll be making some necessary arrangements."

Colleen's voice had a commanding timbre as her brother came on the other end of the line. "Family conference, Ryan. At home. Now!" She hung up imperiously.

"What's going on, Uncle Brian? Dad?"

Bill looked to Brian for support. The cardinal cleared his throat. "I'll do my telephoning." He smiled, turned, and left for the back of the house.

"What's going on, Dad?" Colleen asked coolly.

"Well, Colleen, I need to go to Rome."

"When, Dad?"

"Tonight."

"Why the big rush? I mean, what has Uncle Brian got to do with it?"

"Well, impossible though it may seem, I've been elected pope."

"P-p-p-p-pope?" Colleen screamed with laughter. "Daddy, stop kidding me." She calmed down. "There's no God, no virgin birth to begin with. But I guess popes get good money. How did you get the nod? They were looking for another fisherman?" She saw the pain in her father's face but couldn't stop one last barb. "Dad, remember what happened to the last fisherman who left his family and traipsed off to Rome to become pope? He got nailed upside down to a tree!"

The depth of his daughter Colleen's hurt and loss of faith when her mother died had never been so apparent to Bill Kelly. Then she became serious. "Dad, if you have to go to Rome on business, no problem. Between Ryan and myself we can hold the fort here. I get back and forth to classes at college in time to see that Roger and Meghan get fed and go to bed and do their homework." Colleen's eyes sparkled. "I'd love to visit Rome sometime. My course in Renaissance Art and Lit has taught me what to look for in the museums."

"If all goes well, you'll have an apartment in Rome whenever you want it."

"Daddy, how exciting! What kind of job has Uncle Brian found for you? It seems like a tough time for him to visit us. Must be important."

"I'll let him explain when the others get here."

Ryan arrived within ten minutes of receiving the call from Colleen. Bill thought it best to explain to his two oldest children, before the two younger ones arrived, what might be about to take place.

Ryan was delighted at being immediately promoted to captain and Colleen assured her father that the house and family would be well looked after. It seemed so far-fetched, so impossible that their father would actually become the pope, that they considered it a family joke, not to be mentioned to anyone without explicit instructions from Bishop Sean Patrick.

In awe of his decision, Bill Kelly was still trying to explain it to Brian. "I didn't know exactly how to react to what I knew was an apparition of Our Lady until I saw you. Now I am positive that, as Shakespeare put it in *Julius Caesar*, 'There is a tide in the affairs of men, which, taken at the flood, leads on to fortune. Omitted, all the voyage of their life is bound in shallows and in miseries.'" Bill turned to Brian and Colleen. "Can you understand?"

Colleen turned a wry smile to Brian. "My father is quite the poet, no?"

"And now, Your Eminence," Bill asked, "where do we go from here?"

"I don't know the final result, but your next stop is Rome. And we can't go together. Even though you were elected, the cardinals might figure out a way to go back on their protocol. But if you feel God calling you so urgently, and"—his tone betrayed genuine awe and wonderment—"in the light of this astounding conclave, then be assured I'll do my part to put you on St. Peter's throne."

Bill nodded. "Your reward is in heaven, Brian."

"He's sounding like some kind pope already," Colleen snorted.

Cardinal Brian Comiskey leveled a long, deadly serious gaze at his old friend. "I know you are and always were a serious-minded fellow, Bill. But what you are embarking on now will change everything forever. Are you ready for the criticism you and your family will endure, justified or not?"

Bill nodded slowly, somberly, and bowed his head.

"This is the highest-profile position and you will be wide open to constant criticism and abuse from the enemies of the Church. Look what the press does to the priesthood and the profile politicians, never mind the pope. One slipup in your family and it's instant and sustained headlines. Are you absolutely convinced that you know what you are doing? Are you prepared to share the consequences, good or bad, exhilarating or soul-searing, that will shape your life from this moment on?"

Bill drew a deep breath. "I am more aware than you can imagine of what I have chosen to confront in accepting, in not denying, this God-decreed mission. Without realizing it, I have been preparing for this quest most of my life. But without my children I would be hard-pressed to carry out this mandate. God's call, perhaps."

Ignoring the plea, Brian continued relentlessly. "Others, I'm sorry to say, will grumble that it is the Devil's handiwork."

"I'll make them understand that God's joke is in reality God's call," Bill pursued.

"So it is, then," Brian breathed. "All right, let me make a plane reservation for myself on the evening flight to Rome and then call back the gentleman you are going to get to know very well these next few days. If the conclave abides by its rules, this gentleman, the American ambassador to the Vatican, will be extremely important in your life. Are you ready to meet him over there tomorrow? Ambassador Kirby will see that you get there, if you still choose to accept the offer. And bear in mind, dear old friend, the college of cardinals could yet rescind it."

"Brian, I believe sincerely that I must go. If God changes his mind, then it is not that I will have spurned him."

"All right," Brian sighed. "OK. The worst that can happen is that you get a free visit to Rome." He realized that in all liklihood the story of the conclave farce must eventually surface. But he was counting on being back in his relatively quiet native Ireland when the news broke. And Bill would secretly have arrived back in Buzzards Bay as clandestinely he had reached the eternal city.

"Now, do we have time for some of Colleen's lobster stew before I am off?"

The telephone ringing in his room at Logan Airport's Harborside Hyatt Hotel interrupted the noon Channel 4 news broadcast Ed Kirby was watching. An interview with Cardinal Comiskey from that morning was the lead story. Knowledgeable people whom the station contacted for their expert and considered opinions offered wild speculations. By then it was known that Comiskey had been driven to Fall River to meet with the respected Bishop Sean Patrick. Was some information needed about Boston's Cardinal Cushman, as he was on the verge of being elected, that only Bishop McCarrick could supply?

The *Boston Herald* and the *New York Post* reported that a highly placed source had been informed that a major scandal was unfolding within the Church, and that Cardinal Comiskey had come to the United States carrying $50,000 to try to settle it before it became public.

Another story amused Kirby when he read in the *New York Times* that the State Department had been trying to locate him to help explain the confusion at the conclave. An unnamed top State Department source said that he had left Rome and they didn't know where he had gone. Nobody had suggested, however, that it had anything to do with the papal election.

Kirby was deeply concerned at the article. Although he had spent several years successfully turning back State Department efforts to discredit him, it was disquieting to once again read himself publicly targeted by the denizens of Foggy Bottom with innuendos that indicated he was not doing his job.

The ambassador was following all developments closely as reported in the Rome press. He had read the newspaper reports on his flight from Rome and was watching reruns of the airport interviews with Brian Comiskey. Each statement the cardinal made was notable for its dearth of information.

On the second ring Kirby snatched the telephone up. Brian was returning the call put through to the bishop. He listened attentively as Brian relayed his instructions.

"It's lucky I went to college in the area you're talking about," Ed said.

"You once told me that the best place to go to college to get a good education and play big-time college basketball was Providence College, so I knew you were familiar with this area," Brian replied with a laugh. "Now I'm going to put you on with Bill directly. The two of you decide where you should pick him up in a rental car."

When Ed Kirby had finished speaking to Bill Kelly, he went into action. He was an old hand at working out travel plans incognito, having been both the key member of the Democratic National Committee during two presidential campaigns and a streetwise Chicago politician. He'd had to make travel plans for Vice President Humphrey in the 1968 campaign during the violent anti-Vietnam protests by Students for a Democratic Society radicals. His vast experience had made him a very alert and expert planner.

For a reason Ed could not fathom, Comiskey wanted a New England fisherman named Kelly brought to Rome immediately and in great secrecy. Had he not known his fellow Irishman so well he would have thought the cardinal was playing games with him, perhaps using the ambassador to throw off the scent of the press bloodhounds.

✛ ✛ ✛

In Buzzards Bay, Brian's last attempt to dissuade Bill proved unsuccessful. With steadying hugs from Meghan and Colleen Kelly, Brian left the house. It remained sunny this memorable October fourth, the feast of St. Francis of Assisi. Brian felt he had executed his assignment as well as it could be done.

Bishop Sean Patrick was waiting as Brian, smiling and nodding to the horde of journalists who had tracked him down to Fall River, laughed inwardly. The press had missed turning up even a hint of the real story in Buzzards Bay. Father Charlie Burke was standing with Bishop Sean Patrick. The cardinal climbed out of the car he had borrowed earlier and strode toward them.

"I guess you won't have any time to visit with us, Brian." The bishop glanced at his watch. "It may take a while to get to the airport in this afternoon traffic." Brian turned to Father Burke. "Charlie, could you wait in the car for me? I just need to speak to the bishop a moment."

"Of course, Your Eminence."

Inside the bishop's residence Brian pulled a long white envelope from his jacket pocket and handed it to the bishop. "I'm sorry about the reporters and cameras all over your residence, Sean. Put this in your desk drawer and don't take it out until it's time to open it."

"And when will that be, Brian?"

"I know it sounds odd, but I'm sure you will know exactly when to open it. Trust me on this one. And, Sean Patrick, let me apologize again for not being able to spend some time with you on this special day."

As Sean Patrick slapped the envelope meditatively against the palm of his left hand, Brian left the perplexed bishop looking after him and walked out to his car.

The ride to the airport with Father Burke broke all records. They left a wake of pursuing media vehicles and made it all the way to Quincy, on the outskirts of Boston, before being stopped by a state trooper. The combination of a Roman collar, a short explanation and a supportive officer facilitated a high-speed run through the Ted Williams Tunnel and over the final mile to Logan Airport. Cardinal Comiskey thanked the trooper, noting that he had forty-five minutes left before takeoff time.

He checked through the ticketing area, then sat down in the boarding area of Alitalia Airlines. He would have liked to meet with Ed Kirby on the Cape, but the ambassador and Bill Kelly were on a tight schedule themselves, driving to Kennedy Airport in New York in time to catch the late flight to Rome. Besides, the chances of being seen by the press and perhaps being traced to a meeting with the ambassador would have been deadly, both for Kirby's diplomatic status and the media speculations on what the cardinal and the ambassador were doing together in Boston during the conclave at the Vatican.

With practiced answers, Brian did his best to fend off the questions of reporters who had staked out Logan. Then he was escorted to a private room, where he plopped his tired body down on a seat. Waiting for the boarding call, he dozed off. Startled, Brian awoke, looking down at the floor in front of him and noticing polished black shoes and uniformed trousers. He looked up into the smiling face of a middle-aged pilot.

"*Buonasera*, Your Eminence. You look like you could use a friend. I'm Captain Maroni. I'll be flying you back to Rome. Let's get you on board right now." He extended his hand to help the tired cardinal to his feet, picking up his small bag and heading for the boarding gate.

The aggressive reporters seemed to reluctantly accept that there was no new information forthcoming. Most of the press picked up their cameras, microphones, and notebooks slowly after leaving the boarding area. Among themselves, they speculated on what significance, if any, might be attached to the cardinal's trip to Fall River and his mysterious visit with an unknown family on Cape Cod. Others discussed the possibility that either Cardinal Cushman of Boston or Bishop McCarrick of Fall River was in some way connected to the election of the new pope. They realized that Boston was playing a big role in the election; they just couldn't figure out who and why.

Hardly had the media reported Cardinal Comiskey boarding the flight in Boston for his return to Rome when Father Farrell was back in the media limelight. His educated reasoning was broadcast around the world. He was convinced the new pope would be an Italian but made splashy sound bites by saying, "Cardinal Cushman of Boston, an intelligent and pious priest, is noted for his fund-raising expertise, and is the possible new pope. The Church worldwide needs to meet its humanitarian obligations with its limited financial resources, so somebody who could raise considerable amounts of cash is essential to lead the Church into the new millennium." Farrell had certainly used his Chicago Irish political instincts to catch the media's attention.

BILL VISITS ROME 11

Not a little mystified by the reasoning behind Cardinal Comiskey's summoning him to Boston, Ed Kirby dutifully followed the plan as Brian had concocted it. He checked out of the hotel a bare two hours after he had registered, picked up a rental car, and made the hour's drive to the Lizzie Borden Café in Fall River. Ryan Kelly was to drive with his father to the famous restaurant, just off the main interstate that would take Bill and Ed Kirby to New York and JFK International Airport.

Kirby was well acquainted with Fall River and the city of Providence, Rhode Island, from his college days and had no trouble finding the appointed meeting spot. He parked directly in front of the entrance to the restaurant and, after taking a long look for reporters, opened the car door and stepped out onto the sidewalk. A tall, lean man with a weathered face and graying hair, dressed in a dark suit, walked out to meet him immediately. He was carrying an overnight bag.

"Ambassador Kirby, I presume." He grinned.

"Please, get in the car, Bill," Kirby answered. "We're on our way to Rome via New York, Kennedy Airport."

Bill walked around the car and opened the front door, stowing his bag in the backseat. In a jiffy they were on Interstate 95 heading south for New York. Ed opened the conversation. "Brian asked me not to give you the third degree, so say whatever you feel comfortable with."

"Well, first I need to express the gratitude both Brian and I feel toward you personally. He never really thought his mission would end this way. But, just in case, he knew he would need you."

"Bill," he began, "Brian didn't give me much information, so I really don't understand what is going on. It is only a matter of time until the wrath of Foggy Bottom will fall upon me again. I'm glad, of course, that it is all for a good cause. I would hate for the desk at State to be right when next I get castigated for being too damned independent, or too close to the Vatican point of view."

"I don't know what will happen in Rome," Bill said. "But either way you will have done a great service to the Catholic Church. It may or may not be recognized."

"Service is important to me."

"Brian will explain it all to you when this blows over."

"I'm sure. Now let me tell you how we are going to handle the TWA flight to Rome tonight and get off without attracting attention. Fortunately, you have a valid passport. With the help of Tom Meagher from Chicago, Chairman of TWA, we can board without my full name being entered on the passenger manifest. In Rome I'll get you through customs quickly, and we will go to my residence, called Villa Richardson. Once there, it's all up to Brian. I'll have done the job he gave me."

"If this all works out, you just might be a hero down there at the State Department."

"Are you kidding? Not on your life!" Ed snapped. "You never get rewarded for doing a good job but you do get punished when you make a mistake. Most diplomats unfortunately take the safe 'middle' course and do nothing." The ambassador chuckled to himself. "A former governor of your state and a good political friend of mine, John Volpe, became ambassador to Italy some years ago. When he heard I was going to the Vatican, he called me and said, 'Ed, the career diplomats have foreign service degrees, but they are without either loyalty or common sense.' I have learned for myself how right he was."

A long silence ensued as Ed drove along the John Lodge Connecticut Thruway that would eventually lead them to New York and JFK International Airport. Then the conversation continued. "I won't even try to guess why Brian is bringing you to Rome," Ed Kirby sighed. "By the way, here it is October fourth and I see in the newspapers the Red Sox have missed the playoffs again. But the Patriots are four and one and leading the division." Ed warmed to his favorite subject after politics. "You remember that year when my Bears cleaned their clocks at the Super Bowl in New Orleans?"

Kirby's switch from present circumstances to sports was a welcome change in subject for Bill Kelly. They talked sports and then some politics as the ambassador drove toward New York. Bill noticed that Kirby started blinking from time to time and seemed to be getting road tired. "Would you like me to drive?" he asked.

"No, I'll make it. One more hour and we'll be there."

"By the way, when did you leave Rome for Boston?" Bill asked.

"Ten A.M. this morning, that was four A.M. in Boston. I checked into the Harborside Hyatt Hotel at about eleven this morning and called Bishop Murray. That's five P.M. in Rome. By the time I talked to Brian at your place it was after twelve noon. I got my instructions from Brian and picked you up at three o'clock in Fall River, nine P.M. in Rome. Now it is, let's see"—he glanced at the dashboard clock—"six P.M., that's midnight my time. Eternal Rome is just starting its nightlife. The restaurants have been open a few hours. Tough to get used to these changes."

"You've already had a full day," Bill marveled.

"I didn't take my usual run this morning—saving all my energy. We'll be on the eight o'clock flight tonight for Rome in good time and back at my place before eleven tomorrow morning. We should get a few solid hours sleep in first class, and you'll be ready to do what Brian has in mind by the noon vote in the conclave."

"I can hear you speculating, Mr. Ambassador." Bill chuckled.

"Well, as a born-and-brought-up Chicago politician, when I see certain things happening during the election process, I have to draw my own conclusions. And I must say, although the inference is hard to ignore, it seems as downright improbable as anything I have ever heard."

There was a long silence between the two of them as they stared out while passing Shea Stadium. Kirby started to mention the infamous 1986 Mets–Red Sox World Series but caught himself, realizing that this was a sore spot with New Englanders. Finally they approached the outskirts of JFK Airport.

There was no doubt in Ed's mind that in some arcane manner, Bill Kelly had become the leading candidate for pope. The concept was almost unbelievable. Did the college of cardinals really believe that with the number of fallen and disillusioned Catholics in the world, more swept away from the faith every day, they could turn to the laity for their Church's new leader? A leader who would restore the faith of the financially, politically, socially, and ideologically oppressed? Was the Church seeking a pilot whose personal sufferings reflected those of the ordinary people in the pews? The concept was perceptive and innovative, but its implementation seemed nigh unto unimaginable.

Ed parked the rental car at Hertz. After sloppily signing the credit card slip, he and Bill were driven to the TWA terminal, where Ed contacted the supervisor, an affable disabled Vietnam veteran from Brooklyn named Ed Hunter. They worked out the details of first-class ticketing, keeping Ed's name off the passenger manifest until after the plane was airborne. Any one reporter seeing the name of the ambassador to the Vatican on the passenger list could cause him considerable trouble and raise questions that, for the moment, were better left unanswered.

Gratefully unnoticed, Ed and Bill were escorted to the jet by a passenger manager and shown to their first-class seats. Ed recalled a previous trip on the same jet with the deceased pope, on his second to last visit stateside. They had sat together talking politics on the way back from a World

Youth Conference in Denver. Was he once again flying with a pope back to Rome?

Dead tired, Bill settled his tall frame into the wide, comfortable seat as the enormous jet filled with passengers. Shortly after eight P.M. the flight took off and headed out over Long Island Sound on its route to Europe.

Ed checked his watch. "Two A.M. in Rome. The city is jumping. I hope my daughter is home. When I'm away she thinks she can get away with staying out late with her friends at Miscellanea Café, near the Pantheon. She's a great kid. Thank the Lord we can really trust her. I've been lucky with my children. Rome has a different clock for the young than any other place in the world."

Bill sighed. "I know the problem. My daughter Colleen, just twenty-one, attends our community college, and I have to discipline her some-times for breaking our curfew." He sighed again. "But she is a wonderful young lady, trying to replace her mother for the family. If only..." he paused. "If she could just make her peace with God, who she says can't exist. A kind God wouldn't have taken her mom. And in that mood she comes home after midnight all too often."

Ed nodded. "Young people don't realize the trouble they can get into out late. The drug situation has changed everything in one generation."

"And they resent you telling them," Bill replied.

Again, Ed Kirby heard a calm but incredulous small voice within him asking, *Can this common fisherman, with such prosaic human problems, really be our next pope?* It seemed too practical, too rational, too good and simple to be true.

From the usual sumptuous hors d'oeuvres and wine list, Ed Kirby let the hostess bring him a glass of wine with dinner. Bill Kelly ordered a double Irish Mist after the plane had reached cruising altitude. Kirby had gone for twenty-four hours without sleep and he was more tired than he knew, uncertain of the results he might expect from this latest absence-without-leave from his post.

Undoubtedly, the embassy DCM had tried to reach him and was ask-ing questions. He visualized J. Calstrom Seedworth already furiously pounding out a memo to the effect that for one entire day, the ambassa-dor to the Vatican had not been at the embassy and was unreachable at the residence. With equal certainty he knew that the memo would already have been leaked to the hostile Chicago press who had been critical of his mayoral initiatives and strongly opposed to his lunch-bucket positions on most issues. Later the *Washington Post* would pick up the leak.

Nevertheless, relaxed and enjoying this respite in their odyssey, Ed knew instinctively that Bill was, in some unfathomable manner, up for the papacy. Then he remembered Brian Comiskey's hint that any advice of a practical nature Ed could offer to Bill would be gratefully received.

"You know, Bill," he began, sipping his wine, "all politics, and that goes for Church politics, is personal. When you run for office you have to remember one thing: Everyone is interested in jobs, either for themselves or their relatives or their close friends. And nobody wants to lose a high-level job, or any other job, for that matter. If I were trying to take over as governor or mayor, or member of the U.S. Congress, I'd make it known immediately that nobody was going to lose his or her job or position of authority. Not only that, I would always be available to discuss their job status. And it's the same thing in the Vatican. People will transfer their loyalty from one pope to his successor almost overnight."

Ed finished his wine and came out with a final profundity. "If they think they can manipulate you, they'd rather see you in charge than someone they know they can't manipulate." Kirby turned in his seat, a thin smile on his lips. "Know what I mean?"

Bill nodded. "Thanks, Ed. Let them think they can push you around, actually appear to be pushed around—at first. Once you're in solid, you can clamp down."

"That's the way, Bill. Make your enemy think you're his friend. Everybody wants authority. Let 'em think they're all going to be boss of something. That's how you manipulate the manipulators."

"Right, Ed. I'll remember that. Job security."

"Right. Put it on your bumper sticker." Now he had done his best for Cardinal Comiskey, the Church, and Bill Kelly. At least for this one day.

Ed Kirby finished his second glass of wine and almost immediately fell asleep. The hostess cleared his tray and slipped a pillow behind his head, exchanging an understanding smile with Bill, who was not used to enjoying public officials' airline perquisites. The furthest place he had gone recently was Walt Disney World in Orlando, Florida, with Mary and the kids before she had died.

Later Bill turned off the light above his seat and, closing his eyes, began to meditate deeply on what Ed had said. How would he handle the questions sure to be asked him at the papal conclave? And that was assuming that he was even recognized and permitted to defend his various positions as pope-elect. How such a drama could have unfolded at all was God's mystery. But he, William Kelly, ordained priest—albeit lapsed, but still a brother—would not, could not ignore what he knew had been a sign from the Holy Spirit that he had been the one chosen to serve.

DEPUTY CHIEF OF MISSION 12

✠ J. Calstrom Seedworth, the deputy chief of mission and number
two in the Vatican embassy after the ambassador, was going
through one of his periodical indulgences in the "poor me" syndrome as he pored over the latest cable from the Vatican Desk at
the State Department. He, who had majored in language studies at
Princeton, the super-elite Ivy League university to which he had won a
full scholarship, was presently relegated to subordinate status behind this
Irish big-city politician whose Catholic school credentials were, in Seedworth's opinion, not comparable to his own. Edward Kirby, appointed
ambassador over several substantial financial contributors to the party
and State Department career employees, was obviously far less qualified
in Seedworth's mind than proven professionals like himself, who, at age
forty, was now leading the pack, ripe for advancement.

It was eight A.M. in Rome when this particular cable arrived, two A.M.
in Washington. The desk at this very late hour was asking Kirby for his
best guess as to why it was taking so long to elect a pope and who the
leading candidate might be. It also inquired about the breaking news
story that a prominent cardinal, Comiskey of Ireland, had committed an
unheard-of breach of conclave protocol and had left Rome for Boston
while the college was still locked in conference.

For two days Kirby had not appeared at the embassy, working he
claimed, at his residence office. Seedworth, his courtly manner of speech
always slightly exaggerated, had called the residence and was told by
Patrick, the ambassador's assistant and only temporarily employed by
State, that the ambassador was in conference and would call back. The
DCM had replied that the Embassy Desk was anxious to get a reply to
their cable immediately. It appeared that some sort of crisis was occurring
at the conclave after six days of deadlock, and, with Comiskey in Boston,
it was important to know what was happening. Meaning now.

By noon he had still not heard from Kirby, and with only two hours
until the Washington early birds showed up at their desks at eight A.M.
and a scarce three hours before the more established State Department
regulars made their nine o'clock appearance, he dictated a cable back to
the desk reporting that Kirby was nowhere to be found. At that point

Seedworth had the embassy transportation director order Claudio, the ambassador's driver, to report to the DCM. Already Seedworth was writing one of his confidential reports and evaluations on embassy affairs, this one examining the ambassador's being AWOL at a critical juncture in Vatican history.

Reluctantly, Claudio appeared at the embassy, having left Kirby off at the airport. In response to the DCM's stern interrogation, Claudio could report only that he had driven Ambassador Kirby to catch a plane that had left at nine or nine-thirty in the morning. Its destination he was unable to say, but the ambassador had mentioned that it was a mission of no little importance.

Seedworth checked all the flights leaving at nine or nine-thirty. There was a flight that left for Nice, France, at nine-thirty, one departed for Boston at nine, and a third headed for Dublin at nine-forty-five. Embassy transport had no record of the ambassador being ticketed for any of the three destinations.

The flight to Nice was a connector to Monte Carlo. While it would have been unlikely that Kirby could have taken a flight to the States without his being listed on the passenger manifest, which he was not, a flight to Nice could easily be booked under an assumed name. Aer Lingus would not give the embassy any information on who was aboard the nine-forty-five flight to Dublin.

Was Kirby visiting someone in Monte Carlo at a time when he would not be missed? Or maybe a gambling casino? Was he traveling to Ireland to catch up with old drinking buddies who were scheduled to attend the All Ireland football championship?

When it was nine A.M. in Washington, Seedworth called his boss at State's Vatican interest section. This was another career officer who deplored the plethora of political appointments at ambassadorial posts around the world. The DCM reported the latest information on Kirby, a prime target in the department's effort to embarrass the present administration and in particular its choices for high diplomatic appointments.

"Good show, Seedworth," the DCM heard himself complimented from afar. "Keep developing a complete report on Kirby. Meantime I'll turn on the 'confidential source' heat here in Washington. Be ready for calls that come through to you as a result of, let's say, an 'unfortunate leak.' Make certain that all calls from the media go directly to you. And see if you can pin our friend down to the Nice or Dublin flights. Good show!"

The next call made by the DCM was to Villa Richardson, where, once again, he reached Kirby's assistant. "Patrick, Cal Seedworth here. Anything new from the ambassador?"

"All I know is that he is on an important United States mission. I'm sorry I can't be more specific. But I really don't know anything beyond that."

"I understand. Probably something so confidential he can't let us in on it just yet." The DCM's voice fairly bubbled with understanding and faith in whatever it was the ambassador was undertaking for the embassy and his country. "I don't mean to be presumptuous," he continued. "It's just that I am getting cables from the desk asking about Cardinal Comiskey's surprise visit to Boston. And State does know that Ambassador Kirby is close to this cardinal. So naturally I'm taking some heat, but it's all part of my job." He sighed. "Don't worry, Patrick. I'll answer the cables as best I can. We must protect the ambassador. But please ask him to contact me at his earliest convenience."

"Sure will, Cal. I appreciate your concern. I'll keep in touch."

+I+ +I+ +I+

Hanging up, Patrick thought he was going to throw up at that line of bull. He was, however, deeply concerned about just how J. Calstrom Seedworth was going to use this unexplained absence against his boss. Patrick had no idea exactly what Kirby was doing, but he knew it was very much in the line of duty. He knew that the DCM, wrapped in a mantle of resentment, would use this particular absence to the detriment of any political appointee to any top embassy post. It also meant that if the ambassador were to be recalled, the DCM had access to all the ambassador's perks, plus the money and car.

+I+ +I+ +I+

Back in Washington, the State Department specialist in leaks to embarrass political appointees was hard at work, in this instance on the phone to the *Washington Post*. "Hello, Jerry. You know who this is. Deep Throat Two. Listen, I have a tip. We've lost Ambassador Kirby again. Yeah. And this time when all hell is breaking loose. Cardinal Comiskey of Ireland has left the conclave at the Vatican for Boston, and—"

He paused after Jerry Taylor said, "We know all about that one. Stew Peadman is covering it from Boston."

"Yeah, but do you know that with a Vatican crisis brewing we can't find Kirby? We think he might even be in Monte Carlo or Ireland. At any rate, he's AWOL once more when we need him. This may be the time when another reprimand isn't enough. The word is coming down from the top that he may be recalled. Maybe fired."

"Sounds interesting. Exclusive to us?"

"As far as we're concerned, yes. Just keep that recall statement coming from a high-ranking, reliable source at the State Department who prefers to remain unidentified. You know the drill, Jerry."

"I'll have to call Rome, of course," Taylor said.

"Of course. Do you want the number of the embassy and the ambassador's residence?"

"Sure. And what's the name of the local DCM?"

Five minutes later the *Post*'s Taylor was on the phone to the U.S. Vatican embassy. Then, after calling the residence and speaking with Patrick O'Hearn, reaching the U.S. Information Agency in Rome, and checking with the White House press secretary, he wrote a breaking story from Washington regarding Kirby's absence from post. He was writing his exclusive story.

Seedworth smiled. "He won't survive this one."

✛ ✛ ✛

In the White House, meanwhile, a concerned assistant press secretary, Art Jones, was in the chief of staff's office with the news that the *Washington Post* was running a story indicating that U.S. Ambassador Edward Kirby was on the verge of being recalled from the Vatican. This at a time when at any moment a new pope was about to be elected. Jones was concerned because he was a close friend of Kirby's. He knew the damage the story could do to Kirby personally, as well as the collateral embarrassment it would bring to the president.

The chief of staff, sizing up the political ramifications of such a story, particularly if the State Department did something foolish like confirming a recall, went directly to the president in the Oval Office. Surrounded by his top policy staff, including the national security adviser, the president listened carefully to the assistant press secretary. Then, after a pause, he passed judgment on the situation.

"You know as well as I do that the State regulars have no loyalty or much political sense at all. Ed Kirby has had to defend us here to his friend, the pope, against what the curia deem our liberal and anti-

Catholic ideas. I don't have to repeat to you that the conservative Republicans over there on the Hill are one hundred percent against abortion and gays in the military." The president nodded at his personal assessment so far.

"Our conservative enemies on the other side of the aisle hold many other views in common with the Church leadership in the United States. They seem to share a strong sense of Catholic values with the pope. Now here comes one Democrat, Ed Kirby, advocating what is important to the pope and the Church, which is human rights, religious freedom, health care for the poor and needy, plus he's strongly pro-life. We can't afford to lose the Catholic vote; it's too important to the Democratic Party's success."

The president fixed his advisers, one by one, with a watery stare. "Who kept the Catholic vote from swinging Republican? Ed Kirby, that's who. State has no more idea of political reality than my dog. In fact, Buddy has more sense than those hired cow-handlers. And yet they wonder why the executive has to have political appointees to hold his foreign policy together—politically and financially," the president added with a wise nod. "Over at Foggy Bottom they've all married each other's first cousins. It's no wonder they all look like the inbred dry sticks they are."

The president paused, taking the measure of his advisers. "I don't know where Ed Kirby is now, but I do know that he has more damn political savvy than any of those birdbrains at the department. What a cesspool of media leaks those hypocrites are!" He grinned broadly and winked at his Peace Corps director, Mike Gearson. "Probably while those small-minded idiots are tearing him down, Ed is with the next pope right this minute."

Since such a speculation was, on the face of it, preposterous, nobody in the Oval Office bothered to challenge the president's latest whimsical conjecture. But it closed their case that the president still retained full confidence in Ambassador Kirby and his political value.

The *Washington Post,* by now well primed by DCM Seedworth, who had agreed to inform them only as an unnamed source, had by day's end wrapped up its story about Ambassador Kirby's alleged disappearance from the Vatican scene. Cardinal Comiskey was televised at Cardinal Cushman's residence on Lake Street in Boston holding a morning press conference, and then had eluded the press until joining the Franciscan bishop of Fall River just prior to catching his plane back to Rome. All this time Kirby had been clearly out of the loop.

At the hour Kirby and Bill Kelly were boarding their night flight to

Rome, there was a top-level meeting at the undersecretary of State's office with certain officials sharing a deep interest in the Kirby situation. A special assistant to the national security adviser had been called to the meeting and had delivered the White House stand. The president remained fully confident in his ambassador. When advised of the ambassador's absence from his post he had remarked that if he knew Kirby, the ambassador was "probably at that very moment with the next pope."

"The president won't be able to ignore the *Washington Post* article," the Vatican officer snapped at the absurdity of the statement. "I'm sorry, but whatever it was Comiskey was doing in Boston, Ed Kirby was unable to give the department a clue. Tomorrow, we'll tighten the noose," said the desk officer in a low voice.

THE NANCY REAGAN SUN ROOM 13

All night on the plane, Bill Kelly rehearsed what he would say if, indeed, he were called before the assemblage of cardinals. He reviewed what Kirby had told him and recalled a statement about actors: "The next performance is the most important one of your life." It all seemed so unlikely that he felt he was dreaming aboard his trawler, the *Mary One,* and that this particular day, from the moment he had docked yesterday morning, had never really dawned.

He fell asleep, to be awakened by the first call for breakfast as the fierce morning sunlight pierced through the airplane window. He looked across the sleeping Kirby, then out the window, and saw, for the first time in his life, the spectacular white-topped Italian Alps spread out below. He held to the breathtaking sight for some moments and then began saying the Rosary with the beads Brian had traded him just a few hours ago, hoping for strength and guidance.

Ed Kirby had also awakened. He gratefully sipped the orange juice in front of him. Then he turned to Bill in the aisle seat and smiled. "Well, we've done everything Brian asked of us and for whatever higher power is working through him. I guess it's His call what happens next. Not Brian's. Not ours."

"Amen, Ed," Bill replied.

When the plane landed at Leonardo da Vinci Airport in Rome, Ed Kirby had arranged that he and Bill would be the first passengers escorted to the debarking ramp. They were immediately led through customs and immigration, carrying their overnight bags. They were led out to the sidewalk, where the U.S. embassy car and Claudio, the ambassador's driver, were waiting.

Claudio's first words, in broken English, were, "The DCM wanted to know where you were. I tell him that I am sure ambassador knows what's best for America. This makes him mad at me." Claudio grinned broadly.

The car was well on the way out and heading toward Villa Richardson before the last TWA passengers had left the plane. The drive to the residence took less than half an hour, and by ten A.M. Kirby was showing Bill to the front door. Kathy Kirby and daughter Maureen were at the door to greet them. The women knew only that Bill Kelly was a close friend of Cardinal Comiskey's and a deep-sea fisherman from Massachusetts.

Kathy and Maureen welcomed their guest with a kiss on each cheek, an Italian custom Bill had never experienced before. Kathy told him that a box from Brian had been delivered just half an hour earlier and was to be given to him. She pointed to the neat box resting on the hall table with a Roman tailor's label on it. Ed excused himself, leaving Maureen, Kathy, and Bill to chat in the Nancy Reagan Sun Room. In his office he dialed the number that Brian had given him and found himself talking to Monsignor Cippolini at an office in the Sistine Chapel. "Please tell Cardinal Comiskey that Ambassador Kirby called to let him know that the package he has been expecting from the United States has been delivered," Ed said succinctly.

"His Eminence left word that when you called, Mr. Ambassador, to please send the gentleman to my office here at the Sistine Chapel. And, Mr. Ambassador, please be certain he immediately opens the box delivered to your residence this morning."

"I will send him down to you with my driver shortly, Monsignor," Kirby replied. He picked up the package left for Bill. In the sun room, Ed Kirby found him talking animatedly with Maureen and Kathy. Already they'd discovered that Maureen and Bill's daughter Colleen were the same age. Maureen was telling Bill about the excellent school she was attending, Marymount International School, and mentioned that Sister Ann Marie, the principal, was from the same Irish county that her grandparents were from.

"There are many good schools here," Maureen declared.

"Bill," Ambassador Kirby interrupted, "the cardinal wants you to open this now before we deliver you over to him. Let me take you up to a guest room so you can refresh yourself." Bill followed Ed upstairs and into a guest room with a scenic view of St. Peter's resplendent in the midday Italian sunlight.

"Come on down whenever you're ready, Bill."

In the sun room the ambassador held up a hand against the flood of questions launched by Kathy and Maureen. "We'll all see soon enough why Mr. Kelly has come to Rome. As soon as he is ready, I must have Claudio drive him down to Monsignor Cippolini."

"I wonder what Cardinal Comiskey sent over to him," Maureen mused.

"I expect you'll find out. And don't be surprised."

Ida, the Filipina housemaid, brought in a pot of tea with four cups. "Ed, I'm glad you're home," Kathy said as she poured. The ambassador began to relax.

"I'd like to drive down with Mr. Kelly," Maureen said. "It is my turn to keep Marymount's vigil in St. Peter's Square for the election. I want to see history in the making."

Meanwhile Bill Kelly, upstairs in the guest bedroom, was having his own concerns about a new pope. He sat on the edge of the bed and slowly opened the box that Brian had sent. He gave a half smile, which quickly faded as the cassock seemed to stared back at him. "God, what am I doing here? I must be crazy." He reached out and touched the cassock. It had been so many years, often full of guilt, since he had worn a cassock. It sent shivers down his spine. He slowly withdrew the cassock from the box. A tear began to form in one eye. Reaching to wipe it away, he looked at the dampness on his finger, then opened his large hand to view the roughness. "These are the hands of a fisherman...not a pope." He stood up and let the cassock fall to the floor. He was totally lost. His mind went blank: even prayer could not come. Then a picture caught his eye. He slowly moved toward it. A man standing on the shoreline pulling in a full net of fish while Jesus looked on. The caption read: PETER THE FISHERMAN. It was settled at last. God was still talking to him. He reached down for the cassock.

✠ ✠ ✠

"You may very well be part of that history, Maureen," Ed said in a low tone. The two women followed his eyes, and both let out gasps. Bill Kelly slowly walked into the room wearing a black cassock adorned with the red trim of a monsignor. He was carrying a neatly tied file folder under his right arm, which he set down on the hall table.

"It fits you well," Ed managed. "I wonder where Brian...It's your size, all right. There is hardly a cardinal, monsignor, or even a priest in Rome as tall as you."

To a startled Maureen and Kathy, Bill said, "Sorry if I shocked you. I was a priest for six years before I married Mary. I guess Brian wants to remind someone, as the saying goes, 'Once a priest, always a priest.' "

"Claudio will take you to your next stop. By the way, do you mind if Maureen goes down with you? She somehow thinks a new pope will be on the balcony before sunset today."

"I would be most appreciative of her company," Bill replied. "In fact, I need it."

Kathy stared openmouthed at the imposing figure Bill Kelly presented, standing in their sun room doorway wearing the long black cassock and

Roman collar. Bill, aware of the startling effect of his sartorial transformation, strove for a moment of levity. His fingers tracing the red cord outlining his vestment, he quipped, "This is the fastest promotion to monsignor any ex-priest was ever given!"

"With more to come, I vow." The awe in Ed's tone was almost palpable. He raised his voice and called for Patrick in his cubbyhole office down the hall.

Bill took a cup of tea from Kathy and sipped silently for some moments, then set it down as Patrick came in. "Patrick O'Hearn, this is Bill Kelly," Ed said. "We just flew back from New York together."

Patrick reached for Bill's hand and shook it. "Monsignor, a pleasure."

"Good to meet you, Pat," Bill boomed heartily. "And to tell you the truth I don't quite know what or who I am at this moment."

"Patrick, get your camera and take a roll of pictures of Bill here with the rest of us."

"Yes, sir. I'll go find it. I'm glad you're back."

"Imposing house," Bill commented. "What a view of Rome!"

"This is the Nancy Reagan Sun Room," Kathy explained. "Our first ambassador to the Vatican was a great friend of President Reagan's and was appointed by the president. When Mrs. Reagan decided to visit, the ambassador's wife had this room completely built onto the residence for her at considerable expense. Those new picture windows were put in, and this southern California style furniture. Light, airy upholstering replaced the original, old-fashioned, heavy stuff."

"I trust the First Lady enjoyed it as much as I do," Bill remarked, taking in the authentic beauty of the room and the view through the windows.

Kathy laughed deprecatingly. "As it turned out, Nancy had two cups of tea, stayed for three hours, and that was the last she ever saw of her room."

"Then the State Department found an excuse to replace the ambassador, a political appointee," Kirby added. "He went to Libya on a confidential mission at the president's request, and when the State desk found out about it, they leaked it to the press and the ambassador was summarily removed. He fell on his sword to protect the president."

Patrick returned with his camera to shoot the pictures Ed had requested, wondering why the ambassador wanted pictures with a monsignor. In short order he snapped a dozen of Bill with Ed, Kathy, and Maureen and then several of Ed and Bill together. Then Ed snapped one of Bill and Patrick and the photo session was over.

"With all we've been through these past twenty-four hours, it would be a crying shame to be any later in getting on with our mission," Ed suggested.

Bill turned to Maureen. "Shall we set forth, then?"

"Sure thing." She paused a moment, her eyes taking in the formidable figure, then said hesitantly, "Bill?"

"Right. Please never forget to call me that—come what may. OK?" He picked up his overnight case and the manila folder.

Kirby walked out to the car and instructed Claudio to take his passenger to the side emergency exit of the Sistine Chapel, there to introduce him to the Swiss guardsman, who knew where he should be escorted.

Smiling, Ed turned to Bill. "You'll like Monsignor Cippolini. He will be expecting those documents." He tapped the file folder.

On the street, Maureen stepped into the backseat and Ed gripped Bill's hand. "I don't know anything officially," the ambassador said, "or unofficially either, for that matter, but I gather that it might not be entirely inappropriate for me to say to you, 'Feed my sheep, Peter.'"

Bill's face was suddenly illuminated as a smile shone from his eyes and lips. "Ed, you just gave me an idea!"

"What's that, Bill?"

"You'll see!"

Ed Kirby watched as the embassy car drove off. He smiled at the likelihood of his daughter being very much a part of the history of this day.

Inside, Patrick answered a phone call in the ambassador's office.

Elizabeth Redmond, AP Rome-Vatican bureau chief, was calling. At first, Patrick said the ambassador was too busy at the moment to talk with the press.

"Well," the AP woman snapped, "I just thought he might like to have me read the opening paragraph of a story in the early edition of today's *Washington Post*."

"Why don't you read it to me," Patrick suggested.

"It starts out with a question. 'Kirby to be recalled from the Vatican?'"

"Hold it!" Patrick exclaimed. "I'll get the ambassador."

"Yeah, he might want to hear what State's saying about him over there."

Patrick quickly summoned Ed Kirby, who exchanged pleasantries with the AP bureau chief and then listened to the feature story. "AWOL?" Ed exclaimed. "Monte Carlo? Ireland? Where did they get that garbage?"

"Unidentified reliable sources," the reply shot back.

"Look, Elizabeth, this is way off the mark. Why does the press believe these self-serving State Department bureaucrats? They spend their time talking to the press on background and they don't know what the hell they are talking about. I'll never understand it. I had a choice to make: play it safe and do nothing, or take a chance and help a friend and be loyal to my Church and country. And if something phenomenally extraordinary happens at the Vatican you can call me for an explanation."

"Sounds to me as though you have one hell of a story no matter what happens," the bureau chief commented.

"Well, there is such a thing as total secrecy within the conclave."

Smelling the most important story breaking within the Vatican in many years, Redmond tried to pry it out of the ambassador, but with no success. "Just call me if something breaks beyond this *Post* story business," Kirby said.

"Can you answer the allegations? Off post without permission? Did you drop in at Monte Carlo via Nice?" Redmond pursued.

"Unequivocally, no. I'll tell you as much as I can as soon as I can." Kirby hung up and looked at his loyal young assistant. "If this situation doesn't work out and I can't explain where I've been the past couple of days, I'm in deep trouble. Any word from the conclave?"

Patrick shook his head. "I can see the chapel down below us from upstairs, but no white smoke."

"I hate to think of the president greeted by this mess when he comes in from his morning jog. Conclave secret or not, I am going to have to explain to him what happened and leave it up to him what he wants to tell anyone else!"

"Let's hope he doesn't ordinarily read the newspapers before he goes out running," Patrick said.

NO NEED FOR MORE VOTES 14

Two hours before Ambassador Kirby and Bill Kelly arrived, Cardinal Comiskey was being driven from da Vinci Airport to Vatican City. Making all the preparations on the car telephone for Bill Kelly's arrival, Brian directed the motor pool driver, Tony, to take him to the side entrance of the Sistine Chapel. Outside stood a Swiss guard, with whom Brian exchanged a few words as he stepped out of the Vatican Mercedes. Then he approached the chapel's emergency door that would lead him back into the conclave. Monsignor Alonso Cippolini stood up from his desk to greet him. "So glad to have you back, *Eminenza*! I hope everything went well...whatever you had to do. You have been the most famous face on TV since you departed."

"Yes, Al, it's a media circus. I have one more item for you. A certain Monsignor Kelly, an American from Massachusetts, is bringing some important information to us. Ambassador Kirby will confirm by phone when Monsignor Kelly is coming. A couple of hours, Al."

"Massachusetts. Now I am understanding—a little." He smiled knowingly.

"I left instructions with the captain of the Guard at the gate to bring him straight to this door when he arrives. In your own charming way please make him feel comfortable until I come out and get him."

"Certainly, *Eminenza*. Will he be staying? I mean, do you want me to prepare a room for him at the new Vatican hotel?"

"No, Al. He may already have arrangements made."

Smoothly Cippolini unbolted the door, bowed graciously, and smiled. "Have a fruitful day, *Eminenza*. I hope the information you are expecting will get us a pope soon so we can put this long conclave behind us."

"I also, Monsignor," Brian echoed. With that Comiskey passed through the door and breathed a sigh of relief as he heard the bolt close behind him. A triumphant if enigmatic smile played across his face as he considered the anxiety his fellow princes of the Church had undergone. They had no idea what he had experienced while away from them. Of course, they had no real reason to be concerned. They all knew that he had been sent merely to explain the "joke" and the "problem" to some poor American fisherman. Of course, Mr. Kelly's refusal had been automatic!

As Brian walked in, Cardinal Rostia, smiling and extending his hand, was the first to greet him. "I trust your trip was successful and that we can put this whole nightmare behind us?"

In the Sistine Chapel, Cardinal Motupu and the other black cardinals clustered together, anxiously staring at the two. Brian's grin broadened as he caught the eye of the lead African delegate and gave him a wink, which immediately brought wide, toothy smiles of comprehension on the part of this new faction seeking change.

Everyone in the august conclave believed he alone was doing God's work and that, hence, God was working through him. Each believed his individual opinion was God's opinion, and, therefore, even if his thinking might be at total variance with that of any other princes of the Church, that God, at least, was on his side.

They are all correct, Brian thought. *God will take us and work with us come what may. We are his children. He is capable of considering all our views and opinions, then of getting it to work out and to move us ahead in time.*

"You did your work most expeditiously." As Cardinal Robitelli turned toward his table facing the chairs arranged for the cardinals, Brian reached out and laid a hand on the *carmelengo*'s shoulder. Robitelli was now clearly back in charge of conclave proceedings.

"Please, Your Eminence, may I speak to you for a moment? It is vitally important that I tell you about the mission."

The *carmelengo* showed his vexation that his conclave might be delayed for even another minute. "Not now, please, Comiskey. I'll have you give your little travel talk as soon as we get back into session." With that he turned and walked briskly away.

What a fatuous snob, Brian said to himself before he could stop the thought. *Very well. OK. I'll give my 'travel talk' later. But 'little'? I doubt it. It will be the most momentous travel talk in Catholic annals since Peter walked from Galilee to Rome.*

✠ ✠ ✠

Two Swiss guards on duty who recognized U.S. diplomatic plates on the big bulletproof American Cadillac waved the official embassy driver, Claudio, through the Porta di Sant'Anna. He drove up toward the Sistine Chapel and stopped in front of the side entrance.

"See you later, Maureen," Bill said as he stepped out of the car. "I hope you have your historic day."

"Maybe I'll see you later if you'll be staying on?" Maureen replied. "I'll make you the best *olio e aglio* you've ever tasted."

Bill smiled enigmatically. "What happens to me from this moment on is in the hands of God. I will, of course, assist Him in making His will my own in every way possible."

Maureen gave him a questioning look but found it hard to reply as Bill repeated his name to the guard at the door.

"Yes, Monsignor Kelly. I have been waiting for you," the multihued-uniformed guardsman said. "Brian Cardinal Comiskey asked me to show you into Monsignor Cippolini's office at once."

Beyond the side entrance to the Sistine Chapel the guard stopped at a large desk, where another Swiss guard wearing a contemporary officer's uniform sat on duty. "For you, Captain," the first said, handing him a note. "Cardinal Comiskey of Ireland gave this to me less than an hour ago."

The captain read the note, looked over at the imposing cleric in front of him, and reread the paper. "You are Monsignor William Kelly?" the captain asked sternly.

"Yes, I am!"

"Have you documents to prove that?" the captain challenged.

"Yes, of course." Bill put his folder down, reached for the passport he had obtained when he attended a fishing conference in the Azores several years before, and handed it over.

The captain looked at the picture, a hint of a smile on his face. He rose, extending his hand. "Welcome to Rome, Monsignor. Follow me, please."

Bill picked up his folder, pocketing his passport, and followed through a short, ancient hallway until they reached the desk of Monsignor Cippolini, who scrambled to his feet.

"Here is the monsignor that Cardinal Comiskey has told you to see." The captain turned to Bill. "I'm led to presume you must be carrying important documents in that folder."

"I presume so," Bill replied levelly. With that the Swiss guard turned and moved swiftly down the hallway.

"My name is Monsignor Alonso Cippolini." He shook hands with the anxious Bill Kelly. "Cardinal Comiskey asked me to receive you. Ah, something to eat, *caffè* maybe, while we wait for the signal?"

"I'd love coffee and any kind of roll."

Monsignor Cippolini picked up the phone and gave the order, looking at Bill with an engaging grin. "The Americans and other English-speaking just call me 'Al.' I must confess I'm as curious as the captain was as to what's in that apocalyptic folder. But I'm sure with all the trouble Brian, I mean Cardinal Comiskey, went through, we'll know soon enough."

Al's Italian accent was charming, Bill thought. "Yes," he replied. "I'm sure the cardinals will be anxious to see me—with this folder, of course. Monsignor—call me Bill."

"Right, 'Bill.' We'll sit here at my desk. You can have your *caffè* and rolls and we can make talk until the phone rings."

"Thanks, Al. It's good to meet a thoughtful person now, at this moment."

"I am from Sicily, but of course I love Rome. Rivalry, you know? Is this your first visit?"

"That's right. Maybe you could tell me a little bit about your work and what goes on in this place," Bill suggested.

"If I did that, Bill, you'd have a long beard and cobwebs before I finished. But I think I could give you a mental tour before they call you. When they are done maybe we will go out to one of my favorite little restaurants for a late lunch." Monsignor Cippolini turned as a waiter brought in a continental breakfast. "If you are going to be here a while longer I will show you the best restaurants in Rome. The best are also the least expensive."

"Thanks, Al. That would be helpful indeed." Bill sipped the coffee and munched on a tasty, sticky Italian roll.

Inside, the princes were waiting expectantly, some apprehensively, to hear Brian's account of the aftermath of their ill-advised "joke" before casting their ballots anew. Various groups were already seated in their places, openly discussing the next ballot despite the rules. Every cardinal was by now eager to put an end to this conclave, to get out of his Vatican prison and speed back to his own semiprivate world again.

Within minutes after the last cardinal was in his place the *carmelengo* tapped his wooden gavel on the table before him. "Dear brothers, I know you are all anxious to get our business concluded, so I will not slow you down save to allow our brother, Cardinal Comiskey, a few moments to tell us all about his trip. We are well aware of the pressure he was under the moment he left our presence. I, for one, am particularly proud of him for the near-incredible speed with which he carried out this most difficult assignment. Let us give him a warm welcome back."

"*Bravo, bravo!*" echoed in the chapel.

Restrained but intense applause greeted their momentary hero. When the clamor began to subside the *carmelengo* tapped his gavel again. "So, dear brother, before we begin our voting, would you take no more than fifteen minutes to bring us all up to date?" The *carmelengo* seated himself.

Cardinal Comiskey felt the butterflies in his stomach and a constriction in his throat as he stood up. To everyone's surprise he strode to the front of the chamber and turned to face them. "Dear brothers, I feel any account of my journey would be superfluous. The only thing necessary to say, and I certainly did not expect I would be saying it..." He paused, as though incapable for a moment of making the pronouncement. Then, "There will be no need for another vote. Bill Kelly has accepted the papacy!"

The shocked silence was suffocating. Slowly minds began to absorb the meaning of this declaration. *"Mio Dio,"* were the first words uttered as one cardinal blessed himself with the sign of the cross.

Nervous laughter, mingled with a subdued mumbling, was cut off abruptly by Cardinal Robitelli. Without rising, he blared out at the bowed head before him. "Please, Cardinal Comiskey, the 'joke' has gone far enough. We will have no more of it! If you think this gathering is a joke, be seated and we will get on at once with our work."

Brian turned his head slowly, and the *carmelengo* mentally shuddered at the withering contempt of his stare. "You are right, Your Eminence. The 'joke' is over, and it is on us. God is my witness, and I am not in a jesting mood."

The *carmelengo* was on his feet now as he suddenly realized along with the others in the room that there was no smile on the face or jest in the words of their Irish colleague. "Impossible, Comiskey! What did you say to that man? What are you trying to do to us?"

Murmurs arose, some angry, from several areas in the room. Only the black cardinals from Africa and America, seated in their own enclave, indulged without constraint or fear in joyous expressions and nods among themselves.

Brian could see that he needed their attention in the Sistine Chapel to complete his task. "Sit down, Eminence!" his voice whipped. "I will inform you what occurred." The totally uncharacteristic turnabout had its desired effect. The *carmelengo* fell back into his seat, dazed by his junior's outrageous rebuff. Silence, and all eyes were glued on the now isolated figure confronting them in evident pain.

"First, I apologize to you, Cardinal Robitelli, for my outburst, but I felt it the only way I could deliver this most unique of messages. I must explain to all of you exactly what happened, no more and no less.

"My trip to the United States, as we all expected, was fraught with confusion and bewilderment. But I was blessed with the help of Bishop Murray of Boston and Bishop McCarrick of Fall River. When I arrived at the Kelly residence, Bill Kelly had just returned from a long fishing trip."

Brian paused and searched his audience for understanding. "Now, please pay strict attention to what I say. It is of the utmost significance." All the cardinals, some in a kind of agony, leaned forward to hear the next words. "I went down to the dock to greet him. When I got within five yards of him he caught sight of me. He dropped the nets he was repairing and cried out to me in a shocked voice, 'Oh, my God! So it's true!' His words stunned me totally." Brian held the rosary he had given to Bill all those years ago, suddenly as bright as new, tightly in his right hand and mustered all the sincerity, emotion, and inner truth he could command.

"I asked him what he meant by those words. After some fumbling around he quite reluctantly admitted to me that he had dreamed, envisioned, perhaps had even experienced, an apparition from Our Lady of Fatima. She was appealing to the people of the world to recognize the new challenges to the Church. She implored the lowly fisherman to become a fisher of men's souls."

Brief murmurs arose in the assembly as Cardinal Comiskey paused and then continued. "I sat down with him on the side of his boat and tried to explain my purpose in coming and the bizarre manner in which his 'election' had transpired. But the more I spoke to him about how impossible this situation had become, the more evidence he provided me for believing that the Blessed Mother Mary somehow had spoken to him beforehand, and he would not be dissuaded from accepting."

As Brian continued with ever-greater fluency to recount the conversations and events that had taken place the day before in Buzzards Bay, individual whispering coalesced into a steady murmur around the chamber.

"And that, brothers, is what leads me to believe that through our blundering and our floundering here, or perhaps in spite of it, or perhaps because of it, the Holy Spirit has in very truth spoken to us in this conclave!"

With his last words Brian walked slowly over to the Bible that was placed beside the voting chalice and placed his hand, still holding the rosary, on the book. "So help me, God, I have witnessed the truth, the entire truth, and nothing but the truth." He kissed the Bible and walked quickly back to his seat.

A few cardinals began to talk quietly to each other. They were surely, terribly, at a loss. Finally, a stunned Cardinal Robitelli stood behind his table and tapped his gavel. His mind was searching for words. As was the case with most of the assembled Church princes, he was trying to determine how to repudiate the accounting that Cardinal Comiskey had rendered.

What had happened was blatantly inconceivable. Worse, it was suspect. Yet, like all the rest in the room, the *carmelengo* felt an inner tug at his conscience—or was it his soul? All of them had experienced what each believed to be direct communion with the Holy Spirit in some way, at some time, in some place. Could this be another one of those circumstances? They were suddenly, instantly, caught between two worlds. It was one thing to preach love of God or say that He had spoken through His Scriptures. But it was another matter entirely when a mere mortal stated that Our Lady had spoken to him. Who did this man think he was? Yet had not each one of them been similarly called to the religious life in the first place?

Robitelli looked out at the assembly. He could announce a recess. They were all anxiously waiting for him, their leader, to clarify this situation. "Dear brothers, I'm...well, at a loss to know what to say. And you know I've seldom been at a loss for words."

He waited for help in the expected response. None came. He coughed to clear his throat, stalling for the inspiration that eluded him. Finally he reverted to the tried and true solution to any dilemma: Pass the buck, or blame the messenger.

"Cardinal Comiskey, I can't believe that you allowed this to happen! You should certainly know how to convince a layman that any high post, let alone the papacy itself, is far beyond anything he could imagine or merit. I hold you personally responsible for this situation. My God! I wish I had been granted a chance to speak to this upstart, Mr. Kelly. Things would have been different."

Cardinal Comiskey, mortally affronted, had expected something like this, and was prepared. Standing before the cardinals, he glanced around the assemblage, then stared back at the *carmelengo,* a smile of impending vindication on his lips. The *carmelengo* again unwittingly had ensnared himself. "You have appealed to Caesar, to Caesar you shall go!"

"What in God's name—? Are you—?"

"No, Your Eminence. It occurred to me the request you made might fit St. Paul's appeal. You want to speak to Bill Kelly? You want to tell him why he shouldn't dream of taking advantage of what you consider our mistake? Fine. I believe Bill Kelly should be waiting in Monsignor Cippolini's office at this very moment. Allow me to summon him."

A stunned *carmelengo* glared back at the more youthful cardinal standing before him. Chuckles, impossible to interpret, rose here and there. Then some mumbles, followed by a few hand claps.

Cardinal Motupu leaped to his feet. "Yes, Brian." He looked about at the cardinals, all of them now fascinated with the turn of events. "Let's meet the pope and hear what he has to say."

It was evident Motupu had enjoyed this shot. "*Sì, sì.* Yes, yes," other voices joined in. "Let's see him. Let him be heard."

The gravel sounded sharply. The *carmelengo* was attempting to regain some order, to reestablish control. "Brothers, we cannot be hasty! If Mr. Kelly is here, ought not we to decide first what we want to say to him and convince him how to give up his mad ambition to—"

"Not unless Mr. Kelly is present," Motupu countered. "Do we have to sneak up on the man and betray him like Judas did, before attempting to destroy him? No, I say! Let's have an open and honest discussion with him present, in front of us. Then let God's will be done."

Applause rang uncharacteristically from the assembly along with cries of "*Sì, sì.* Yes, yes, bring him in!"

The *carmelengo* at once perceived the futility of any more attempts that might further erode his control over the proceedings. Despairing, he banged the gavel for order.

"Very well, brothers. Cardinal Comiskey, please go for your Bill Kelly."

WEAKNESS REACHING OUT TO WEAKNESS IN LOVE 15

Cardinal Comiskey responded with alacrity to the conclave's request. He had played his part well in accordance with his conscience and was anxious to get the monkey off his back, allowing the assemblage to deal with Bill Kelly in its own way. The light of battle animated his eyes as he approached the emergency door.

Yes, Brian thought, *they will have to deal with him, true enough, but the Bill Kelly I know will want to examine the deck before the cards are played.* His heart quickened when he picked up the phone and called Monsignor Cippolini.

"Yes, Your Eminence, I have him seated here at my desk. Do you want him or just the papers?"

"Papers?" Brian asked absently. "Oh yes, the papers. No, bring Monsignor Kelly to the door."

Brian waited a few moments before the knock sounded. He opened it to see Monsignor Cippolini with Bill standing beside him. "I see you made it all the way." He nodded approvingly at Bill Kelly, resplendent in the long cassock Brian had gone to some trouble to find for him. "Well, my friend, the cardinals would like you to come before them...and to present the papers you brought," he added for the benefit of Monsignor Cippolini. "I trust you had no trouble gathering them."

"None, Your Eminence."

The cardinal turned to Monsignor Cippolini. "Thank you for your assistance, Al. You will consider this to be conclave work and discuss it with no one."

"Certainly. I understand completely. And Bill, when your errand is completed, it will be time for me to take you to lunch at that restaurant I was telling you about."

"Al, don't wait too long." Brian chuckled. "There may be many questions asked. Let's go in, Bill. Not to keep my esteemed brothers waiting!"

Bill finally found words. "God, Brian, do I feel out of place."

"You hardly look it. Take it easy and remember: you're the biggest guy in the place, literally and figuratively. Be respectful. Keep your temper! I suspect they are as nervous and confused as you are. To tell the truth I'm utterly and completely mixed up myself. But I just now presented your views as you did to me on your dock. Just yesterday," he marveled. "God, it seems like an eon ago. I'll stand behind you, don't worry."

Bill could only nod as they approached the entrance to the famous Sistine Chapel. He felt his face flush crimson as he gazed out at the battery of eyes fixedly staring at him. The few moments of silence were then broken by some quiet and admiring murmurs at this would-be pope's imposing appearance. "My God, it is John Wayne," someone whispered in the silence.

The Sistine Chapel! What an awesome and breathtaking sight. Like a movie extravaganza. He half expected to see Anthony Quinn, Gregory Peck, or Charlton Heston come winging down from the ceiling. He lowered his eyes to Michelangelo's magnificent and brilliantly restored *Last Judgment* on the far wall, overcome for a moment by the sheer brilliance and meaning of this Renaissance masterpiece, but then quickly recovered, to give the appearance of being firm, steadfast, and confident. *I must survive,* he told himself. *Please, Our Lady, give me strength.*

The *carmelengo* advanced, extending his hand. "*Benvenuto al Vaticano.* Welcome to Rome, Mr. Kelly. My name is Cardinal Robitelli. We don't wish to frighten you. We are at bottom a friendly group of men and most willing to discuss some issues of importance with you."

"Well, if that's the case I'm feeling at ease already."

Smiles of condescension and relief, some of pity, dotted the assembly as the *carmelengo* coughed and got down to business. "So, as you know, Mr. Kelly...Bill...we have...that is, some serious reservations concerning you...er...as pope. The cardinals would like to ask you questions concerning...er...your qualifications." The *carmelengo* stood beside Bill Kelly, facing the seated group. "Who would like to be first?"

Cardinal Willeman, as anticipated, was the first to lift his hand and be recognized. "My question is a simple one, Mr. Kelly. Allow me to call you 'Bill.' You are a widower with a family. Have you thought in full depth how this would affect the Church? Even how it would affect your family? Granted, we had a few married popes hundreds of years ago, but modern history has shown us that marriage is unsuitable for anyone in such a responsible position. We here represent the Church inasmuch as we have dedicated our lives completely to God. Our vows of chastity, of obedience, are our witness to that particular commitment. I understand that you originally made that very same commitment but failed in it. Now you are a layman, I think, despite your monsignor's vestments, and you have a commitment to your family. A good father, no doubt. That is why many of us feel you are initially unfit for this august, even final, office."

Standing beside the *carmelengo*'s desk in front of the cardinals, Bill nodded thoughtfully. He took a deep breath and began the most important performance of his life.

"Thank you for stating your opinion in such a direct manner, Your Eminence." Smiling, Bill said, "I rather suspected the subject would be brought up." The cardinals clearly appreciated the fact that, at the very least, Bill had a sense of humor. "I'm glad it was the first question, so that we can clear the air in that regard. I will say only this. I have the highest respect for the rules of God and His Church, but I don't feel that celibacy has anything to do with love and commitment to God and His Church. Jesus had no problem appointing a married man to be his first pope. 'On this rock, Peter, you will build my Church,' He directed."

Bill paused to gauge the effect of that hoary argument for marriage within the clergy. "In regard to purity," he continued, "I would remind you that I was an active priest for six years. I sat in rectories and monasteries and heard the issue of the laity discussed openly around the table. It was one of deep concern and extensive inquiry within each group. While I obviously love my late wife and children, I love Christ also with all my heart and soul and want to serve him and the people of His Church."

Again Bill took a moment to gauge the reaction to his argument before going on. It seemed to him that he had captured the attention of the college. The facial expressions of many of the cardinals showed Bill the discomfort he was causing, shedding unwelcome light on a controversial issue within the Catholic Church, namely the subjugation of women. Nevertheless, he relentlessly decided to pursue the question of celibacy, which he had suspected while on the plane would be among the first arguments raised against him by the conclave.

He glanced around the half circle of cardinals concentrating on his every word. "The facts are, it seems to me, that the overwhelming majority of priests and all of the higher clergy are caring, decent, dedicated souls who would never purposefully sexually harm anyone. But unfortunately it only takes a few to tarnish the reputation of the many. I know that. You know that. But to keep God's Church strong, the people outside must know it too."

Bill spread his hands out in a take-it-or-leave-it gesture. "So that is my answer to you as honestly as I can give it. I see no moral problem in a married pope, or a married priest. But then again, that is a decision to be made by God, and we must pray for guidance." He gestured for the next question.

As soon as the cardinals had caught their breath, Cardinal Cordeiro of Central America was recognized. "Mr. Kelly, may I ask...since leaving the active priesthood have you continued to be an active member of the Church? I mean do you go to Mass regularly? Say your prayers? Try to serve the Church faithfully?"

Bill nodded. "Well, I trust so. Being a fisherman I sometimes am unable to attend Mass on Sunday. When my boat is in port I attend Mass. Not because of any Church law but because I know for certain that I am the one who benefits, not God."

A few murmurs of "Well said, well said" were heard from the black contingent. But Cardinal Cordeiro did not feel satisfied and pressed on. "But don't you think, Mr. Kelly, that if someone is serving God, or feels the call to serve, his daily life should be much more active within the Church?"

"Well, now that you mention it, Your Eminence, I totally agree with you. That's why I'm here! And that's why I work hard for my Church back home. And I do it in a quiet and unassuming way. I guess you could say weakness reaching out to weakness in love. That is the face of the Church we must display. I'm reminded of the quiet but wonderful work Paul VI did on behalf of handicapped children."

Cardinal Cordeiro sat down. Cardinal Motupu was recognized next. "Bill from America, I first want to welcome you here. I tend to agree with most of what you have said, especially your words on the Church helping the weak. But I would like to know your views about how you would see yourself handling the awesome responsibility of being pope. I mean, how could you possibly make all the necessary office appointments that a new pope must make in order to continue the ever-ongoing work of the Church? As you are no doubt aware, all offices end when the pope dies. They must all be reconstructed."

"Thank you for asking such an excellent question, Your Eminence. I was thinking about that on the way over here. I recognize my defects and limitations. So I thought that I would just trust that the people our beloved Pope John Paul II selected were the finest people available for those posts. At least at first, I would leave everything and everyone exactly as it was and they were when he died. There will be no shift in authorities. The jobs in the curia will not change, not at first. But I will listen long and carefully to every cardinal in this conclave as we begin to shape future lines of authority. Together we will decide on who will do what jobs here inside the Vatican. As I say, everyone will be heard, and, since I have no preconceived ideas on personnel, any ideas proposed by individual members within this college of cardinals will have equal weight. I would depend on the cardinals who work here to be my teachers and to help me adjust to the office."

Cardinal Monassari stood up and was recognized by the *carmelengo*. Brian wished there was some way he might warn Bill that this question or statement would be slanted toward Monassari's continuing to exert his personal power based on his influence at the news-making Vatican Bank.

"Mr. Kelly"—he emphasized the Mr.—"Vatican finances have been a source of contention for most of the last century, especially since the period before, during, and after World War II. There were allegations that the Vatican Bank harbored Nazi gold and money. And so forth. More recently there was speculation about a criminal conspiracy involving forged and counterfeit bonds deposited with the Bank used as collateral for various loans. As the member of this conclave closest to the operations of our Bank, I would like to know how you would deal with these outside charges, which come mostly from anti-Catholic sources. And perhaps concerning administration of the Bank and our finances in general."

Bill sensed a trap laid out for him. He hazarded a cautious but positive approach to combating the obvious corruption that had plagued Vatican banking connections for most of the century.

"Your Eminence," he began, "I have found it necessary to pay a great deal of attention to the financial matters of a certain business and a certain industry in America—that of fishing. I am not naive in recognizing fiscal misappropriations. I shall pay stringent attention to other Vatican issues. But I will be mindful of those members of the curia, and of their supervisors in this body, who have given so much of their energy and wisdom to administering the vital aspects of the worldwide Catholic Church and its government, the Holy See."

Pasquale "Patsy" Cardinal Monassari nodded in preliminary satisfaction. With these words it was suddenly evident that a whole new attitude of acceptance was developing in the assembly. Heads turned, nodded, whispered. His few bold statements of concern for the weak had intrigued the liberals. Leaving the posts as Pope John Paul II had filled them intrigued the traditionalists. A few old conservatives thought they saw their chance ahead to manipulate the new pope to their philosophy.

A feeling, perhaps the breath of the Holy Spirit, seemed to be indicating this might indeed be the perfect time for a layman who was also an ordained priest to rule. It would surely amaze, startle, and perhaps even reawaken the faithful. They would see for themselves how concerned the magisterium really was to have them participate more fully in the life and voice of the Church. No matter that some of them viewed the pope as a mere figurehead, like the queen of England. They, and a friendly magisterium, would remain the moving power. All, perhaps, would be well. The Holy Spirit, as it had through the centuries, still spoke through them!

Robitelli was quick to pick up on this shift in the atmosphere when Cardinal Monassari sat down and no more hands were raised. He tapped his gavel lightly. "Brothers, we seem to have come to some kind of consensus. May I see at once a show of hands of those who are opposed to Mr. Kelly?" No one found himself able to stir. The die had been cast.

With a sigh the *carmelengo* rose. "The original vote stands, then! No changes are necessary. The integrity of the rules has been preserved." He paused and gave Bill an approving look. "Except for one omission in procedure, we have a pope!"

Cardinal Motupu, almost succumbing to a sense of accomplishment, suddenly jerked his head up combatively. "Omission in procedure?" his voice cracked out.

Cardinal Comiskey also betrayed an attitude of alarm not lost on Robitelli. "Yes," the *carmelengo* answered. "The pope, of course, must also be the bishop of Rome. Yet Bill here is not even a bishop."

Silently, almost menacingly, Cardinal Motupu stood up and walked over to where Bill was standing. He gestured toward the empty chair beside the *carmelengo*'s desk. "Sit down, Bill," he said in a friendly tone of voice.

Bill did as he was bid and without further ado Moputu placed his hands on Bill's head. "As cardinal I consecrate you Bishop William Kelly."

Immediately Cardinal Comiskey wordlessly laid his hands on Bill's head. And then, with a confidential smile, he pressed the rosary he had given Bill when they graduated from St. John's back into his hands. Robitelli was next, inaugurating a procession of cardinals as one by one they laid hands on Bill's head in silent consecration and fealty to him as bishop of Rome and pope.

Unbelievably, it was over! After two taps of the gavel Cardinal Robitelli announced, "My responsibility as *carmelengo* is finished. We have a pope. Please rise, Your Holiness, and tell us your name." Loud applause and laughter, even shouts, rang within the hall for several minutes. When it had settled down the cardinal stepped from behind his table.

"Brothers, as continuing Vatican secretary of state, unless the pope changes his preferences, for we all know a pope is not bound by promises made before he officially takes over his position..." The cardinal gave the new pope a questioning look, and Bill Kelly shook his head. "As secretary of state I suggest that we now take some time to decide exactly what I am going to say to the crowd outside and, through the media, to the watching world before we get round to sending up white smoke." He turned to the pope-elect.

"Your Holiness, what name will you choose? As you know, that is the custom."

All the friendly smiling eyes were turned to the new leader. Bill nodded. "I will take the name of the first Vicar of Christ, who like myself was a fisherman and a married man with children. Peter! I am Peter II!"

A brief, sharp shock—some of the cardinals obviously thought that assuming the one name that no other pope had ever had the temerity to consider bordered on sacrilege—was followed by tearful applause. Perhaps they did not have as much control over Bill Kelly as they had thought. More astonishing, however, was the suitability of this name for the coming new millennium.

Cardinal Robitelli began formulating the short but crucial speech he would deliver to the hundreds of thousands of faithful who had patiently waited for days to hear the announcement. A deep, collective sense of accomplishment was enjoyed now by the college of cardinals as it realized that it was actually doing something never done before, or considered a possibility for many centuries, namely enthroning a pope of the laity who had been ordained.

A second revered custom was suggested to the new pope. He must be fitted into a white cassock. The Gammarelli brothers, fifth generation of a family of Vatican tailors, were let into the Sistine through the emergency door. They carried several cassocks of varying sizes. Thinking that Robitelli had surely been elected they proffered the garment tailored to fit him, but when confronted with the tall, strapping, burly fisherman, Peter II, they were embarrassed and dismayed. However, they quickly set about tailoring two white cassocks into the largest one ever known to have been made, using a corner booth of the chapel as their workshop. Peter the Second was soon clad properly for his presentation to the teeming crowd waiting outside in the famous St. Peter's Square.

As these preparations proceeded, Brian Cardinal Comiskey was on the emergency telephone calling Monsignor Timothy Shanahan, rector of the North American College just a few blocks from Vatican City. The moment Bill Kelly had signified his desire to accept the papacy; Brian had tapped Shanahan as the one man most competent to become private secretary to this first, relatively untutored, American pope.

Robitelli then borrowed the plain gold wedding ring Bill was wearing. "The Vatican jeweler will have the 'fisherman's ring' ready by tomorrow."

"Then, Your Holiness, we must all individually step forward, kneel, and kiss the ring as a show of our unity and fealty," Cardinal Comiskey explained.

"I respect your customs," Bill replied, resplendent in the newly fitted white cassock, "but I must confess I don't feel very comfortable with all of them. Tell you what, Brian," he confided, "I'll accept it all as you say this first time, but if I find them too hard to deal with I may end up putting the ring in my hip pocket."

Laughter again filled the room as this colloquy was repeated. The cardinals seemed to be enjoying this artless new pope. Each cardinal came forward, pausing to speak to him. Holtz of Belgium was the last to engage Pope Peter's attention. Cardinal Comiskey winced, knowing Holtz was a hard-line traditionalist and undoubtedly profoundly disturbed by the abrupt and totally unexpected turn of events.

"Your Holiness," Brian overheard Holtz address the pope, "I am by nature so set in the traditions of the Church that I would beg to hear your view on what you honestly think about papal power and jurisdiction. How will you attempt to make your authority recognized and accepted by the people?"

Brian was quick to come to the assistance of his friend. "Your Eminence, the pope has stated he needs our help in all areas of Church affairs. I think that's an unfair question to ask of him so soon."

"It's OK, Brian. I can speak for myself." Bill stepped up to the podium vacated by Cardinal Robitelli, and silence quickly descended on the clamorous conclave.

"I don't have all the background of you fine, learned, and dedicated Churchmen, but I suppose I could offer you an analogy, as Christ himself did so often through his parables. I believe that we have many examples of the Church as the bark of Peter, since he himself was a fisherman. Well, I'm a fisherman also. Professionally so. I recall the day that my father gave me my first boat to captain. It was after I was laicized, and I had no little concern about an ex-priest being in charge. I asked him straight out, 'Dad, how do I go about telling my crew that I'm the captain?'

"My father looked me in the eye for a moment, then said, 'Boy, you just go and do your job as best you understand it.' To quote my father exactly, he said to me the following, which I never forgot. 'Son,' he exclaimed, 'if you have to explain that you are the captain, you are already in deep trouble with the crew and may as well hang it up.'"

Bill smiled apologetically. "Peter I never got over his direct fisherman's language either. In any case, I found out in due course that merely taking over worked out very well."

Cardinal Holtz nodded as he seated himself. Brian seized the moment to break in. "Well spoken, Your Holiness." He clapped loudly. The others, enthusiastically if now somewhat automatically following his lead, confirmed his statement and fell into line.

Assured finally that a new pope had been positively elected by the cardinals, a Sistine Chapel official burned all the ballots that had accumulated from the "joke," adding the chemical that sent a rush of white smoke billowing up the chimney.

✦ː✦ ✦ː✦ ✦ː✦

All the speculative babble in St. Peter's Square was abruptly brought to a halt when a call came from one of the camera crewmen stationed outside the Vatican. White smoke pouring out of the chimney! The conclave was over! A great event in the world had taken place. Newsrooms were busy worldwide and TV stations were going to cut into whatever programming they were broadcasting to switch to the Vatican. Soon the new pope would come out on the balcony to give the faithful his customary blessing.

It was after three P.M. in Vatican Square, nine A.M. in Washington, as Ed Kirby heard his assistant, Patrick, shout down the hall from the Nancy Reagan Sun Room, "Hey, Ambassador! White smoke!"

Ed Kirby found himself laughing as he pictured the scene at the State Department. The European Desk officers would be just assembling to chortle over one more nonconforming political appointee on his way out. Or so they thought! Then he turned his attention to the main event.

Ed and Catherine, with Patrick, watched the television to see close up who would emerge on the balcony below to address the faithful, Maureen among them, crammed by the tens of thousands into St. Peter's

Square. Was it really possible that Bill Kelly of Cape Cod would indeed be introduced as the new pope? And if it wasn't, would Ambassador Kirby at least be able to verify the story of his assistance to the conclave and Cardinal Comiskey? Or must that remain a secret to cover up the cardinals' "joke," which Ed was beginning to feel was no joke at all but rather some act of divine intervention? In any case, if it was not Bill Kelly who emerged sometime within the next hour, Ed Kirby knew that his fledgling diplomatic career was over. He began to ask himself about the next office for which he would run. Maybe Congress, where he could be the harasser rather than the harassee of the arrogant State Department.

The cardinals, led by the pope and guided by the Sistine Chapel official, began their procession out through the back. They crossed the Regal and Ducal Halls of St. Peter's Basilica toward the loggia, a central balcony overlooking the spreading square filled with over two hundred thousand faithful—Italians, foreign pilgrims, and tourists gathered to see and hear the new pope.

Along the processional route Brian, walking closely beside the man who was once Bill Kelly, now Peter II, whispered softly to him, "We will make one stop along the way and let the others proceed."

As they passed the offices of the curia between the Sistine Chapel and the basilica, Brian entered a small reception room that he had designated and, taking the pope by the arm, led him away from the others. "We'll catch up with you," he said to a surprised Robitelli. "I need a few words with the Holy Father."

Robitelli obviously was not pleased but could say nothing to his pope, who had acquiesced to Cardinal Comiskey's suggestion.

Away from the procession, Bill found himself facing a pleasant-faced priest, a man of about fifty, he estimated, almost as tall as Bill though little overweight, with thin, graying light-brown hair.

"Bill, this is Monsignor Timothy Shanahan, originally from St. Louis but currently the rector of the North American College—NAC, as we call it."

"Your Holiness," Shanahan murmured as he knelt and took the pope's hand to kiss the ring, which was not yet in place.

"Tim, a great pleasure to meet you," Bill said.

"Tim is also a longtime friend of Ambassador Kirby's," Brian explained. "I know that Ed will join me in expressing great confidence that Tim, if he can bear to leave the college, would be your ideal private secretary and mentor to you in your early days here."

"All right. That's just the kind of support I need at this moment."

"Bill," Brian said, "Let Tim Shanahan here serve you in the way he knows best, following protocol that nobody understands better than he, as rector of the college teaching young priests here."

"Whatever you say, Brian. That is, until I get the hang of things around here and can take care of protocol myself."

"I will be honored to be of service, Your Holiness." There was a sincerely respectful timbre to Tim's voice, and he clearly appreciated Bill's usual openhearted, ingenuous approach to any potential new associate.

Brian began, "I thought that Tim could give you some pointers on your first pontifical talk to the world. Meaning right now, Bill."

Bill looked with pointed interest at Monsignor Shanahan, who smiled back. "I surely will not pontificate," Bill declared. "Never have, never will."

"That's certainly the right attitude to keep, Your Holiness. Please go out and be yourself. Be the fisherman turned pope we haven't had since our first leader, two millennia ago. Instinctively I sense that you bring us a new soul. I believe that the Holy Spirit prevailed in this conclave, as it did when Pope John Paul II was elected. At that time Communism was the blight on the world and only the prayer and courage of that Vicar of Christ could have ended it."

Shanahan's gaze searched Bill's eyes. "This time, certain challenges and actual threats on the Church we know will need to be addressed in the new millennium and we will need a man who speaks for the average Catholic who has now, somehow, miraculously been delivered to us. Family deterioration, Islamic fanaticism, the Russian Orthodoxy, plagues are all afflicting humanity like AIDS in Africa. It will take all the resolve of Pope Peter II to save the Church and the world from the terrors that threaten them all."

"Tim, that's quite a mouthful. I don't know how to say it, but I guess I can get your point across. I'll start out with a few words in the very bad Italian I learned from my fishing crews."

"Please be yourself and in your own vernacular say what you believe. The people will rest easy knowing that one of their own is at the helm. Always remember, Christ chose you, not the other way around."

Cardinal Robitelli appeared at the door. "Your Holiness, the world outside waits to meet you."

"Be right with you, Your Eminence. Come on, Tim, Brian, let's greet our people."

Word rapidly spread through the Eternal City as new crowds swarmed into St. Peter's Square to get a glimpse of their new pope. With bands playing and the crowds jostling, at precisely four P.M. the balcony door of the basilica pulled open. The massed faithful were awed and then fell silent when they saw Secretary of State Cardinal Robitelli step out. This itself was a surprise. Traditionally the first cardinal to appear would introduce the new pope, and it had been taken for granted that Robitelli was the front-runner. So much for the predictions of cognoscenti like Father Farrell.

The next moment was even more disconcerting. The cardinal did not announce at first the customary *"Habemus papam!* We have a new pope!"* Rather, he raised his hands to motion for silence and tapped the microphone to make sure it would amplify him sufficiently. He seemed more in a sermonizing mode than about to make a momentous announcement.

"Dear friends of the Church," he began, "we have caused you such anxiety and wonderment. You have been waiting patiently on us during this extended conclave. I mention also a necessary trip undertaken by Cardinal Comiskey of Ireland. We in the magisterium of the Church can tell you now that we were in these, as in other important issues, seeking enlightenment from the Holy Spirit on how best to serve the Church and its people. God alone makes the fitting choice for St. Peter's successor."

The cardinal paused and his eyes traveled over the huge crowd looking up at him from below. "In my lifetime," he continued, "I have been amazed how the Holy Spirit has given us such great, holy men in sometimes startling ways. But today I have such incredible good news for you that we find it necessary to…how shall I express it…lead you, our beloved laity, gently into our interpretation of God's will."

Once again the cardinal, spacing his words to carry, benignly turned his head from side to side, gauging the temperament of the multitude below. "You are all aware of the increased role we have asked you, our lay people, to take within the Church since Vatican II. We, as the Church hierarchy within the Church, have felt often that no matter how hard we've tried, a great gap slowly has grown between the clergy and the laity. This last gathering of the college of cardinals took our concern for the laity as its centerpiece. After much, often heated, debate we finally concurred the Holy Spirit had indeed revealed to us the way to bridge this terrible gap. Thus, dear brothers and sisters, in the name of Christ, I have the providential honor of announcing to you that a layman and former priest—not one of the cardinals—has been elected our new Holy Father!"

The awesome effect of these words was like nothing that ever had been experienced in St. Peter's Square before. The multitude, even the news media, stood spellbound in wonderment. Cameraman Augusto Dante from the Vatican TV station, Tel Pace, was so stunned that he failed to focus his camera on Cardinal Robitelli. It dipped down instead to a crowd of people standing at the fountain of St. Peter's that included Maureen Kirby and her group from the Marymount School in the fore-front. Their looks of amazement and disbelief said it all. The silence was the forerunner to a great explosion. Slowly the words began to filter through numbed minds that could barely comprehend what they had just heard.

Some began to mumble softly. "What did he say? A layman? Former priest? What does he mean?"

Robitelli allowed his statement to exert its full effect on the crowd and then concluded: "My dear friends, may I present to you, from the United States of America, His Holiness, Pope Peter the Second, an ordained and later laicized priest, a true fisherman in the tradition of St. Peter, our leader and founder pope. *Habemus papam!*"

Maureen Kirby found herself trembling. She was standing in the square with her classmates from Marymount. They had been there long before the puffs of white smoke flew skyward above the Sistine chimney, hoping to catch a glimpse of the new pontiff. Maureen's mind darted back to her father's mission and his return with Bill Kelly, metamorphosed from fisherman to monsignor, who had allowed her to call him "Bill."

Well, Cardinal Robitelli had not appeared in the white cassock! He had visited the residence and Maureen had a fairly good idea of what kind of pope he would make. From what she'd heard at home and from Vatican denizens she knew, this was all to the good. He was an old hand set in traditional ways, hardly understanding of her youth culture. But whoever the pope would be, she could now always say she had been in the square that day to see him. Someday, too, she would find out what was written in the documents that she had seen Bill carry into the conclave. It was all secret, but one day he might tell her.

"Bill! *Mio Dio!*" A scream of surprise, shock, and joy was wrung from a stunned Maureen as Peter II came onto the balcony, clothed in his hastily but meticulously tailored white cassock. Julie Rogers, a geometry teacher at Marymount, stared at the usually rather reticent young woman in astonishment but said nothing.

"I drove with Bill—Pope Peter—to the Sistine Chapel this morning," she shrieked. The young students were certain they had not heard her correctly amid the cheering of the crowd.

"What did you say, dear?" Sister Teresa asked.

"Just welcoming Bill, the new pope!" she replied. This was no time for explanations. Maureen reached into her pocketbook and withdrew a small cellular phone and dialed her father's private number at the residence while staring intently at the balcony.

In the awed silence that gripped the square, Maureen heard the number buzz and her father answering.

She spoke to him, crying out over her cell phone that it was indeed Bill Kelly on the balcony. He said he knew. Ed Kirby saw his fisherman acquaintance on the TV screen just as his daughter's call came through from the square. Instantly he turned to Patrick. "Take the film down to the AP Rome bureau. Stay with them while it is developed, and after they've picked a couple of pictures of Bill and myself for their story, bring the film back here. Tell Elizabeth Redmond I'll call her with the details as soon as I talk to Washington." Ed's heart was glad, he felt secure in the knowledge that he had helped to accomplish something very important and significant.

He strode from the sun room, where the enraptured chanting from the Vatican could be clearly heard. *"Viva il papa! Viva il papa!"* The over-flowing tens of thousands gathered in St. Peter's Square rejoiced as they had never rejoiced before. A barrier many centuries old had abruptly and totally unexpectedly tumbled down. High above the elated throng stood one of their own, a onetime layman, and they themselves felt elevated. The more they thought about it, collectively, the more excited they became.

Once safely ensconced in his private office, Ed Kirby put through a call to the White House switchboard. It was just after ten in Washington when his call was transferred to the office of the White House chief of staff. A deputy was on duty and Kirby asked to be put through to the president. The deputy had obviously read the morning paper and was reluctant to put Ed through. The Oval Office might now be off-limits, and his boss was out.

Ed explained. "Look, I was unavailable yesterday because I was escorting the new pope from Massachusetts to Rome. I know all about the *Post* story and I want to tell the president who the new pope is—an American, for starters."

The news surprised the deputy to the point that he opened up. "The president is over at the Pentagon. Scout's honor. We do have a slight crisis going on, as I'm sure you know."

"Then put me through to the First Lady. It's damned important!"

There was a hesitation on the line. Ed's voice uncontrollably rose an octave. "It's important that the First Lady herself hear what happened and that she tell the president." He paused to let his voice calm down. "It's your fault if the president is asked a question by the national media before he hears directly from his ambassador. I was with the dark horse from his home on Cape Cod to here last night."

In less than three minutes, Ed Kirby had the sympathetic ear of the First Lady on the telephone as he explained the entire situation. In the background Ed could hear the coverage on a White House TV set of the scene happening immediately below his residence in the square. When Kirby had finished explaining to the First Lady, she was enthralled with the story. "I'll brief the president immediately. I'm sure he'll want to talk to you directly, Ed."

"I'll stand by at the residence to wait for his call—even at the risk of being accused of deserting my post at the embassy," he chuckled.

Now that he had reported everything to his boss at the White House, he picked up the phone to reach the AP bureau chief. For ten minutes he briefed her on the story until Catherine came in, a grin on her face.

"Mr. Seedworth to see you, Ed."

"Tell him to wait." Back on the phone, Elizabeth Redmond thanked him for the exclusive pictures of Kirby and Bill Kelly.

"It's the biggest Vatican story we've moved since the Turk tried to kill John Paul II."

"Glad to help. Just be sure to send back the negatives with my assistant."

"Will do. And AP will be moving the first paragraphs in a couple of minutes. Wait till my pals at the *Post* read this!" she chortled.

In the sun room, Calstrom Seedworth was waiting for Ed, an innocent smile on his face. "Mr. Ambassador, we missed you yesterday."

"Cal, what about this story in the *Washington Post* this morning?" Ed asked abruptly. "What's this about Nice, Monte Carlo, and Ireland?"

"A call came in for you yesterday from the *Post*. I told them you weren't here. The driver said he had taken you to catch a nine-thirty plane. They probably checked and found one leaving for Nice. You know these press guys." He stared out the window and down at the Spanish embassy, where many diplomats were standing on the roof observing the excitement around St. Peter's Square below. Then he added helpfully, "I've asked the embassy press clerk to find out everything possible about the new pope for transmission to Washington."

Kirby nodded noncommittally. "I understand that AP is putting out quite a story on our new pope. You know, how he arrived here in Rome so secretly this morning." The hint of a smile flickered over his face. "They have researched some detailed background material on Mr. Bill Kelly." The DCM was beginning to sense that there might be a considerable and embarrassing gap in his perception concerning the ambassador's absence.

Catherine came back into the sun room. "That call you were expecting is coming through."

Ed turned back to the DCM. "You might get ready for a press conference about six P.M. when I'll explain where I was yesterday. Have it at the Cardinal Baum Room at the embassy."

Before the startled DCM could reply, Kirby was striding out of the sun room and down the hall again to his office. He was resolved to let it all hang out with the president, let the chips fall where they may. This was no time to protect innocuous conclave secrets with the State Department setting out to destroy him.

⊶⊷ ⊶⊷ ⊶⊷

It took half an hour before some semblance of order was restored in St. Peter's Square. When he thought he could be heard, Bill Kelly stepped closer to the microphone.

He began his talk in the simple Italian and Portuguese words he had picked up from many years of dealing with the immigrants who took the most humble jobs he could give them in his small fishing fleet. "My dear brothers and sisters," he began in Italian and then switched to Portuguese and to English, "I cannot say why the Holy Spirit has led these cardinal princes to select a poor and humble fisherman like me." From an utter ecstasy of jubilation the crowd was reduced to silence, absolute in its contrast to the uproar of a few seconds before.

"Like the first fisherman, Peter, I feel more like saying 'Depart from me, oh Lord, for I am a sinful man.' But I know that being a poor sinner myself, Jesus Christ is the only one I can turn to. So I have accepted both His love and His cross." Seeking to identify himself with the people of the Church in a spiritual as well as personal way, Bill glanced down at the one line in Italian written on the small piece of paper Tim had handed him and said the words which in English meant "Weakness reaching out to the weak in love."

"In the days to come," he went on, "you will learn every smallest detail of my life. So let me conclude with my sincere blessing."

He paused and smiled benignly. "I have decided to use my own words. May our beloved Savior bless and keep each and every human being on the face of this Earth. May he grant us the grace to live together in peace! May the families of the world grow in God's love like the Holy Family. And may we all learn to know and love Christ as He knows and loves us." Pope Peter II continued to wave as he departed the balcony and stepped back into the basilica. Only those cardinals near him could see the tears flowing freely from his eyes.

As Peter II disappeared from view, the crowd, which now reached all the way up Via della Conciliazione to Castel Sant'Angelo, began and continued to chant and sing long into the night. As Vincenzo, head cook at

Sabitino Ristorante at Piazza Santa Maria in Trastevere, said to a group of pilgrims from Manchester, England, "I have never seen Rome like this before, and I was here when the Allies liberated us in June of 1944."

The celebrations continued into the night like a Roman festival of ancient times. Enterprising hawkers had already taken the first available picture of the new pope from the special edition of the afternoon newspaper, *Il Tempo*. A life-size cardboard replica of Peter II with the Statue of Liberty in the background had been mounted. They were shooting pictures with their Polaroid cameras at twenty thousand lire a copy, finally running out of film as the excited spectators crowded about to make this historic day and night a personal thing. Everything American was selling out, even the remaining pirated Elvis Presley CDs and tapes down at Il Colosseo.

✠ A sense of shock gripped the Catholic world at four P.M. in Rome when Pope Peter II had been presented to the huge crowd in St. Peter's Square. It was ten A.M. eastern standard time in the United States. In Fall River, Boston, and Washington, D.C., successive waves of the concussion were especially resounding.

Ambassador Kirby's nemesis at the State Department listened, horrified, as the department's assistant director of public affairs read the first two paragraphs of a story moving out over the AP wire. "The *Post* just called about the Kirby recall leak and asked if that information is still operative in view of this AP story. It seems that the ambassador personally delivered the new pope from his home near Boston to the Vatican," the information officer said. "What's my answer? The *Post* guy told me he had called the White House and heard that the president was very pleased with Kirby's performance."

The Vatican Desk officer shouted at his assistant, "Is there a cable from Kirby explaining anything?"

"Nothing. I checked around."

Then came an exclamation from the information officer. "Oh, bloody hell. A picture is being slipped in front of me. It shows Kirby and Peter II at the ambassador's residence this morning just before William Kelly was elected pope. Kelly's wearing a priest's cassock."

"Get Kirby or the DCM, Seedworth, on the direct line," the desk officer commanded. "How could Seedworth screw this up so? The *Post* will look like a bunch of asses, just like us."

The president of the United States was winding up a meeting as his chief of staff reported the latest from Rome. Already the First Lady had summed things up for her husband after talking with Ed Kirby.

"An American pope, a widower ex-priest!" the president exclaimed. "Delivered to the conclave by my ambassador. Didn't I say Kirby was 'with the next pope' when those State idiots couldn't find him? Wonderful! Here's a God-given opportunity to divert media attention from the last remnants of that impeachment trash." He was referring to certain final Republican attempts to keep the scandal ongoing. "The talking heads will have to find something else to gossip about. Every big-time editor in Washington knew what previous presidents were up to, but they looked the other way because they liked them personally. I am going to nominate Kirby for the State Department's highest award."

"The Jefferson Medal?" The press secretary who was present shook his head. "Don't you think that's a bit much? I mean, there'll be a revolt at Foggy Bottom. They'll turn the press against you if you anger and embarrass them too much."

"They need to be shaken up," the president growled. "Regularly."

✠ ✠ ✠

An awed silence settled over the chancery in Fall River as the TV carried exclusive reports about the news from Rome, where it was now midafternoon. Disbelief and a sense of unreality disconcerted Father Raphael. He was conscious of the backside of his bishop flying out the library door toward his private den and then pausing. Bishop Sean Patrick turned to face the awestruck priest.

"Ralph, get my car out and leave it running. NOW!" He entered his sanctuary and scuttled over to the big mahogany desk. Jerking open the middle drawer, he extracted Cardinal Comiskey's white envelope. He was not surprised now to read the message the cardinal had left for him.

✠ ✠ ✠

"Sean," it instructed him, "as soon as you hear the news, get to the Kelly home and provide protective shelter for Bill's children. Do whatever is necessary to help them. I will see to your expenses. And pray for Bill. He will need all the help he can get from all sources when you read this and know what has happened. Thanks, Brian."

Even before Bishop Sean Patrick had opened the envelope from Comiskey, he was complying with the instructions. His first move was to call the commander of the Massachusetts State Police, Bill McCabe of Charlestown, to provide protection for Bill Kelly's family. Then he called the Kelly house and reached Colleen, who by now had recovered from the initial shock.

Bishop Sean Patrick promised Colleen he would be at the Kellys' home within the hour. He told her to take her phone off the hook until he arrived.

Father Raphael was standing beside the car as the bishop emerged from the rectory. "Want me to drive, Bishop?"

"God no, Ralph. I need you here to answer the phone and the doorbell."

"What do you want me to say?"

"Anything. Anything. I'm not here…whatever. I've got to get to the Kellys'. Call you when I need you."

Leaving his assistant trembling at the thought of handling the press and the crowds sure to descend on the pope's home diocese, the bishop eased in behind the wheel of his car and, quietly praying for heavenly supports, sped off in a cloud of dust. His prayer was answered when he turned onto Interstate 95 toward the Cape. A state police cruiser was up ahead, giving someone a speeding ticket. Bishop Sean Patrick pulled over quickly and jumped out to see Trooper Joe Collins whirl around, staring at him. Miracle of miracles, not just a trooper but also a parishioner from St. Mary's in Fall River!

"Joe, I need help. I need to get to Buzzards Bay posthaste. Know what I mean?"

The trooper nodded, looked back at the stopped speedster, and warned, "Slow down. Now get going."

Turning from the driver he had halted, who was gratefully moving away, Joe called out, "Follow me, Bishop. Stay close."

The cruiser's blue lights flashed as the bishop struggled to keep up with the trooper. Twenty-five minutes later he was shaking the hand of Trooper Collins on the main street of Buzzards Bay. "Thanks, Joe. I'd appreciate it if you would follow me and stand by the home we're about to visit."

"What's happening, Bishop?"

"No time to explain now. Turn on your radio and you'll find out." Bishop Sean Patrick sped off down the back road to the Kelly house and dock with Trooper Collins behind him. Colleen Kelly came out to meet him.

"Welcome to our humble house, Bishop. So good of you to come. I have the kettle on for tea or coffee if you wish."

"Thanks very much, Miss Kelly."

"Call me Colleen, Your Excellency. Dad always tells me friends should use first names."

"Well, I agree with that, especially given present circumstances. Please call me Sean."

Trooper Joe Collins emerged from his car. "Bishop, I heard the news. Wow! I can't believe it! I don't know what to say! Anyhow, I figured the Kellys might need a bit of protection, so I called my sergeant to let him know I was taking on the duty. I'll be here until my relief comes at midnight, Miss Kelly. No one gets near your house without permission."

Touched, Colleen replied, "Dear Lord, what can I say, Trooper, except thank you so much. Will you come in for some tea or coffee with us?"

"Thanks, no, Miss Kelly. When the media arrives I can best handle the show out here."

"Thanks for your thoughtfulness, Joe," the bishop broke in. "We'll need some time to decide how to handle these people." He followed Colleen into the house.

"Please sit at the table, Your Excel…Sean," Colleen corrected herself. "I want you to meet my younger brother, Roger. My sister, Meghan, is at school, but should be home as soon as her teacher gets the news. My older brother, Ryan, is a fisherman like our father and is on his way to Georges Bank. I think he'll call us on the shortwave radio when he hears the news. We didn't really believe Dad when he told us where he was going or why. I guess I am a bit confused," she ended helplessly.

"Colleen, I'm as baffled and amazed as you are. But I do know that if your father was picked by all those cardinals there must be some reason for it." The bishop thought about his statement for a moment, watching as Colleen took a kettle off the stove.

"From what Cardinal Robitelli said on the balcony at St. Peter's," the bishop continued, "they have had more interest in the laity than I could have ever imagined! There have been lay popes before. But most were men from powerful and influential families."

As Colleen poured the hot water into the teapot she discerned a note of wonderment in the bishop's voice.

"This is so vastly different," he went on. "Like, well, like choosing the first fisherman, Peter, I guess. Choosing him all over again."

Colleen nodded and turned toward the kitchen door. "Roger," she called. "Please come out here and say hello to Bishop Sean Patrick."

A ruddy face emerged from the bedroom area.

"Hi, Roger," the bishop said. "I'm happy to meet you. Would you like to sit down with your sister and me? We can discuss what has taken place today in Rome and how we feel about it."

Roger sat down quietly and looked warily at the table. Colleen finished pouring tea for the bishop and herself.

"Well, Roger," the bishop began, "may I ask how you feel about your dad being made pope? It certainly sounds like a scary thing to me. I never would have imagined him being made pope of our entire Church."

At that moment Meghan Kelly burst in the front door of the house. She saw her brother and sister sitting at the table with Sean Patrick. Her eyes fixed on the bishop, she cried accusingly. "I don't want my dad to be a pope. All the kids at school will terrorize at us. Why does he want to do it? I want my dad at home, like always."

The bishop slid his chair closer to the children. "Kids, I know this must be very hard on you. I am as amazed and puzzled as you are, and I doubt we will ever know exactly how your dad got to be pope. I have known your dad and his close friend Brian Cardinal Comiskey for many years. Perhaps all those cardinals in Rome wanted a good man of the people like your dad to help make the world a better place to live in. I'm sure that's why Cardinal Comiskey came this far to see him."

"Yes," Roger interrupted, "it's Uncle Brian's fault. I hate him! I hate him!"

"No, no, Roger, it's not his fault." Colleen turned to the bishop. "Tell him, Sean."

"Your sister is right, Roger. The cardinal—'Uncle Brian,' you called him—he alone could never make your dad the pope. That would be the choice of all those cardinals in Rome. It seems like they must have wanted to elect a layman for a reason we may or may not discover one day. They probably discussed many, many fine laymen from all over the world that various cardinals knew. And think of this: Your Uncle Brian must have been able to convince them what a kind, loving, decent man your fisherman dad is, and they were so impressed that out of all possible choices they came down on the side of your dad. But I'm sure he will be calling here very soon and wanting you to go to Rome to live with him there."

"Is that right, Bishop?" Meghan asked breathlessly. "We can go to Rome?"

"Meghan, don't worry. Your father is working on that right now and he'll call you soon. If he wants you there tomorrow I'll arrange everything. I'll even take you over to Rome myself if that's what you three want."

"Will we have our own bedrooms?" Roger asked, acceptance slowly settling in.

The bishop chuckled. "Why, certainly, Roger. Maybe even two bedrooms!"

"Wow!" Meghan smiled. "Is it a big house he lives in?"

"Yes, Meghan. It's very big. It will probably take you a month or two just to find your way around."

"How big is it?" Roger asked.

"Well, from what I know of the place, I think there are about fourteen hundred rooms inside the Vatican. I'm sure they'll have plenty of space there for you. It has its own post office, railroad station, movie theater, and supermarket. And you can learn all kinds of things from your dad's new friends there. So please, just try to be happy for your dad. He has a very hard job. And if the kids in school make remarks about it, you can tell them about your big new house. Okay?"

Meghan and Roger looked at each other happily. "All right." Meghan smiled.

Bishop Sean Patrick turned to Colleen. "It seems to me I heard that you have a problem with the Church, Colleen."

"No problem whatsoever, Sean," she replied coolly. "I don't go anymore. I guess you could say I'm an atheist of sorts. Or perhaps merely an agnostic."

Sean Patrick recalled Brian's mentioning how hard Colleen had taken her mother's death and how she had lost faith in God because of it. He could only think to say, "We must talk sometime about that."

To the bishop's surprise, the Kelly children gave him a hug.

"Why, thank you, kids! Incidentally, would you do me a very special favor?"

"What?" they chorused.

"Well, it's this. I may be around here for a while...visiting you until you go over to live with your dad. Would you mind calling me 'Uncle Sean'?"

They looked at each other and smiled broadly. "OK." Their personal crisis seemed over for the moment.

"Oh dear," Colleen exclaimed. "I forgot you told me to leave the phone off the hook. I better hang it up now in case Dad is trying to call." She walked over to replace the receiver on the hook. Before she made it back to her chair the phone rang. She ran back, hoping to hear her father's voice.

"Hello, Colleen Kelly speaking. Who? Oh, yes, I am. No. I mean look, I need some time...Hold on, please." She cupped her hand over the mouthpiece and looked up at the bishop. "It's the *Cape Cod Times*. What do I do?"

Bishop Sean gave the matter some careful consideration. "They'll be all over you, even if an entire state police battalion surrounded this house. You've got to get through a first meeting with the press as soon as possible. After that you can routinely refer them to my diocese and I will clear with the Vatican every question they may have after you make your statement."

Colleen sighed. "You're right, Sean. Shall we make it three o'clock this afternoon?"

The bishop nodded. "Yes, by all means today. Three in the afternoon. I'll help you draw up your statement."

Colleen removed her hand from over the phone. "Hello. Yes, come over today at three in the afternoon. If you really are who you say, you can spread the word. We'll talk to all media people this afternoon at three."

After a pause Colleen's voice turned vehement. "No, definitely not now! Please, understand that this is all coming as a shock to us. We have to get prepared." She politely but finally restated the three o'clock time, gently placed the phone down, and turned toward the bishop. "You want that coffee now, Sean?"

SETTLING IN 18

As Pope Peter II returned from the first universal blessing of his new career at four-thirty, he was surrounded and congratulated by a number of the cardinals who had been the most supportive of his papacy, especially Cardinal Motupu and the five other black Churchmen. Some of them, like the pope himself, were wiping the remains of tears from their eyes.

Brian could not resist a natural impulse born of years of close friendship. He reached out and grabbed Bill and gave him a big hug. "God bless you, Bill. I'm so proud of you. Were you scared out there?"

Bill regained his usual comfort zone and grinned conspiratorially. "Only the launderer who does my underwear will ever know." His remark brought a burst of laughter.

Robitelli maintained a somewhat more distant demeanor as he advanced to shake the pontiff's hand. "Your Holiness, you must be starved. Your dinner for the cardinals is scheduled for six-thirty. After Mass tomorrow morning everyone returns to his assigned duties."

"Gene, thank you. And please call me whatever name you feel most comfortable with. And, by the way, as we say out on the sea, the sun is definitely over the yardarm."

At Cardinal Robitelli's questioning glance Bill chuckled. "That means it is after noon and we would all appreciate a good drink."

Robitelli laughed and smiled warmly. "Your Holiness, I'll see to it."

With the secretary of state leading the way, the pope and Brian followed toward the large study for a drink. Suddenly Bill stopped and grabbed Brian's arm. "Oh, for heaven's sake, I almost forgot, Brian. Could you find Monsignor Cippolini and ask him to join us for dinner?"

Brian colored, as he noticed the cardinals who were with them had heard the request and were looking askance. "Well, Bill, this affair is usually—that is to say, always—limited to just the cardinals who have had to endure their long captivity in the conclave."

"I see. Look, I was invited out by Monsignor Cippolini before you led me into the conclave, so I have to return the favor. He thought I was delivering some documents and then I'd be back out. Now, just this once can we allow him to join us? I hate to break my promise to him."

Brian hastily departed to find Monsignor Cippolini. Bill felt a friendly hand patting his shoulder and turned to see the smiling face of Cardinal Motupu. "Pope Bill, Monsignor Cippolini should sit next to me. He has invited me to dine with him many times also."

"Great, Cardinal. What's your first name?"

"Augustine is my Christian name. 'Gus' for short, with friends."

"Okay, Gus, thanks for the support. Brian told me you had something fundamental to do with this 'joke' thing. I confess I know nothing about you, or any other cardinal except Brian, for that matter. Tell me, are you a brainy Vatican hand or are you, say"—Bill grinned broadly—"an affirmative-action cardinal?"

Motupu roared with laughter until tears came to his eyes, while the cardinals nearby regarded him nervously. "Dear Lord, I love sincere, honest talk like that, Bill. As a matter of fact I fit quite comfortably into the token mold. But I now see some hope for the future." He lowered his tone. "And I'll be wanting to visit you sometime and discuss my thoughts on the subject."

"Please do that! When you place the call just tell them the pope asked you to contact him and needs to talk to you—immediately."

Cardinal Motupu nodded wisely. "You know more about the chain of command here than you let on, Bill."

"Remember that my closest friend is a cardinal. My wife always tortured him with piles of lobster and apple pie till he confessed many Vatican secrets."

"Lobster and apple pie! What a way to suffer."

"He endured it well. All those years of religious discipline." The pope smiled.

⊹⊱ ⊹⊱ ⊹⊱

The media was frantically trying to make some sense of what had happened in the conclave. How could it transpire that a layman, albeit a former priest, had been elected? What disturbed them most was that for the first time in recent history not one cardinal had said any more than the standard "We cannot discuss what transpires in a conclave."

The local Italian newspapers and TV consortium were only temporarily frustrated, they thought. Cardinal Angellini sat on the company's board and was their inside man. The consortium had given a sizable donation to his favorite charity with the tacit understanding that he would pass along important details of what happened inside. With the resulting stunning conclusion of this historic conclave, Angellini's story would be worth all the support and favorable media attention he had received over the years from the press. A news courier was dispatched to his apartment near the Vatican to retrieve the scoop of the century. After a short wait, he was handed an envelope by the cardinal's assistant, which he quickly pocketed, and hastily returned to his editor's desk. The editor was all smiles as he opened his treasure. But the smile turned to a sour droop of the lips as he pulled out a short missive that read simply, *"Sorry, we are not, as you know, allowed to discuss conclave affairs."* It was evident that each cardinal was determined to abide by the rules.

✙ ✙ ✙

Cardinal Comiskey returned with the news that Monsignor Cippolini, extremely reluctant at first, would join them for dinner with great pleasure. Alone with Brian, the pope then remarked, "I could sure use a touch of the Bush about now."

"I'll see that Old Bushmills whiskey, black label, is added to the pope's private wine stock," Brian promised.

"Please, Brian, stay here and help me. I need someone close by. We can appoint another bishop or cardinal to your post in Armagh."

Brian shook his head. "Forget it, pal. I love my country and my priests and my people. I can best serve my Church there. I could never work here in the curia. It's too crowded with sycophants and bureaucrats"—he grinned at his old friend—"as you will soon learn."

"Well, I am the pope, you know. I could order you to stay."

"Yes, you could, but I also know you won't. Listen sharply to Ambassador Kirby and let Monsignor Shanahan, that college rector, be your closest guide. I would have suggested that you have him moved permanently to the Vatican, but it's possible he can be more valuable if he is not openly perceived by others as an éminence grise. Trust him above all others no matter what their cursed rank. Shanahan and Kirby are currently the keys to your success and, I might add, survival. Ed, I know, will not resign his ambassadorship as long as you need him."

They walked down the corridor and were met by the ubiquitous Cardinal Robitelli.

"Ah, Comiskey, I knew you might be here. Listen, the media people are here and driving me to distraction looking for some sort of 'political' explanation. Since you were the one everyone knows left the conclave and evidently went to fetch His Holiness, I thought you might satisfy them by coming up with some...vague...er...general statements. I'm sure you can think of something."

"I owe you that much at the very least, *Eminenza*. Where are they?"

"In our communications office. I told them you'd be along shortly."

"I'll talk to them. Please show the pope his apartments so that he can make some necessary phone calls. I'll go get this thing over with. See you soon at dinner, Bill." Brian hastened out the door, down the long marble stairs, and across St. Peter's Square to the communications office.

A round of applause greeted him as he entered the room, taking him entirely by surprise. There were media people he had known for some time, smiling and cracking jokes at his expense. "You rascal, Your Eminence, are you responsible for this? How did it happen? Who else was in the game? When did you decide on a layman?"

The cardinal raised his arms for quiet. "Dear friends...please understand that this was the work of the Holy Spirit. Besides, I am bound by conclave rules. I can't give you all the answers. It must be self-evident that we had a lengthy discussion about the role of the layman. But remember again, it's the Holy Spirit who guides our actions."

"Who were the other candidates?" a reporter shouted.

"I can only give you this one name since he was the one selected. Certainly many, if not all, of the cardinals in the college know many upstanding men who might be worthy of consideration. The fact is that we settled finally on William Kelly, and he accepted our offer." Then, after a pause and an inadvertent shrug of the shoulders, "Although it will now and in the future probably render him no little sorrow and pain."

He hesitated and then continued confidently. "You will not have great difficulty finding out about the man, but let me give you a brief sketch of the background of our new Pope Peter II. The then Father Kelly and I went through the seminary together. We were so ordained. After six years' active ministry Father Kelly applied for and received dispensation from his vows. He returned to Cape Cod, Massachusetts, to work with his father as a professional fisherman. All this time he was busy taking special care of immigrant children, Portuguese children in particular. He married a young lady from Ireland whom he had met while a priest, and they were happily married for seventeen years until his wife's tragic death due to cancer. They have four children, whom I'm sure you will meet soon via American television. All the details of how they will live together here will take some time to work out, I know. We were aware of the possible—I should say definite—shock it will have on the faithful. But the ending of the Latin Mass was a rough hurdle for them, and they handled it with considerable grace."

Brian paused and sensed that a more generous explanation was expected by these experienced Vatican reporters. "Remember also," he added, "we did not proceed contrary to Catholic tradition. William was, and thus always will be, a priest. We settled, I guess you could say, on a halfway measure. He has a lifetime of experience, both clerical and lay. Who knows, perhaps someday this simple layman, like St. Peter himself, will become a great pope. He certainly has always been a great follower of Christ."

Cardinal Comiskey smiled and paused. Then, "That is all I can give you now." With that the cardinal hastened out the door and the media scrambled to use the available phones. Those who had been videotaping were off to screen the surprising update over the networks.

✠ ✠ ✠

Cardinal Robitelli led Pope Peter away from the cardinals still milling around the conclave area in the Sistine Chapel. "Please, this way, Your Holiness, and I'll show you your apartments and how to use the telephones here. I imagine you may want to, ah"—he paused over the troublesome concept—"call your children."

"Yes, I certainly must! They will be terribly worried and anxious by now."

They entered the apartment, majestic in its simplicity. The cardinal turned to the pope. He was very grave. "Your Holiness, let me be frank with you. This whole affair flies in the face of everything I have believed during a lifetime of service. I'm sure the Church will adapt to you as it has adapted to certain"—he again paused, choosing his words carefully—"distinctive, even 'anomalous' popes through its two millennia. But for my own peace of mind, you should know that I did not in any way agree with the proceedings of this day. From what I have heard and seen thus far, I feel that we probably are not going to find ourselves in agreement on most important or perhaps even trivial matters. I am a convinced traditionalist and very much set in my ways. So, if you prefer, I would be more than happy to step down as your official secretary of state. My personal advice would be yours always. In the official role we would be constantly associating with each other, virtually every day. I am anxious to clear the air on this matter."

Pope Peter smiled benignly and sympathetically at his cardinal. "No,

Secretary Robitelli, it is, I think, vital for the stability of the Church that you remain secretary of state. Brian told me that you were never one to conceal your true outlook and that you spoke your mind honestly and forthrightly. I see now and for myself that he is correct in this assessment." Their eyes met in a moment neither would ever forget.

Robitelli, touched, nodded in agreement and the pope continued. "I need a man of your caliber close to me. It is true that we will disagree, but that will give me a chance to assess the other side of any argument. I'm going to depend on you to run the business and government of the Church for some time. I need to learn what I must do here. I know that all of you see me as only a figurehead." He shrugged helplessly. "Fine. Maybe that's all I'll ever be, but maybe I can give you...justify myself along the way." Looking directly in his eyes, Bill, mustering up what sincerity he could, said, "Cardinal Robitelli, I want you to know that I believe that what happened was the work of God. I am going to try as hard as I can to serve Christ and His Church as best as I humanly can. I will never intentionally bring shame to the Church. As God is my judge."

A subdued secretary of state could only summon a slight smile, but he felt an enormous weight lifting from his shoulders as the pope continued speaking.

"I fully intend to explore avenues and concepts that may be of benefit to the Church, and especially the laity. So please feel free to disagree with me as vehemently as necessary when we meet for our private discussions." He smiled, nodding his head as though in benediction.

"And now," Bill said briskly, "let's see how those phones work. I need to blow some kisses across the ocean to my family."

Cardinal Robitelli, satisfied, explained to the pope how to make an overseas phone call through the switchboard. "I'll be back to take you to 'the last supper'...with the cardinals, that is." He chuckled and left Bill Kelly alone, puzzled at the remark, to talk with his family.

"Colleen, is it you?" His voice was unsteady as his call came through. "All OK?"

"I miss you already, Daddy. How are you holding up?"

"Fine. Is everybody there?" He listened. "Ryan is out on the trawler, eh? Testing the new generator. Good man! I was going to do that myself today. Put Roger and Meghan on."

He listened a moment. "Who? Oh, yes, your Uncle Brian told me the bishop would probably be there, so lean on him for support. How are the other kids handling it?"

Bill nodded at the phone as though Colleen could see him. "I expect

Cardinal Robitelli, secretary of state here, will be discussing all that with me tomorrow. We'll have everything set here when you can come. Yes, honey, I will have someone look into the school situation. Ambassador Kirby's daughter attends Marymount, a fine school here in Rome, and she loves it...I will miss you until then too. But we have to take this thing one step at a time. Just pretend I'm out on one of those longer fishing trips."

Then, moments later, "Hello, Roger...Yes, I'll be in touch with you about your quarters when you come to stay here. Lots of room. Sure, you can skateboard for miles. Put Meghan on...Hello, dear. Yes, I'll e-mail my address at the Vatican. You can send me a daily report. I haven't much time now. Put Colleen back on, please."

"Hi, Dad. Don't worry about us...No, Ryan doesn't know yet. Unless he has the boat's radio on the news station." She listened to her father's next question, and the contumacious expression which Roger and Meghan instantly recognized seized her face. They looked at each other helplessly. Their big sister was the same age their mother had been when she had married their dad. Colleen reminded them of this reality at any breach of sibling discipline.

"No, Dad. I won't be there this Sunday—any more than I have been to Mass for two years." Colleen's tone had an unmistakable edge. "I love you, Your Holiness, but I can't be a hypocrite just because you have this new job." She took a deep breath. "Wouldn't you like to talk to Bishop Sean Patrick? He's being very helpful to us."

Back in the Vatican, Bill Kelly's features momentarily betrayed anguish. "Sure, put him on. I'd love to. Yes, hello, Bishop! Listen, Brian always told me you're a very special priest. I appreciate all you are doing for my family, and that's an understatement. I'm sorry about Colleen's attitude. Maybe you can do something to soften her attitude towards God. Hey, could you work with me over here? I mean it...I need someone like you."

After a moment Bill went on. "I know, but even popes need loyal people they can identify with. That's certainly what John Paul II did. Well, I can see why you won't want to be a cardinal just yet...Yes, and please think it over. People calling me 'Your Holiness' makes me feel quite odd. After all, it's only been a few hours since I was a New England fisherman traveling to Rome. But I'll still call you Sean...Okay? I guess I will get used to it after a while. Let me talk to her now. Yes, Meghan. Love to all of you. I don't want to use up the whole Vatican phone budget in one day."

He heard his daughter's voice. "Yes, Meg. He is obviously a dedicated priest and a straightforward guy. So it's six hours' time difference. Just say what you think and feel to the press. We've got nothing whatever to hide, so let it all hang out. Except"—he paused a moment—"tell Colleen to be careful. I mean that. It is important to me now. None of her atheistic stuff. 'Bye sweetheart. I'll call tomorrow. I have an official dinner coming up. Don't forget, when you all land at the airport I'll run up to the plane and give you a big hug!"

Pope Peter II hung up, sighed mightily, and looked out the window onto St. Peter's Square. Thousands of people still lingered there, singing, delighted to be witness to this seeming miracle and state of ecclesiastical disarray.

An air of unreality descended upon him as he cast his eyes about his apartment at the Apostolic Palace. So chaste, so abnormally antiseptic despite its elegance. He noticed among the beautiful silver and gold religious relics that filled his bedroom a hand-carved wooden replica of "Our Lady of Fatima Appearing to the Three Children" resting on the dresser. His crew had presented it to him on his fifth anniversary as captain of his late father's fishing fleet. He remembered how Mary used to hold it when she would dust the bedroom. He had obviously slipped it subconsciously into his kit, and Brian had put it on his dresser here.

Bill knew with a pang that he was going to need the help of Our Lady of Fatima more than ever before. But his devotion to her was already strong. He felt comfortable talking to her regularly as he used to do so often on those long fishing trips out on the bank. He chuckled, imagining how the kids would soon "modify" the apostolic apartments, and he wondered if here you could get lobster and Guinness stout and catch the Red Sox on TV.

WASHINGTON ROCKS 19

Neither DCM J. Calstrom Seedworth nor his secretary was able to field the volume of telephone calls swamping the U.S. embassy switchboard. Phones and all other resource systems, including U.S. Marine Corps guards, had long been downsized by the State Department to a point where this embassy didn't have the capability of coping with the press, public, as well as the security of the U.S. Embassy as professionally as did other, more favored diplomatic posts.

Seedworth had just heard about the photographs of Bill Kelly with Ed, Kathy, and Maureen Kirby taken by Patrick at the residence a few hours before the pope's elevation. They were now displayed on all the national TV news shows. Next morning, he knew, every paper in the world would carry them on their front pages. The line from the Vatican Desk in Washington was now open, the desk shouting for more information—where, by the way, was the ambassador?

+I+ +I+ +I+

Kirby was at home, but that line was perpetually busy also. Only the White House knew Ed's private number. When it rang, Kirby tensed and snatched the phone from its cradle in time to hear the president laughing. "This morning I said you were recalled," the president chuckled. "Tomorrow morning they'll publish our leak, namely that I'm nominating you for State's Thomas Jefferson award!"

"I am indeed honored, Mr. President! But don't draw extra flak from those Foggy Bottom career types. Their philosophy is say nothing, see nothing, hear nothing. That way they don't have to do anything."

"They have no imagination," the president growled, "or loyalty. They undermine all my appointments. Don't take it personally, Ed." The president paused, then asked, "Look, how did you pull this thing off?"

"I went AWOL, Mr. President. It was the only way."

"Well, the 'Ed and Bill'—or should I say 'Ed and Peter'—show is taking the world by storm," the president chortled. "It's completely replacing certain 'right-wing conspiracy' lies about me. Even Rush Limbaugh didn't mention my name today. That's a first. Now, Ed, I want you to stay at the Vatican. I don't know how it happened, but this is the most interesting news out of there since Henry the Eighth turned Protestant." He paused. "Don't quote me on that!"

"No, sir." Ed Kirby tried to hide his distaste.

"You are doing a hell of a job, Ed. So is your family. Nice picture of the three of you with this fisherman, Kelly, before he became Peter II. Catholics over here will love it."

"Mr. President, I think the time is right to have a word with my DCM and get a few matters straightened out. For one thing, he's been writing his own efficiency reports and signing them. From now on, I'll write them and sign them. That will shake things up a bit."

"You are chief of mission. You have just pulled off the hat trick, an outstanding job. Go to it. Be the pope's best friend. And get him to say something positive about our administration. I need all the help I can get these days."

"Thank you, Mr. President." The ambassador shook his head as he hung up. *The president wants the pope to say something positive about him, while the Church in America is on the warpath against him about abortion!* he thought.

Patrick walked into his office. "The phones are off the hook at the embassy and also here. Every newspaper and TV station on earth wants to interview you. Will you hold a press conference?"

"Ask the DCM to call State. I don't want to give them another excuse to fry me!"

"I'm glad you're having the press conference at the embassy. It would be politic to have Mrs. Kirby and Maureen on hand, too."

"Damn, I wish I could reach Comiskey."

"That's easy. He's on his way up here to see you before the pope's dinner with the cardinals. He flies back to Ireland tomorrow."

"Get Maureen on her cell phone and have her come back now. Please send the cardinal in as soon as he gets here."

✝✝ ✝✝ ✝✝

In response to the call from Patrick, working the residence today, DCM Cal Seedworth began the process of getting through to the Vatican Desk in Washington about the press conference the ambassador had requested to be held at the embassy. The desk officer reminded his DCM that the ambassador could not take it upon himself to call a press conference without planning it with the public affairs officer at State in Washington.

"Seedworth, I'll check it out. Hang on or I'll never get you back. The PAO is calling."

Seedworth held the telephone to one ear and picked up another ringing instrument. "Yes!" he barked. "We're discussing the conference now. No, I can't tell you how it happened. The ambassador himself will answer your questions soon."

A strangled cry over the line the DCM was holding open with Washington distracted him. Seedworth abruptly turned his attention to the desk officer.

"What?" he gasped.

"PA just got a call from the *Washington Post*. They were checking on a White House leak that the president is nominating Kirby for the Thomas Jefferson."

"Oh, no! Son of a bitch!" Seedworth groaned. "He'll be out of control."

"Let him have his conference, but write the opening statement yourself. We'll do damage control from here."

The DCM was shaking with apprehension as he hung up. He had been outmaneuvered by a rotten political appointee.

•‡• •‡• •‡•

Patrick came in to Ed's office to say that Cardinal Comiskey had arrived and Seedworth needed to speak to him about the press conference.

Ed nodded. "Send in the cardinal while I talk to our DCM."

As Kirby reached Seedworth on the direct line between the residence and the embassy, Brian Comiskey thrust his head in the office doorway. Ed waved him in as he relayed on the phone, "Yes, I think six is a good time for the brief. That's noon in Washington. We'll catch TV news all over the U.S. and give the morning papers plenty of time for stories. We'll make the European media just in time so they can hit their TV evening news and headline the morning papers."

Kirby detected a sharp intake of breath on Seedworth's end, and his voice took on a sharper edge. "Actually, maybe I'd better have Patrick call the media and set the show up here at the residence."

"Ambassador, let's have it at the embassy—to show that we're still in the loop," Seedworth importuned and hastily apologized for any irresolution he might have projected. "Will anyone from the Vatican be along?" he asked.

"Will Cardinal Comiskey be there?" Ed repeated Seedworth's next question, glancing at Brian. The cardinal shook his head firmly. Ed smiled and nodded. "No, Cal," he said into the phone. "He won't be there. He's already spoken to the press. I think I'll handle the press alone."

"I'm on it, Mr. Ambassador. We'll use the Cardinal Baum Room, just as you said."

"Sounds good. I'll be there at"—he glanced at his watch—"five-forty-five."

"You want the full treatment, sir?"

"Too late for the wine-and-sandwich routine. Just make sure the microphone is working." He hung up and turned to Brian. "Don't you want to come, say a few words and answer some questions?"

"No way, my friend. I paid my penance just now with them. And please don't expose any conclave secrets you may have picked up."

"Brian, we've known each other for years. And these past two days have been something else. You know you can trust me."

"Look, tell it your way. You don't know how Bill got elected within the conclave. Nobody outside knows that. You only know that I asked you for help and you obliged."

"Suppose Bill had refused, as you expected he would?" Ed held up a restraining hand. "Don't worry, I'm not going to spill any conclave secrets." He paused. "But I do owe the president an explanation. He backed me all the way. State had already leaked word of my recall when Bill and I finally got back to Rome. If he hadn't been elected, I'd have come back alone, and the leak about my being fired would have ended up as fact. There was no way I could have explained things."

"The cardinals are grateful for your help—and silence."

"So, are you planning to stay on for a while to help the pope get adjusted?"

"He doesn't need me as badly as I need Ireland. I have done my work. It's up to the pope himself now. I requested that Tim Shanahan call you if the pope needs political advice."

"I appreciate your faith, but Tim can do infinitely more. He'll be a big asset to the pope."

"Exactly, Ed," Brian agreed. "Timmy is the right man for Bill now. But I'm ahead of you. Tim has already talked to the pope. I'm not from Ireland for nothing. Let's have a taste of the Bush and I'm off to the pope's dinner. Then I'm back to the Auld Sod."

"Sorry to see you leave, old friend. But I'll keep on top of Bill's problems as they come up. Now, let me lead the way to the sideboard and we'll have that good-bye toast. Should I see any trouble on the horizon, I'll call. I still wish you would stay around a little longer."

"No. I've done everything I can do to promote God's will. Now it's up to Bill and the Holy Spirit."

Ida, the housemaid, was standing in the doorway. "Will you be having dinner after the press conference, Mr. Ambassador?"

"No, thank you, Ida. Mrs. Kirby and I will have to grab a pizza and a glass of wine at Campo de' Fiori and watch all the people walk back and forth."

He put his hand on the cardinal's shoulder and steered him toward the Nancy Reagan Sun Room. "The sideboard lies ahead."

BUZZARDS BAY 20

At twelve noon in Washington an anxious group of bow-tied and miniskirted young State Department careerists were gathered around their TV sets to catch whatever snippets from Ambassador Kirby's six P.M. press conference in Rome might get through on the news. The Vatican Desk officer, Skiddy von Stade, and his staff were particularly anxious to hear what their newest "out-of-control" envoy might choose to impart.

Also watching the news that noon were the Kelly children, except for Ryan. Bishop Sean Patrick was with them. Live from Rome, Ambassador Kirby explained succinctly how Cardinal Comiskey of Ireland had asked him to go to Boston and escort William Kelly, a Cape Cod fisherman, to Rome.

"Did you know he was about to become the next pope?" a reporter asked.

"No, it seemed to me beyond the bounds of reason," Ed replied.

"Did you notify the State Department you were going to meet Mr. Kelly?"

"I was asked by my Vatican contact not to do so," Ed answered casually.

"So you ignored protocol and flew off on your own?"

The questioner seemed a replica of his press antagonists at home. "In a manner of speaking," Ed replied nonchalantly. "I felt I was serving my country."

"What happened when you got to Boston yesterday morning?" another reporter asked.

"I arranged to meet Mr. Kelly in Fall River, Massachusetts, and drive him to JFK Airport."

"Did you know you were escorting the next pope?"

"As I said, it seemed highly unlikely, but I couldn't understand why else I was bringing a fisherman and, as I discovered, ex-priest to Rome during a papal conclave."

"When did you notify the State Department of your self-appointed mission?"

"It wasn't self-appointed. I called in my DCM, acronym for deputy chief of mission, after hearing speculation that I had perhaps taken a plane to Monte Carlo or some other destination. One report had me going to a football match in Dublin with Irish friends."

The camera cut to a chagrined-looking Seedworth and then swung back to the ambassador.

"When did you realize Bill Kelly would be the next pope?"

"I wavered in that direction when I saw him wearing a monsignor's cassock left for him at my residence."

A voice burst out from the back of the knot of reporters and cameras. "Did you know that the president has nominated you to receive the Thomas Jefferson Medal, the State Department's highest award?"

"The president mentioned it to me on the phone this morning."

"Do you expect to maintain a close relationship with Pope Peter?"

"Look, it's my job. The late pope and I were personal friends. It's important to the diplomatic relationship between our two governments." Ed was trying to downplay the personal relationship.

Back at the State Department, those concerned with the Vatican assignment were worriedly mumbling to themselves. "Seedworth is a fool," von Stade rasped. "Or at least he was fooled."

✠ ✠ ✠

In Buzzards Bay, Colleen, Meghan, and Roger, with Uncle Sean, had been listening to Kirby's press conference intently. Now, with their own press conference less than three hours away, Bishop Sean Patrick cleared his throat. "My guess is he's not the most popular ambassador with his colleagues at the State Department."

"Darn it, he did what he had to do," Colleen declared. "I'm so sorry I didn't see him when he picked Dad up in Fall River."

"Look outside!" Roger shouted as he peeked out the window. "Already all kinds of TV cameras and people. Colleen, are we really going to be seen all over the world like on real TV shows?"

"I guess so, Roger," she sighed. "Dad will be watching, so be good and don't do anything foolish."

"Gee, Meg, too bad Ryan isn't here to be on TV," Roger said. "When will he get back?"

"That's up to him, Roger. He's been out all day making sure the engine is good for another year of fishing. It was the last thing Dad asked him to do in case he needed money for a big overhaul. When we talked on the shortwave I told him to make up his own mind. He is captain now. And he's not happy about being the center of attention—the pope's oldest son and a fisherman like his dad, and of course like St. Peter."

⊷ ⊷ ⊷

As Ed Kirby was finishing up his press conference, the pope's dinner for the cardinals was under way in the elegant dining room between the basilica and the Sistine Chapel. The 119 voting cardinals, along with some older ones disenfranchised by age, were at the various banquet tables. Some of the tradition-bound elderly prelates seemed more than slightly discomfited at seeing the pope flanked by Cardinal Motupu and Monsignor Cippolini.

Several tinkling taps of a spoon on a wineglass by the ever businesslike Engenio Cardinal Robitelli, now reappointed secretary of state, commanded the cardinals' attention. "Dear brothers, I am so glad that we can all share this time with the new pope before you return to the work God has assigned you."

Robitelli, *carmelengo* until the election was finalized just a few hours before, looked about the ornate dining hall, fixing his gaze on one cardinal after another. "The more I have seen and heard over the last few hours, the more convinced I become that the Holy Spirit has spoken to us." He caught Bill's eye and smiled. "Just as His Holiness, our Pope Bill, once guided his fishing boat safely to shore with his friends in Brian Comiskey's little homily. I also believe that with God's grace and the support of all of us in this great hall, he will be able to guide the bark of St. Peter to safe harbor." He paused once again, looking at many of those present. "As Bill, our second Peter, promised those endangered priests when their ship foundered, 'Follow me, and I will make you fishers of men once again.'"

Robitelli raised his glass. "So I propose this toast of welcome to Bill, Pope Peter II, to pledge to him our everlasting support throughout his reign."

The cardinals all stood with their wineglasses held high and toasted the pope. *"Salute! Salute!"*

Bill was covering his mouth to hide a smile as he and Brian exchanged glances. Cardinal Motupu noticed both. As the African prelate seated himself, he turned to Bill. "I noticed your amusement when the boat was mentioned. Did Brian leave something out of the infamous story?"

"Well, as a matter of fact, yes," the pope confessed. "You see, the boat sank about fifteen yards from shore. We had to wade ashore and have the boat towed in the next day."

"Oh, my goodness!" Motupu grinned. "So much for the bark of Peter."

"But indeed all of them are fishers of souls today."

Listening attentively Monsignor Cippolini began to piece together portions of what had occurred in the conclave that resulted in Bill's election. "Your Holiness," he assayed tentatively, "when the cardinal led you away into the chapel I had a strange thought: Wouldn't it be bizarre if they wanted to see you rather than the papers you were carrying?"

"Of course you were right, Monsignor. It was bizarre and confused. But that's past now. We can laugh for a while and accept the result."

After the sumptuous Italian meal of *carciofini e funghetti' sott' olio, zuppa di cipolle, risotto alla milanese, ipoglosso, patate arroste,* topped off with tiramisu for dessert, final toasts were downed. Most of the cardinals were suddenly anxious to start packing for the escape from their Sistine Chapel imprisonment after an early Mass the next morning. The newly constructed Santa Martha Hotel within the Vatican walls had improved the housing conditions for the cardinals spectacularly, but they were all eagerly looking forward to returning to their principalities. Their particular areas of authority throughout the world had been unattended and their power delegated for too long as it was.

Pope Peter glanced at his watch and noticed it was close to nine in the evening, three o'clock back "home" in Buzzards Bay. He had determined earlier that the press conference held by Bishop Sean Patrick and Bill's family would be telecast live in Rome. With Brian, Motupu, Cippolini, Robitelli, and Tim Shanahan, he retired to the papal apartments to see how it went.

✠ ✠ ✠

The chaos inside the Kelly home was interrupted by a knock at the front door. Colleen opened it. The large figure of Trooper Joe Collins loomed in the doorframe. "Miss Kelly, it's about that time. Remember what I told you. If you start feeling uncomfortable with them, just give me the nod and I'll have you back inside here in no time. Bishop Sean Patrick is out there letting them know they need to be very proper. He may be able to deflect some of the heat. But I guess you already know that it's you they want to see."

"Yes, Trooper. Thanks." She turned to Meghan and Roger. "Okay, Roger, let's go out and get this over with before I develop an ulcer." They emerged from the house to find Bishop Sean Patrick at the edge of the porch fending off a rapid fire of questions thrown at him amid a swirl of cameras, microphones, booms, and men and women pressing forward as the family came forth.

Seeing the Kellys, the bishop turned and raised his hands for quiet. "Please, ladies and gentlemen. Realize that the Kelly children here are bound to be a bit nervous with all this commotion and excitement about their father's unprecedented elevation. Let's try to do it the way they do at the White House. I'll point to individually raised hands and that person can ask his or her question. Following this format, I'm sure most of your concerns will be covered. So—"

He pointed to a woman reporter and the noise subsided.

"Colleen, may I call you by your first name?" Colleen graciously nodded. "When did you know that your father was going to be made pope?"

"When that cardinal came out and announced it on TV. The same as yourself."

"But you must have known something before that, Ms. Kelly."

Another reporter chimed in. "Cardinal Comiskey came here, we now assume, to tell your father he had been elected. Can you tell us how that came about?"

"I don't have the slightest idea." The sincere puzzlement on Colleen's face and in her tone gave authenticity to her answer. "My guess, as you heard Uncle Brian—uh, Cardinal Comiskey—say on TV, is that they discussed many different laymen in the conclave and for some compelling reason decided to vote for my dad."

"How do you feel about your father being made pope, Colleen?"

"To tell the truth I am confused, numb, and at a loss to understand how or why and even whether this happened. All I can say for certain is that I love my father, Bill Kelly, very much. Whatever job he chooses to do is his business and not ours."

"You say 'job,' Ms. Kelly," a stern male voice called from the rear of the knot of aroused journalists. "Do you consider the papacy just a 'job'?"

An obstinate expression spread across Colleen's face, and her two siblings shuddered.

"It is obviously what our father has chosen to do for rest of his life. If it makes him feel fulfilled, that's great!"

"But as a Catholic isn't it thrilling to be the first person on earth to be able to say, 'Hey! My dad is the head of the Church' and be your father's hostess at Vatican dinners?"

"Lucrezia Borgia could say that almost half a millennium ago when she was poisoning her father's enemies at Vatican dinners."

The unexpected answer to such a gracious question caused an uncharacteristic silence among the media representatives. It was followed by a flood of speculative queries punctuated by an authoritative shout from the rumpled female reporter representing the local *Buzzards Bay Journal*. "Colleen, I just called Father Milligan. He says you haven't been to Mass with your family in the two years he's been our pastor. Are you going to start coming now?"

"It's been more like three years," Colleen answered forthrightly. "A couple of weddings, three to be exact. But not since my mother died of breast cancer at age thirty-five have I attended Mass." Colleen turned to face a barrage of questions, pointing to a middle-aged man wearing thick glasses who seemed sympathetic.

"Colleen, do you believe in God?"

"I don't know," she replied tartly. "I used to, until Mom died." Standing before the crowd of reporters and TV cameras, Colleen presented a vulnerable yet unshakable figure.

At that, Bishop Sean Patrick moved forward, both hands held high, shutting off the high-decibel interrogation. "I just talked to the Holy Father an hour ago. If you'd like to ask about his reaction to this enormously unusual day, I will take your questions."

The bishop pointed to a persistent reporter, who called out, "Have the youngsters spoken to their dad since he was elected pope?"

Bishop Sean Patrick put a hand on Meghan's shoulder, and she clearly replied, "Yes, he called me shortly afterward."

"What did he say to you?"

She smiled a moment and then colored. "Why, he said the same thing he always says when he calls me on the shortwave radio from the fishing banks. 'I love you, and miss you.'"

"What about the young son? Roger, is it?" a woman reporter called out.

The bishop placed a hand on the boy's shoulder and pushed him forward. "You talked to your father, Roger. What did he tell you?"

"He said there was lots of room where he is and miles where I could skateboard." Laughter arose from the group of journalists. They all seemed to come to the same conclusion. There was no hidden agenda with the new pope's children. They were plain, honest young people who had gone through a family tragedy and seemed unimpressed if confused with their new circumstances.

"Bishop Sean Patrick," a reporter called out, "Cardinal Comiskey stopped at your residence before coming here. May we know what you discussed there?"

"Yes, certainly. There was merely a simple request. 'Sean, may I borrow your car?' "

"That's all?" an incredulous voice called out. "Come now, Bishop, you're pulling our leg."

"No, really. I was more curious than you people here were. And he gave me the same reply as you got from him. A conclave secret. He wanted to borrow my car to visit his friends, the Kellys, before flying back to Rome." Bishop Sean Patrick laughed deprecatingly. "I know most of you guessed that either the archbishop of Boston or I had been chosen as the next pope. Since I knew I wasn't worthy, I speculated that it must have been the archbishop. He's a great man and well respected in Rome, America, and throughout the world. Like the rest of you, I was totally in the dark. The only thing I had was a sealed envelope the cardinal handed me when he returned. He said to keep it in my desk until it was time to open it. When I questioned him he said I would know for certain the moment it needed to be opened. Naturally, I understand what he meant when I heard the announcement of Mr. Kelly's election. I didn't have to read the letter. I knew he was instructing me to be of whatever assistance I could to the Kelly children. And here I am."

An assertive female voice rose above the murmurs. "Colleen, what do your brothers and sister really think about your dad being the Holy Father?"

Colleen laid a hand on Roger's shoulder. "Tell them what you think. Other than skateboarding."

"I miss my dad. I just want school to get done. Then we can go and be with him."

"Is that true, Miss Kelly? Are you children going to Rome to live?"

"Yes, we are!" Roger's voice rang out. "And Uncle Sean said maybe I could have two bedrooms."

Smiles appeared on the faces of the reporters, and TV cameras zoomed in on the young boy. A microphone was thrust at him. "How old are you, young man?"

"I'm fourteen. I'm in the tenth grade."

"And who is Uncle Sean?"

Roger pointed at the flushed bishop. "Him."

"Are you related to the bishop?" a reporter shot out.

"No, not by blood," the bishop answered for Roger and then continued. "I guess it's a special gift the children gave to me. Cardinal Comiskey is a longtime friend of Bill and the late Mary Kelly. He performed their marriage ceremony, baptized their children, and spent some vacations with them. The children have always called him Uncle Brian. I became part of the family a short time ago," he said with a pleasant grin.

Then Meghan cut in, moving closer to the TV cameras. "Can I wave to my dad and say hello?"

The cameras zoomed in on her and a reporter held the mike close to her face. "Sure, honey. Go ahead."

"Hi, Dad, I miss you. I love you."

"Yeah, me too, Dad," Roger broke in, waving to the cameras.

Colleen also waved. "We all look forward to being with you, Dad. Please forgive me for saying what I did. But I can't be a hypocrite. Maybe I can change someday." She turned from the cameras and started to slowly walk toward the door, followed by Meghan and Roger. The reporters and cameras followed closely until three state troopers cut them off.

"Sorry folks, that's all the Kellys want to say. Please respect their privacy."

Colleen turned and stared searchingly into the camera. "I expect my dad and I will have some interesting philosophical and religious discussions when we get to Rome."

"Colleen," a reporter called out, "are you an atheist?"

"Like I said," Colleen called back, "the way things are, I wouldn't want to make any enemies with whatever or whoever is ahead of us."

"Colleen, are you pro-life or pro-choice?" a woman's strident voice hurled at her.

Colleen smiled coyly. "I don't know. I haven't had to decide yet. 'Bye, everybody."

Expressively, she raised her eyes skyward. As she ducked back into the house the press of the world knew they had one feature attraction in the new pope's family. Things would never be mundane with this one around!

As Meghan stepped through the door, followed reluctantly by Roger, who was enjoying the attention being showered upon them, the reporters turned to the bishop, standing protectively before the front of the house. "Bishop McCarrick, can you give us some more information?" another woman journalist pleaded. "I just flew in here from Chicago to cover this unprecedented story."

The bishop stared back. "To be perfectly honest, we would only be venturing into the realm of hypothesis," he replied. "The situation is unique in Catholic procedure and history as we know it. I might suggest that you get in touch with some of our historians, who could provide you information on past laymen who were made popes." He shrugged expressively as cameras whirred and clicked in the midafternoon sunlight. "I never bothered to pay much attention to that kind of thing when I was studying for the priesthood."

A stricken expression flitted across the bishop's countenance. He added hastily, "Not that I personally, nor, I believe, does any other American Catholic bishop, entertain in any way views contradictory to the decision of the conclave in Rome." Abruptly the bishop turned and passed the troopers into the sanctuary of the Kelly home.

The many local neighbors and other onlookers were slow in dispersing, reluctant to miss any part of this unique American drama as all the journalists present grudgingly accepted the fact that the all-too-brief interview was over. Only one camera crew gave desultory attention to the tall, strapping young man as he appeared from somewhere below the Kelly home. Over his shoulder was slung a duffel bag.

Trooper Joe Collins confronted the purposeful youth. "And just where do you think you are going, mister?"

"Into my house. I'm Ryan Kelly."

Instantly the newspeople recognized the oldest son of Pope Peter II. The trooper glanced down at the glassine pad of photographs in his hand. "Well, your face fits, but what happened to the long hair? It looks really wild in the picture your sister gave me."

"I went to the barbershop and had it cut," he snapped. "It didn't seem right for the pope to have a long-haired son captaining his fishing ship. May I pass now?"

Collins smiled and stepped aside. "Be my guest." As Ryan stepped up onto the porch, three alert reporters and a MSNBC cameraman and his crew scrambled to get near him. "Mr. Kelly, could we talk to you a moment? What do you think about your father being made pope?"

Ryan stopped, threw his duffel bag down, and smiled directly into the camera and at the reporters. He seemed to be enjoying the attention. Raising his hand, he flashed what he imagined was a papal-type blessing. "Peace and good fishing," he intoned. "We're going to need both if I'm going to keep the bark of Peter the Second afloat. I don't figure that being the pope's son will get me any higher a price on my fish in New Bedford, so when I go out tomorrow I'll have to hope that Jesus will lead me to enough fish to almost break my nets like he did for the first Peter. In other words, Daddy needs a new generator for his boat," he explained.

"Are you a Catholic, Mr. Kelly?" a reporter asked.

"Of course. And on those long fishing trips with Dad he sometimes forgot he wasn't a priest anymore, especially if we were out on Sunday. Why do you ask?"

Then a smile of comprehension spread across his face. "Uh-oh! Colleen has been giving you her take on the religion thing." A serious expression replaced the grin. "Well, you have to understand her feelings when our mother died. They were really terribly close, my sister and our mother. Colleen was just seventeen when we lost Mom. She's never forgiven God."

The bishop stepped through the doorway into camera range. "Hi there, Ryan. I'm Bishop Sean Patrick." He extended his hand.

Together they answered a few questions from the gathered reporters until they heard Colleen call out from inside the house. "Trooper Joe, Uncle Sean Patrick, please end this meeting."

Between the bishop, Trooper Collins, and his backup state troopers, the reporters were cleared away, and Sean Patrick went back into the house. "A hectic first meeting with the press, to say the least," he observed. "If you don't need me anymore today, I'll head back and get some of my own work done before dark. You have my number."

"We're fine now, Uncle Sean." Colleen took his hand in hers. "Thanks again for your support. We are so grateful."

They stood up and Meghan gave him a hug. The bishop responded in the only way he knew how. He traced a sign of the cross on her forehead. "God bless you, Meghan. As I said, feel free to call me anytime if you need help or have any questions you think I can answer."

Bishop Sean Patrick left the Kelly household and walked toward his car. Trooper Collins was politely moving the last of the reporters and camera crews away from the lawn. "Hi, Bishop. May I ask how things are going with the kids? That Colleen is a piece of work, isn't she?"

The bishop sighed. "I'm glad I won't be in Rome when she hits the Vatican"—he swallowed hard—"to join her father, the pope."

"The neighbors are sending over some nice prepared dishes so the Kellys won't have to cook meals," the trooper observed.

"Good." The bishop chuckled. "Last I heard, Colleen was starving. Are you going back to Fall River now that the excitement is over?"

"I need to do some paperwork here and wait for backup help."

"Good Trooper. See you in Church."

✦✦ ✦✦ ✦✦

In the apostolic apartment at the Vatican, Pope Peter II sat uncomfortably watching the sporadic press coverage of the papal family on the television set.

"Should be interesting when your young Colleen arrives," Brian remarked.

"The others will have to control her," Bill acknowledged. "She is at a rough age. Thinks she knows it all."

"Meghan and Roger came through it very well. And Ryan looked sharp with his new haircut," Brian observed. "And I was glad to see Bishop Sean Patrick beside them all the way. Your family is in for considerable attention and under great pressure."

"Yes," Bill breathed heavily, "and they seem up to it. Ryan, though! He seems to have become a responsible captain overnight."

Robitelli stood up. "I'll be here in the morning, Bill. I'm more than afraid the Vatican will never be the same again."

"And neither will he," Brian chuckled, as he and Bill watched the weary secretary of state close the door.

"A touch of whiskey?" Bill suggested.

"I'll get it. I found out where the papal store is kept."

✦✦ ✦✦ ✦✦

Peace of a sort settled on the Kelly household. Ryan left to attend to the boat at the dock below. Over the next several hours, until nightfall, a number of cars came to deliver neighbors' gifts of love—flowers and food. By eight-thirty, Colleen, Meghan, and Roger were deeply engrossed in a game of Scrabble. Life was beginning to return to at least a semblance of what it had been before Brian Comiskey arrived. As evening fell, the doorbell rang.

"Go see who that is, Colleen."

"Okay, Meg. Maybe someone bringing dessert to that grand supper." She opened the door to see a swarthy, heavyset young man with a two-day growth of black beard standing there holding a box in his hand.

"Hi there." Colleen smiled. "Can I help you?"

"Yes, I have something for you." The man held out a box. "Lemme bring 'em in."

Meghan and Roger looked closely to see who was bringing them more bounty. They did not recognize the face, and Colleen started to ask his name but was cut off in midsentence. The box dropped to the floor. The intruder had a pistol in his hand.

"Now, let's not have any trouble, folks, and no one will get hurt," he growled.

Meghan screamed and moved to shield Roger.

"Stand still, little girl. I warn ya."

"We don't have any money here," Colleen cried out.

The intruder moved to the chair where Roger was sitting. "You may not have any, but your old man sure as hell does. I've heard all about the millions the pope has. So you can call your old man and tell him to get up a million bucks, quick, if you want to see this kid alive again. And no cops!"

"No, please, take me, not my brother!" Meghan cried.

"No, take me," Colleen broke in. "He will be a problem for you, and my sister will need to be here to phone Dad. I'll be no problem to you."

"Forget it, ladies, and shut up." He grabbed the boy by the arm and yanked the frightened child from the chair. "Come on, kid, we're going for a ride. I'll call you in one hour, Kelly, and remember, no cops or you'll never see your brother alive again." He moved cautiously toward the door, an eye on the women as he held the gun to the boy's head. He turned as he reached the door. "I mean business, girls. So don't screw with me. Out the door, kid!"

The pale sisters watched their brother thrust through the door. Then it happened. Suddenly the boy disappeared. The would-be kidnapper went crashing to the floor of the porch, the heavy boot of trooper Joe Collins smashed down on his gun hand. The startled young goon looked up to see the barrel of a police .38 revolver inches from his face.

"Even breathe heavy and I'll blow your head off. Just give me any excuse!" Two more troopers were now on the man, handcuffing him behind his back.

A tearful Meghan rose from her chair.

"Stay still, Miss Kelly. Just give us a moment to get this piece of garbage out of here. Roger is okay."

Within two minutes the hoodlum was subdued and in a police car and the happy, crying siblings were hugging each other. "Oh God, Trooper Joe," Colleen cried, "how can we thank you enough? How did you get here so soon? I mean, how did you know? Good God, I'm so shaky I need to sit down."

"That's a good idea, Miss Kelly. Welcome to celebrity time."

The Italian sun shone spectacularly through the windows of the Vatican apostolic apartment as a persistent knocking on his bedroom door awakened the new pope. Bill rubbed his eyes, and Cardinal Robitelli entered in response to his invitation to come in.

"I'm sorry to disturb you, Your Holiness. I let you sleep a bit later because I thought you might be very tired after these last, or should I say first, two days." He came closer to the bed. "I have asked Monsignor Cippolini to say Mass for you when you are ready. Or would you like breakfast now?"

"I should attend Mass first, I guess. I suppose that's what the pope usually does?"

"John Paul II rose at five-thirty, prayed, and said his own private Mass at seven. He breakfasted at eight and began his daily schedule at nine," Robitelli replied.

Bill sat up and thrust his feet on the floor and into his slippers. Then, glancing at the bedside clock, he exclaimed, "Seven o'clock! I haven't slept after five-thirty on a workday in years!"

"I assume," Robitelli said dryly, "that it's been many years since you've said Mass, so I assigned Monsignor Cippolini to run through the process with you. You appear to have a good relationship with him, and he's a knowledgeable man." What he did not say, although Bill sensed his motive, was that he would control Cippolini and, as secretary of state, he felt the need to exert as much authority and influence as possible. "He'll act as a tutor. He speaks English very well. Also, he is a Scripture and Church scholar."

"Thank you, Eminence. Most thoughtful of you." Bill paused a moment. Then, "Brian Comiskey suggested I meet frequently with Monsignor Timothy Shanahan. You remember him. He was here...."

A frown flickered across the cardinal's patrician features. "The rector of the North American College is indeed knowledgeable and busily engaged in running his institution." Robitelli continued, "An Italian, Sicilian actually, Cippolini is surprisingly familiar with the ins and outs of the American Church as well as Vatican affairs. He is a talented linguist who will help you learn Italian, an important accomplishment for a non-

Italian pope. We went to unusual lengths to retain such a man as a permanent member of the curia."

"I'm thankful for that!" Bill said warmly.

The secretary of state nodded. "At Cippolini's diocese, in Sicily, they had counted on getting him back after his studies were completed. It took a request by Pope John Paul II himself to keep him. We rewarded him by designating him Monsignor. He can be more than a mere help to you." Robitelli smiled sadly. "Some people have not taken him seriously because of his often casual, Sicilian appearance and his notorious familiarity with the local restaurants, but he nonetheless graduated at the top of his class at the Pontifical Gregorian University and in virtually every advanced study group in Rome. A bright man indeed, with certainly a bright future."

"Fine, fine, Gene—if you don't mind me calling you that?"

"I can adjust to it in private, Your Holiness. 'Gino' is our word for 'Gene.' But in public we need to use the proper titles of office, if you agree with me." A perfunctory smile, then, briskly, "Before I busy myself with the stacks of backed-up paperwork..." He reached under the folds of his black cassock and retrieved an ivory-colored business-size envelope that bore a large red seal across the flap. "This was given me by our late Pope John Paul II to be handed only to his successor. It was for his eyes only, now yours. Any others with whom you feel you might share this vital message can be given this missive."

Somewhat awed, Peter II reached for the envelope. Suddenly he had the distinct impression that Robitelli resented handing it to him. He realized that Robitelli had been convinced that only he was entitled to receive the envelope as John Paul II's successor.

Robitelli continued briskly, "Many documents require your signature. I trust you will sign those I feel need approval as quickly as possible. I'll explain any others you may want to know more about as we go along." He paused, and then in a tone of satisfaction added, "With Cippolini for Scripture and language and—" He was just going to name another staff person for the pope when Bill Kelly abruptly interrupted.

"And with Monsignor Shanahan as secretary."

Affronted, Robitelli stared in disbelief and could only mutter, "But—"

Bill broke the tension by saying, "I am extremely grateful for your understanding of my preliminary problems here, *Eminenza*." He smiled at his sudden recollection of the deference to Rome young seminarians learned. "In ten minutes I'll be ready for chapel."

There was one item needling the profound sense of peace enveloping the new pope as he finished preparing for Monsignor Cippolini's Mass. Robitelli had been all too set to dismiss Tim Shanahan, who both Brian Comiskey and Ed Kirby felt was best suited for becoming the most influential member of the new cabinet.

For a moment Bill regarded the wooden carving he had packed unwittingly with his belongings when he'd left to meet Ed Kirby on the way to Rome. Our Lady of Fatima and the three peasant children to whom she had appeared in 1917 in Portugal stood on the austere bureau at the foot of his bed. Bill propped up the envelope from his predecessor against the carved grotto.

When the Portuguese crewmen of his fishing fleet had presented him with this carving, Bill thought it was impossible that he would ever actually read the words dictated by Sister Lucia to her bishop. However, after the recent release of the third prophecy, given that day to three children in a field outside the northern Portuguese town of Fatima, the pope enjoyed the new attention given to Our Lady. Now, the third millennium had actually broken. Peter II knew he must read this portentous document with more care. But first there were the contents of the envelope bequeathed him by John Paul II to be absorbed.

The Kellys had a friend who owned an antique furniture shop on Cape Cod. He often spoke to Bill and members of his crew about the third prophecy, wondering what events it foretold. The first prophecy had concerned the end of World War I, the second the end of Communism in Soviet Russia. The third prophecy was only recently made public, and some authorities still debated its true meaning. Others predicted a great threat to the Church and the world coming from the East. Wasn't this what Our Lady herself had said to Bill Kelly only a few days before? John Paul II, more than any world leader save former president Ronald Reagan, had deflected the second near-disaster as a prime mover in the Soviet overthrow. But what now after the third prophecy?

A few Swiss guards and several Vatican household retainers attended Monsignor Cippolini's Mass, possibly to make the pope feel as though he were not the only one late for the prayers.

It all reminded Bill of the tranquil days at St. John's Seminary in Boston, where students were cut off from the world, enjoying their island of isolation with no interruptions from the outside. For a moment he meditated on how different the seminary chapel and this private Vatican chapel were from the half-empty Churches most laity knew.

True, a few Catholics made retreats on occasion, but fewer ever experienced this kind of serenity in prayer. Bill remembered the quiet and profound peace out at sea just after a storm. He glanced down at the small shelf in his prie-dieu and noticed a pad and pen. Quickly he jotted down *"Shanahan"* as Monsignor Cippolini's strong voice from the altar interrupted his reflection.

"Brothers and sisters, let us begin. In the name of the Father and of the Son…"

Pope Peter found it impossible to concentrate on prayers as his mind kept slipping back to the envelope propped up on his bureau. He was the first to hurry from the chapel when Monsignor Cippolini finished Mass. Now he had two immediate objectives: to talk to Monsignor Shanahan and, even more urgent, he felt, to read his predecessor's epistle.

He made short work of the continental breakfast brought to him at his desk and, with trembling hands, applied an ornate letter opener to the underside of the red seal, breaking the envelope open. There were three pages of tightly spaced, handwritten manuscript. It was the first time he had actually seen the former pope's handwriting. Staring at the meticulous script, his eyes crinkled as he tried to understand the sentences before him.

Bill Kelly sighed helplessly. Of course, the words were in Italian. He had never learned to speak more than deckhand Italian and certainly never to read it. He took the first sentence and copied down each word in letters he could read and then went to an English-Italian dictionary he had located among his office reference books. Word by word he began to decipher the former pope's message. Half an hour later he managed to read the first sentence, a welcome to the papal successor.

Obviously Bill Kelly could have called in any number of his people, from Cippolini to Robitelli, for a quick, clear translation. But he didn't want to be forced to reveal the pope's message to anyone but himself, at least not until he understood its purpose.

He guessed that the deceased pope had wanted his successor to make up his own mind how much of this missive should be passed on to any others. The pope had written that he did not wish even his faithful scribe, who translated all his directives from Polish to Latin and other languages, to learn the exact nature of this "letter of warning," as Bill interpreted the word *avviso*.

For two hours, during which he warded off intrusions on his solitary perusal of the message's opening, Pope Peter painstakingly struggled with the Italian, unraveling the meanings and intimations Pope John Paul II had intended to convey. Bill jotted down the disclosures as he struggled like a child with them, word by word.

The fact that only one living person—perhaps two, unless Bill himself deemed otherwise—would know the contents of the pope's epistle lent moment to this painful process. And still, he realized, he was missing the little ironies and gentle derisions which only familiarity with Italian might render clear.

For two and a half hours he struggled to comprehend the three pages. He realized he had gained only a superficial knowledge of the intent and meaning of this communication. Yet he sensed it might be the most important aspect of the last pope's legacy. The intent itself came through explicitly. The *avviso* was never to be made public. Bill grinned as he held up two fingers and recited an old mantra about secrecy: "If two know— that's eleven."

The disclosure was indeed a warning. *Avviso* meant to him: "Be advised." It was in Italian because the pope apparently expected an Italian cardinal would succeed him. The Polish pope must have realized that he was an anomaly in a more-than-four-hundred-year line of native Italians. This was an oddity unlikely to recur despite John Paul II's efforts to stack the national origins of the college of cardinals against the seemingly inevitable election of yet another Italian.

Twice during these two and a half hours of isolation he had created for himself, Bill's concentration had been disturbed by soft knocks on the door, to which he responded with pleas for continued solitude. Finally, with a sigh, he picked up his gently ringing telephone. As he suspected, it was Robitelli, anxiously inquiring whether His Holiness needed special guidance on any matter.

"Give me another few minutes, Gino. I'll call you." He replaced the receiver without waiting for a reply.

With a sigh Bill folded up the parchment, put it back in the envelope with the broken red seal, and tucked it into a marked manila folder keeping his notes in front of him. He placed the folder into a drawer of his desk, which had a key protruding from the keyhole. He locked the drawer, placed the key in the pocket of the pants he wore under his white cassock, stood up, and walked to the window overlooking St. Peter's Square.

At least he now comprehended what the former pope was trying to impart! This millennium into which the new pope would lead his great Church was fraught with danger and a certain unvarnished evil. The Polish pope had been a practical man, unrelenting in his quest to firmly establish traditional Catholic values worldwide. He had fought an evil revealed in three parts at Fatima and destined to destroy the world if allowed to continue unobstructed. He had barely come away with his life, but he had won temporarily. The assassin had fired unsuccessfully and Communism in most of the Western world had since been eliminated.

But forces of this evil remained implanted and deeply rooted within a corner of the Russian Orthodox Church, part of the *avviso* seemed to tell Bill. The pope and the Roman Catholic Church were the enemy. Catholicism and most other competing religions had been banned from Russia by the state Duma in 1997. The continuing indicators had been apparent when, in 1999, the Russians and their Orthodox Church had allied themselves with former Balkan Communist rulers to destroy, massacre, and "cleanse" certain countries of European Muslims and those Catholics, including priests, as were housed among them. Even as the would-be assassin had come out of Bulgaria, so the Catholic Church faced dire prospects for its continuing preeminence in that tortured and dangerous region.

The three prophecies of Fatima, now revealed, and other appearances of the Holy Mother had made clear the extent of the dangers faced by the Church and all mankind, threats to the world that would come to pass unless the Church could liquidate, not merely overcome, this evil cloud lurking at the opening of the third millennium. The former pope had believed implicitly that Our Lady of Fatima had indeed saved his life, even though the third prophecy predicted otherwise.

He had bent over on this day of the feast of Fatima to look at the emblem on the dress of a young girl commemorating the Holy Mother's appearance. The assassin's bullets had missed the pontiff's head but wounded him in the body. Alois Estermann, commander of the Swiss guard, had thrown himself over the killer and saved the pope's life. And Estermann himself became the victim of the Evil Spirit when, twelve years later, still commander of the Swiss guard, he and his wife were murdered in their Vatican quarters by a deranged young guardsman who then killed himself—the first ever suicide or murder recorded of a Swiss guardsman.

Bill, now in full contemplation, was startled by the pope's dogmatic view of the struggle between good and evil in the universe. He was amazed by the way the pope tied earlier prophecies to immediate events. Yet he had seemed to imply that the third prophecy at Fatima by the Holy Virgin was not the end of the dangers to the Church.

As Bill had laboriously translated the Italian words into their English equivalents the hair on the back of his neck stood up. The epistle stated that Orthodoxy in the East, fundamentalism among the Muslim nations, remaining communism, and apathy within Catholicism's most powerful nation—America—stood ready to cripple the Church in the new millennium.

The pope had gone on to write (as closely as Bill could make out) that there was imminent trouble not revealed in any of the prophecies of Fatima. War, pestilence, and widespread genocide would occur in the early twenty-first century. This had certainly begun, the pope noted, citing that half the population of Africa would die of genocide uprisings and the disease of AIDS if these evils were not stopped. What he saw at this moment seemed a fourth prophecy not widely revealed. The last and final battle between Christianity and Islam would be waged during the early days of the new millennium. Baghdad would be wiped out and a million soldiers would fall as the Cross of Christendom replaced the Crescent of Islam.

There was more, but Bill could not cope with it, since he was unsure of the accuracy of his translation. But essentially he read into the message that, as the first pope of the twenty-first century, he himself would be embroiled in the constant war of good against evil and that, as such, his own survival was uncertain.

"Enough!" he heard himself say aloud. There were more specifics with which he must deal within this letter of warning, this *avviso,* but that would come later, when he had someone he could trust read the epistle. "Shanahan," he murmured. In any case, his impression was one of caution, even fear. He accepted the letter's overwhelming prediction that if he served the Holy Spirit as intended, he would not live long.

Pope Peter turned from the pleasant view of the square. Walking back to his desk, he picked up the phone. Sister Miriam, the assigned secretary, answered.

"Put through this telephone call for me, and when I'm finished tell the cardinal secretary of state he can come to the office." Bill, dazed by what he understood to be the sense of the communication transcending life and time sent to him by his dead predecessor, sat down and waited.

Maureen Kirby peered out her bedroom window toward St. Peter's, still feeling the exhilaration of the historic events of the day before. She relived the moment when she had seen Bill Kelly emerge on the balcony. It was still hard for her to believe it had occurred. As the sun rose higher in the sky above Rome, she wondered when she would see "Bill," the new pope, again. What would she call him? "Your Holiness," of course, but the familiar first name of "Bill"? She thought of trying to telephone him, but the thought of getting through the Vatican switchboard to the pope was too daunting to contemplate. She remembered how difficult it had been for her father to reach the president when Pope John Paul II wanted to talk to him, so she imagined that it would be practically impossible for her to get through by phone to the pope even though he was just down below.

As she was wondering how to explain to her schoolmates and headmistress, Sister Ann Marie, her short but, as it seemed to her, close relationship with the new pope, the private residence telephone rang. Maureen picked it up. "*Pronto,* Villa Richardson," she said.

"Just a minute, please," came an impersonal female voice. "To whom am I speaking?"

"This is Maureen Kirby, Ambassador Kirby's daughter." Then she heard the call being transferred at the other end of the line.

And suddenly the warm, New England–accented voice boomed on the telephone, "Hello, Maureen. This is Bill! How have you survived these last twenty-four hours?"

"Bill!" she shrieked. Then, "Your Holiness—"

"Remember the last thing I said to you?"

"Of course, Holy Father. It's just that this is all such a shock. I mean..."

"Understood—and likewise. Is your dad home? OK, do me a favor and ask him if he can see me today with Tim Shanahan and, yes, Brian Comiskey before he heads back to Ireland."

"I'll sure do that, Holy Father. Just as soon as he comes in."

"And Maureen, I haven't forgotten your promise to cook me your specialty dinner."

"Anytime, Holy Father. Anytime at all."

"As soon as my kids get here, we can all have dinner together."

"Sounds great. Can't wait."

"Got paper and a pen handy? I'll give you the private number."

She wrote down the number. "I'll try to reach Dad on his cell phone."

"Thanks, Maureen."

Kirby was attending a meeting with World Vision representatives on the hunger crisis in Africa when his cell phone buzzed.

"OK, Maureen. I understand. Put the number next to my office phone."

Kirby left the meeting, returning to the residence. The call to the apostolic apartment went directly through to the pope.

"Your Holiness, it's so good to hear from you! Yes, these have been hectic days for both of us. I'm happy that things are working out, so far."

Ed listened to the pope's request. "Yes, of course I'll be there, and I'll call Tim and make the arrangements. I'll drive in with him to avoid being seen."

Monsignor Tim Shanahan was obliged to cut the class in "Epistles of the Apostles" he was teaching at the "Greg," as the Gregorian Institute was fondly known, in order to meet with Ambassador Kirby before their papal appointment. Cardinal Comiskey had, of course, alerted him to Bill Kelly's mentoring needs the day before.

"I am not sure of the welcome I'll receive from Robitelli, who I hear will continue on as secretary of state," Shanahan began as he sipped a cup of tea with Kirby in the Villa Richardson sun room. "I take a far more freewheeling approach to ecumenical education than that approved by the Italian traditionalists."

"I gather Bill sensed something of the sort when he brought up your name," Kirby remarked. "But you two will understand each other perfectly. Aside from Notre Dame and Columbia, you had the advantage of being brought up in a good Catholic working-class St. Louis family and your father worked for Anheuser-Busch. You have the credentials to act as Bill's Vatican navigator."

"Your assessment of the situation eases my mind, Ambassador. I love what I'm doing, but if the Church calls, I'll answer the call."

"Brian and I are in total agreement. It would be ideal if you could move to the Vatican and take over Pope Peter II as a full-time job"—Ed saw the pained expression that came over Shanahan's face and quickly retrenched—"despite your devotion to NAC."

"Not only that, Ambassador, I could well upset the delicate balance between this—to understate the matter—unorthodox papal succession and Vatican bureaucratic stability as symbolized by the present secretary of state."

Now it was Kirby who expressed dismay, and the rector of NAC continued hastily. "However, as I told him personally yesterday, I stand ready to do whatever His Holiness desires. NAC is only a few blocks from the walls, if initially it proves better not to relocate inside. Perhaps at some point, if it is deemed appropriate, I can become a Vatican resident."

"I believe Cardinal Comiskey could agree to such an initial arrangement." Kirby glanced at his watch. "Well, if you are ready we'll drive down now to the Vatican. Monsignor Cippolini has left word that he'll expect us without advance notice."

A tall, slightly rotund cleric in a simple black cassock, Tim and the ambassador drove through the gate in Tim's run-down, beat-up Fiat. Ed Kirby had to admire, as he had so often since coming to Rome, the freer, energetic, vigorous quality of the younger clergy of the new millennium. The Church had changed since he was a devout Catholic boy, not eating meat on Friday and fasting, not even water allowed, from midnight Saturday to Mass on Sunday morning. But still, many devout and dedicated young priests like Shanahan were always there to answer the call of the Church. Kirby registered Tim's proven brilliance, yet here he was driving a decrepit car in a foreign country over three thousand miles away from his family and friends.

Monsignor Cippolini greeted them at the entrance to the apostolic apartment and led them up the marble staircase to the third floor, then down the corridor to the pope's private chambers. He knocked gently on the double door. A nonclerical aide silently directed them into the pope's library. Moments later Peter II entered. To Monsignor Cippolini Bill said, "Al, try to see that we are not disturbed?"

"Yes, Your Holiness. Will you want tea perhaps? *Caffè*, juice?"

"Maybe later," the pope replied. "Thank you."

Cippolini nodded and excused himself, closing the door behind him as Bill turned to Ed Kirby. "Thanks for getting Tim here to me. We hardly had a chance to say two words when we first met."

"Those were hectic moments, to say the least, Your Holiness," Tim acknowledged.

"Brian Comiskey is a great admirer of yours."

"I've had the honor and the pleasure of knowing the cardinal for several years."

"Yes. Well, the purpose of this visit is to set up the lines of communication between the two of us. You understand, of course, that I need a sort of spiritual guide for my new surroundings, and I hope you will try it out for a while. I know how much you love your present assignment, but I need some stability around here as I settle in."

"Your Holiness," Ambassador Kirby interrupted, "I've gone over that ground with Tim."

"And?"

"In a nutshell, Tim realizes that a degree of opposition might be generated by having too many Americans around inside the walls. He feels he may be able to do more to help the cause by staying where he is. He shouldn't appear to be part of your inner structure here, at least for the moment."

Bill gave the rector a questioning look. "Do you feel that I am going to be boxed in? All my incoming calls go through the Vatican switchboard and I don't know where all else. Same with outgoing calls. I asked for a private outside line and number this morning. It didn't seem to be a very popular request. I mean, after all, John Paul II brought all his Polish loyalists into the Vatican. He even had a Polish cook." They all laughed.

"Naturally, Pope Bill, your secretary of state wants to know everything you are doing and thinking," Tim said. "It's been his standard operating procedure for years. And you did the right thing keeping him on. For now, that is."

"Well, Tim, Brian Comiskey and Ed Kirby feel you are the answer to my lack of experience. No pope, particularly the first American, should be without an American top adviser with your expertise. If you can teach the young lads studying to be priests or teach advanced Church study and what the hierarchy of the Church is all about, I guess that I can learn from you as well."

"Robitelli can't complain too bitterly if you decide you want to consult with a fellow American who is experienced in Vatican tradition," Kirby pronounced.

"We'll see," Shanahan cautioned. "You will all too quickly learn how easy it is to upset the curia and its leaders, the cardinals who want to run this place." He cocked his head and gave the pope a shrewd look. "If you want me to accept the assignment, I'll do it. But if things get too hot or uncomfortable for you, please whisper in my ear and I'm out without a peep! I ask only one favor: On my day off I like to walk around Rome visiting Churches and museums wearing my St. Louis Cardinals baseball cap and brandishing my Irish walking stick. And I'm a big Mark McGwire fan, so a photo of the all-time single-season home run king will be prominently displayed in my Vatican office as it is at NAC."

"The walking stick is fine, but I am a Red Sox fan and will never forget what the Cardinals did to us in 1946 and 1967." The pope stuck out his hand, however, and Shanahan warmly grasped it back.

PETER II AMONG THE TOURISTS 24

A week had passed since Bill Kelly was elected pope. Tim discreetly moved down from the Gianicolo and NAC to act as the closest person next to the leader of the Catholic Church. Tim's reputation was well known, so the transition was going more smoothly than anyone would have imagined. Some privately might have hoped he would fall on his face, but as yet that didn't appear to be happening.

The media by this time had researched every available source of information on "Pope Bill," as friends referred to Peter II, even ferreting out records at his seminary. He had been at the top of his class both academically and athletically, along with one other, Brian Cardinal Comiskey, his fast friend as well as one of the youngest bishops of Ireland before rising to the status of cardinal. Already a TV movie of the week had been written based on Father Kelly's romance with the Irish colleen for whom he had sought and received dispensation of his priestly vows.

Secret Service agents and state troopers in the United States were assigned to protect the children of the head of the papal state. They found themselves hard-pressed to keep tireless media representatives from photographing and trying to interview them. Ryan found it prudent to spend most of his days and nights out on the bank. Roger, as the youngest, was the most vulnerable prey of these news hawks' tireless search for yet-unpublished tidbits concerning Pope Bill's life in Rome.

Conjecture based on the meager facts available concerning a fisherman and his family were exploited daily on radio and TV talk shows. A certain unprecedented mystique began to form after this first week of Peter II's reign.

As happens in circumstances that exert a fascination on a worldwide public, people resorted to their normal local attitudes to form their opinions. The older ones, ever increasing in number, were the more traditional Catholics who opposed any kind of change in birth control policy, who could not and would not countenance married priests or female priests, and for whom marriage outside the faith and the capricious annulment of a marriage remained anathema. Their view of Pope Peter II was passionately negative. He was the usurper perhaps, the agent of evil, who had somehow been able to worm his way into commandeering the highest office of their Church. So be it, they said resignedly. God had saved Catholicism from evil popes, even married popes in the past. He would do so again.

The liberal faction of the Church saw the elevation of Pope Peter in quite another light. To them it was the work of the Holy Spirit guiding the Church in its preordained way, as he had always led it before. "The Lord works in mysterious ways his wonders to perform," were their watchwords. For these realists and forward-looking Church members, an era for rejoicing and great expectations had dawned at last.

In the end there remained the common man in the street who only made a comment when his living was materially affected. For these "people in the pews," life meant just going to work, going home, watching TV, and having a few drinks with friends. It didn't mean much to them either who or what was going on in Rome. They went to Church on Sunday, or Saturday evening, and contributed their tithe because it was an ingrained habit. Go to Church or go to hell. Take your choice. Even a fool like Pascal, the French philosopher, was wise enough to bet on the former.

Bill Kelly was not unaware of all these attitudes within the Church. In his new position of power he had his finger on everything happening in the world due to the vast communications network the Vatican had at its disposal. He was becoming more conscious of why it was that many popes seemed to spend so much time in prayer. How could mere humans deal with it all? Most of the world was in violent turmoil, either economic conflict or bloodletting strife. Most people were starving, either literally or for a better way of living, as they sought the means to buy those goods and services that made for a few fleeting moments of happiness. Those at the top of financial and social affairs maintained an iron grip on their lucrative stations in life, fending off the many who strove to approximate their freedom and success. Materially, the rich were getting richer and the poor poorer and nobody else cared very much about either extreme on the human spectrum.

Cardinal Robitelli was now overtly demonstrating why so many had considered him the best-suited Roman cleric for the pontificate. He spoke with the total voice of authority in every circumstance and informed his Vatican colleagues that the new pope was slowly learning the process but needed more time to attain the self-confidence necessary to begin public appearances and discussions with various Vatican officials. The cardinal, perhaps prematurely, was truly enjoying his newfound role as puppet-master. It was a measure of Tim Shanahan's tact and quiet behind-the-scenes manipulations that few, if any, close to the curia noticed the gradually escalating power of this self-effacing although effective éminence grise.

Still, a twinge of discomfort stalked Robitelli whenever he discussed Church affairs with Bill Kelly. The cardinal's years of contact with the public had honed his powers of observation. He was fully aware that while this proletarian American "fool" continued to smile and agree with each point he made, wheels were spinning in his head, storing up information for future discussion and manipulation. The pope frequently asked questions that seemed to have an ultimate negative intent. What did the Jews think of this? How did non-Catholic Christians feel about that? How could he learn more about the other side?

Pope Bill, as Peter II was frequently called, was not your ordinary stupid man. He was a scrutinizer, seldom if ever satisfied with one answer. And now, with the rector of NAC mysteriously appearing beside and behind the pope, where would it all lead? What would this man do when his day came to take over? Would he take over? Would he content himself with being just a figurehead managed by a curia, which, of course, Robitelli ordinarily ruled? Only time would tell.

Was there a way in which the cardinal could turn that time to his own advantage and machine all the parts of the Vatican apparatus into an entity so formidable that it couldn't be shifted or tampered with? Could he make the Vatican impervious to the aggressive Pope Peter II that Robitelli strongly suspected he soon would have on his hands? Reaching that objective would require skill, even subterfuge, but if it meant saving God's traditional Church, he was more than willing to sacrifice himself.

And, of course, there was another presentiment slyly intruding on the cardinal's mind, one he was unwilling to entertain on the conscious level but that he could not exorcise, try as he might. Could it be that a working-class layman was indeed God's choice for pontiff? That Bill Kelly, or indeed any number of other possibilities like him, would in the future be the ones to please the Holy Spirit? If so, God had been forced to go to unimaginable historical lengths to make his wish known and finally accepted. Was "God's joke" in actuality God's only available instrument or weapon left for communicating his sacred wishes to his sacred conclave? Certainly it had not been Comiskey's intent to bring Bill Kelly's name before the conclave anyway, other than in a purely metaphorical manner of speaking.

✤ ✤ ✤

A pressing matter now demanded the cardinal's attention. He called the pope and arranged to meet him after his daily Italian training session with Monsignor Cippolini. It was three in the afternoon when he knocked on the open door of the pope's private office.

"Come in, Gino." Bill's usual smile greeted the cardinal as he entered. "Now, what is this very important matter that we need to deal with?"

"Well, er, Holy Father, as you may know, there is another title bestowed on the pope upon his election. He is also 'bishop of Rome.'"

"I thought we took care of that in the conclave," the pope replied.

"That was a secret, like everything that happens in the Sistine during the conclave. It took care of the cardinals who elected you. But now we need to let the Catholic world know you have been ordained a bishop."

Bill, prepared for a petulant inquiry regarding the *avviso,* was relieved when he replied. "Yes, Cippolini mentioned it as he tried to get my tongue working around the Italian phrases I would have to say. What do we need to do?"

"Usually those promoted to the office of bishop spend a week in retreat before the ceremony. We have deliberately delayed your formal installation as pope until you are made a bishop. It seems more fitting and in line with tradition."

"May I ask, Gino, what the ordination of a bishop entails?"

"After a retreat the rite of ordination usually is a solemn celebration of the Eucharist, with several bishops present to assist."

"How is that different from simple ordination to the priesthood?"

"Well, naturally it is one step higher. It is the 'fullness' of the priesthood."

"Is it really necessary to have several bishops, Gino? After all, we have already had a hundred and nineteen cardinals consummate the deed."

"That was in secret. But to be exact it only takes one." He paused. "But that seldom happens except, say, in some Third World country where there are few bishops present to celebrate. The pope will then designate some individual bishop to perform the rite. But when performed under full ecclesiastical direction, it is a beautiful ceremony that has matured over many centuries."

"I'm sure it has. But I am of the American school, inspired by our great naturalist and philosopher, Henry David Thoreau. 'Simplify, simplify.' I remember our canon law professor telling us that all the ceremonies and words were only trimmings. That to be ordained a priest all that was absolutely necessary was that the bishop have the intention to ordain and then simply lay hands on the person's head. It was the 'laying on of hands' that conferred the priesthood. Is not the rite for the office of bishop exactly the same as for the priesthood?"

A wry expression crossed the cardinal's face. "Well, yes," he said hesitantly, "it is the same, now that you mention it. But we are not talking of the minimum necessary but about the beauty, the magnificence of our Vatican Church ceremonies."

"Thank you, Gino. I just wanted to know how different it was from the priesthood. It's always important to know the details of things, don't you think?"

Pope Bill smiled gently at the consternation clouding Cardinal Robitelli's countenance as he took his leave. "I must be going now, Your Holiness. I'll be in touch regarding all this as soon as we can work out the details you consider so important. By the way, how are your meetings with Monsignor Cippolini going?"

"Very well indeed. He is wonderful to talk with and full of amazing and interesting facts and figures. Thanks truly for recommending him to me. Tim Shanahan is working out well, too."

"Glad you're pleased with Al. Do you have anyone in mind to provide you your retreat? You probably don't know many good retreat masters here. I could recommend a few if you wish; you could review their backgrounds with me."

"This is so new to me that I need to think it over awhile. I'm not sure I want this to drag out. I'll just do it quietly and get it behind me. May I let you know tomorrow?"

"Most certainly. I'll drop off a list of those recommended retreat masters to Cippolini." Robitelli stood a moment as though there were another matter he wanted to bring up. The pope indicated with a nod and redirection of his attention toward the door that the meeting was over. With a slight shrug the cardinal turned and left.

No sooner was the pope alone again than he began jotting his thoughts down on paper. He read them over slowly, then reread them. Finally he crumpled the paper and threw it into the wastebasket. Reaching for the phone, he smiled again. "Please put a call through to Cardinal Comiskey in Dublin and get word to him that I'd like to speak to him as soon as possible."

He placed the phone in its cradle and, rising from his chair, walked to the French doors looking out over St. Peter's Square and pushed them open. Sightseers were wandering around staring at the various architectural masterpieces. One of the tourists taking pictures suddenly raised his hand and waved at the pope. Evidently his high-powered lens had been focused on the balcony door of the papal apartment. Bill waved back. This long-range observer motioned to some of the people near him, who looked up and began to wave also.

Bill noticed that one member of the group was carrying a sign that said ST. JAMES OF NEW BEDFORD LOVES PETER II. He remembered that he often attended Mass at St. James on holy days and Sundays, or after returning from fishing trips with his crew. Following Mass the crew would then go to the Portuguese Club for pizza and beer.

Impulsively Bill decided to walk outside and say hello to the group.

Strolling past the Swiss guards, he was met with looks of shock and disbelief. "Your Holiness," one of the guards stammered in surprise, "you must not go out without our making the necessary preparations."

"Oh, it's OK. I'll only be a few minutes," Bill replied airily as he walked down the long marble stairs onto St. Peter's Square, almost a head taller than the last two Swiss guards at the door, and moved toward the fountain where the New Bedford group was staring up at his apartment window.

The pope noticed the group had increased in size as more passersby were attracted to the small crowd. *Oh God! What have I done now?* he thought. *Well, let's see what comes out of it. I've been cooped up inside too long anyway.* He sauntered over to the crowd, followed anxiously by several Swiss guards.

Glancing back at the contingent of worried sentinels, he said, "It's OK. Don't be worried." The captain of the sectional guard quickly approached him. "Your Holiness, where are you going? May we help you?"

"I just want to go out and chat with some friends of mine from America—New Bedford, actually," he replied with a grin.

"Your Holiness, I...er...I know this is all very new to you, but please understand. We are charged to protect you. The pope never goes anywhere anymore without protection. We need to plan ahead. Like the Secret Service does for your president."

"Oh, I'll be just fine. I will only be a few minutes."

The startled guards followed closely behind the pope, motioning to other guards as they passed. The group he had waved to ran to meet him. The guards stepped in front of them, battle-axes crossed, to halt the surge.

"Stop!" one shouted.

A momentary stalemate ensued. Bill Kelly walked slowly to the guards and said, "It's OK."

The confused Swiss sentinels glanced at their captain, who signaled them to attention. "Please, Your Holiness, be careful!"

"Yes, yes." He noticed numbers of guards encircling the group.

Pope Peter II walked slowly into the visitors, shaking hands as he moved. They were delightfully confused, not knowing if they should bow, kiss his ring, or kneel. He sensed their air of uncertainty, but told them how pleased he was to see their poster. All the tourists told the new pope how proud they were of him.

The ice melted immediately as the visitors gathered around him like tourists visiting a shrine. They introduced themselves, posed for pictures, and began to swap stories about the New England coast from New Bedford to Cape Cod. But when he observed the crowd gathering beyond the circle of halberd bearers he felt it would be wise to return to his prison before causing any more trouble.

"I'm sorry I can only visit with you for a short time. I'd much prefer to join you in a local café and all of us could have a glass of wine together. But I really have to leave now."

"Please, Your Holiness, may we have your blessing?"

Everyone around him dropped to their knees. He blushed at their show of simple faith. "I have to tell you, my friends, I feel quite humble giving you a blessing. I believe that the pope is merely the servant of the servant of God. I should be asking your blessing. So let's compromise. I'll ask Our Savior to bless you if you all ask Him to bless and aid me."

His eyes searched heavenward as he raised his hand. "Lord Jesus, I beg you to send your blessings on these good people who have so clearly shown their deep faith in you by coming all this way to visit this beautiful basilica and your humble servant."

As he finished the blessing he dropped to a kneeling position and bowed his head. Many had tears in their eyes. This man was very different from what they had expected. Was he saintly, or perhaps a bit too simple and humble?

Pope Peter arose, waved good-bye, and turned back toward the Apostolic Palace, followed closely by the unnerved Swiss guards. A somber Cardinal Bellotti stood in the entranceway watching him return. "Your Holiness, I'm sure you impressed the people, but you must realize you could have been in terrible danger. You recall what happened to Pope John Paul II. Please try to remember we have customs here based on years of experience. We certainly want you to meet and bless the people, but we also want you to stay alive. I, for one, am not anxious to be shut up in another conclave! The last one was enough for me!"

"Sorry, Cardinal. I know you are right and I respect the difficult job the guards have on their hands. Maybe I need to adjust more than I really want to. Pray for me, *Eminenza*. I am a stubborn man," Bill confessed.

The cardinal bowed as he watched the pope wend his way back up to the papal apartment, leaving the embarrassed captain to try to explain to his superiors what had just happened.

As the pope entered his private office the answering machine was blinking brightly. He pressed the button to answer whoever was on the line. "Your Holiness," the Vatican operator reported, "Cardinal Comiskey called but you did not answer, so I assumed you were busy. He stated he would be at his residence for another hour."

Within two minutes Brian was on the line. After the pleasantries Bill said, "I need to ask you a favor, Cardinal Comiskey."

"Just say the word, Your Holiness, and I'll do what I can."

"You have, of course, ordained many priests into the episcopacy, as well as bishops."

"If this means you have approved someone on my recommended list for the vacancy in Galway I'd be more than delighted. Just send me your official announcement and I'll make the arrangements."

"I don't know about any lists yet. In fact, I don't know much about what goes on here at all. I'm still in boot camp. I want you to come to Rome to perform the rite. Can you fit it into your schedule as soon as possible?"

"I could come this Friday. But why me? You have closetsful of bishops right there."

"Because I want you to consecrate me in this public ceremony, Brian."

"You?"

"Yes, you know...His Holiness Pope Peter II, Bishop of Rome! I need to be consecrated out where anybody can see it happen, not just in the secret conclave. Church regulations, you know."

Brian laughed. "Oh, yes. But I haven't received any announcement. When does the big event take place?"

"Look, Brian. There isn't going to be any announcement or any big event. I don't want to complicate this. Just come here and I'll explain everything. OK?"

"Well, you're the pope. What can I say? See you in two days, buddy... I mean, Your Holiness."

"See you Friday. Now good-bye. God bless."

As he replaced the phone a smirk flashed across his face. "We'll just see what happens when this request gets out."

The knock on the door to his apartment that Pope Bill was expecting—dreading, really—came late the following morning. A determined-looking Cardinal Robitelli entered the room. "Your Holiness," he began. Now Bill knew he was in for trouble. Most of the week the secretary of state addressed him as "Pope Bill" when they were alone, as they were at this moment. "Excuse me for bothering you before our scheduled appointment this afternoon. Cardinal Bellotti told me what happened in the square. You must realize you have caused some serious difficulties not only for us but for the guards also."

Bill bowed his head, accepting the chastisement, but said nothing.

"We are more than willing, anxious in fact, to assist you if you wish to meet people, but such meetings always take place in a private audience where they can be controlled. Not everyone in the world loves the pope and the Church, you know. You could have been in terrible danger. It has happened before."

Bill nodded somberly, recalling vividly the message and words of Pope John Paul II's *avviso* to his heir. If he did his job, it said in effect, he would be in danger at all times. The assassination attempt in St. Peter's Square had occurred on the anniversary of the original Lady of Fatima apparition.

"Please allow us to assist you with security. The reason for this period of adjustment is to help you understand your role as head of the Church. It may seem the Swiss guards are a mere decoration, and we sincerely hope that is all they need be. But they are well-trained soldiers, equal to any in the world. They'll die for you, but they expect you to give them a fair chance to stay alive as well."

Bill's planned rebuttal to the cardinal's scolding faded swiftly. "I was out of line. I'm sorry for that," he said contritely. "I'll try to do better."

"You must learn of the outstanding history and work of the Swiss guard, Your Holiness," Cardinal Robitelli reproved. "I'll have Monsignor Cippolini give you a complete history of them, right up to the present moment. Suffice it to say, those fluffy uniforms cover more than undergarments. I assure you those guards that formed the outside circle around you yesterday were well equipped to deal with any situation. Also, there were men in positions you would not notice, ready to respond to any emergency."

The cardinal paused to see if he was getting his message across. "It is not something we are happy with, Your Holiness. It is, however, part of the world we must live in." He smiled at the humbled pontiff. "To be honest, Your Holiness, I thought I was going to be in for a verbal battle. Thank you for your consideration. Perhaps you fail to appreciate the significance of all our traditions even as Pope Peter II. The robes, the miter, all serve to remind us of God's authority and power."

For a moment Bill was tempted to give the cardinal the Polish pope's *avviso* to read, but some instinct told him, *Not yet.* Instead he asked, "What of the authority of the many millions of people whom we serve in God's name? The 'people in the pews,' as we used to call them. Particularly in America, these masses are questioning the basic traditions sometimes taken for granted. No less a political American icon than Senator David Lane, from one of our richest, most powerful Catholic families, called some Roman Catholic traditions, and I quote him, 'Catholic gobbledygook' and called himself a 'cafeteria Catholic.' He'll decide which teachings of the Church to follow."

Cardinal Robitelli ignored the barb. "They have had no training in Church history. Please understand that we need to be firm to these traditions just as each of us was while rising up the ladder of authority. We have a glorious history to live up to." He smiled patiently at the pope, who was listening intently to his words. "I hope you will allow our learned historians to give you further instruction so that we may come to some agreement on these issues. We must have order and discipline in our ancient traditions."

The cardinal paused in his lecture, seeing the pope's face flush and his eyes narrow and harden. There was no hint of agreement. Robitelli began to feel quite uncomfortable as Pope Peter rose from his chair and leaned his hands on the desk.

"Cardinal, I have read a great deal of Church history. Not only written by Catholic and Protestant historians but by just plain old everyday historians who, incidentally, had less of an ax to grind or point to prove. Maybe, just maybe, you are the one who doesn't see clearly. Maybe you have only one quite narrow view of the entire tapestry. The word 'religion,' as you know, comes from the Latin *ligio,* which means 'to connect.' As ligaments connect our body parts. As I see it, you don't completely connect. The fancy robes and miters and titles have more to do with earthly authority than with God's Church. I think the feudal Middle Ages is where all this hierarchical pageantry comes from."

Pope Peter stared at his uncharacteristically cowed Vatican secretary of state and added yet another thought. "Good God, 'Your Holiness,' 'Your Eminence,' 'Your Excellency'—it makes me want to throw up my hands in frustration." Bill paused to bow his head, realizing he might have gone too far, perhaps allowed himself to be too forceful.

He raised his head and stared into the eyes of the bewildered cardinal. His mind spun as he searched for words. Suddenly in a rush they came. "Tell me, Your Eminence, do you recall what Our Savior replied when questioned by the young man? 'Good master, what must I do to be saved?" Bill paused but did not wait for a reply. "I believe he said, 'Why do you call me good? No one is good...only God.' If Jesus abhorred the idea of being considered better than the rest of mankind, then what are we talking about? Sometimes I feel that tradition is an excuse for not doing something that needs getting done. God is not Church tradition. He is always NOW! Everything is in the Present to him. By emphasizing tradition we avoid responsibility for all new, forward action."

The two Churchmen looked each other in the face. Bill began to feel his mouth had betrayed him again. "I'm, I'm sorry if—"

The cardinal lifted his hand to interrupt. "Please, no more." He turned and left the pope's office.

When Cardinal Robitelli failed to appear for his usual midafternoon meeting, Pope Peter began to have qualms of conscience about his sudden outburst a few hours before. He felt at sea in a world with which he found it difficult, nearly impossible, to come to grips. He placed another call to his faithful friend in Dublin, only to hear the operator report that the cardinal was unavailable.

"Do you wish to leave a message, Your Holiness?"

"No, thanks. I'll speak to him tomorrow when he comes here to see me." He hung up the telephone and began pacing despondently back and forth over the length of his office. He tried to pray, but nothing seemed to help. He dropped into the seat behind his desk and reached for the telephone.

"Please place a call to my home in Massachusetts and buzz me when you get through," he requested. Fifteen minutes passed before the buzzer sounded. His heart quickened its pace as he anticipated the comfort of his children's comments on his general situation.

"Your Holiness, your son Ryan is on the phone. He states that your other children have gone shopping. Do you want to speak to him?"

"Yes, thank you." He heard his son's voice over the line. "Ryan, how are you, boy? Good...No, I just wanted to gab with you kids. I miss all of you. I was feeling a bit down so I thought you all could cheer me up. How is the fishing?...Yes, it must be hard. I can't expect you to easily understand why I did this, son. I know Uncle Sean tried his best to explain. No, I can't say I'm enjoying myself. Please don't be sarcastic. It has nothing to do with 'enjoyment,' son. Just my own feeling that this is what I am called to do at this point in my life." He pictured his son on the other end of the line.

"It's asking a lot of you to run the business, I know. But you're a grown man, Ryan. And I have the greatest confidence in you. I've written you a long letter about the business. You are to be the owner, son. The same as when my father turned it over to me when I gave up the priesthood. Manny and Jerry will help you. Yes, I know you'd be happier to have me. It was sudden for us all but I really know this is where I need to be, where I belong right now..." He hesitated a moment.

"Your sister said you were pretty upset about the girls and Roger coming here to live and you staying. Please try to see it in the light of your faith in God. I know you will make a good boss and treat the men as equals. And tell the guys that I send my very best...What? Yes, it should be easy enough to find some medals and send them a special blessing. I'll get you some medals of St. Peter, a fisherman like us, Ryan."

For the first time that day Pope Peter laughed aloud. "He said that? That's funny. Stan is Jewish, you know, but if he wants a medal, he gets one! I'll tell the engraving department to make me a nice big St. Abraham medal for Stanley. How's that?

"No, I never heard of him either but I can take care of that. I'll just declare him a saint. I'll have the medals in the mail this week. Tell the others that Uncle Brian is coming to see me tomorrow. And Ryan, when the press folks contact you, just remember you are the pope's son and don't swear at them." The pope laughed at his son's reply. "I'll call and tell you all about Uncle Brian's visit."

The pope felt better as he hung up but decided to go to his private chapel to see if God was in a talkative mood.

He knelt slowly, breathing deeply as he looked up at the tabernacle. What was there to say? His depression returned as he tried to articulate his dilemma. "Look, I'm not asking for visions or miracles. Just tell me what I should do. How can I settle these issues I'm supposed to settle? I used to think You gave special knowledge to the pope. If You will help me, show me the way, I'd really appreciate it." Silence seemed to muffle the chapel. He felt devoid of inspiration. He put his face in his hands and let taciturnity envelop him. He lost track of time until he felt a hand on his shoulder. He turned and looked up into the ascetic, aristocratic face of Cardinal Robitelli.

"Your Holiness, sorry to disturb you. I want to apologize for leaving so abruptly."

"It was my fault, Gino. I was far too outspoken. I don't know what came over me. So much change and pressure, I guess."

"No matter. I recall we had originally agreed to discuss our differences. I should have heard you out. I am aware of your point of view. We can go over it tomorrow if you wish."

The pope rose from the kneeler and seated himself in his chair. "I've been thinking about my consecration as bishop."

"Oh?" the cardinal responded cautiously, seating himself beside the pope.

"I have asked Cardinal Comiskey to come here tomorrow. My plan was to have him consecrate me a bishop and skip all the ceremonies."

"I suspected you might be thinking along those lines."

"I suppose the idea upsets you."

"In some respects. But there is sense to it. Under the circumstances it is best not to make your consecration too public, or not public at all. Totally private, in fact. Do what God guides you to do. You are the pope, after all!"

Bill still felt the cardinal's hand on his shoulder as Robitelli rose to leave.

"I've seen other popes and brother cardinals with that look I now see on your face, Your Holiness. I'm not preaching, just imparting a thought someone told me years ago when I was praying for guidance. Our God is a God of silence. He speaks only in silence." With that Robitelli was gone. Bill Kelly bowed his head and closed his eyes, absorbing the chapel's tranquillity.

It was eleven the next morning when Cardinal Comiskey arrived and was escorted up to the papal study. "Brian, come in, come in!" A delighted Pope Bill hastened to greet his best friend, reaching out to give the cardinal a hug and a crushing handshake.

"Glad to see you, Your Holiness. You don't look any the worse for wear. Is your new 'job' agreeing with you?"

"If that's a fact then I can thank Tim Shanahan, and of course you and Ed Kirby for bringing him swimming into my net, so to speak."

"I am indeed happy to hear you say that. Has he actually moved into the Vatican?"

"Not yet. He feels for the sake of harmony he should be readily available but that a gradual intensifying of his influence will better serve the cause."

Comiskey frowned and then nodded. "Yes, I suppose he's right. We don't want Robitelli and the rest to get their noses out of joint just yet."

"For certain everything is much more complicated than I ever dreamed. I came here hoping to do real good for our Church in the world. Now I feel I'm just trying things that will cause the least amount of harm. Tim keeps telling me to hold on and everything will work out just fine."

"We can't please everyone, Bill. Just get as much information as possible before you make a decision. Then pray to God it turns out right."

Bill allowed a half smile to cross his lips. "I'll try to remember that, Coach."

"And now, Your Holiness, when do we perform our little ceremony? This afternoon? This evening?"

"Brian, I hope you'll understand. I have decided on a Mass in the private chapel. After I receive the Holy Eucharist, just lay your hands on me to consecrate me a bishop and that will be that!"

"What? What do you mean?"

"Just what I said. No frills. The basic form that the early Church followed. It is valid, you know. Bishops are priests, after all."

"Yes, I guess that's true. But have you discussed this with Robitelli? Or with the other bishops and cardinals here?"

"I discussed it with Tim and he said the plan was just what he would have suggested. Yesterday I told Gino what I wanted. To my amazement, he agreed. And just before you arrived he phoned me to say that at a general meeting with many of the bishops and cardinals they too agreed. Those who wish to attend the Mass are welcome. It will be at noon and lunch at one. OK?"

"Wow, you move fast! Do you think I have time to go to the bathroom?" They laughed and embraced once again.

"The chapel at noon, Brian. Keep it simple...no sermon."

+I+ +I+ +I+

The chapel, surprisingly, was filled with several cardinals and bishops and numerous clergy, all of whom were staff in the Vatican. They had evidently been informed by Cardinal Robitelli of the momentous event, reduced to ceremonial insignificance at the pope's request, that was to take place. Many came out of curiosity, to be able to later say they had been present when Pope Peter had been ordained bishop of Rome. Monsignor Timothy Shanahan sat unobtrusively at the back of the chapel.

Several of those present came forward after the short ceremony to kiss the ring of the newly made bishop. When the celebrant and the new bishop sat down to lunch they had to insist on a reluctant Tim Shanahan joining them. Brian was the first to comment on the disdainful attitude of some of those in attendance. Bill was quick to brush it aside. "I think it's much too early to make anything of their seeming condescension, Brian. Remember the confused attitudes we had when the Church switched from Latin to the vernacular? I can expect the same. I am a renegade around here."

Pope Peter held up his wineglass in silent salute to those before him at the luncheon. Robitelli had made a last-minute excuse for not being among them. Taking a long swallow, the pope continued, "They'll either accept me in time, if I toe the mark, or"—he smiled wanly—"increase their prayers to the Holy Spirit to take me to my eternal whatever."

Shanahan leaned over. "That may be right, Your Holiness. But you are the pope, regardless of what the people attached to this reverent place may feel about you. You may have noticed that Cardinal Robitelli excused himself after you and Cardinal Comiskey insisted on my presence at this table."

"They should show a little respect for the papacy, at least," Brian grumbled.

"Down, boy." Bill grinned. "Cool it. When this lunch is over we can go sit in my library and have a little schnapps or Irish Mist to settle the stomach. Do you want to stay for supper, or do you have to get back?"

"Needless to say, when I left Dublin, I thought I was in for a long, drawn-out affair, so I canceled all tomorrow's appointments. Satan at work again!"

"The Holy Spirit at work again! We can have some real time alone together," Bill said in pleased tones.

After the luncheon Bill led Brian and, with some insistence, Monsignor Shanahan back down to the apostolic apartment. He poured a liberal Irish Mist for each of them, and after a few minutes of relaxed banter, Brian asked Tim outright how he was doing as the pope's closest adviser.

"At all times I am trying to anticipate our next problem and steer His Holiness here away from it." Tim sipped his drink. "Until now he has taken my advice. But the less I am seen exerting a strong influence, the better I can serve him."

"That has to be corrected," the pope said. "As soon as possible we should make Monsignor Shanahan a bishop with an official post inside where he can advise me every day as my private secretary."

"I agree," Brian said heartily. "We're the Irish Mafia."

"As your adviser, let me suggest you wait on that," Tim told the pope. "The correct moment will no doubt arrive, but it sure isn't now." All three took a healthy sip of the Mist to let this sink in.

There will never be a more propitious time than now, Bill thought in this moment of warmth shared with his two most trusted advisers. "There is another bit of information," he began hesitantly. "I have shared it with no one, although Robitelli certainly is aware of what is causing my concerns even if he does not know precisely what they consist of."

"Please, Bill, there is no time like this moment," Brian urged.

Monsignor Shanahan put the empty glass down and turned attentively to Bill, anticipating an unburdening of some of the pope's seldom-revealed anxieties.

"I call it the warning, *avviso,* from my predecessor."

Bill went on to describe the way Robitelli had presented him with the sealed document. He was conscious of it resting securely in the desk across the library from where the three were seated around a low table. Bill explained to his two closest advisers how he had painstakingly, word by word, roughly translated the Italian writing into English.

"Here, I'll show it to you," Bill said impulsively. He put his empty crystal glass down and, placing his hands on the arms of the chair, started to push himself up to a standing position.

"A moment, Holiness." Monsignor Shanahan's voice cracked as he put out a hand to restrain the pope. Bill sank back in his chair, leveling a questioning stare at Tim.

"Have you told Cardinal Robitelli what is in this warning, as you translate *avviso?*"

"No, I have not. He has been on the verge of asking me several times, but I managed to turn him off the matter."

"Your Holiness...Bill." There was urgency in Brian's tone. "Tim is thinking that before you actually allow us to see and read this message, you should at least let the cardinal secretary of state be the first to know what the contents are. If, as you say, the advice from John Paul II is not to let anybody read it but to keep its message clearly in your mind, that's fine. But to let us read it, even though we're dying to see it, before discussing the contents with Robitelli would be an error in tactics."

Bill knew his two advisers were correct. "Robitelli will, then, be the first to actually read the *avviso.* It will give him an opportunity to say 'I told you so' when he brings up my little solo walk around St. Peter's Square, of course."

"How's that, Bill?"

"The *avviso* in effect tells me that if I follow the Holy Spirit's plan for my papacy, I will not live longer than it takes to fulfill my mission here. He wrote that Our Lady of Fatima, working against the third prophecy, saved him from dying that day in the square when the Turk shot him. He then lived to rid the world of Communism to fulfill the second prophecy of Fatima. But with his *avviso* revealing that the greatest loss of life to genocidal behavior, disease, and famine ever seen on Earth will happen at the start of the third millennium, I must work fast to accomplish my mission here." The pope shrugged in resignation.

The three were silent as the mood in the room changed. Bill Kelly smiled cheerfully and poured another round of Irish Mist. "So now you are up to date on the bishop of Rome. I will take your advice as soon as it seems a convenient moment and give Robitelli a copy of the *avviso* to read. And then I'll feel free to let you two in on it."

"Which reminds me," Brian said, "now that I have completed my duties as celebrant, I must see Robitelli to find out if the curia have gotten around to approving one of my three candidates to replace my auxiliary bishop, who passed away this September."

"I was thinking about that. Why do these things take so long?"

"A mystery to rival the Trinity, Bill. It's always been that way. I remember when my bishop told me I was on his recommended list. It took a year before he received the decision."

Bill shook his head. "Ridiculous! May I ask who on the list you personally favor?"

"A lowly Father Crowley. Monsignors McCarthy and Donnelly are darned good men. But if I were told whom I might choose, Crowley would be my man. Of course, they're long his superior in rank."

"What if you didn't have to choose, Brian?"

"What do you mean?"

"Well, say you needed three new bishops. Would you consider those three your best choices, or begin selecting some other men as well?"

"Now, look." Brian breathed heavily. "That's an impossible dream, three new bishops. But yes, I would definitely nominate those three."

"You mean you really need three bishops but only ask for one?"

Brian laughed. "Poor Pope Bill. Well, you'll learn one day how slowly things happen around here in the Vatican. They like to play it safe."

"Baloney, Brian. If I ask my first mate to choose a new first mate for one of my boats I sure would not tell him I'd take his choice 'under advisement.' That would be a direct slap in the face."

The pope reached out and pressed a small button at the edge of the end table. "Let's just see what we can do about these various great and sundry mysteries."

In moments a knock was heard on the door. "Come in, come in, Sister," Pope Bill called out and stood up as a middle-aged nun entered the room.

A "liberated nun," Brian noticed. Perfect attire for a working secretary. The traditional nun's habit would preclude efficient shorthand, typing, and office work. Cardinal Comiskey also rose.

"This is Sister Miriam, my secretary and the world's fastest shorthand specialist."

The nun colored as she bowed to Tim and shook hands with the cardinal when she saw no ring to kiss. "What may I do for you, Your Holiness?"

"Please be seated and take down this official letter for me."

The nun seated herself, opened her pad, and was ready to write. The pope began to dictate, a sly grin on his face. "This document is to confirm that His Holiness, Pope Peter II, has approved for the office of bishop in the Church the following priests." He turned to Brian. "What are their first names and middle initials?"

"But you can't, I mean you're not—"

"Your Holiness," Tim added urgently, "as your secretary adviser I agree with Cardinal Comiskey. This is bound to have unfortunate repercussions at this time. One now, the other two down the road would be much more advisable."

"I'm the pope, remember?"

Brian nodded in wonderment. The full names were entered. Pope Peter continued to dictate. "These three priests are needed to assist the Church in Ireland and will be consecrated to the bishopric at a time and place to be decided upon by His Eminence, Brian Cardinal Comiskey, primate of Ireland. Said cardinal will also have authority to decide in which areas these bishops will serve for the betterment of the Church following their consecration. Signed and sealed, et cetera." Bill turned triumphantly to Brian.

Tim Shanahan sighed, shook his head, and then shrugged in resignation.

"Dear God!" Brian exclaimed. "Can you do this?"

"I just did. You know the pope has the authority here."

Sister Miriam flashed her first tentative smile at the bewildered cardinal.

"Yes," Brian conceded, "I know that. But think of the trouble this may cause. I mean, isn't this just a little hasty?"

"My dear Cardinal Comiskey, do you mean to tell me you have been wasting the pope's precious time with small talk and did not mean what you said?"

"No, of course not, but—"

"Good. Then it's done. Sister, please give me three copies of that on my official letterhead and I will stamp the Vatican seal on them."

"Very well, Pope Peter. I will return in fifteen minutes. Excuse me." She stood up and retreated backward through the door.

"Well, all I can say is thank you," Brian, bemused, said. "You have no idea how much this will upgrade our faith in Ireland."

Tim shook his head. "I hope you don't create problems with the magisterium here. You surely will hear from Robitelli."

Brian's gaze went to the door through which Sister Miriam had disappeared. "The good nun certainly does seem to be super efficient, as you said . . . all business."

"Yes, but there is something missing. I can't put my finger on it yet. She seems . . . well, somehow uncomfortable with me. I suppose it's the fact that I'm a layman—or was. She reminds me a bit of my son, Ryan, the only kid of mine I could never read."

True to her word, the sister was back in fifteen minutes. Brian happily patted his Vatican letter as he put it carefully into his jacket. "Thanks again. You're not doing this merely because we are friends, are you?"

"Of course, it's always easier to do something for a friend. But if a need makes itself known I see no reason not to address it immediately. I just may send out a few feelers to some of our other cardinals, like, say, Motupu, and see if I can help them."

"Well, all I can say is, good luck. If I don't see you again I'll assume they have thrown you into the moot," he quipped.

"You mean the moat, our beloved Tiber into which the Borgias threw the bodies of certain beloved cardinals who disagreed with them, or whose lands and possessions they appropriated?"

"No, although that, too. The history of the Church is bloody and profane. But I was referring to the 'moot point' where nothing can really ever get done," Brian commented. "Our business is finished. I'll now return to Dublin a little early, if you don't mind?"

"No, I don't. But you'll miss a perfect Italian meal. Monsignor Cippolini is taking his mother and sister, who is a concert pianist, and Tim and me out to eat at a great restaurant nearby. And don't worry. I planned it with the Swiss Guard, so I'll be protected."

"I heard about your little excursion out into the wicked world. Seriously, though, remember the cautionary advice from your predecessor. I'd love to be a fly on the wall when Robitelli finds out what you've done for Ireland. That might be a good time to tell him about, or show him, the *avviso*."

Bill grinned broadly. "I'll just say, 'Gino, tell me who you selected for the bishopric in Dublin?' Then when he mentions any one of the three I'll just say, 'Why, you know, I agree completely with you. I also chose him and gave Comiskey an official letter saying so.'"

Brian threw up his hands. "God help us...another Boston Irish politician!"

✢‡✢ ✢‡✢ ✢‡✢

Brian left Rome. Pope Bill waited for the other shoe to drop. That Cardinal Robitelli would try to inflict serious consequences for the pope's temerity in taking it upon himself to appoint three bishops out of hand was a foregone conclusion. Was there a madman on the premises?

Inexorably, but three full days later, Bill learned how far the tentacles of the magisterium could reach. His Friday meeting with Cardinal Robitelli gave him reason to regret his spontaneous use of the power vested in him as pope. He resolved henceforth to curtail his exuberance and behave more circumspectly when dealing with his curia.

Almost the first words out of the cardinal's mouth when they were alone together were "Your Holiness," the sure signal that chastisement was in the offing. "I have received word early this morning," he continued, "that you have given Cardinal Comiskey permission to consecrate three priests to the office of bishop in Ireland. Bishop Wu, director of personnel at the Vatican, was shocked and nearly broke down over the news. And I must agree with him! Let me ask you, who else now will want a half-dozen or so more bishops?"

Cardinal Robitelli peered owlishly at the pope for a moment. "This is a most dangerous move you have made. No one will argue the fact that you have the authority to appoint bishops," he added hastily. "But previous popes have always been very careful to discuss each new appointment to that high office with the prefect of the Congregation of Bishops and the cardinal secretary of state. We like to think that we work here as a team, brothers joined together to assist each particular diocese throughout the world. It is forever necessary to examine carefully the background and ministry of each candidate to determine how he has progressed as a loyal witness to the tenets of our faith. I feel—nay, I insist—that you should at least afford us the respect of discussing your concerns before making any major changes!"

Pope Peter was embarrassed not only by his precipitous action but also by the open, if not hostile, manner in which the cardinal had expressed himself. He searched for the sentiments he had been composing to use in his defense when this inevitable moment of conflict arrived.

"Your Eminence, I confess I do not totally understand your process of appointing bishops. I can't help but detect a certain, shall I say, 'contradiction' in the process. Brian Comiskey was obviously a worthy candidate for bishop and then for cardinal long before I came. Therefore, why should his recommendations be questioned? Perhaps because of his part in the elevation of Bill Kelly?"

Robitelli shook his head in exasperation, and the pope continued. "Is there a need to limit the authority to a small group here that knows very little, extremely little, about the troubles in Ireland? Does the curia here somehow have better skills at judging who is suited to be a bishop there?"

When no answer was forthcoming, Bill finished his reply to his secretary of state. "I do not apologize for this action. But I apologize sincerely for not letting you know of my resolve. I promise to keep you and the curia apprised of my intentions in the future. If you convince me that any contemplated action of mine will cause serious harm to the Church, I shall heed that advice."

Still Cardinal Robitelli maintained his silence. But Bill was not finished. "Incidentally, I spoke to Brian this morning and learned that the curia agreed with his first choice for a new bishopric. With regard to the other two, please ask Cardinal Comiskey to come here and discuss with us the monsignors I agreed to consecrate. If you can show good reason why they should not be appointed, and if Brian cannot justify them, I will withdraw my approval. Fair enough?"

The cardinal slowly rose from his chair, a half smile on his face. "I presume there is no way I can argue with that. It seems the ball is now not squarely, but obliquely, in my court. As you football people say in America, 'the best defense is a good offense.' Allow me to contact Cardinal Comiskey later this afternoon."

Pope Peter nodded his assent. A nagging question had flashed through his mind with increasing frequency. He had never, one on one, directly confronted Robitelli with this suppressed doubt about his miraculous election. Now seemed to be the moment when the truth might emerge.

"Your Eminence." The pope underscored the seriousness of the concern he was about to express as he looked up at the cardinal secretary of state, standing attentively in front of his desk. Robitelli stiffened, sensing the gravity of this moment. "I would like to have an indication of the consensus of the cardinals, an agreement you personally may or may not share wholeheartedly, in respect to the status of Pope Peter II."

Robitelli's eyes glittered, his body tense as he concentrated on his pope's words.

"In short," Bill Kelly asked levelly, "do you believe that the Holy Spirit, in the form of this 'prank' I've heard referred to as 'God's joke,' truly picked a lowly New England fisherman, Bill Kelly, to be Christ's Vicar on earth? Do you believe that God would go to such extraordinary lengths as to trick His own conclave into voting for me? Then send word to me, on a fishing boat at sea, to be prepared?"

When Robitelli, now standing before the pope, did not reply immediately, Bill continued the probe. "As far as I know, the details of Bill Kelly's election have never been revealed outside the conclave itself. To this day nobody knows how it happened that the sacred college of cardinals elected this laicized priest, Bill Kelly, myself, to the throne of St. Peter. Do you cardinals feel that, if the truth were out, the college would never be taken seriously again? Are you all so frightened of your collective irresponsibility being discovered by the people in the pews, that you put up with me until this foolishness can be rectified?"

Before Robitelli could consider an appropriate answer, Bill Kelly continued, voiding his psyche of the most troublesome concept presently disturbing him. "I wonder how you can keep the Church in line if you do not believe, as I do, that God chose this present pope, Peter II. If there were serious doubts that the Holy Spirit entered the conclave, if it is widely believed that my election was a mortal mistake, I believe my reign as pope would be as short as that of John Paul I, namely thirty days. I do not employ a medieval food taster, but my children are coming here to join me and I do not want any similar tragedy to occur."

Robitelli, for a moment terrified at the implications of this soliloquy, reached down, placing his hands on the pope's shoulders. "Bill, if I did not believe with my heart and soul, as you do, that this was indeed the work of the Holy Spirit coming to the conclave and then to you out on your boat, I could not allow such a charade to have occurred in the first place. We are all truly convinced that it was no joke, no accident that you were brought to us by God himself. As was expected at the conclave, the Holy Spirit indeed came among us and chose you to lead. In the same way He came to us twenty-five years ago and we chose an obscure Polish cardinal who became Pope John Paul II, who peaceably rid the Western world of Communism."

The cardinal glanced at his watch. "Oh, my! Now I am due at a meeting of the curia on this subject of Irish bishops. We have to assume, Holy Father Bill, that the Holy Spirit chose to create three new bishops in Ireland." He squeezed Bill's shoulders affectionately.

Eyes misting, Bill watched as the secretary of state made his exit, as always in charge of the situation at hand. *Well,* the pope thought, *another time will suffice to talk with the cardinal about the* avviso.

THE CATHOLIC FIRST FAMILY 26

The next month flew by for the new pope. Cardinal Comiskey was awarded his three bishops, and Bill was leaning more and more heavily on Tim Shanahan for advice on everything involving Church politics: when to meet with whom, what the international press was saying. The former rector, now a close papal confidant, was also conducting a sub-rosa investigation of the controversial Vatican Bank. Bill respectfully consulted daily with Cardinal Robitelli, keeping a low profile at the Vatican. He so attentively studied Italian in Cippolini's private language course that he was soon able to understand the letter from John Paul II in all its nuances and made up his mind not to reveal its details to anyone for the time being. His forerunner had requested that the details remain secret until the pope deemed it necessary to reveal them.

On rare occasions he and Tim dined out at quiet restaurants despite Robitelli's disapproval. Ambassador Ed Kirby had arranged for Armed Forces Network reception in the pope's study so that he might watch American college and pro football games on television. Tim would consult Ed once in a while to evaluate media coverage of the pope's first days at the Vatican. By and large the world press had been rather favorable, even in usually hostile countries like France and England.

Bill worked assiduously on the final planning of the yearlong celebration of Giubileo 2000, which would actually run well into 2001. It would affect millions of pilgrims during the dizzying months ahead. The ancient city hadn't nearly the infrastructure, hotel rooms, or public transportation to adequately accommodate so many people. A major debate was continuing in the Italian Parliament as to whether or not such great financial expenditure should be approved or the taxpayers should be spared a huge outlay of public funds. However, if the world economy remained strong, the millions traveling to Italy would bring billions of lire pouring into the economy.

Vatican officials were working closely with government officials at the Quirinale and Campodoglio on a daily basis. The pope was also consulting with Israel's chief rabbi in Rome on the Church's responses to the many books and negative news articles on the Holocaust and how Pope Pius XII and the Church dealt with it during the World War II period.

Many Catholics had felt that great strides had been made in Jewish-Catholic relations under the previous pope, but tensions still existed. As the rabbi put it, "Many Jews throughout the world, especially in the United States, believe the Church continues to refuse to come forward and acknowledge that Pope Pius XII could have made considerably greater efforts to help save more of the six million Jews killed under Hitler during the war years."

This opinion was usually driven by highly visible best-selling books and TV documentaries. It was almost as though no matter how much proof or documentation the Church shared, it didn't make any difference. Many Church scholars could only conclude that the enemies of Pius had their minds made up and didn't want to be influenced by the facts.

Soon the middle of December was upon Pope Peter II and a quiescent media found itself stirred to life by the prospect of the pope's family arriving in Rome, an unthinkable event in modern history. The media reviewed in caricature the lives and likenesses of women who had lived with various popes as concubines from medieval times onward. Lucrezia Borgia, daughter of Pope Alexander II, received close and detailed scrutiny. Anticipation heightened perceptibly.

The fact that a pope and his children would be living in Vatican City generated continuous speculation on talk shows; the stain of a married clergy was dinned in op-ed pages by feminist groups and anti-Catholic zealots. As anticipated, activists, naturally feminists and women's groups, began openly to question the Church's position on the nonordination of female aspirants to the priesthood. They saw this period of change as their long-overdue, historic, God-given right.

One major American newspaper, which recklessly reported that marriage annulments for several prominent Catholics had been purchased from the Church, cited Senator Lane's separation from his wife, with three children left in limbo. Headlines and editorials proclaimed that this issue was the new pope's biggest challenge. They did not fail to mention that Lane was from the pope's home state. The Church's firm positions on artificial birth control and abortion reopened old wounds, not surprisingly, and heightened the ongoing verbal jousting. Liberal activists felt that this was their opportunity to move the Church in a more progressive direction. They summoned Hollywood celebrities, now self-proclaimed "lapsed" Catholics, to invoke their celebrity for radical change. All these currents weighed heavily on Pope Peter. Would he end what some termed in the media the "hypocrisy of Rome"? John Paul II's *avviso* warned of increasing apathy and unrest in the American Catholic Church. On the positive side Pope Peter noticed that several of the cardinals and bishops were nonetheless sincerely inquiring about the health and welfare of his family, offering to help in any way.

Finally the morning of the family's arrival in Rome was imminent. Pope Peter began to feel more than a touch of anxiety and excitement at the prospect of seeing his children again. Some of the Vatican establishment felt that it would be improper for the pope to go to Leonardo da Vinci Airport to welcome his family as they came off the plane. Among other things, it was argued that popes had never gone outside Vatican City to greet visitors before. They had always come to him.

Bill Kelly would, of course, hear none of it. He insisted on being at the airport and in the same suit that he had worn when he left home. He was to be plain Mr. William Kelly going to collect his kids.

Thus he sat nervously in a parked limousine, guards unobtrusively stationed about, his chauffeur at the wheel, watching the plane from Boston touch down. In frequent conversations Bill had learned that Tony Maroni, the driver, had four children nearly the same age as his own. There was always something for them to talk about. Tony was in his glory, later boasting about his conversations with his good friend, Pope Bill.

The pope's heart began to pound as the big plane pulled up to the ramp. Special preparations had been made by Alitalia to stop a distance from the normal deplaning area so that the Kellys could descend directly to the limo and get out before the regular passengers disembarked. It was also a plan to keep the ever-voracious media at a distance.

As soon as a member of the landing crew nodded to Bill, he was out of the car and standing at the bottom of the ramp the moment it was pushed in place. As the door opened, his children stood waiting. They descended the stairs, and then came the hugs and kisses for his two youngest, Meghan and Roger.

Then Colleen glided down the steps, looking about her regally. "Hey, Papa, how's tricks?" She stepped onto the tarmac and kissed his cheek and hugged him. "Ryan sends his love. He'll be thinking of us here in Rome as he pulls up his nets on the bank." Bill grinned and turned his little family around, facing the faraway terminal, conscious that the long-distance lenses on scores of TV cameras from around the world had zoomed in on them from the outer gallery of Leonardo da Vinci Airport.

"Wow, Dad," Meghan exclaimed, "this is as big as the president's limo. I saw it in the movies. Is this one bulletproof too?"

"Yes, I guess so, sweetheart. I hope to God we never have to find out." The children were introduced to Tony, and Roger sat up front with him.

Meghan and Colleen sat in the backseat with Bill, Colleen riding backwards on the jump seat.

"Dad," Roger said, "Bishop Sean Patrick—Uncle Sean—said your house is so big I might even be able to have two bedrooms. Is that so?"

"Well, it certainly is big. But why on earth would you want two bedrooms? Twice as many to keep clean."

"But Uncle Sean said we'd have maids to take care of everything."

"No way, pal. The offer was made, but I told them my kids were highly trained and would never think of having someone else make their beds and clean their clothes. I even had a washer and dryer put in our apartment so you can keep your clothes clean just like at home."

After they left the airport Bill turned to his daughter. "Colleen, you have been rather silent. What do you think of Rome at first glance?"

"It's interesting, Dad."

"You don't seem too excited, baby. You didn't have to come, you know. If you feel uncomfortable in this center of religious fervor you can go back anytime."

"No. I want to visit you and see what the Vatican is all about. I plan to stay through the Christmas break, and I hope you can get me into the Vatican Library so I can see all the art and read some of those centuries-old books. My major now is art, you know. I really find it interesting."

"Well, you're in for a special treat here with all the museums. You'll never run out of things to do and see. That's a guarantee. By the way, I got you a special gift. You'll find a new computer in your room."

"Wow! Thanks, Dad. I was going to bring mine but I thought you might have an extra one kicking around. You said it was special?"

"Well, it's hooked up with the mainframe in the Vatican Library. Everything in the place is on that computer. You'll obviously want to visit the museums firsthand, but you don't even have to leave your room to delve into any books or letters you want to read. Your computer has official clearance to see almost anything." Ruefully he thought of the highly classified documents, the third prophecy of Our Lady of Fatima, for instance, and the *avviso*. He was holding out sharing the *avviso* and the original parchment of Lucia's memory of the Fatima prophecy with anyone.

"Neat!" Colleen exclaimed. "Oh, Papa!" She gave him a kiss.

"Now, about your belief, or lack of it, in God, which you shared with the world in that press conference, which is being replayed in Rome," Bill began.

"I know, I know. Look, I'm sorry my views aren't the same as yours." She sounded truly contrite.

"All I'm asking is for you not to make a big deal about what you think, whether to the press or inside the Vatican. I love you as my daughter and that's that."

Roger interrupted with an exclamation from the front seat. "Oh, wow, Dad! All of a sudden motorcycles are in front of us and police cars in back of us."

"That's our security escort, Roger. They'll keep the cameras at a distance."

"I'll keep my thoughts to myself," a contrite Colleen promised. "The press has already been prying into my whole life, and Mother's death, in newspapers and on TV. Your Vatican associates must know all about me and us. I just want to visit my dad and do some research for a possible master's degree. All I ask is that they don't treat me like a child."

The pope laughed. "Maybe you have a point, Colleen. I must introduce you to Maureen, Ambassador Kirby's daughter. She's a great young woman and you probably have a lot in common. She also knows every disco in town."

Colleen smiled broadly and nodded as Meghan broke in, excitement in her voice. "Look how old these buildings are! They're magnificent. What's that one? I've never seen so many fruit stands and all those people shopping. I think I can see St. Peter's from here."

"We're changing the usual ride from the airport to give you a more scenic route," Bill proudly announced. They drove around Rome for an hour, visiting historic sites—the Colosseum, Trevi Fountain, the Spanish Steps—and stopped in for gelati at the Piazza Navona.

"Will we be restricted where we can go inside the Vatican?"

"Not really, Meghan. All those pictures you sent me of you have been copied and distributed to the Swiss guards and Italian police in the vicinity."

"Are they going to follow us around like in school?" Meghan asked.

"How did you know about that, young lady?" Bill asked.

"We knew some of the new teacher assistants were really police," Roger replied.

"And I spotted a new 'student' at college," Colleen added. "That doesn't happen in the middle of the semester. He was cute. He looked like twenty but he was really thirty. I made it easy for him. It was like I was going steady with my security guard." She gave her father a sly wink. "Are there cute Swiss guards?"

Bill shook his head. "You all will be the death of me yet."

"I hope our luggage was picked up," Colleen said.

"All taken care of, including the UPS stuff you sent a few days ago."

"My skateboard?" Roger asked anxiously, kneeling on the front seat and facing backwards. "I said two whole Rosaries for it to get through. Isn't that good?"

"Great, Roger. It's good to know that God has a concern even for skateboards. I'll ask Monsignor Cippolini if there is a patron saint for skateboarders. I should think they need one as much as any soldier going into battle."

Tony pulled the limousine to a stop inside the Vatican, and a youthful Swiss guardsman in his red-, yellow-, and blue-striped uniform stepped forward and opened the car doors. "Welcome to Rome, Colleen, Meghan, and Roger. We're sorry to hear Ryan is not here."

Colleen took the proffered gloved hand that helped her out. Once outside they followed their escort to the residence entranceway. Colleen stayed close to the young guardsman bringing up the rear. With a coquettish smile she asked him, "Can you tell me how old I am? I forgot."

The guard smiled back. "You're recently twenty-one. I'm twenty-three." He winked.

"Wow, Dad," she called to her father. "I'm going to like this place."

By five-thirty they had met Cardinal Robitelli, who greeted them officially on behalf of all the Vatican personnel. After a short investigation of their bedrooms they gathered in the refurbished family dining room for supper.

Monsignor Tim Shanahan stopped by, bringing with him Italian pastry.

"And I took the liberty of ordering sloppy joes and french fries for you kids," Bill announced, "so the change in venue would seem less traumatic." They eagerly began to devour the contents of both large platters.

"Your first 'infallible' judgment, Your Holiness," Colleen quipped.

"Not so perfect, Colleen. What kind of pope would forget to say grace?"

When they finished eating, Meghan tipped her chair back and patted her belly. "That was great, Dad. Like a real restaurant. Will we always have meals served like that?"

"Only until you kids do your own shopping and learn where everything is." Bill pushed back his own chair. "Well, gang, what say we go rest our stomachs in the papal study, now to be called the family room. There are only three English-speaking TV channels here in Rome at the moment, so you guys will have to be selective. If we have major disagreements, I may be able to put a small TV in each of your bedrooms to keep the peace."

Within an hour of sitting down, jet lag set in; heads began to nod. "Kids, you must be tired from such a long trip. By now your bags are in your rooms. Roger, your skateboard is stored in your closet. Leave it there until I find a place for you to use it."

The children confirmed their father's diagnosis, saying they were going to take a nap for a few hours. "We didn't get any sleep coming over because we were excited and watched a movie." Words tumbled from Roger.

Colleen had already explored the papal quarters and picked out the room she liked best. Roger and Meghan found the rooms in which their luggage had been placed. Colleen helped her brother and sister get settled and met Maria, the housekeeper assigned to their quarters.

"I thought we were on our own, without help," Colleen said when, to her delight, she found their rooms ready and their beds turned down.

"Well, you'll find Maria very helpful. She doesn't speak any English so you'll have to learn Italian."

"I have already started," Colleen answered. "I think I'm going to like it here."

AT HOME IN THE VATICAN 27

The world within the Vatican was an entirely new experience not only for the Kelly family, but also for the official papal household. One morning after the pope's early Mass, Meghan Kelly swept into what had become the family room, formerly the study of the expanding apostolic apartment. She sat on a sofa next to her father, who had slipped into black slacks and a white open-neck shirt.

"You know, Dad, I was afraid we would be making the clergy a bit uncomfortable here." Bill gave her a questioning look. "With the exception of Monsignor Cippolini and Monsignor Tim Shanahan, I was afraid they would resent us for moving in here and forcing them to deal with things that haven't been seen here since those early Renaissance popes who had wives and children, the ones mostly ignored in modern Vatican history books."

"And my friend and sometime adversary, Gino Robitelli?"

"He seems more or less like the others. Whether just priests or monsignors, bishops or cardinals, they all seem glad to see us."

"I'm glad you feel comfortable, Meghan. I, too, didn't know exactly how a pope, *en famille* as the French put it, would be regarded. Just yesterday I asked Gino to say something about it."

Meghan smiled. "Even after you and cardinal Robitelli have disagreed, he couldn't be more respectful of the rest of us. What did he say?"

"Well, the clergy we see around this place actually welcome the opportunity of being with laypeople. Ultimately a lot of them look forward to working in parishes, hearing confessions, baptizing babies, confirming family members, helping the sick and the dying. They actually like working with families, especially young people."

"I guess they'll all adjust in time to popes having families in a modern Vatican."

"You may just be right, Meghan. I do recall that Robitelli himself said something to that effect the day after you kids arrived. We've got to work on it."

Curious, Meghan asked, "Oh? And what was that?"

Bill blushed as he thought back on it. "He said he's noticed a change in me since my children arrived. He said it was like the glow he remembered in his parents' eyes, something he had long since forgotten. We discussed the possible differences in the minds of married people. It had kind of slipped my mind, Meghan. Child-rearing has many challenges and pressures, but the feeling of a father working to overcome the difficulties of money, paying the bills, bringing up the children—that's the essence of parenthood. To change the subject, how is Colleen adjusting?"

"She is finding much of interest, of course, in the libraries and museums. And it seems she and Maureen Kirby are becoming friends."

"That reminds me, we must have the Kirbys over to dinner."

"Yes. Whenever you say, I'll help arrange it, Your Holiness." Meghan reached out and took her father's hand. "Do you sometimes feel bad now that you had left the priesthood and got married?"

He gazed at his beautiful young daughter and kissed her lightly. "Never, Meghan."

A loud bang on the door interrupted their conversation. "Bill! Meghan! Come quick! Roger is hurt!" Cippolini shouted. Startled, Bill and Meghan sprang to their feet.

"What's happened, Al? What's wrong?" Bill gasped.

"He was skateboarding down the hallway on the first floor and he ran into one of the Swiss guards. He may be hurt, Bill." Monsignor Cippolini was visibly shaken.

They hurried out of the office and downstairs to the scene of the accident. A small crowd had gathered to assist—or perhaps to gape—at the unusual accident to the pope's son.

A more composed Monsignor Cippolini kneeled beside Roger, holding his handkerchief to the boy's head. "He should be fine, Bill. It's a nasty gash on the head. The nurse is on her way."

The pope kneeled beside Cippolini and looked down at his young son, lying stunned and bleeding on the marble corridor floor. "How did this happen?" he asked.

"From what I can gather," Cippolini explained, "Roger was trying out our long winding hallways with his skateboard. Then he ran head-on into one of the guards coming around the corner to investigate a 'strange noise.' Roger slammed into him, and the battle-ax scraped his head."

The pope looked down at his son, who was trying to hold back his tears. "Roger, I thought I told you—"

"Dad," Meghan sharply cut him off, "please. Not now. Just thank God he's all right."

Sister Maria, one of the Vatican nurses, pushed her way muttering through the surrounding crowd. She used her short body to muscle a path to the fallen boy. Then, with a grunt, she lowered herself to the floor beside Roger.

She spoke rapidly in Italian and then, realizing it was the pope's son, switched to English. "Well, now, let's have a look at this cut, young Roger. I'll be careful."

Roger nodded, even though grimacing with fear, as the nurse slowly pulled the handkerchief back to view the damage. Then she looked up and met the searching eyes of the worried father.

"He'll need some stitches, Your Holiness, that's for sure. Let's get him to the infirmary. I'll call the doctor. I think he's up at the Guard infirmary." Maria grinned mischievously. "He's probably taking care of the other casualty."

"I'm sorry, Dad," Roger moaned as he looked up at his father.

"It's all right, son. Don't worry. Let's go get some stitches like you had the last time on your knee."

Roger reached to touch his head but was blocked by the nurse. "Aw, do I have to?"

Bill grabbed his son's hand. "Yes, you have to, pal. Be a brave boy now. Meghan is going with you."

The boy was helped to his feet and slowly walked alongside the nurse, gaining moral support from his sister.

Monsignor Cippolini glanced up at the pope as they returned to his office. "It sounds like he's had stitches before, Bill."

The pope smiled ruefully. "That seems to come with the territory for small boys, Al. I'd venture to say he's been sewed up five or six times. So he's a pro at it. Thanks for looking after him." The anxious look returned to his face as he sat behind his desk. "Incidentally, how is the poor guard? I almost forgot about him."

"He'll be fine," Al Cippolini assured the pope. "Roger was going pretty fast and hit him in... well, let's say the lower half. A few of his countrymen helped him off while needling him with their little quips. He was trying to apologize, but it wasn't his fault."

"Thanks, Al. Let me know his name. We'll invite him to dinner some evening so the two warriors can shake hands and be friends again." He sighed deeply. "Meantime I'll quarantine the skateboard for the duration. I guess it's my fault. I told Roger I would find him a place to use it and haven't quite gotten around to it."

A slow smile brightened Al's visage. "I'm supposed to know this place better than anyone. I think I know a few places in this vast complex where the young man can practice his skills."

"That would be appreciated, Al."

"Well, please don't forget, you are the pope. I think we may find a guard with a little time who might be able to supervise his demonstrations."

Bill smiled appreciatively. "That would be great if you could. I must move on quickly now. Tim Shanahan is coming to discuss some Church history. Do new popes get a chance to peek into the family closet?"

Flustered, Alonso Cippolini said, "I don't know anything about that kind of thing, Bill. It's not my area."

"Well, you've got me saying Mass again, in Italian and English. That's pretty good."

Meghan pushed open the door and interrupted them breathlessly. Bill gave her an alarmed look. "Is Roger okay?"

"He's coming along fine. I dropped by the apartment and on our private voice mail there was a message from a Cardinal Motupu in Angola. He asked if his message could get to you personally and privately." She glanced at Cippolini questioningly.

"It's all right, Meghan. Gus is concerned about a certain cardinal intercepting my messages."

Meghan handed her father a note. "Here is the routing of his number. He said he'd wait until he hears from you."

Bill took the slip of paper and turned to Cippolini. "Al, would you excuse me, please?"

"Of course. I hope all is well in Africa." The monsignor stood up and left the room immediately.

Bill gestured for Meghan to sit down beside his desk and picked up the phone. It would naturally get back to Robitelli that Motupu had gone around the approved routing. The call must be urgent and personal.

Soon Motupu's high-pitched voice was coming over the phone. "Your Holiness, I am sorry to bother you outside protocol but I felt it was important. I never had a chance to brief you personally on certain African affairs, and Robitelli unfortunately never got around to paying much attention to our continent."

"Go ahead, Gus. I'm listening," Bill invited.

"I can't tell you too much on the telephone. I'd like to see you personally."

"Is it truly that urgent?"

"I think so, Bill. It is a situation that has been festering here for the last half century. I had hoped that it would die out with the collapse of Communism."

"Can you tell me any more?"

"On these lines out of Africa there is no such thing as security. Get Monsignor Shanahan to tell you what he knows about things here in respect to certain Christian religious rivalries. That's all I can say in these circumstances."

"When do you want to come, Gus?"

"The sooner the better."

Bill glanced at the calendar before him. "Can it wait until after the Christmas holidays? This is a busy time for me, and I'll be saying Mass and greeting a lot of folks."

"It's waited this long; a few more weeks won't make a great big difference...I guess," he added doubtfully.

"Any hint so I can be prepared?"

"Check your files on Russian Orthodox African intervention. And see what you can find on the Patriarch Alexis and a certain Bishop Yussotov, sometimes known as the 'Mad Monk of Odessa.' Anything more will have to wait until I can see you."

As Bill hung up, an alarm went off in his head. For a moment the *avviso* flashed through his thoughts. The Orthodox Church and the patriarch suddenly took on meaning in light of a passage in the previous pope's warning. He noted with relief that Tim Shanahan was coming for one of their general consultations. Impatiently, he read a memo from Cardinal Robitelli regarding the next scheduled meeting he must attend before he would have a chance to discuss Motupu's call with Tim.

"*Archbishop Enrico Locatelli, the socially progressive papal nuncio in Washington, constantly agitating for social and economic justice, is upset about the way things are going in America.*" The memo indicated that the pope's representative in the United States needed to confer on the fact that American bishops were having a difficult time keeping the flock united.

By the time Archbishop Locatelli was announced, the pope had managed to don something resembling formal attire after having been more comfortably dressed all that morning. Bill rose to meet the nuncio as he entered the richly appointed papal library. By force of habit the bishop, a short, plump, and fussy individual, dropped to one knee, reaching to kiss the fisherman's ring. Both flushed slightly as the bishop rose.

"So glad to have this opportunity to meet with you, Your Holiness. Sorry about the ring business. I was forewarned that it bothers you."

"I'm likewise trying to adapt. Please be seated," the pope replied.

The nuncio cautiously made sure not to seat himself ahead of the pope. "Thank you, Your Holiness." He winced again as the words escaped his lips. "Oh, sorry about that. I hope you understand how much emphasis we put on showing the highest respect for the representative of Christ on Earth."

The pope let a long breath flow from his lungs as he tried to adjust his own mindset. "I know, I know. Whatever makes you feel the most comfortable."

The archbishop cleared his throat. "Well, Pope Bill, as you know I personally came here to see Cardinal Robitelli—and yourself—to try to impress more firmly upon your minds that the Church in the United States has for some time been drifting toward a potentially debilitating state of affairs. The U.S. government, including both political parties, is generally walking away from the concerns of the needy and the poor. This is placing a greater burden and more responsibility on private charities, especially the Churches. Catholic Charities in cities like Chicago and Boston are now practically the safety net for the poor."

The archbishop paused to gauge the effect of his situation on the pontiff. "There is marked division when the bishops meet for their annual conferences. Everyone is sincere, I know. But I see an increasing dissatisfaction, even fear, creeping into their various presentations. They are under great challenges and are meeting more while accomplishing less." He gave the pope a questioning look. "I was hoping that perhaps, finally, a strong stand from Rome, some sort of definitive pronouncement, would make them regroup and get on with the business of bringing all alienated souls—the homeless, drug addicts, fallen-away Catholics, all of them—back to Christ." He stopped abruptly and stared at the pope.

"Well, well," Bill muttered, clearing his throat and fumbling for words. "No one can argue with that. Of course, Cardinal Robitelli has apprised me of some of this. I have even met with several bishops and cardinals here to come up with solutions."

The nuncio plunged ahead with his argument. "On the social front, they have fewer dollars and more needs. Charitable giving overall is down. People are not contributing and they have had to close hundreds of inner-city schools and Churches. They just can't afford to keep them open! The Catholics with money have gone out to the suburbs; charter schools are opening up everywhere, taking students and dollars out with them. The politicians are afraid of the antiChurch groups and liberal media so they don't want to go out front on school vouchers."

Locatelli stared almost accusingly at the pope, who replied apologetically, "Naturally, I admit I haven't been much help. My knowledge of ecclesiastical affairs is still limited. But I do receive a great deal of input from the American bishops. Secretary Robitelli is putting reports together for me to sign as a sort of...what do you call it...'rescript'?"

The archbishop smiled involuntarily at the pope's attempt to search out the right word.

"It's called an 'encyclical,' Pope Bill." The pope's face reddened. Archbishop Locatelli continued. "We feel that an encyclical would be the most powerful way to press our point further, and would clarify our stance on all related issues. Do you agree? To define and clarify once and for all Church's responsibility? I read part of the paper that Cardinal Robitelli is writing. Very good."

The pope frowned, aware that he was not yet in the loop. Here was a man meeting with him for the sake of courtesy, because he was pope. They apparently didn't consider his opinions relevant yet, he realized. And he was an American! His mind began to assimilate previous information that Cardinal Robitelli had mentioned and the *avviso*'s warning concerning his native land. He had never been informed, actually, about the underlying issues involved.

When Bill Kelly became angry, his mind accelerated like a computer. An idea formed four squares in his head. "Say, Your Excellency, did you ever read or hear how some people try to learn God's will by flipping open the Bible and choosing a random passage to see what it says?"

The archbishop stared at the pope in disbelief, remembering St. Augustine. *Robitelli is right*, he thought. *This upstart is a gadfly.* He shifted, uneasily but smoothly, in his chair. "Why, yes, Pope Bill. I have heard about that. You know, St. Augustine. I have done it a few times myself...as a young boy."

The pope reached for the huge Bible resting beside a pile of papers on his desk. Archbishop Locatelli watched in amazement as the pope leafed through the Bible, lifted it, and then let it drop loudly on the desk. His forefinger came down on the open book, and he bent over to see what revelation it would offer, not noticing the archbishop shaking his head in astonishment.

Locatelli thought he might as well humor his deranged pontiff. "What did God tell us? Any solutions to our problems?"

The pope looked up momentarily and back down. "I don't know exactly. 'Tell Pharaoh to let my people go!'" he recited loudly.

The two men looked at one another questioningly. "Maybe try two out of three, Your Holiness," Locatelli swallowed and suggested. "Sometimes these things take time."

The pope seated himself in his chair with a slight grunt. He looked at the archbishop, then back at the book. Suddenly the light seemed to dawn. He settled back in his chair, eyes closed. Locatelli nervously watched someone who seemed lost somewhere in his thoughts. "Eh, Pope Bill," he prompted, "are you all right?"

The pope's eyes abruptly opened, looking straight at the nuncio. A smile curved his lips. "Yes, Your Excellency, I'm fine. Now I think I see our answer."

The nuncio uneasily shifted in his chair again, not sure of his ground as the pope continued. "I think we should look at that statement in a more contemporary and spiritual sense. As if we are pharaohs."

The nuncio's brow furrowed noticeably. "I'm afraid you've lost me, Your Holiness. What do you mean, 'we are pharaohs'?"

The pope pushed himself up and out of his seat, walking toward the window behind him. He stared out at the blue sky. After a few moments he turned around to face the nuncio again. "Don't you see? Who was Pharaoh? A man of power and authority. He pushed poor people around. He couldn't find any solutions either, because he couldn't look at other people's problems, only his own. To keep the old customs going. The old ways. To separate rich and poor...slave versus master...whatever. Even the miracles Moses performed couldn't alter his mind, or his heart. Maybe that's what's wrong with this whole setup, Your Excellency. Maybe we need to really become more understanding of those homeless people, drug addicts, and inner-city poor. We need to be less pretentious about what we are doing. By our action or by our lack of action, by our misdirected action, we hold God's people in bondage." He pointed his index finger directly at the archbishop and his voice quivered. "Tell them to let my people go!"

The archbishop sat mesmerized. His mind kept reverting from a review of the pope's words to the confidential conversation he had recently held with Cardinal Robitelli before leaving his ornately decorated office. "The man's a nut, a total nut."

In silence Locatelli sat gathering his thoughts as he watched Peter II move away from the window to sit down. He waited while the pope dried his eyes and reached for a pen and paper. Suddenly the nuncio felt sorry for this poor fisherman who had been thrust into a foreign environment with absolutely no idea how things worked in the vast, Byzantine complex of the Vatican. His own innate goodness urged him to help. He began impulsively.

"Well, Pope Peter, I must say you have a very interesting way of interpreting this passage. I'm not sure it suits our situation. We have always set up soup kitchens and clothing bins where the poor can come for help. It costs us a great deal of money to rent buildings for shelters for the destitute. Our people in the field are pushed to the limit donating to others without enough to take for themselves. I don't see how we can do more. But I admire your deep concern for God's people."

Archbishop Locatelli paused, becoming aware that the pope was not looking up at him as he spoke but was silently scribbling something on a pad in front of him. The nuncio waited for some sign of recognition. After what seemed forever the pope looked up.

"Open your Churches, Your Excellency! Open the Churches and schools and leave them open...all the time!"

"What?" the archbishop mumbled in bewilderment.

"Are you deaf, man? I said open the Church doors and leave them open."

"We can't do that," Locatelli snapped, shocked. "They would come in and steal...make a total mess of the place. It's impossible!"

"You see," Bill shot back, "always concern for our possessions. Let them take the candlesticks or whatever else isn't glued down. Then we won't have to worry about them anymore. Yes, that's it! Apostolic poverty. Like the old days, when I was a boy. We stopped by our Church anytime to talk to God. Don't you remember? It's exactly what set us apart. It could, should, be like that again! Everyone will know that they can find refuge in the Catholic Church. I don't believe it would be all that bad. People respect property if it is theirs. Let them know it is theirs. In time they'll get used to it. Maybe the other denominations will do the same. We don't serve *things*, Archbishop Locatelli. We serve *people*. We need to address those people, discover their problems and how we might help them."

The nuncio, stupefied, was left speechless. He didn't know whether to reply or to run. The pope made the choice for him. "Discuss my idea with Gino Robitelli and the finance staff. Then maybe we can kick it around and come up with some realistic conclusions before you leave. Thank you for coming here to fill me in on my native country's problems."

Bill followed the nuncio, who was beating a hasty retreat to the door and all the while glancing back uneasily at the pope.

"And I deeply appreciate your courageously expressing your concern about American Church leaders. I agree the Church must fight in the political arena for what we believe in, and I strongly believe that U.S. leaders cannot be cafeteria Catholics either. They can't choose which issues are politically popular, like AIDS, housing, and health care, then take a walk on other Church issues that are less popular. Everyone wants to be a leader, but they only want to lead on certain issues. Like they say at the Portuguese Club in New Bedford, 'Everyone wants to go to heaven, but nobody wants to die.' It seems to me that the United States needs a pro-life, pro-family, and pro-needy political movement!"

By then the nuncio had fled down the corridor, taking the first turn that would put him out of sight.

THE EASTERN ORTHODOX CONSPIRACY 28

Bill chuckled to himself as he watched the black-and-red-swaddled archbishop virtually fleeing down the long marble hall leading ultimately to the Sistine Chapel. The usually taciturn Swiss guards were looking after him, openly puzzled. Tim Shanahan glanced at the unnerved nuncio quizzically.

"What's with him?" Tim asked as he entered the outer reception room.

"I'm afraid I made a suggestion that sounded as though I advocated the Church sharing its wealth with the parishioners," Bill confessed. "Come on into the library. Fortunately, I have no other appointments this afternoon. Some tea and Irish bread, Tim? My daughter Meghan baked it last night. The Irish nuns here love it."

"Sounds lovely." They entered the secure, bug-free apostolic library. Instead of retreating behind his desk, Bill took a seat on the sofa, gesturing to Tim to sit in the facing armchair. He wasted no time getting to the topic concerning him most. "Gus Motupu called. He couldn't talk openly on the phone but he needs to see me as soon as possible."

Tim nodded. "From sketchy news reports and what I hear from my own net, the Church, Cardinal Moputu in particular, has big problems in Africa."

"I keep current, Tim. What am I missing?"

Tim took a deep breath. "It all goes back to World War II and, of course, Pope Pius XII."

Bill nodded thoughtfully. "From the *avviso* I know that events of half a century ago are shaping our destiny in the new millennium. My predecessor has warned me."

Tim gave the pope a questioning glance. "The *avviso*?"

"I finally cracked the code." Bill grinned. "Learned Italian, that is."

"You still haven't shared it?"

"Robitelli keeps asking, but I told him John Paul II did not want it made public. Some of what the pope confided flies in the face of his own public stance. For instance, he never wanted to criticize the Eastern Orthodox Church even when he knew the patriarch was responsible for outlawing Catholicism in Russia and the continuing campaign against our Church in the Balkans, despite John Paul II's missionary visit to Romania."

"He told you that in this *avviso*?"

"He wrote that and more in full confidence that it will never be published."

"Any other information you would like to"—Tim's voice took on an ironic tone—"communicate to your 'private secretary'?"

"Certainly. The time has come for me to share his revelations with a few trusted people. The pope was shocked and horrified when the Russian Orthodox patriarch refused to join him in protesting Serb conduct in the 1999 war in Yugoslavia. The Serbs turned thousands of people in Kosovo out of their homes and country. They froze and starved these victims of religious and ethnic persecution, which the Russian Church could have prevented by joining the pope's call for a Serbian cessation of the war. The Orthodox leadership in Moscow showed their true colors by not telling its Belgrade adherents to stop persecuting, driving from their homes, and killing all the ethnic Albanians, who are mostly Muslim, they could find. A terrible revenge for past centuries of Muslim outrages against Christians, no doubt. But as Pope John Paul said about capital punishment, an eye for an eye merely means two people are blinded, not one."

Both the pope and his top adviser were silent for some moments. Then Bill said, "The message of the *avviso* unequivocally states that it will be John Paul II's successor's job to steer a course between Muslim extremism and the Eastern Orthodox Church in the Balkans. The danger may be great. It might take the reigns of two or three popes, 'short ones,' he wrote ominously, to succeed in bringing peace between regions, which, he pointed out, was far from accomplished in his own reign." After a long, contemplative pause, Bill observed quietly, "Now you tell me about the relevance today of what happened over half a century ago."

"I'll sum up the situation as briefly as possible, Bill."

"Take the time you need. Gus has a problem he can't even talk about over the telephone. By the time he arrives here, I need to be aware of all the ramifications of whatever difficulties he finds himself confronting."

Tim nodded and stood up, walking over to a mahogany table on which were arrayed certain personal artifacts. He picked up the carving dedicated to Our Lady of Fatima. "Here is the crux of the problem that faced us midway through World War II and confronts Africa today. It concerns the message Our Lady gave to three Portuguese children in the year 1917."

"I'm deeply concerned about what remains the third secret's revelation," Bill said. "But it seems every time I ask to see if there is any more information following the message dictated by Sister Lucia, some Vatican excuse surfaces. Cardinal Robitelli doesn't think I'm ready for it and that only he should deal with it. That's just speculation on my part, but I'm certain I'm right."

Tim smiled. "Back at the height of the War in 1942 and '43, the Vatican was virtually held hostage by Hitler and the Nazis." He examined the wood carving a moment. "The second prophecy warns us that Russia, unless converted, will ultimately prove the cause of world destruction. Pius XII concluded because of wartime suffering in the then Soviet Union that a part of the prophecy—the beginning part—was coming true. That was, quote, 'Only if Russia were changed would there be peace in the world,' unquote!"

Tim flashed a mischievous grin at the pope. "I'm afraid Pius XII jumped the gun a bit when he announced in a prayer broadcast about Europe that in effect 'Russia will be converted and there will be peace.' The Nazis linked this apparently pro-Russian prayer to the Allied invasion of North Africa and a general marshaling of religious forces throughout occupied Europe favoring the Russian side. The overall feeling among people in the pews was that Communist Russia would be reconverted, and, thanks to Russia, after the war there would be a spiritual renewal throughout the overall Christian Church. That being so, the Communist danger did not really, ultimately exist.

"The pope's interpretation of the second Fatima prophecy was seized upon by the Nazis, especially in light of their defeats on the Russian front, as a wave of Catholic-inspired anti-Nazi sentiment generated throughout the world, particularly in Italy. This general belief would adversely affect the German war machine—or so the Nazis felt." Tim Shanahan replaced the carving on the table and turned back to the pope.

"When the war was actually won, Stalin recognized the power of religion to influence the masses. He wisely gave the few Orthodox bishops left in Russia permission to elect a new patriarch. Pius XII's prayer hailing the conversion of Russia—mistakenly, as it turned out—had rekindled a European-wide interest in Christianity. The second prophecy of Fatima was cited as giving strength to the notion that Christianity had defeated Nazism."

Bill fixed Tim with a mock baleful stare. "Get back to Gus Motupu. How does this business with Pius XII almost sixty years ago impinge on Africa today, in the twenty-first century?"

Tim turned away from the grotto image. "From that prayer to the fall of Communism in 1991, Russian Christianity Eastern Orthodox style became resurgent, accepted increasingly by the Iron Curtain rulers as an important, even necessary, 'opiate of the people.' "

The pope frowned and shook his head. "Like most Americans I was under the impression that active Christianity of any sort was nonexistent in the Soviet Union."

Tim smiled grudgingly. "Brezhnev, as atheistic as Stalin, recognized the value of using the patriarch and certain Orthodox bishops as a force augmenting the KGB to gain control over a vast African population and render it ideologically associated with both Russian Orthodoxy and Soviet Communism.

"It was this duplicitous power, blessed by the patriarch's missionaries on the one hand and the atheistic KGB on the other, which still poses the long-standing threat to Cardinal Motupu and his young fellow African priests. Gus fought the Communists from the African Patrice Lumumba University in Moscow, which trained African youth to be Communists. The Orthodox Church, working toward the same goal, struggled to convert African people to a Russian style of Christianity. All these forces were working for one strategic purpose: control of the mineral and oil wealth of the 'Dark Continent.' Only the pope in Rome and his field representatives, priests, bishops, and cardinals held Catholic missions and their African faithful together. The pope had now made his inroads into Communist domination of Poland and all of eastern Europe.

"Thus in 1981, the Communists, directed by Moscow and operating out of the Balkans, Bulgaria to be precise, dispatched Turk Mehmet Ali Agca to assassinate Pope John Paul II in Rome itself. Fortunately, the assassin picked the anniversary of the Fatima apparition for his deed. An instant before the bullets would have struck his head, John Paul II leaned forward to bless a girl wearing the icon of Fatima on her dress!

"Although the pope was struck in the body by two rounds, his Swiss guard was able to wrestle the Turk to the ground, disarming him. John Paul II survived, ironically flying in the face of the third Fatima prophecy, and it set back the Communists and the Orthodox Church considerably."

Tim leaned down toward the pope. "But the successors to the Communists and the Russian Orthodox Church are trying to gain control in Africa to this day, Pope Bill. They have succeeded in strengthening the Orthodox Church at home, and several years ago, a law was passed in the Russian Duma weakening or prohibiting all other religions in Russia. I will be interested to hear how Motupu is doing against the advance of the Russian Church in Africa."

"So will I," Bill replied.

"I shouldn't be surprised if Motupu asks you to go to Africa."

"And if I appear successful, then may I expect a visit from another Mehmet Ali Agca?"

Tim Shanahan turned deadly serious. "We live in the most dangerous of times, Your Holiness. But I wouldn't even try to tell you to stay well guarded at home. I know you are an activist—a danger to yourself, perhaps, but you will do what you feel is necessary, go where you think you are needed."

"When was it—in the beginning of 1998 that Pope John Paul went to Africa?"

"Correct, almost three years ago. Since then the so-called Democratic Republic of Congo has emerged, along with a powerful oil-rich Angola, to say nothing of Nigeria. The genocide in Rwanda went on unabated. And the crisis of AIDS and disease is as big a threat to their society as the demise of the family in the economically and technologically advanced United States. AIDS has reduced life expectancies in many African nations to less than half of what they had been not long ago. Augustine Motupu will be able to tell us more of how the Russian Orthodox Church is progressing."

"Robitelli tells me, despite the *avviso,* that we are on most cordial terms with the Russian Church."

"We'll find out from Cardinal Motupu what the real story is in Africa." Then, after a reflective pause, Tim chanced an observation. "It has been called to my attention that Patsy Monassari has been getting cozy with the Orthodox Vatican representative here and his colleague, Bishop Yussotov, the Mad Monk of Odessa. My sources tell me the monk, as everyone refers to him still, makes frequent trips between Rome, certain African destinations, Moscow, even America—Chicago, to be specific, according to Kirby."

"You seem to have your own intelligence service," the pope remarked.

"Well, Your Holiness, in this new capacity which Comiskey and Kirby thrust on me, I feel that to be effective, I have to be informed on what goes on. I kind of miss being a history teacher. But this job is certainly intriguing."

"Is it less interesting to be a history maker?"

DINNER WITH THE KIRBYS 29

The holiday spirit of the Christmas season in Rome is far less intrusive than the commercial circus to which the average citizen is subjected back in America—more about family and tradition and less about gifts and parties.

It was on a mid-December morning that Ed Kirby, his wife, Kathy, and their daughter, Maureen, now a senior at Marymount International High School in Rome, drove to the da Vinci Airport to meet the other Kirby daughters: Julie, twenty-three, a graduate student at the University of Chicago, working part-time at a Chicago law office; Nancy, twenty-one, a senior at Salve Regina College in Newport, Rhode Island; and Kate, nineteen, a sophomore at Providence College. All were arriving on TWA from Chicago via Boston. Their two sons, Ed Jr., twenty-seven and a navy officer, and Ray, twenty-five, owner of a Chicago pizza restaurant and an avid Cubs fan, would not be arriving until just before Christmas Day.

The Kirby girls greeted the household staff at Villa Richardson upon their arrival, updating everyone about how they were doing in school. Nancy said she had nothing to wear a couple of evenings from now to the big U.S. Marine Corps Birthday Ball at the Excelsior Hotel on the Via Veneto, and had to buy a new dress.

When three Marines stationed at the Rome embassy had met Maureen a few weeks back at a popular nightspot—Ned Kelly's Australian Bar—they asked if her sisters were coming over for the Christmas holiday season and invited them to go to the ball as their dates. The ball was a very special event, with the Marines dressed in their formal blue uniforms, swords and all. The talented Italian Carabinieri Band, with some sixty members, provided music annually.

Ambassador Kirby enjoyed a very special relationship with the marines, always attending their events and regularly playing basketball with them to keep fit. The Kirby girls had attended the big ball in the past and knew that they were in for a real treat. As a matter of fact, Ed Kirby was scheduled to receive the U.S. Marine Corps's "outstanding service" award, for upholding the very professional relationship that existed between the old U.S. embassies and the Marine Corps. When the State Department decided to cut back on security and downsize the marines at the Vatican embassy, it was Kirby who strongly protested against it. The Rome embassy and all the other embassies throughout the world had marines guarding them, and so should the embassy to the Vatican. The State Department responded, "Our budget was cut, and the Vatican embassy is less important than the Italian embassy." That comment provoked open resentment at the Holy See, despite the special, personal relationship Ambassador Kirby and his wife had established with the pope himself. United States and Vatican relations, as important as they were, were not a priority at the State Department.

Now, when Nancy said she needed a new dress, the other three girls chimed in as well. "Let's go now before the stores close for supper," said Katie. The four went running down Via Giacomo Medici to Via Garibaldi and took the bus in short order to shop for dresses at Via del Corso. By eight o'clock, just before the shops closed, they had bought three beautiful dresses on sale at the Lisa Spinnelli and Bellini shops on the Via Condotti. The week before, the dresses had cost L250,000, said the saleswoman, but this week they were on sale for L150,000. The girls stopped at Campo de' Fiori to get some ready-made Roman pasta before heading back up the Janiculum Hill to the Villa Richardson.

"You all got phone calls from the marines!" their mother announced. "They are looking forward to seeing you. They will stop by tomorrow night at seven to escort you to the ball. Call them tonight if you care to, at the Marine House. Let's see, I have their names right here...Jackie Killcommons, Jeremiah Foley, and a Jamie Long. They sounded very nice on the phone. I often meet them down at the commissary. I think I know all three. Kate, call Jackie Killcommons and tell them to meet you tomorrow in the lobby of the Excelsior. It's easier on them to meet you there, not travel all the way up here."

After unpacking their suitcases and once more surveying their new dresses, the young women turned on the radio for some Italian pop music before succumbing to jet lag and to sleep. Tomorrow was going to be a big day and they wanted to conquer their jet lag as much as possible.

Early the next morning Ida, the Filipina housekeeper and cook, knocked on Katie's bedroom door with a smile. "Flowers for the girls," she said, barely able to hold back her exuberance. She repeated, "Flowers for the girls!"

The Marine Corps Ball always turned out to be the most colorful social event the Kirbys attended in the course of their five years in Rome. This one was no exception. They danced and sang all night until the "Marine Corps Hymn" and "God Bless America" drew everything to a close.

The next day would prove to be even more eventful. It was the feast of Our Lady of Assumption, an Italian holiday.

Every year on the feast of Our Lady of the Assumption, following Mass at the North American College chapel, more than six hundred seminarians, friends, American nuns, priests, and American Catholic Church leaders living in Rome would take lunch in the spacious dining room. Traditionally three toasts were offered. The first one honored the pope, the second recognized the president of the United States, and the third was for the North American College. A leading cardinal usually raised his glass to the pope. This year he was Carlo Maria Cardinal Martini, of Milan. The second toast, which in previous years according to custom the U.S. ambassador to the Holy See offered to the president, this year was a somewhat more delicate matter.

The American president had not only vetoed the bill banning partial-birth abortions a second time, thus permitting abortion of a fully grown unborn baby, but one of the liberal members of his administration even publicly ridiculed the Catholic Church in America. His words were, "The Church only cares about a baby before it is born, not after."

The statement was not only inaccurate and highly offensive but an insult to the majority of people in America who were pro-life. And so, this third millennium year, it was decided that the college would not ask the U.S. ambassador but invite Mrs. Kirby, very popular at the college, to do the honors. Monsignor Timothy Shanahan, the rector, had been called on by Pope Peter II to serve as his chief of staff, yet continued to be active in the college and thus was responsible for the invitation to Mrs. Kirby. American Church leaders had hoped that Mrs. Kirby's toast would not mention the president by name, but instead toast "the people of the United States."

Mrs. Kirby, not being an overly political person, thanked everyone for inviting her and expressed how honored she felt. She said that in all the years her husband had been mayor of Chicago, she had never been asked to speak before such a large audience. Looking out at the nearly all-male crowd of cardinals, bishops, priests, and seminarians, she said, "Monsignor Tim, dear friend, as a woman, I am pleased to present this toast." Looking directly at the affable Shanahan, standing next to her, she continued, "This proves you're such a good, open-minded, progressive 'liberal feminist'!"

Tim turned beet red. He reached for the microphone and replied, to the delight of all there, "Mrs. Kirby, I've been called a lot of things in my day, some of which I can't repeat here, but never have I ever been called a liberal."

This brought the house down. Kathy continued with her toast after the roar of laughter stopped, lifting her glass to the audience. "Today is very special for all of us in the U.S. but especially for mothers, for it is the Blessed Mother whom we honor today.

"Let me toast Mary, and your mothers, who have worked hard and sacrificed much to prepare you to come to this great college, thereby to serve God and country.

"Let us also think about the mothers back home who have sons and daughters again facing armed conflict in the Balkans and all mothers who at this time face pain in their family, depression, separation, poor health, death, and some even loss of faith."

She paused, then added, "And lastly, to the U.S., including its elected president and all officials trying to exercise their authority with justice and compassion. Finally, may we see God in each and every human being? *Salute!*"

"*Salute,*" the gathering responded.

Brother Damien, in charge of the college library, said later, "I've been attending this celebration for decades, and never have I been so moved or enjoyed myself as much as today. I see now why Kirby won so many elections in Chicago. Why wouldn't he, with a wife like that? What an absolutely wonderful person!"

But the excitement was anything but over. Halfway through lunch, Fabio, one of the ambassador's security guards, proceeded to the head table to tell Ed Kirby that there was an important telephone call. Fabio had a message from the switchboard operator saying that Ed was to expect a call from the president in ten minutes at Villa Richardson. Kirby told Kathy that he would be back shortly. The North American College was only two minutes from the residence. A few minutes after arriving, the call from the president came through.

"Ed, Prime Minister Bob Mulval of Haiti and his wife are on their way to Rome. He wants to meet the pope and his Vatican officials and talk about the new crisis situation in Haiti. He needs the Church's help. Take care of him. I want to settle this Haiti thing once and for all. The Black Caucus is on my case, driving me crazy. Please pick him up at the airport and bring him over for dinner to your house, OK?"

"Sure, Mr. President," Ed assured his boss.

His driver got him back to the college just as lunch was ending. Ed told Kathy and his daughters what had happened. Mrs. Kirby had given the residence staff the holiday off. The Kirbys themselves were scheduled to attend a party at the Spanish ambassador's house at Piazza di Spagna, the Spanish Steps. The pope went there each year to crown the Virgin Mary with roses. It was always a big event and several thousand attended. After the ceremony, the pope lingered to greet people.

"I don't know what we can do," Kathy Kirby despaired. "All the stores are closed and we have no food in the house. It is always bought fresh daily. We don't even have bread or a good bottle of wine."

"Look, Mom, don't you worry. We'll take care of everything. Just be there with your guests for dinner at eight," Katie said.

Kathy and Ed trusted the look of determination in her eyes and the resolute expressions on their other daughters' faces also. Acceding to long-tested family resourcefulness, Ed and Kathy shrugged and went on with their schedule for the rest of the day. They attended the Spanish ambassador's reception. They chatted with the pope, introducing several Americans who were at the ceremony.

It was now time to pick up the prime minister of Haiti and his wife at da Vinci Airport and check them into the Grand Hotel, and then bring them to the residence for dinner. When they arrived at the hotel, several media people had already heard about the Haitian visitors and began hitting the ambassador with questions about their mission, the chronically unstable situation in Haiti, and if the prime minister was going to meet the pope. "Is the U.S. sending troops to Haiti again?" shouted one reporter.

The prime minister dodged these queries about as well as anyone could. He was not a politician but a prominent businessman, a neutral currently acceptable to all sides in the never-ending Haitian political struggle among strongmen for power and for the concept of a democratically elected government.

Finally the nearly exhausted prime minister, his wife, Kathy, and Ed arrived at Villa Richardson. The first thing he said when he walked into the Nancy Reagan Sun Room and saw the bar all set up was, "Great, a drink. This is exactly what I need." He asked the young lady behind the bar if she spoke English or French, and she nodded. *"Oui, Monsieur. Tous les deux."* The prime minister requested a double scotch and water and had finished it before Mrs. Mulval and Kathy Kirby had completed their brief inspection of the residence.

When the two couples were finished with a tour of the garden, Mrs. Kirby was informed that dinner was ready. The men spoke mostly about politics and of Bob Mulval's recent visit with the president at the White House. Kirby had already instructed his DCM to work on setting up appointments the following day for Prime Minister Mulval with the cardinal secretary of state and other ranking Vatican officials. At the end of the evening the prime minister and Mrs. Mulval thanked the ambassador and his wife for their hospitality and for a wonderful dinner.

Kathy looked at Ed and smiled. "Should we tell them?"

"Why not," the ambassador agreed.

"Tell us what?" the Mulvals wanted to know.

"Well, when the president called today and asked us to do everything we could to assist your mission, we were caught off guard. We were attending an important luncheon at the North American College and, following that, we had to attend a reception at the Spanish ambassador's palace to meet the pope. When we found out you were coming and the president wanted us to invite you over to dinner tonight, well...today is a holiday. We had given our staff the day off, and they have no telephones. The stores were closed. The staff shops daily for groceries, so we had no food in the house. When our daughters heard of our dilemma, they said, 'Don't worry about it.' They told us to continue on, and they would take care of everything. So it is they who did all the work and preparation."

Listening to all this while serving after-dinner cordials was daughter Julie.

"This is Julie," Kathy said.

"Very happy to meet you, Julie," said the prime minister. "Thank you for dinner. It was wonderful. Where are your sisters? Do you think my wife and I could meet you all?"

"Of course. I'll go get them. They are down in the kitchen celebrating the achievement with Fabio and Gerry."

"Fabio and Gerry? Who are they?"

"Oh, the Italian security officers who helped us with the cooking and actually getting the food."

"Let's get them up here as well, then," said the prime minister.

As Julie was running down the stairs to the kitchen, Bob Mulval said, "We have a saying in Haiti, 'Never let more than one person in the kitchen at a time.' I'm curious, since I've already counted six cooks."

Just then four lovely young ladies and two older gentlemen walked self-effacingly into the capacious living room. The prime minister and his wife greeted them.

"This was a wonderful dinner and evening for us here in Rome. We thank you." Mulval applauded. "We didn't expect such *de la coeur* or 'from the heart' hospitality. But I am curious to know—if, as your mother said, you had no food in the house and the stores were closed, how did you manage to create such a superlative dinner?"

They all looked at the youngest daughter, Maureen, who in her last year at Marymount International School in Rome had become the true Italian connoisseur. "Well, Mr. Prime Minister, it's something like this. We borrowed the chicken and veal cutlets from the U.S. Marine House. The tomatoes and lettuce we got from the Benedictine nuns just up the street. You can always find potatoes in the Irish ambassador's house, just down the street. The Russian ambassador gave us fruit and a bottle of vodka, and said 'Compliments of Boris.'"

"The Russian ambassador is a former press secretary and close friend of former President Yeltsin," Ed explained. "In writing his biography of Yeltsin, which was very critical of the Russian Duma, a draft copy prematurely leaked out. Boris had to get his friend out of Moscow quickly."

"The wine was easy," Maureen went on. "The older Italian men down the street who play bocci leave the wine in a big wooden cask in the shed where they play cards."

"This is fascinating. Perhaps we should make a movie," the prime minister laughed. "The only problem is nobody would believe it."

"But the sauce for the veal was delicious. I never tasted anything so good. How did you make that?" Mrs. Mulval enthused.

The girls looked at Fabio and had a hard time holding back their laughter. "Maybe he could tell you."

Fabio, who was satisfied standing in the background, nervously explained in broken English. "I don't speak good English."

"He just doesn't want to tell where we got the sauce," Maureen chuckled. "It came from his Italian coworkers guarding Oscar Luigi Scalfaro, who lives three streets away. He's the president of the Republic of Italy."

"Maybe the president not have too much sauce with dinner tonight." Fabio laughed with the Kirbys' dinner guests as the latter headed back to their hotel.

The next morning a giant fruit basket and a plant were delivered to the ambassador's residence with a handwritten note from the prime minister of Haiti and his wife.

It was nice to discover firsthand why America is so great. It's the creativity of its young people. Thanks for the lovely evening.
Bob Mulval.

A few months later Kirby was attending a function at the White House when the president grabbed him by the hand and said, "I meant to drop your girls a note. That was a great thing they did for our country. The Haitian prime minister felt very positive about his visit to Rome and has been very cooperative to deal with ever since."

Pope Peter II was all smiles as he knocked on his oldest daughter's door within the papal apartment. "Colleen, are you alive in there?" He winked at Monsignor Cippolini, standing close at hand, proud of his accomplishment soon to be revealed.

"Perhaps she is out, Your Holiness. It is ten-thirty."

Bill grinned and gave a loud bang on the door. Muffled sounds of movement on the other side of the door, fumbling fingers on the knob, and finally a sleepy-eyed Colleen opened the door a crack, her hair a total wreck, her face like mashed potatoes. Limited night attire drew a cough from the shy monsignor as he turned his head about to look at nothing in particular.

"Good news, baby," Bill greeted her cheerfully. "Monsignor Cippolini has found you the perfect room for meditation. Want to see it?"

The zombie came to life. She flew back inside, leaving her father caught between smiles of helpfulness for his daughter and of embarrassment for Cippolini.

"Too bad you weren't watching, Al. You would have seen what we might look like when we rise from the dead. I can safely predict she will be ready in ten minutes or less. I suspect she had a big night with Maureen Kirby and their friends at Oliphant's, the American sports bar, and maybe they then went to Ned Kelly's." Bill clucked his tongue. "The culture here is so different. Many of the places these kids go to socialize don't open until eleven P.M. If they get home by two in the morning their parents are lucky. Ed warned me, but I couldn't believe it until I had to experience it for myself. Some night I'll have to go out in disguise to see what it's all about."

"I'll escort you. It's quite a sight."

"I'll bet. Let's finish our coffee."

Not at all interested in coffee, nevertheless the befuddled monsignor had an excuse to remove himself from the scene of his confusion. Just nine minutes later Colleen strode into the family room. Al glanced up in amazement as she made her entrance wearing a long, free-flowing sari covering her from neck to ankles. Her hair was swept back, held by a large clip that matched the dress.

"Oh, Alonso, do you have a room for me? Dad said you could do anything!" Her enthusiasm engendered a big hug, rekindling the blush he had tried to deny. Bill Kelly grinned widely, enjoying his friend's innocent confusion.

"*Après vous,* Alonso. We'll have a look at the room you've located for this brat."

Within five minutes they were in another set of the myriad Vatican hallways. As they reached the halfway point in the corridor, a Swiss guard standing at one of the doors snapped to attention.

"This is the one, Bill. I trust Colleen will like it."

Al Cippolini opened the door and stepped back. Colleen's eyes flashed instant approval. It was evident Alonso had done more than merely find a spare room. A window at the far end was dressed with a multicolored film to give the impression of a stained-glass window. A large round Oriental rug covered the marble floor in the middle of the room. The high ceiling with ancient frescoes rose above the small study once used by Church leaders waiting to meet the pope. The only furniture was a small wooden desk and chair pushed back out of the way against the front wall, which was decorated in cheerful paper depicting birds in flight.

Bill watched his daughter slowly walk to the center of the rug. She paused, and then seemed to float down into a lotus position. The pope gave his friend the thumbs-up sign as they backed out, closing the door.

"Al, you really know how to do things correctly. You hit the nail on the head." The pope looked at the young guard, standing like a statue beside the door.

"Please be at ease, young man. Your name?"

The previous pope had evidently never questioned the startled guard. He struggled to speak, but the words seemed frozen. Bill waved his hand in front of his face and broke the spell. "Why, my name is Jan, Jan Christensen, Your Holiness." He resumed his imitation of a statue.

Bill could only smile at the poor boy with amusement. "Jan Christensen, my daughter Colleen will be using this room, perhaps on a daily basis, for...ah, meditation, I guess. I hope you will be sure no one disturbs her. OK?" He noticed a hint of pain, or perhaps frustration, on the young man's face. As always he felt the necessity to investigate its meaning. Bill Kelly always felt uncomfortable making others uncomfortable. Hence dig deeper, press on: "Speak up, young man. What's the problem?"

This assault from the commander-in-chief was too much for even the inculcated discipline of a Swiss guard. He lowered his eyes and commenced fidgeting with his belt. "Well, er, I'm sorry, Your Holiness. I, er, well..." Then suddenly he seemed to find the power that lay hidden within and straightened up. "To tell the truth, I was wondering if I could sometime perhaps ask your daughter to go out on a date with me?" He then let out a loud exhalation like someone who had surfaced from a twenty-foot dive.

The pope grinned. Now it was clear. "Popes are supposed to have spiritual power, young Jan. I'm not sure fathers have any power at all. Here, why not give me that blade, and you ask her yourself." He reached for the battle-ax, which the guard immediately released. Then the pope turned the knob on the door and motioned for the stunned guard to enter, closing the door behind him and looking at Al Cippolini, who gasped at the proceedings.

The pope came to attention, gripping the battle-ax by his side. "Love is a many-splendored thing," he quipped, as straight-faced as possible. Both men smiled and waited with quiet anticipation to learn the outcome within. A few moments later the door opened and the young guard walked out. The look of confusion on his face dissolved the pope's grin.

"Jan," he asked anxiously, "what's the verdict?"

The guard seemed more confused than ever. Rubbing his chin with his hand, he searched for words. "I don't know, Your Holiness. I asked her if she would consider going out on a date with me. She glanced up and said...I think it was something like...'Wow, cool, man! Far out.' Then she just went back to rearranging the desk and chair."

The pope laughed and handed the halberd back to the guard. "You'll have to pardon my daughter, Christensen. It took me as a parent a long time to decipher the term 'cool.' She thinks you're 'far out,' which means you are 'far in.' Come by the apartment at six this evening. She has accepted your invitation. It will give her something to look forward to after our first audience with the public this afternoon. To tell you the truth, I'm delighted, Jan. Now, if you will, please see to it that no one disturbs her until it is time for the audience."

The attitude of the young man had become one of total dedication. He would defend the pope, his possessions, and his beautiful daughter to the death. Stepping directly in front of the door, Jan stood at attention and set his jaw. "Your Holiness, no one gets by here."

Pope Bill slowly departed with Al. The monsignor, now courting a smile, shook his head. "I would give even money that a military tank would have a hard time confronting that fellow now. Love is not only splendid, it's electric. Now we can get ready for your first audience." Al gave Pope Bill a worried look. "Are you sure Colleen will be all right at the audience? I mean"—he rolled his eyes expressively—"no surprises?"

Bill's lips compressed a moment, and then he shrugged. "Surprises? I can't guarantee anything. But she will not embarrass the Vatican."

✦⊦ ✦⊦ ✦⊦

"Colleen, please. Not to be nervous," Bill urged as they were driven the short distance from the Vatican Palace to the entrance of the Paul VI Audience Hall, filled to capacity with people eager to see the pope's family.

"I am not nervous, Dad," Colleen pronounced. "Meghan and Roger aren't either. It is the Vatican regulars that are doing the shakin' and sweatin'," she chuckled. "Let the people, the laity, get a look at us and adjust to this new millennium situation."

The Kelly family faced more than an initial meeting with the people in the pews. Television cameras would be elevated above the audience hall in glass-enclosed side booths. The entire world was going to witness the first papal audience of the widower pope and three of his children.

Walking onto the elevated stage, both Bill and Meghan began to have "pregame jitters." Amazingly, Colleen seemed not to have a worry or qualm in the world as she strode across the stage like a runway model at a Paris fashion show in a new black dress Maureen Kirby had helped her buy. It was both demure and exciting on her full body, contrasting with her blond hair. Roger looked out curiously over the audience.

A table with a number of chairs behind it faced the audience. A tapestry-like tablecloth depicting the Holy Family in the manger reached to the floor, serving also to hide microphone wires and the feet and legs of those who would soon be sitting there. Three chairs were placed for interpreters; the center chairs would seat the pope and his three children. The audience rose to show respect and applauded warmly.

The pope pulled out a chair on either side of his thronelike seat and gestured for each of his daughters to sit down. Roger sat next to Colleen. Glancing off to his right, Bill noticed that Leonardo Cardinal Bellotti was standing alone, like some dark specter, in the wings of the stage, almost out of sight of the large gathering of people. Here he could unobtrusively observe the pope's first public audience. The man was an enigma to Bill Kelly, obviously providing a set of eyes and ears for Robitelli. Even Cippolini seemed surprised to see the tall, black-haired, sharp-featured, angular cardinal surveying the large gathering with gleaming black eyes. Bill knew only that Bellotti was a Vatican expert on canon law.

Bill sat down and the children followed suit, coolly regarding the expectant throng excitedly chattering away. Monsignor Cippolini, taking over as master of ceremonies, tapped the microphone. "Please be seated," he asked the crowd, which was mostly standing and gawking at the Kelly family. Then, without further introduction, he announced, "Pope Peter II will introduce himself and" he gulped audibly "his immediate family."

Eschewing the usual procedure of introductions by a cardinal or bishop, Bill Kelly opened the proceedings himself. "As you are aware, when I was elected the two hundred sixty-fifth pontiff of the Catholic Church, I took the name Pope Peter II because, like the first pope, I was a fisherman, and I had a family. As is also well known by now, my name is William Kelly, and I was an ordained priest for seven years until I fell in love and married a beautiful girl from Ireland. Mary Kelly gave me four wonderful children and was a loving, caring wife and mother until tragically she died three years ago of cancer.

"As it was with the first Pope Peter, two thousand years ago, and almost every lay member of the Church since then, I, too, have had children to bring up and educate, a business to run, and bills to pay. I share your problems, your joys in your children, and the personal tragedies that happen in every human's lifetime. I think that in many ways, I am you and you are me."

He paused a moment, surveying the largest audience he had ever in his fifty-seven years stood before. His welcoming smile seemed to catch the heartbeat of the multitude for a trice before he continued to address the eager crowd. Many of his enthusiastic listeners had waited since early morning for a seat to hear and see the new pope introduce himself and his family.

"To my left is sitting my daughter, Meghan. She is just eighteen. Beside her is Roger, a fourteen-year-old bundle of energy. The bandage you see above his eye is the souvenir from a skateboarding expedition about the Vatican hallways yesterday, during which he collided with a Swiss guard. The guardsman is expected to be back on duty by tomorrow."

Pope Bill smiled broadly at the laughter from the audience, warming to this totally unexpected and already historic first papal audience by the new pope. "And now let me introduce my beautiful daughter Colleen, sitting to my right. She is twenty years old, majoring in Renaissance art and literature at her college back in America, and already a habitué of the Vatican museums and library." He reached out his right hand to her. Colleen took it and stood beside her father a few moments, again revealing her statuesque beauty to the admiring audience. In any other milieu appreciative whistles would have sounded forth, but in this Vatican setting sensitive sighs and murmurs emanated from an already enraptured crowd.

"Colleen has an older brother by one year, Ryan Kelly. But my son Ryan, like the son of Peter I, is obliged to remain far from Rome, tending to the family fishing business."

Allowing the audience to absorb the charm of the papal family a few moments, Bill Kelly seated Colleen and once again looked out over the now thoroughly enchanted holiday congregation. He paused meaningfully, eliciting an expectant silence from the rapt crowd.

"I would be negligent and thoughtless at this moment if I failed to tell you about the mother of my four children, my wife of eighteen years, Mary Kelly. She was visiting her uncle, the pastor of the Church where I was serving as curate. Priest or pagan, I fell in love with her, and she with me. I applied for a release from my vows. In due course I was laicized, eight years after my ordination. Mary and I were married by my seminary classmate, now Brian Cardinal Comiskey of Ireland. I took up the family business, fishing while Mary and I brought up the children, all but one of whom is here before you."

Bill gestured at his children, seated on either side of him and staring up at their father adoringly.

"Then, just three years ago, Mary was tragically taken from us. But the entire Kelly family has worked hard to keep the household together, and we will continue that tradition here at the Vatican as our first Christmas season in our new home comes around."

The pope cleared his throat, looked down at the prepared statement on the table in front of him, and began to read.

"I am humbled by the fact that your love for God and your deep faith brings you here to the resting place of the apostle Peter. Your sincerity convinces me more than ever that our faith is far from dying. Over the years pictures I have seen of so many coming to Rome to pay their respects to the pope, or the office he holds, have awed me. I know, of course, that you are really now paying your respects to Jesus Christ and His family, whom we honor always, but especially at the time of His birthday and the Sunday after Christmas, the feast of the Holy Family."

The pope looked up from his prepared talk and put the typed sheets down.

"Since you are all here to see the new pope and his children, it is my belief that rather than hear me read a canned speech, you must all harbor concerns and questions you are hoping will be answered. To make sure that this happens I am going to turn over the meeting to you who have come from afar to partake of the Christmas spirit in the place where, for two thousand years, it has been fostered, kept alive, and celebrated. Therefore, my daughters and son will devote this first audience to you of the laity, for whose benefit and spiritual guidance the Vatican, the pope, and all the cardinals, bishops, monsignors, priests, nuns, and clergy are presumed to exist."

From the corner of his eye Bill noticed Bellotti shaking his head slightly. At first the audience of several thousand sat stunned, but in a few moments, as Bill cast his eyes around the throng, he sensed the wave of new interest this extemporaneous approach to his first papal audience was generating.

"So now, if you like, the children and I would be more than happy to answer any questions you may have," he concluded.

Hands soon shot up all over the room. Monsignor Cippolini, playing his role of the man for all occasions, stationed himself at the base of the podium. He strolled toward one woman conveniently sitting on the aisle close to the front of the auditorium. She seemed eager for the opportunity to have her question answered. He handed her the wireless microphone he was carrying. She smiled triumphantly at being selected to ask the first question. Pope Bill sighed silently. He had learned to recognize newspaper reporters instinctively.

Standing up, she held the microphone close to her mouth so that her words resounded throughout the hall. "As a fellow American, Miss Colleen Kelly, I have seen you on television back home on Cape Cod in Massachusetts. You first mentioned that you thought it would be very hard for you, and the other children, to make the adjustment of being uprooted and moved to Rome. I also believe that on more than one occasion you forthrightly told people interviewing you that you did not attend Mass, nor have you been a practicing Catholic since your mother died. I believe you have been described as feeling that God, if he exists, deserted you and your family. May I ask how you are feeling about that now?"

Pope Bill immediately took the initiative. "Before Colleen answers that," he said into his microphone, "let me say I am glad you asked that question right off the bat, so to speak. Allow me first to make a brief point."

He smiled and nodded in friendly fashion to the questioner, looking her in the eyes as she seated herself. "The death of a parent at a young age is always a shock to a child and particularly grievous for a young adult who has just become best friends with her mother. Mary, when she died, was thirty-nine, Colleen was seventeen. But I'll let Colleen explain her relationship with God for herself."

The pope handed the microphone to Colleen with his left hand, patting her on the shoulder with his right.

Colleen, holding the microphone well below her chin, showing off her regular, clear-cut features, stood up and faced the huge audience in the Vatican's largest auditorium.

She paused a moment, as if savoring the spectacle. Then, "Yes, I expect I do owe the Christian world an explanation for some of my remarks immediately after my father's elevation to pope from laicized priest and fisherman."

A natural performer, Colleen moved gracefully from behind the table to the front of the dais. Standing alone, yet with all the presence of a diva completing the lead aria in the first act of a grand opera, she smiled broadly and began.

"I have heard whispers from Vatican sources comparing me to another highly visible daughter of a famous pope."

She smiled as the audience, mostly tourists and Italian residents, gasped. Almost all were conventional Catholics with little knowledge of Church history beyond what they were told by their parish priest and read in their Bibles. The thought of a married pope shocked them; indeed a widower pope with children was almost beyond the pale—one reason for the standing-room-only turnout today.

"That particular pope," she continued, "born Rodrigo Borgia near Valencia, Spain, became Alexander the VI. His claim to fame, beyond total political corruption, was dividing up the New World discovered by Christopher Columbus between Spain and Portugal. His daughter, Lucrezia Borgia, lived and did her thing right here at the Vatican from 1492, when her dad became pope and she was married for the first time at age thirteen, until her father died in 1503. Despite Lucrezia's reputation, until her death at thirty-nine she conducted the greatest court in Italy for artists, writers, and musicians at Ferrara, the dukedom of her third husband. That, by the way, is the name of the car I hope to acquire over here. And let me add, there is no proof that Lucrezia poisoned anyone. History has greatly maligned her."

Colleen smiled. "Not that I am adopting her, or any other papal progeny, as a role model. But Lucrezia did the Vatican proud artistically, although there is little or no history of her being devout or even religious. Lucrezia, one of several daughters of popes, did more than any woman to promote the artistic wealth of the Renaissance, and it was her initiative that jump-started the sixteenth-century aesthetic revolution."

Colleen smiled coquettishly. "I expect to spend much of my time here in the libraries and museums, and it is unlikely that you will hear any more about my religious convictions or lack of them in the coming years."

Unaccountably she caught the bright gleam in Cardinal Belloti's eyes as he stared at her from his stance to her right beyond the pope's table. She allowed two or three silent beats in her locution before going on. "Unless," she continued, "some sort of religious epiphany seizes me by the shoulders, shakes me to the core, and instills the fear and love of God within me." Colleen's smile became an insouciant grin. "Which event is highly unlikely to occur." She turned to her father. "OK, Daddy?"

Pope Bill stood up and, taking her hand, guided his scintillating daughter around the table and back to her place beside him. "We will keep you posted on Colleen's artistic and ecclesiastic endeavors. I suspect it will be the former we will hear the most about." There was good-natured laughter throughout the hall. Colleen had successfully made her religious life a nonissue.

Another questioner, a middle-aged woman whose clothing and bearing suggested that she was Italian, confirmed the pope's hunch when in Italian she asked her question, which was translated over the headsets the children placed over their ears.

"I would like to ask the younger daughter, Meghan, this question. We saw you on television the day it was announced that your father would be our next pope. You mentioned that you thought it would be very hard for you and the other children to make the adjustment of being uprooted and moved to Rome. May I ask how you are feeling about that now?"

When the translation was completed, Meghan glanced at her father, swallowed hard, and then drew the microphone on the table in front of her closer. "To be perfectly honest, at first I did feel as if we had been uprooted, but very soon, with the help and understanding of the people here at the Vatican, both lay and clergy, we soon began to feel welcome and at home."

The ice seemed broken as a mixture of feminine understanding and muted applause greeted this reserved response. She went on. "Naturally, it has been very difficult for us. But I am grateful to the staff at the Vatican for their kindness. They have bent over backward to make things as easy as possible. Dad—" She hesitated. "Pope Peter II and I are both aware that it has been uncomfortable for so many other people as well."

She looked at her father as if he might now lend some help. But he nodded encouragingly and motioned with a wave of his hand for her to continue. Meghan took a deep breath and let it out, relaxing a bit more. "I can assure all of you there was no one in the world more stunned, maybe even frightened at first, by the idea of my father being elected pope than I. Except for my dad, of course." Some further laughter and titters came from the ladies in the audience.

"It was, to be frank, the most unusual experience any of us ever went through in our lives or could imagine any American family with kids our age experiencing. We all decided for ourselves and also as a family that the Holy Spirit somehow had decided this." Meghan paused and stared out at individuals in the audience one by one and then continued.

"And yet we know that many people will always feel we—my father, myself, and my brother and sister—do not belong here." Meghan paused as though searching for a phrase she had decided to use when she had planned her talk. "I will say honestly that we find no comfort in those who mention, even jokingly, that the new pope won't be any worse than some who have held this office in the past and that the Church will survive and thrive as always. All that I have wanted to be is Bill Kelly's daughter and someone he could be proud of. But most of all, I want my mom to look down from heaven and be proud of how we have made her feel."

Meghan's apparently unrehearsed speech left the room wrapped in silence. Bodies began to shift, uneasily, in their seats. Total honesty seemed to have disarmed most of those present.

An Italian woman asked about how the other children were doing. A few more polite questions, difficult to understand even with the help of the interpreters, were asked and answered by Meghan and Colleen Kelly.

Young Roger replied with warmth and charm to the question directed at him. "What are you going to do about the Swiss guard who cracked your head, young man? Have him sent home?" The not-so-jocular question was put to the pope's youngest son.

"I have apologized to him for being the first skateboard artist to cruise the Vatican's marble hallways and not warning the commander of the Guard," Roger replied. "I offered to change places. He could take the skateboard, I'd hold the battle-ax. But Eric said no, he'd feel safer with his halberd." Roger's zest charmed the audience.

At a signal from Monsignor Cippolini a young man midway back in the crowd was next to be recognized. The youthful questioner took the microphone somewhat nervously. He was tall, with long blond hair neatly brushed back, stylishly attired in a dark suit, a white shirt with a button-down collar, and a conservative tie. "Pope Peter, I'm not sure I belong here or should even be speaking, but because of all the background news we have heard of you back in the States I feel compelled to ask you this question. You are very aware of the sexual urges in most people. I am conversant with the Church's position on homosexuality. Do you foresee those teachings changing to accommodate people like me?"

From the corner of an eye Bill saw Bellotti's hands rise and cover his face. Cippolini, supervising the microphone handlers, seemed to blanch and speculate on how to get the microphone away from the lanky youth. Hundreds of heads in the crowd turned to the questioner, many with evident disgust.

Bill Kelly shifted uncomfortably in his seat and glanced at Meghan for support. Her eyes were closed, head bowed. Slowly Bellotti's fingers opened as his black eyes focused on Bill's reaction.

The pope cleared his throat sharply and, half smiling, tried to answer the question. "I confess, my friend, that I have not had much time to review the subject myself or with the bishops of the curia since I arrived here. I am aware that homosexuality is and has been a matter of deep concern with the Church. The Church has always held that the union between man and woman and the procreation and education of children was the primary responsibility of marriage. The importance of that relationship in the eyes of God cannot be overemphasized. So I can't at this time give any additional statement as to what further instructions may be coming from Rome."

Cardinal Bellotti seemed to draw a more relaxed breath and his hands uncovered his face. Cippolini could do nothing but stand in the aisle close to where the youth was listening to the pope's discourse.

The pope gave his questioner a forgiving smile. "This probably seems just my official way of avoiding the issue, so if I may I would like to offer you the feelings that Bill Kelly had on the subject of sex before he came to Rome. But as a Catholic one can hate the sin, but love the sinner."

He waited a moment before proceeding, noticing a sudden wave of interest sweeping through the several thousand people in the audience. "I had the distinct feeling when I was in the seminary that sex was a very uncomfortable subject in the Church. I guess it is common knowledge that sex is accepted as necessary to keep the human race going, but that those who live a life of chastity are more 'pure' than married laypeople. It was my own dear wife who pointed this out to me sometime in the sixth month of our marriage. She told me that somehow she got the feeling that when we made love I acted like I was doing this dirty thing called sex, but smugly I could get away with it because I was married now."

A titter arose from the audience, but the pope continued with his explanation. "It took me a while, with some counseling, to get my head screwed on right. So, yes, I do understand about sex urges, but due to my own upbringing I have only one view of sex." He stared out at the audience. "That is as a relationship between men and women."

Pope Bill smiled consolingly at the questioner. "I suppose that means, at least from your point of view, that I can't be objective. But I don't feel inclined to do a scientific study, if you know what I mean!"

Cardinal Bellotti had covered his face again at the pope's candor as laughter rose in appreciation of the joke and the pope speaking his own personal feelings. "From a scriptural point of view, I guess I would be inclined to follow St. Paul's views—that it is not the normal manner of sex. As he said in Romans chapter one, verses twenty-seven and eight..." Once again Bill paused, looking directly at the young man standing in the midst of an obviously hostile audience. "'Men abandoned the natural relations with women and were inflamed with lust for one another. Men committed indecent acts with other men and received in themselves the due penalty for their actions.' I never quite knew what that last part meant. But now that we have the crisis of HIV and AIDS, I wonder if that is what he was talking about. I suppose the only way my theory could be proven would be to dig up some of the ancient grave sites of the early Romans of his time and check to see what the remains might reveal."

Bellotti dug his fingers into his face as the pope went on. "Since Scripture is not taken very seriously in the modern world, I doubt that will ever occur. So all I can say to you, my friend, to give some comfort, is that you continue to pray to Jesus to guide you. God created us all out of love, and you were made in his image just as I was. On my part I will certainly make it known that we need to understand all people regardless of their own views and preferences, even when we don't agree with them."

Bill Kelly bestowed a sympathetic smile on the handsome youth, microphone still in hand, although Cippolini was obviously anxious for the priest in the aisle to retrieve it.

The pope had a few more words of comfort for the unsure youth. "As Jesus said to Peter in the Garden of Gethsemane, 'The spirit is willing but the flesh is weak.' We all need God's grace and strength to be what he wants us to be. God bless you for your question."

The young questioner turned to his equally attractive male companion as he relinquished the microphone. "Well, not exactly what we wanted to hear, but at least some understanding...I guess."

Bellotti removed his hands from before his face and glared at Cippolini in the aisle, trying to choose the next questioner with more care. From the raised hands in the audience Cippolini spotted an elderly harmless-looking gentleman and signaled the young priest in the aisle to hand the microphone to him. The old man grasped it purposefully and stared at the pope as Bill strained to see and hear where the next question might come from.

In a stern, powerful voice the interrogator began. "Mr. Kelly." He paused as a gasp of dissent at this disrespectful address swept the audience. "Don't you feel a measure of shame at the fact that you betrayed your priestly vows to become a married man?"

Dead silence once again. Only Bellotti smiled in acquiescence. Several angry faces turned to the man who had asked such an impertinent question. Others bowed or shook their heads as if to block the moment out. Two people in the room responded immediately. One was a Swiss guard who began walking toward the questioner in the event he had more than asking a rude question on his mind. The other was Bill Kelly, sitting calmly and looking at the gentleman still standing there, confronting him.

"Why, yes, sir. Certainly I have always felt ashamed of that, and of the many other sins I have committed during my lifetime. But I believe God is loving and forgiving and that he continues to love me and all of us despite our myriad imperfections. I thank God for giving me another opportunity to serve you and His Church." Some in the audience, moved with emotion, rose to their feet and applauded.

The man now holding the microphone spoke again, with evident pain. "One more question." His voice rose and cracked slightly. "Do you forgive me for asking that question?" He handed the microphone back to the young priest, who was still startled by the colloquy.

Bill looked at his daughters, then at his audience. Meghan grasped his hand as he regained his composure and leaned forward toward the microphone in front of him. "My friend, there is nothing to forgive. Perhaps you have satisfied the doubting experienced by the many who are pained by my election. All you got was a simple fisherman—Bill Kelly."

The direct assault proved fortuitous. As if on signal, more among the audience began to clap. The applause lasted at least half a minute, though it seemed an eternity. Al Cippolini caught the pope's eye, and, by his nod of approval, Bill knew they were out of the woods. The audience was suddenly developing a rapport with the Kellys.

Questions turned to the children, husbands and wives, skateboards and stitches, the oldest daughter and how she was faring in Rome this Christmas. Finally the question Bill had hoped would be asked was posed to Meghan.

"Miss Kelly, have you ever thought you might be considered to be something like the American president's daughter? A First Daughter?"

Thoughtfully Meghan admitted that she had given consideration to just this; she had worried about what sort of role she should play in the world as, indeed, a First Daughter of sorts. "I have never been a person who wanted attention. However, even before our plane landed in Rome, an idea came to me about trying to play a small role to stop all wars."

She glanced about an enthralled audience. "I have not had the chance to discuss this with my dad or anyone else for that matter...But I thought I might invite the other First Children of the world to the Vatican and have them all persuade their parents that war should not be allowed in the world. As I settle into being the daughter of Pope Peter II, I wonder what I can do to keep alive the hope I think all children in this world share. We do not want to be sent into another war. Any ideas the people of the world might have on accomplishing this goal will be appreciated, studied, and sent to qualified men of the Church, including my dad."

On cue from Monsignor Cippolini, Bill rose from his seat. "You have made this audience a heartwarming event for my children and me, and we are grateful." He raised his hands out toward the audience. "May the love of the Father, Son, and Holy Spirit descend upon you and keep you and protect you and your families. Remember to pray for us. There is much that has to be done. Too many people are suffering in our world. I personally am overwhelmed by it." He turned to assist his daughters. As they walked off the stage, the pope paused to glance at Monsignor Cippolini, who seemed to be waiting for the signal.

"Bring him to me, Al, if he's willing." Meghan looked at her father, puzzled. "The old gentleman, Meghan." He bent close to her ear. "He's a former priest."

Meghan was startled. "What?" She clucked her tongue. "Takes one to know one." She watched as Monsignor Cippolini hurried up the middle aisle.

+I+   +I+   +I+

It was now six o'clock. Jan Christensen knocked on the door to the papal apartments, unprepared for the surprised stare of a fellow guard posted outside. Meghan let the young man in. "Hi, Jan. Colleen said we should expect you. She'll be with you in a moment." She ushered him into the family room, where Roger was busily engaged in a video game. "Roger, come and say hello to Mr. Christensen. He's come to take our big sister out for dinner."

Roger stood up reluctantly, bothered that his video game had been interrupted. He stuck his hand out, and it was lost in the grip that met his own. "Hello, Roger. I'm glad to meet you. One of my fellow guards says you have a tough head." Roger was not a little awed by this paragon of health and strength, his tight-fitting sports shirt revealing such conditioned muscles.

"You ever slash anyone with that ax you carry?"

Meghan flashed a reproving glare at her brother. "Roger, mind your manners!" She turned to Colleen's date for the evening. "Mr. Christensen, pay no attention to him."

Jan smiled at Roger. "Those things are mostly for show. You know, the Middle Ages."

"How will you protect us if you don't have your ax, Jan?" Colleen entered the room, all smiles, wearing a flowered dress that enhanced her figure. Walking directly up to him, she squeezed his arm, letting her hands slide slowly down his side to feel the holster his jacket was hiding. He blushed as he turned to Meghan and Roger.

"So, if you don't mind, we will be off to a little restaurant just off the Piazza Navona. I'll bring Colleen back early, I promise."

"Jan," Colleen appealed, "I'm the big sister here, please. Now let's go, Janny. We have lots to talk about. Sorry Dad isn't here. He's busy doing pope stuff." She winked at her sister and held Jan's arm as they exited the apartment and walked down the hallway.

Smiling, Jan winked at the guard as they passed. Jan's wildest dream, one talked about by many of the guards for hours, was coming true. He was dating the pope's beautiful daughter.

✠ ✠ ✠

In his library Bill sat quietly facing the older, nervous gentleman who had confronted him in the Paul VI auditorium. Milton Drapeaux had calmed down, having told his story. He gratefully sipped a brandy that Monsignor Cippolini had offered him. The history was similar to many Bill had heard, had indeed been part of years ago. A former priest, professor at a Catholic university in Paris, he had been caught up in the early exodus of priests when he married a former nun he had met in one of his classes. Within five years he had lost his newfound mate to AIDS via an unfortunate blood transfusion. Cut off thereafter from family and friends, who viewed him as a disgrace, he had spent the next uncounted years living with his pain and guilt.

He worked at menial jobs to keep from starving. Now he had spent the last of his savings to come to Rome. His hope was to meet this new man in the Vatican who was like him. Perhaps he would understand. He had been there. The pope listened quietly to the man's tale, nodding periodically at some of the more painfully related events. Finally it was all out.

Milton Drapeaux sipped his brandy and waited to discover what Bill Kelly would think of his background. The pope chose his words carefully. "Father Drapeaux, I understand your problems. I have walked in your shoes. Tell me, have you any experience in research? I'm talking about moral theology, which you say was your specialty at the university. I thought you might have some skills along those lines."

The man looked at him, and a gleam of dignity came into his eyes. It was the first time in more than twenty years that someone had called him "Father." "Why, yes, during my summers off at the university I was a loner, not much into the social life, so I volunteered to do research for the other professors. I also volunteered to work with inmates in a men's prison, helping several get high school and university diplomas."

The pope turned to look at his friend and now confidant, Alonso Cippolini. Their closeness made it easy for them to communicate without words.

"As a matter of fact, Father Drapeaux, Monsignor Cippolini and I were only recently trying to find someone who might have the skills and necessary background to do some research for us here at the Vatican, someone who might be able to canvass all former priests still alive. I would like them to consider serving as active priests again, if they meet the challenge. They have much to contribute. As you know, we are short of them."

Drapeaux's mouth dropped open. He stared at the pope in disbelief. "Your Holiness, I was totally unaware that the ban on former priests had been lifted. This is amazing!"

The pope gave a regretful smile to his slightly stunned new friend. "Father Drapeaux, you have to realize that things get done rather slowly here. It's hard to get good help." He turned to Alonso. "Don't tell me,

Monsignor Cippolini, that you didn't get that rescript typed and published yet!"

Cippolini had to cough. It was at times too much even for his quick mind to deal with. Popes were not supposed to lie, much less talk about rescripts that did not exist. He rubbed his mouth to avoid a smile. "Why, no, Your Holiness. We have been so busy arranging your initial papal audience, we forgot about the rescript...put it on the back burner."

The pope smiled and turned to the older, worn-looking man in front of him. "Father Drapeaux, you look like you could use a few weeks to recover from your ill health. Monsignor Cippolini will find you a room here in the Vatican where you can begin to plan your strategy. You may need to brush up on saying Mass again. Despite your sixty-eight years you seem to me to have some good ones left ahead of you. Alonso here will take you to his favorite clerical store; you can choose a new wardrobe. Charge it against the account Al will set up. If you have any questions before you start my research, call Al. He knows exactly what we need. Now, if you would like, we can have some supper with my children."

He paused, shot a look at his wristwatch, and exclaimed, "Darn! Al, I forgot all about our young man coming to pick up Colleen. By now he's arrived, and, knowing my daughter, they're on their way. I got so interested in Father Drapeaux's fascinating story of his life I forgot all about it." He stood up, leading his lost lamb out the door and giving a cheerful, dismissing nod to Monsignor Cippolini en route.

A VATICAN CHRISTMAS 31

Pope Peter II was tallying the overwhelming daily problems facing Augustine Cardinal Motupu in Africa. Fresh outbreaks of the lingering troubles in Ireland were constantly brought to his attention as Cardinal Comiskey did his best to heal never-ending breaches of peace and widening disagreements between splinter groups on both ends of the religious spectrum. And of course right here in the Vatican, he had to face the stern visage of Cardinal Robitelli whenever he proposed something that was anathema to standing dogma or canonical law. Yet Bill Kelly was resolved to enjoy the Christmas season.

The cardinal secretary of state was horrified and angry at the prospect of laicized priests serving in the Church again as newly "active" even though this was now precisely the case at the highest order of Catholicism, the papacy. Robitelli's genuine concern seemed to center on how this 'second coming' as he scornfully referred to the pope's suggestion might affect those thousands of priests who had proven faithful to their vows and also how it might resonate among the people in the pews. Despite Pope Peter II's assurances that the whole project would be accomplished gradually, shrouded in a certain amount of obfuscation, the two men would never come to terms.

Also, Pope Peter had insisted on a more flexible Head of the Papal Household office, with Monsignor Cippolini filling the post. Day-to-day home life was becoming more relaxed for Pope Peter II.

Robitelli, foreseeing dire consequences for the pope's near-heretical initiatives, arranged a private meeting with certain dedicated, trustworthy traditionalists within the Vatican. The conventional-minded Vatican denizens hastily summoned by Robitelli found themselves trapped in something of a paradoxical situation: how to save the Church from this freewheeling renegade and at the same time show obedience to a pope they had themselves recognized as the leader of the Church.

But Peter II was resolved to enjoy Christmas with his family and with friends like Ed Kirby and his family.

The season was well under way when Ryan Kelly arrived quite unexpectedly, to the delight of the rest of the family. Ryan had decided that the loss of a couple of fishing trips to Georges Bank over the Christmas holidays could be sustained. On a sudden impulse he had taken a bus to

Boston, bought a round-trip tourist-class ticket to Rome, boarded an Al-italia flight, and the next thing he knew he was drinking Peroni beer at thirty thousand feet above the Atlantic. A bowl of *gnocchi all'etrusca,* with tomatoes, cream, and cheese—a famous dish of the Tuscan region of Italy—topped off with scrumptious tiramisu, was followed by a few hours of sleep. He was awakened by a flight attendant who asked him if he would like some cappuccino or juice. They would be landing at Rome's Leonardo da Vinci Airport in approximately thirty minutes.

Ryan went through customs and immigration with no trouble, and no one recognized him as the son of the pope. He went to the money exchange and bought a hundred dollars' worth of lire, which he felt should be enough for cabs and expenses. A sharp-eyed taxi driver spotted him as an American tourist and picked him up.

"Vatican...er...*Vaticano,*" Ryan ordered. The driver nodded and began the drive toward Vatican City. As the taxi threaded its way through the outskirts of Rome into the centrum, Ryan expected to hear Christmas carols blasting from stores and watch crowds of shoppers buying presents, Santa Clauses everywhere ostensibly collecting for charities.

He was surprised at the mild, pleasant temperature he was enjoying and the dearth of commercial activity he noticed as they entered Rome proper. What he did see were groups of what had to be mountain people ambling, shambling along the sidewalks and spilling over into the streets. Each small group of three or four men, looking like shepherds, played on bagpipe-type musical instruments. Flapping arms pumped air from sacks and produced a cacophonous sound describable only as very un-Christmas-like. Later he would discover that they only came down from the mountains at Christmastime to play their unique-sounding homemade instruments.

The cab driver shouted spurts of invective out the window of his vehicle at the disorderly groups merrily lurching about the streets. As the driver sped in and out of the heavy traffic in the densely populated city, Ryan could see countless pushcarts with fresh fruit and vegetables. He also observed many cathedrals and Churches—like one on every corner, it seemed—and police cars everywhere. Men were sitting in sidewalk cafés sipping cappuccino and watching women examining the local produce.

"*Sì.* Excuse me?"

"Speak English?" Ryan asked.

"*Sì.* Speaka," the cab driver replied.

"What kind of Christmas spirit you got here? No Christmas carols in the street. No Christmas lights."

That was the final test of the driver's English. "Yeah, *buon Natale.* Merry Christmas."

A few minutes later the cab drove up to a gate. A number of stores faced the entrance gate, which was attended by two colorfully costumed Swiss guards. Looming behind the gate was the Vatican in all its glory. Ryan judged that this was as far as the cab could go. He stepped out of the cab, carrying his suitcase, and pulled out the stack of lire. He read the number on the taximeter and began counting out the bills. He added 15 percent and found that he was almost out of lire. Somehow the cab driver had managed to take him in, but, then, it was Christmas and Ryan would soon be with his father and siblings.

"Yeaha, Christmasa!" he chuckled and approached the guards, who came to attention. Ryan hoped the guards spoke English as he introduced himself. Dubiously they stared at him. Ryan was wearing his one good dark suit, a conservative tie knotted into the collar of his white starched shirt. He was a bit disheveled, he realized, and maybe they could smell the beer on his breath from the flight.

"I'm Ryan Kelly, the son of Pope Peter II," he introduced himself. "Merry Christmas, guys!"

The guards glanced at each other in surprise. The young man was indeed tall like the American pope. But it wasn't their prerogative to let him pass without some proof. Ryan recognized their quandary and showed his passport.

"What's your sister's name?" a guard asked with a grin.

"My big sister is Colleen, and the younger one is Meghan."

"It is strange they did not tell us you were coming."

"This is the Vatican and no Christmas decorations? No lights, no trees, no ringing bells?" He looked about in surprise. "A supermarket and post office at the Vatican?"

"Stand by," the guard ordered mirthlessly. "I'll call the captain."

"I am not expected. This is a surprise visit."

"We do not like surprise," the guard muttered. He unhooked the cell phone from his belt and in an urgent tone of voice spoke into it in a foreign language. After considerable palaver, with the guard examining Ryan's proffered passport, there was a wait while presumably the captain checked out the information he had received.

Stores across the street from the St. Anne's Gate were beginning to bustle with business as Ryan waited patiently for some sign of recognition. Suddenly an official-looking young man in a civilian suit appeared, a broad smile on his face. He held out his hand.

"Ryan, Lieutenant Jan Christensen. You surely have taken your family by surprise. Colleen will meet us at the papal apartments."

Ryan took the outstretched hand gratefully in his and gripped it warmly. "Lead on, Jan. I don't know what was the matter with me, trying to surprise the family here in this place."

"Our job is to prevent surprises, Ryan. Are you ready?"

The gate guards came to attention, halberds held out. "Thanks. See you around, guys." Ryan returned the salute as Jan hefted his suitcase.

Ryan craned his neck, trying to see in all directions while Jan gave him running commentary on what they were looking at. Passing the Sistine Chapel, the library, and the garden walls, they entered a large building in which the papal apartments were located. They strode past another set of brightly garbed guards to an elevator.

Colleen was waiting at the entrance. "Ryan, how wonderful to see you! What a shock!" she greeted and hugged her brother. "Why didn't you let us know?"

"Didn't know myself until yesterday. Then I jumped on a plane and here I am. How is everybody? Where's Dad? How's he doing? I missed you, Col."

"Dad's preparing for Christmas Eve, the midnight Mass tomorrow," Colleen replied. "I'll show you to your room in the apartment."

After Colleen had given her brother a tour of their spacious quarters, already refurbished for family living, and assigned him a guest room, she took him on a tour of the Vatican with Jan Christensen as an escort. In the meantime she had telephoned her friend Maureen Kirby to tell her about her brother's arrival.

Since it was the night before Christmas Eve, Pope Peter II was working with a brace of cardinals on his Christmas Eve Mass and the sermon he would deliver.

Taking time out for dinner, the family ate together and Ryan gave his father a report on the business at home but quickly observed his father's disinterest in the affairs he had cared for so diligently. His only questions concerned the welfare of old hands who had worked for him for so long. Although the pope talked little at dinner about the secular matters concerning him these days, Ryan could see that there was much else on his father's mind, none of it connected with the fishing business. Probably like Peter I; fishing was the last thing on the first pope's mind after he became the Rock on which Christ's Church was founded.

It was after ten o'clock that night when Colleen and a tireless Ryan met Jan for a tour of Rome's vivid nightlife. "We'll start at Michelante's.

You'll love it, Ryan," Colleen enthused. "It's the hangout for young students, Americans and Italians mostly, but others from all over Europe. Maureen Kirby will meet us. You'll like Maureen. She is really like one of us even though her father was mayor of Chicago for years and very important politically. She speaks perfect Italian."

"How are you doing in the language?" Ryan asked.

"In less than two weeks I can get along. Maureen told me just to get out with people and they'll help me with my Italian. 'Mingle and speak,' she said. That's what I'm doing."

Mickey's, as the Roman students called Michelante's, was a revelation to Ryan. It was a real American bar, with college signs hung on the walls. Just then the affable Maureen joined them. A big sign reading ST. JOHN'S UNIVERSITY with hundreds of student autographs on it hung over the booth in which Maureen, Colleen, Jan, and Ryan were sitting, surveying the noisy scene around them.

Ryan watched as young men simply walked over to where two or three girls were sitting and started talking to them. Sometimes a girl nodded and walked out to dance with a young lothario; other times they smiled and shook their heads.

"You just see a girl you like and walk over and start chatting with her?" Ryan asked.

"Everybody is very friendly, especially Italian boys," Maureen replied. "Sometimes too friendly," she mused.

As if to emphasize her observation, a very pretty and full-figured girl with neatly trimmed blond hair who was standing near their table turned suddenly from a swarthy, dark-haired young man who was talking urgently to her. With a look of appeal on her face, she walked up to their table. Ryan smiled at her as she breathlessly asked, "Could I join your table?"

Seeing the hot-eyed young swain behind her, Maureen motioned toward the table. "Of course, come sit down." She turned to Jan. "Could you find a chair for her?" The young guard officer immediately stood up and offered his own seat to the girl, which she gratefully accepted as Jan went to find another chair.

Sitting between Maureen and Ryan, the young woman introduced herself as Paula Novak, a student in Rome from Milwaukee. "I haven't been here too long. I'm studying at Loyola and living in the college hostel, and I'm learning about customs and picking up the language. I read about this place, Mickey's, and it is fun and you get to meet people like you. But just now I felt"—she shrugged—"like I was alone and defenseless. You know, when that guy asked me to go out of here with him."

When Jan Christensen returned with another chair, the young women had already become acquainted. Ryan also found the girl interesting. "I'm not even in Rome for a day and a beautiful girl comes into my life," he chuckled. Then, noticing the Italian youth still eyeing her, he moved his seat possessively closer to hers. She started to tell him about her first months in Rome studying Renaissance art and Colleen joined in.

"Of course there is so much in the Vatican libraries and archives that is not available to the public," Paula remarked. "But just being here in Rome gives you the kind of atmosphere that makes you learn and understand." She laughed deprecatingly. "I'm from a Polish family and my father never heard of Renaissance art until Pope John Paul II became the first Polish pope in history. Suddenly my dad let me come over to pick up a little Polish pride, he said. And then, just after I arrived, the pope passed on before I could arrange to be part of a public audience."

"Do you speak any Polish?" Ryan asked.

"No. But that doesn't mean I wasn't proud of our Polish pope."

Just then several young men stood up from tables and said good night to their friends. One of them walked by the table and winked at Jan, saying foreign words. Jan answered and laughed back at them.

"They are part of the Swiss guard. We have to be back in our quarters at midnight." He grinned broadly at Colleen. "But I have a special pass for tonight."

"You mean you guys have to be like Cinderella? Home by midnight?" Ryan asked.

"Except in certain rare circumstances." Jan grinned and patted Colleen's hand.

They talked at length and sipped on homemade wine, while the boys drank draft beer. Nothing really gets going in Rome until after midnight. Jan told them of the Swiss guard.

"Men from the best Swiss families consider it an honor to be appointed to serve in the Vatican Guard. The prestige lasts a lifetime. We gladly put up with the regulations for a year or two. Our commander is usually from the nobility and a married man with his own Vatican apartment."

"I remember when that terrible business happened," Maureen said. "My father knew Commander Estermann."

A grimace crossed Jan's face. "In the four-hundred-year history of the Guard nothing so bad, so shocking, ever happened."

"I must have been out fishing," Ryan said. "What was it?"

When Jan did not answer, Maureen replied to Ryan's question. "Back in 1998 a disgruntled guardsman murdered the commander and his wife in their apartment and then killed himself."

Ryan nodded but did not pursue the question since it was so obviously painful to Jan. They were all silent a few moments, and then four young men, crew-cut Americans, obviously, came into the bar and looked around.

"Those are some of the marines from the American embassy to Italy in Rome," Maureen laughed. "They're good boys, well behaved."

Curious, Paula turned to Ryan. "What brings you to Rome? Are you studying someplace?"

Ryan laughed. "No. I'm a fisherman from Cape Cod in New England. I'm just visiting for the holidays, and this is my sister."

"Are you studying here, Colleen?" Paula asked.

"I'm thinking of enrolling in Marymount, where Maureen goes."

"That really costs money," Paula remarked. "I was lucky my dad sprang for my college and hostel fees."

One of the marines, neatly dressed in sharply pressed slacks and a long-sleeved, tieless shirt, came over to where Maureen was sitting. "Are you going over to the disco tonight?"

"Probably. I'm showing some friends what Rome has to offer at night."

"Well, save me a spin. See you later."

Ryan leaned toward his sister. "Looks like the crowd here is thinning out a bit. Maybe now is the time to hit one of those discos you were telling me about."

"Ryan, you've been up for Lord knows how long. Aren't you tired?"

Ryan smiled at Paula. "You don't come to Rome to be tired." Then to Maureen he said, "What's that place you were telling me about earlier?"

"There's Radio Londra—in English it means Radio London—and there's also Acav. They are both funky, lively, and fun clubs."

"Paula, will you come with us? Wow! New Bedford, even Boston, has nothing like this." He touched her arm lightly. "We'll drive you home afterwards."

"I'd love that, Ryan." She laughed. "To think I came all the way to Rome to meet an American boy!"

Just as they were standing up to leave, an Italian youth came up to Maureen and kissed her on both cheeks. She was obviously delighted to see him as they exchanged rapid and enthusiastic Italian. Briefly she introduced him as Luigi, a friend from Marymount School. Together they walked the short distance to Radio Londra, where the techno music could be heard loud and thumping half a block away. Luigi led the way in and captured a table for them. As they sat down, Luigi's friend Marco sidled up to them, and they crowded him into the table also. Ryan was amazed to hear his sister, who had been in Rome only a few weeks, talking animatedly in Italian to Marco. As Jan watched protectively, the two Italians led Colleen and Maureen onto the floor, where they danced to the blaring house music.

Ryan and Paula followed onto the floor and danced in somewhat less athletic steps, although they enjoyed being together as much as, perhaps more than, the wildly gyrating couples.

The evening spun on, and then Maureen and Luigi left for another disco. At Jan's insistence Colleen and Ryan agreed it was time to take Paula back to her hostel and go home themselves.

Jan was driving a small black Vatican sedan. Ryan and Paula, sitting in the back, made a date for some sight-seeing the next day, Christmas Eve. Impulsively Ryan invited her to go to midnight Mass at St. Peter's Basilica with him.

"I hear it is always crowed," Paula replied, "but I'd love to spend Christmas Eve with you."

"I have some connections that I think can get us tickets. In any case we'll share our time together."

"I'd love that," she breathed as Jan pulled up in front of the Loyola College hostel and Ryan escorted her to the front door, where they bid one another a chaste good night.

Jan delivered Colleen and Ryan to the apostolic apartment and promised to make himself available next day to take them around town on Christmas Eve.

"That Paula is movie-actress pretty," Colleen observed.

"And she's really nice," Ryan agreed.

"What are you going to do with her tomorrow?"

"I'd like to bring her to the midnight Mass."

"I'll ask Maureen if you can bring her to the ambassador's party at his residence just before the Mass. I know it will be all right. Boy, is that Paula in for a surprise." Colleen laughed. "She hasn't a clue who we are."

Letting themselves in by the main door as two Swiss guardsmen snapped to attention, Colleen and Ryan crept into the papal apartment, hoping that everybody was sound asleep. But Meghan slept fitfully, waiting for their return. Wearing her bathrobe, she met them as they passed quietly through the family room on the way to their bedrooms.

"Gracious, it's three in the morning," she exclaimed.

"And the city is still jumping, Meg," Ryan said merrily. "We sure are a long way from New England."

"It's a good thing Dad is exhausted from preparing for Christmas or he would be standing here giving you two you-know-what."

"Rome is different, Meg."

"Maybe, but we're not, not yet." She tried to frown and burst out laughing. "Dad wanted to send out the guards after you."

"We were with one all evening, Meg."

"And a very good officer he is. But young, too. And I think he's sweet on Colleen."

"If it weren't for Jan baby, we'd still be out there celebrating," Colleen said defensively.

"Well, Dad's asleep and we won't disturb him. For two days he's been working on these Christmas Masses. One of them is for tonight. So I'll see you at breakfast."

CHRISTMAS EVE MASS 32

Pope Peter had practiced with his trusted cardinals and Monsignor Cippolini for a week preparing for the Christmas Eve midnight Mass. Cardinal Bellotti, an expert on canon law, had been assigned to the team by Secretary of State Robitelli, who was anxious that nothing Bill Kelly did as pope would call into question revered traditions strengthened and made inviolate during the last harrowing days of the previous pope. It was, of course, this adherence to hidebound traditionalism, a mind-set secretly held suspect by the majority of the younger, more liberal-thinking bishops and cardinals, that had led to the logjam of the recent conclave. "God's joke," as the unintentional election of Kelly to the papacy was referred to in whispers, was the startling result of this centuries-long crackdown on theological "diversity."

Pope Peter was happy to learn that several cardinals would be concelebrating Mass with him, hoping the mere image of unity would lessen the tensions between them. At the following Christmas morning Mass he was expected to deliver a meaningful homily that would stay strictly within the bounds of orthodoxy passionately reaffirmed in the final days of the previous pope. He had been given models of sermons from over the years, all centering, of course, on the birth of Christ. He sifted through them and selected certain passages meant to catch attention. By Christmas Eve he felt things ought to proceed without a hitch. In Ryan's surprise appearance he rejoiced in that extra pleasure bonus for which he found himself profoundly thankful.

Thus on Christmas Eve morning Bill felt deceptively relaxed and confident. He had revised and studied his Christmas morning Mass notes, now in total conformity with Bellotti's suggestions. The midnight Mass by comparison was hardly a problem. With three cardinals assisting and Bellotti himself delivering the brief homily there was no foreseeable problem—no warning of the challenge he had made up his mind to launch in time against the stifling dogmas Robitelli and Bellotti represented in their persons and ideology. These reforms would have to come a little at a time, certainly. But he would nevertheless encourage change and spur future theologians to take more liberties against present Church doctrine. And he would face the problems confronting Motupu in Africa head on, to help address the devastating toll of human lives from HIV and AIDS all over the continent. It was time to seriously address the health crisis in Africa, perhaps even review the Church's position on birth control information and education. Pope Peter sighed at the difficult prospects he faced and then again resolved to enjoy Christmas with his family.

As expected, Ryan and Colleen slept late. But at nine o'clock his son was sipping coffee with him and explaining his plans for the future of the family fishing business. He then told his father about the Polish-American girl he had met the night before and wanted to bring to midnight Mass.

"Arrange it with Al," the pope told his son. "I've got a pretty busy day ahead. When we get tomorrow's Mass behind us you and I will have the time we need to go over family matters."

He glanced down at the sermon Sister Miriam had aptly typed up and which he had studied and restudied. "Take this, for instance. I went through years of past sermons delivered at Christmas morning Mass by previous popes, trying to discover a common thread to all of them." He sighed deeply and held up the loose pile of typed pages. "I don't know whether all this is one Billy Kelly talking or a distillation of platitudes mouthed by others over the last fifty years."

"I'd rather be out fishing than doing what you are." Ryan stood up. "I'll see you tonight. And good luck!"

The pope smiled a little slyly. "I'll look forward to meeting this girl you seem to like so suddenly."

Ryan's date with Paula was set for twelve noon. He'd consulted with Colleen, who had called Maureen Kirby for advice. Ryan and Paula would take the *treno* trolley to the beach half an hour to the east and sample the mild weather and the boardwalk and have lunch at an oceanside restaurant. Paula had not yet gone there, nearby as it was, choosing to visit later with someone special. That finally happened to be Ryan.

They enjoyed lunch and the sunny afternoon, Ryan being well aware that the best place for him was well out of the way of his father and the Vatican staff. There was not only the Mass but also the pope's small reception afterwards.

"By the way," Ryan said over a glass of wine after lunch, "I have passes for us to the Mass at St. Peter's tonight. Good seats, right up front."

"How did you manage that?" Paula was impressed. "You've only been in Rome for one day and night! At Loyola only a few of the students were able to get tickets."

"You'll see," he replied with a mysterious smile on his face. "First, we are invited to a party at Maureen's house."

"She has a house, a real home here?" Paula asked.

"Her father is with the American embassy," Ryan explained.

"Oh, wow! I sure lucked out last night." They were walking along the boardwalk above the beach. The breeze off the sea was mild. Paula put her arm through Ryan's, leaning her head on his shoulder. They sat down on a bench looking out over the glimmering Adriatic.

"This has been such a perfect afternoon," Paula said softly. "I'm glad I saved the beach for something special."

"So am I, Paula."

"And we still have so much fun and excitement left. Maybe we ought to take *il treno* back so I can nap and get ready. I've been saving something especially nice to wear."

They stood up and walked back to the trolley. "Where is Maureen's house?" she asked.

"I don't know, but we'll have Jan driving us and my sister. They know the way."

"Where are you and your sister staying?" Paula asked.

"We'll go there after midnight Mass. I'd love for you to meet my dad."

"Is he connected to the government? Our government?"

"No. He's sort of independent. You'll see."

"And you have to go back to the States after the holiday?" she asked bleakly.

"I guess. I run the business on Cape Cod so Dad can do his thing here in Rome."

Paula laughed. "Usually it's the other way around. The parents stay home and work so the kids can study."

"Well, you'll understand when you meet my dad. And there is no reason why I can't jump on a plane every so often to visit here with you. This is my first trip to Europe. Already I am beginning to see how my education has been neglected, blighted even."

"I've always wanted to see New England." Paula squeezed his hand.

"I have a hunch you will. Here we are. *Il treno,* next stop Rome."

They boarded and were back in forty minutes. Ryan hailed a cab and delivered Paula to the door of her hostel. He consulted his watch. "See you in three hours, at eight-thirty. Have a good nap. It will be another late night."

At eight-thirty Jan Christensen drove Colleen and Ryan to the Loyola College hostel, where Paula was waiting, and then took them to Villa Richardson on the hill overlooking Rome. As they stepped out of the car Paula gasped. "The American flag. This is the ambassador's residence."

"Right," Ryan agreed. "Maureen Kirby is the ambassador's daughter."

"Oh, I hope I am dressed all right for this occasion."

"You look gorgeous," Colleen exclaimed. "They'll think you're in Rome for the opening of your new film."

Any Christmas cheer lacking in Rome was made up for by the outpouring of seasonal celebration at the Kirbys' residence. Maureen and her sisters had college mates and Chicago friends staying for the holidays. Decorations and balloons hung from the walls and ceilings. Paula, with Ryan and Colleen and Jan, fit in perfectly.

A sumptuous buffet provided all the feasting they could desire, with wine and soft drinks readily available. Paula and Ryan enjoyed meeting the Kirbys' friends and indulging in the festivities until Ed Kirby announced that the midnight Mass would be under way in an hour. Everyone with passes to the basilica should now be on their way.

At Paula's questioning look Ryan produced their tickets and they left with Jan and Colleen to drive down the hill. Paula was speechless when Jan drove them through the Vatican City gates and let them out at the diplomatic entrance of St. Peter's. Chauffeur-driven cars carrying flags of all the nations of the world surrounded the entrance. "I feel like I'm at the UN in New York," Paula said.

Holding Ryan's hand, Paula was swept through the entrance, where their tickets were examined. Inside the famed basilica, Ryan and his new friend were escorted to the front section where guests of the diplomatic corps were seated. Paula stared in disbelief as Ryan escorted her down to the front row, where a priest seated them next to Colleen and two teenagers.

The organ swelled, the choir sang, the Swiss guards appeared approximately ten minutes before the Holy father entered the magnificent St. Peter's, and the Mass was under way. Pope Peter II was seated between two cardinals. One stood up and pronounced a brief welcome in Italian. The familiar lessons were read, and then the pope stood up to read salutations, first in Italian, then in English. He greeted the diplomatic corps and all the other groups of guests who had been invited. Cardinal Bellotti read a homily, and the pope then shortened the proceedings by half an hour, saying Mass.

Seventy-five priests gave Holy Communion simultaneously. It had been Pope Peter's aim to cut down the interminable length it took to get through the Christmas Mass, and he succeeded, much to the relief and gratitude of the nearly three thousand communicants in the basilica who had been invited to attend.

As the basilica crowd dispersed, Ryan and Paula, standing in the aisle, waited for the teenagers and Colleen to leave their seats. Escorted by Monsignor Cippolini, Meghan walked up to them and Ryan introduced Paula to his sister, who greeted her warmly. "Ryan, please bring Paula up to meet Dad and enjoy a little Christmas cheer with us. The Kirbys will be along and a few of the bishops have their mothers and fathers for Christmas."

Jan and Colleen led the way through the quickly receding crowd to an elevator at the rear of the basilica which lifted them to the upper level and the long hallway leading through the offices to the apostolic apartments.

"Ryan, where are we going?" Paula asked.

"You'll soon see."

Swiss guards saluted with their halberds out as Meghan led the way. Doors swung open for them as they walked inside to the expanded quarters. Stewards stood behind the tables of champagne and juice. The room was abuzz with activity. A few members of the diplomatic corps arrived. A smiling Ed Kirby, his family, and their close friends were first among them.

"How did you get us into this party?" Paula asked, now sensing a further surprise. "The ambassador?"

Before he could answer, there was a stir at the door as the halberd carriers came to full salute and Peter II walked in.

"Your Holiness." Monsignor Cippolini greeted him and turned to quickly announce to the teeming reception room, "His Holiness, Pope Peter II!"

Ed Kirby strode over to him, the first to shake the pope's hand American style. Several cardinals had to check their common instinct to kiss the "fisherman's ring" the pope wore in honor of the Christmas midnight Mass.

"A splendid occasion, Pope Bill." Kirby congratulated his friend informally now.

"I was getting thirsty for an Irish Mist. I'm only sorry Brian isn't here, but he has a big affair going for the Irish, Catholics and Protestants. I hope they all behave!" The pope looked around the room and spotted his son Ryan with an especially pretty, light-haired girl. He walked over to them.

"Merry Christmas, Ryan. This must be Paula."

"Merry Christmas, Dad. You did it all just perfectly." The two embraced and Ryan reached for Paula's arm, gently pulling her toward the pope. "Paula, meet my dad."

"Your Holiness." Paula bowed before him, transfixed, not knowing whether to genuflect, kiss the ring, or whatever else.

"You're as attractive as Ryan said." Bill put a hand on each shoulder and pulled her upright. "I look forward to talking to you after I have seen to our guests."

Maureen Kirby walked up to them, took the pope's hand in both of hers, and said softly, "Merry Christmas." She hesitated, then, "Pope Bill."

"Right. Exactly. I'm still looking forward to that Italian pasta you promised to make."

"Anytime."

Cardinal Robitelli had appeared between the Swiss guardsman at the door, and the pope went purposefully across the room. "Gino, Merry Christmas. *Buon Natale*." Then likewise to Cardinal Bellotti. In deference to his always studied demeanor he said, "*Eminenza,* I'm happy you came to this small family reception. Of course you know everyone here."

Bellotti bent slightly as though to kiss the ring and then straightened up. "Your Holiness, a graceful reception. It is little wonder that you shortened the Mass."

The pope chuckled and went about greeting the few gathered members of the diplomatic corps who were present.

Paula put both arms through Ryan's. "My knees are going all wobbly, Ryan. I can't believe this night is happening to a Polish-American girl from Milwaukee."

"Hey, you think you are shocked, what about me? My father, the fishing captain, is Pope Peter II. Impossible—but there it is."

"They'll never believe me back at Loyola."

"Well, don't tell them. How about another small glass of champagne?"

She nodded, still leaning on him, and together they went to the beverage table. "I'm literally weak, Ryan. I can hardly stand up."

"A glass of the French champagne, and it will all be a lark for us to enjoy together." Maureen and Colleen were in animated conversation as they relished being the centerpieces of the party, one the daughter of the U.S. ambassador, the other the daughter of the pope.

"But look, I do have to get up in time for Dad's morning Mass. He's been working on the homily all week with those squares Bellotti and Robitelli," Colleen said.

"Where else are there two embassies and residences, all guarded by local cops, for most of the nations on earth? One for Italy, one for the Holy See?"

Ryan and Paula left the short reception, and Ryan took Paula home by taxi, promising to call her after the Christmas morning Mass.

In the backseat, careening through Rome at almost two-thirty in the morning, Ryan drew Paula to him, kissed her on the lips, and thrilled at the warmth of her return. As they came near the hostel he said huskily, "I wish there was some place where we could be alone. How about your room?"

Paula laughed helplessly. "There is a nun lurking in the women's section all night and there's always a guard on duty."

"Look, somehow we've got to figure out a way to be alone together."

"It will happen when it should, Ryan," Paula whispered.

"Yes, it will," he breathed and they kissed until the taxi stopped and Ryan escorted her to her front door. She opened it and slipped inside.

"Call me tomorrow?"

"I will," he promised.

CHRISTMAS MORNING MASS 33

Pope Peter II was halfway through the Christmas morning Mass that had begun at ten. As his first obligatory Christmas homily approached, he could feel his stomach tightening. He walked over to the narrow podium and looked at the huge throng crowding St. Peter's Basilica. This was a solo delivery, although about forty cardinals, a hundred bishops, and several hundred priests escorted him.

The gathering sensed a certain uneasiness about the pope and tried to mitigate it, remaining quiet, expectant, and attentive. He placed his notes on the gold ledge of the podium and clasped the sides of the frame to steady his nerves. He strove again to remember the public-speaking tips that he had learned years ago in the seminary.

Then it came upon him. He felt the spasm creeping up through his chest, throat, and the back of his nose. His right hand scrambled vainly for the slit in his robe to reach his pocket handkerchief. Too late. The mighty sneeze hit the papers with a blast. His podium was strewn with flying pages. Acolytes, priests, and one or two cardinals joined in a scramble to gather up the fallen leaves. Embarrassed, muffled "oohs" and "ahs" echoed in the nave whilst the pope stood with head bowed, slightly shaking in mild dismay. Within thirty seconds—it felt like thirty minutes—his head of protocol, Monsignor Toug from Hanoi, handed the mixed sheaf back to the pope with an involuntary shrug.

Staring at his notes, the pope finally found breath enough to look out upon his bewildered audience. "So," he murmured, smiling into the microphone, "we have 'blown' our Christmas sermon. I wonder if that other fisherman, Peter, did this."

Some laughter rang out, not a little hysterically, amid the pews. It was the release that both sides needed. Waiting for the noise to settle, he pondered what to do or say next. Nothing came. Then he looked out toward the front row where his family was sitting. His eyes met his younger daughter's. She winked and gave him a thumbs-up. Beside her a bright-eyed Ryan smiled up at him. Colleen and Roger were also attempting encouraging glances up from below.

Bill cleared his dry throat and felt he was back at the helm of his boat somewhere off the Cape.

"Dear friends, we are gathered here to rejoice at the birth of a child, a very special one...Our Savior, Jesus Christ."

Several cardinals straightened up. *God is speaking to his people,* they thought. *Wrong! Maybe not wrong?*

Bill pressed on. "I remember so well the day my wife, Mary, had our first child. So tiny, fragile, beautiful. Babies are a gift from God."

Cardinal Robitelli covered his face with his hands, fearing worse to come.

"I was thinking about this just yesterday, rehearsing my sermon. I took our Bible from its shelf and read every account of Our Savior's birth. And do you know what pierced through to my consciousness? It was the sentence after Mary agreed to become the mother of Jesus. Do you know it?" He smiled.

Few among the cardinals responded. Cardinal Bellotti leaned toward the ear of Cardinal Robitelli. "He's playing school games! What must we do?"

"Let him hang himself," Cardinal Robitelli countered behind a raised hand.

Peter II continued, "The sentence that caught my eye was, 'And the angel left her.' Can you imagine what that sentence means, my dear friends? I tried to imagine how I would have felt...or no, how my Mary would have felt if she were suddenly pregnant and knew she had to come to me and tell me...before we were yet married! A terrible thing. No help or support from anyone. You're absolutely on your own now. And Mary back then? Fifteen or sixteen years old. Just engaged to Joseph. What a terrible burden God thrust upon that poor girl."

He looked down and caught the sympathetic glow shining in Meghan's face and eyes. "My own Mary had that kind of purity and goodness. She could have told you what it felt like better than I."

Bellotti winced again and whispered, "Next he'll be recommending his wife for canonization, and showing home movies. I can't believe this!"

Cardinal Robitelli, white with shame and anger, stared straight ahead.

The pope, now in full command, continued. "I think we should all pause to reflect on this special moment and on the sorrow that the Blessed Virgin endured then. Having to face Joseph, who we know was cut to the heart when first he heard the news." He paused and sighed. "God made those two people pay a very heavy price for the gift of His son in their lives. Perhaps we should think about that price this Christmas morning. If we want the Christ child to return again we'll no doubt have to pay a price. Love does not come cheaply. You mothers know far better than we men the pain of childbirth, and the crosses to bear, day after day, that go with raising children."

Again the pope paused as he contemplated for a moment what no other priest could have experienced, some of his and Mary's trials bringing up their children. "I suggest this 'spiritual birth' of Christ in our lives is the same thing. To raise Him to manhood, within us, has been and will be a long, hard struggle. Oftentimes we won't begin to understand why He seems to be treating us so badly! Let us have the patience in our young people so we'll begin to understand how to have Christ play a most important role in their lives."

The pope stared out over the magnificent Church for a few moments. He caught the eye of a group sitting on the side that stood up and with enthusiasm and visible pride in their new pope joined in the swelling applause.

After Mass Bill walked over to the group he had noticed and met Father Joe Daley and his parishioners from the parish of St. Anthony in Cody, Wyoming. Cardinal Bellotti glanced at Cardinal Robitelli. "Well, did it come out all right? What is your opinion?"

Cardinal Robitelli turned slightly and, still puzzled, replied, "I think...when a sermon, especially a short one, is delivered, we should pay attention and try to learn from it!" Christ was born again safely for yet another year!

A subdued Kelly family exchanged pleasantries with the clergy surrounding them as they made their way with Al Cippolini and Tim Shanahan back to the apartment, where Pope Peter would join them. Bill Kelly, relieved, was suffused with holiday cheer now that his official Christmas functions were behind him.

After the pope had been congratulated he called Ryan over to him. "Son, it's been a busy time for me since you arrived, but with this morning's little recitation behind me, for better or worse—"

"It was great, Dad, really awesome. So short, so meaningful to us all."

"Why, thank you, Ryan. And now I want to devote as much time as possible to the family while you're still here. I didn't ask you, but how long can you stay?"

"Well, I told the crew I wanted to go out again as soon after New Year's as we can get the nets clear and the boats provisioned."

"Since you are over here, I hope you'll stay as long as possible."

"We're getting ready to explore new fishing grounds, further out."

"You have to keep in mind how fast the storms can spring up on you.

And out there some monster waves have a way of towering in from nowhere. They sweep up from the Bermuda Triangle, do their damage, and disappear. Even though you were just in junior high, you must remember the '91 storm, the one they just made a movie about, that took the lives of Gloucester fishermen."

"On another level, Dad, and I hate to bring it up at this time, but there's one wave I know of churning out of our state and heading right at you, here at the Vatican."

"I guess I know what you mean. Young Senator Lane and his contested annulment."

Ryan nodded. "Yeah. Bad situation all around. It's getting a lot of press, and you know the *Boston Globe* loves to beat up on the Church. Lane has been one of their own, but given an opportunity to attack Catholics—especially Irish Catholics—nobody is spared. His former wife has appealed to the Vatican to nullify the annulment because it leaves a marriage of ten years with three kids in limbo. The tabloids and talk shows at home are giving this issue a great deal of attention, and nobody is looking good."

The pope breathed heavily. "It will end up squarely in my lap. Young Lane and his family have supported the fishing association for years. He took on the Canadians when they claimed the banks for Canadians only. He stood up for us in Washington when those corporations tried to stick it to the small fisherman."

"That's another reason why I have to get back, Dad. Business is pretty good except for the quotas, and Lane has been good to us."

"Did he ask you to talk to me about the annulment?"

"No, Dad, he didn't. Just convey his respects."

Bill Kelly reached out and placed a hand on Ryan's shoulder. "I should be sending you to college instead of out to sea."

"I'm no college kid, Dad. I like being the third-generation fishing captain in the family."

"Well, I'm proud of you, keeping the Kelly family business prospering while your dad goes back to preaching."

"Some preacher, Dad." The admiration in Ryan's tone was unmistakable.

The pope then beckoned Monsignor Cippolini over. "Al, have you figured out those excursions for my kids?"

"Yes, I have. Tomorrow, Saturday, you all fly to Palermo, Sicily, to attend an official post-Christmas service. The day after Christmas is also a special holy day throughout Italy.

"You will celebrate Mass Saturday night at my old *cattedrale,* followed by a concert in honor of Festa di Santa Rosalia. It is usually held in July, but Palermo wanted to help shed its reputation as a high-crime and poverty center by inviting you now. Also you will reopen our recently renovated and magnificent Teatro Massimo. Following the concert, a procession in honor of Santa Lucia and a cookout, 'Grande Festa,' is set up at the city park for all the people. That is why our local bishop was so anxious to have your family join him there. Your delegation will stay overnight at Hotel Ariston, then fly Sunday morning by helicopter to Siracusa on the other side of our island to visit its historic British military cemetery."

"What do you know!" the pope exclaimed. "Mary's Uncle Tom was killed in North Africa while serving in the Royal Marines and is buried there. The kids always wanted to visit his grave."

"The archbishop of Canterbury will join you at a special wreath-laying ceremony for all the several thousand British and U.S. soldiers who were killed in the line of duty in North Africa and southern Italy. Then you will drive to Sciacca to visit the Chapel of the Madonna. It is a famous fishing village. The fishermen there claim a bond with you and are honored that you chose to join them. By the way, as you requested, the Jesuit Father Pittau, the president of our Gregorian University here in Rome and your old friend from Boston, will be traveling with us. You will recall that you first met the good father, whose first name is Joe, when he was at St. Augustine Church in South Boston while attending Harvard."

"A most knowledgeable man." The pope nodded. "Especially about Japan and the Far East. He was president of the Catholic College in Japan after World War II. It will be great to see him again."

"You, the two younger children, Monsignor Shanahan, and Father Giuseppe Pittau will fly back to Rome that Sunday night. But Ryan, Paula Novak, Colleen, Jan, and another Swiss guard fly directly to Venice. From Venice they will visit Florence, returning here on December thirty." Monsignor Cippolini, his travel presentation complete, bowed his head as the Kelly family applauded. "I hope it all meets with your approval," he murmured.

"Al, you have done an excellent job in planning such a busy schedule, especially for Ryan and Colleen. Thank you."

Ryan laughed. "For one moment you made me think I am a jet-setter or an independently wealthy man of leisure. I will cram everything I possibly can into the few days I have left in Italy. And when I'm back out hauling my nets and praying no tidal wave sideswipes my trawler, I'll be filled with memories of happy times and romantic Italy to sweeten my dreams."

Bill sat in his chair sipping hot tea, pleased to know that Ryan thought his Christmas sermon had been good. He also contemplated how tough it was for Ryan, suddenly a responsible workingman, to be burdened with the family fishing business and not able to go to college.

Ryan checked his watch. "Dad, I have a date about now. I am giving Paula a tour of the Vatican this afternoon after we have lunch. If you are free a few minutes, I'd like to have you meet her again now that things are quiet."

"Of course, Ryan. I'll be here and free all afternoon and evening."

"I can arrange a lovely luncheon for you at Ponentino Restaurant in Trastevere," Cippolini offered. "And international singer Antonio Furnari is giving a special outdoor concert there this afternoon. He is a friend of Ambassador Kirby and has a great voice."

"I appreciate that, Monsignor. Sounds like fun. You think of everything. If you ever want to become a fisherman I can help you get a job," said Ryan. "It's probably the best route to becoming pope."

Al glanced at Bill to gauge his reaction to Ryan's joke.

·‡· ·‡· ·‡·

With all this activity, Church and family, Bill's head was swimming. Christmas was busy for any pope, but for the first pontiff in several centuries with a family it was proving doubly so. Bill jammed in a briefing meeting with Monsignor Cippolini and Cardinal Bellotti to get an evaluation of how things were going with his Vatican affairs so far. He also wanted feedback on his first papal audience earlier that week.

Overall both Cippolini and Bellotti thought it had gone very well. They replayed the tape recordings that had been made and carefully critiqued them, especially the questions that were asked from the audience, and reached a conclusion for which Bellotti was quick to refer to Scripture for confirmation.

"Something you Americans do too frequently is talk a long time and never directly answer a question. What you say may sound nice, but!"

The pope's eyes narrowed. "I was never one to obfuscate—dodge the truth that is, *Eminenza*. I am not a politician."

"Perhaps," Bellotti replied. But I suggest—" He paused and gave the pope a meaningful look. "Let your answer be 'yes, yes' or 'no, no.' Anything else can be from the evil one. I think that is what you do without realizing it. You seldom hide anything, nor deny anything. I suspect if you make a real effort to say what you feel, not minding if your weaknesses show, you may be better able to win the audience. That, of course, can also present some other problems."

The pope looked quizzically at his cardinal. "What other problems?"

The cardinal smiled, drawing his index finger across his throat. "I must be off now. Enjoy the holidays."

Cippolini and the pope looked after the cardinal as he was leaving, then at each other. "I keep feeling like Robitelli has put an adder in my fruit basket," the pope murmured to himself. "The cardinal is good at helping me with Mass and homilies, and of course his beloved Scripture, but I do not feel he totally has my best interests at heart. I wonder if he'll ever get over the conclave and how I was elected by his sacred college of cardinals."

The children made the most of their holidays together, flying to Sicily with Bill. With great exuberence the Kellys followed Cippolini's Sicilian detailed planning for two and a half days. Then Ryan, Paula, Colleen, and Jan continued on to Venice and Florence before coming back to Rome on December 30 and spending New Year's Eve in the Eternal City, a perfect place to ring in the third millennium. The constant monitoring by the Swiss Guard and Italian carabinieri put a damper on Ryan and Paula. They were together all the time, but it was a problem for them to find the privacy they sought during their whirlwind tour. Nevertheless they enjoyed every moment of each other's company.

After flying into Aeroporto Marco Polo from Sicily, the four went immediately to Hotel Minerva on Venice's Grand Canal. The view with all the boat traffic was memorable and romantic. They sat out on their balcony and drank Campari and soda water before going on a tour of Venice, which didn't get them back in their hotel until after two A.M. By this time they were all exhausted and ready for bed.

The next evening they dined at an outdoor restaurant in San Marco Square and were serenaded by a five-piece band. After dinner it was the Rialto, famous for its markets and for shopping.

Nobody recognized them in Venice. By the time they arrived at Harry's Bar for late-night drinks, the line circled around the corner. Jan showed the maître d' his identification and told him who was with him. The owner came to the door and said it was an honor to have them. He gave them a table in the private dining room, where several movie stars had just come from the International Film Festival. They had late-night drinks and were introduced to Robert De Niro and Sharon Stone, who assured them that, as Americans, they were proud of the job their father was doing. They couldn't order a second drink because they were too exhausted, so they decided to retire for the evening and walked back to the hotel.

It was a wonderful day in one of the world's most fascinating cities. They promised each other that one day they would return. The word "honeymoon" escaped their lips. The next day, after visiting the ninth-century Basilica of San Marco, marveling at the breathtaking view of Venice from the top of the tower, the two couples took separate romantic two-hour gondola rides up and down the Grand Canal. Ryan and Paula enjoyed the complete privacy together, spending more time looking at each other, leaning back, and holding one another, enjoying the romantic setting. Finally, reluctantly, they stepped out of the gondola onto the quay. Even when Ryan was told by the boat's skipper that it cost L240,000 for the ride, he murmured jokingly, "That's about how much Dad pays me a week out at sea."

Late that afternoon, they drove by rented van to Florence. It was six o'clock when they checked in at Hotel La Scaletta, near Ponte Vecchio with its unique rooftop view of the town. Leaving their hotel, they went on a shopping tour of the historic market. Paula bought a leather coat for Ryan and leather bags for her mother at the open market near San Lorenzo. That evening they dined at the outdoor restaurant Acqua al Due and ordered the *assaggio* dinner. They listened to Italian music accompanied by a magnificent female vocalist from the conservatory. They walked away the evening through the winding streets, seeing many American students and tourists and stopping to talk with them. Then there was Gelateria Trianogolo delle Bermuda, famous for its gelato banana, and a street artist drew a sketch of the four of them together.

Next morning, bright and early, they went to the Uffizi Museum, one of the most beautiful art museums in the world. Then they left Florence and drove to Rome, arriving around five P.M.

At the apostolic apartments Colleen plaintively told her sister that they were surfeited with Italian food. "Do you think we could have cheeseburgers, fries, and onion rings? Like we did every Saturday night back home?" Meghan understood as her mouth watered.

Bill, Paula, Ryan, Colleen, Jan, Roger, and Meghan had a lot to talk about that night at dinner, many funny stories—like Ryan getting his pocket picked, and not realizing it until he saw Jan chasing a young boy who dropped Ryan's wallet on the ground, still containing all his credit cards and money. Paula told the Kellys how at first a certain shop owner wanted L150,000 lire for Ryan's leather coat and when Paula said, "No, too much," and started walking away, the shop owner chased after her and said, "OK, one hundred thousand."

Jan recalled how he had asked the pope if he could invite his daughter for a date. He said, "I don't know how I got the courage to ask you, sir, but I'm surely glad I did."

"So am I," Colleen seconded.

At ten P.M. New Year's Eve the foursome said good night, making their way into the city's crowds to experience Rome's way of introducing the year 2001 A.D. Meghan, like most busybodies, expressed concern that they be good and take it easy on the vino. After they'd gone, Bill reassured her that not only would two Swiss guards in civilian clothes follow them at a respectful distance, but Jan was also carrying his handgun. And so they walked throughout the centrum, enjoying the life and splendor of this special night of celebration. Making their way to Piazza del Popolo, they were startled by the traditional throwing of plates and fireworks at people's feet while they walked down the street. The four had never experienced the likes of it and couldn't remember seeing anything akin to it in America or Switzerland.

Later they hooked up with Maureen Kirby and some of her friends at the Night & Day disco. When they got to the door, Colleen told the doorman, "I have a friend holding seats and a table for us." The next thing they knew they were jam-packed together at a table.

Colleen asked Maureen how she had gotten these seats right up front and Maureen said, "Lire talks in Roma."

Jan chimed in, "Like my Swiss guard badge." They danced and welcomed in the New Year in typical Italian style, a Millennium Eve never to be forgotten.

They left the disco while the city was still jumping and couldn't flag a taxi. It was just as well, for they had a chance to walk and share the events of the evening a little longer, until they finally stopped a cab. Cold and exhausted, they nonetheless had a wonderful evening. They dropped Paula off at her college hostel, where Ryan and she kissed a passionate good night and resolved that this was only the beginning. Then the cab drove on to the Vatican.

Pope Peter was prepared to celebrate a solemn High Mass in St. Peter's at ten-thirty New Year's morning. He toasted in the New Year with an Irish Mist after two hours of playing Monopoly with Roger and Meghan, and then they went to bed. Bill slept soundly, not moving; even the riotous sound of fireworks at the nearby Piazza del Popolo failed to wake him. In the Vatican, Bill had learned, you rose early, you worked late, and you slept soundly, not unlike his routine as a fisherman on Cape Cod.

The annual New Year's Day homily was behind him, and Bill Kelly settled down to focusing on the administrative details of the Church at home and worldwide. Despite the popularity and effectiveness of the previous pope, John Paul II, administration had not been his strong point. He was a "big picture" man, not a Jimmy Carter–type leader who, it was said, even tried to micromanage disputes within the White House down to who might use the tennis courts during this or that lunch break.

A trip to Africa, at the urging of Cardinal Motupu, was now anticipated. Cardinal Robitelli was hard at work with Bill on Church matters like papal nuncio assignments to various countries, the Vatican Bank and its investments, or the many religious, political, and constituency groups requesting to meet the new pope since his election. And there was the matter of his first encyclical to be written and released.

Then a day to which Pope Peter had looked forward arrived. A bright smile creased his weathered face as he reached into a desk drawer and took out the folder labeled PRIVATE NOTES. Withdrawing its contents, he reached for his phone and summoned Cardinal Robitelli for a hurried discussion.

Robitelli arrived quickly. "Gino," he was greeted, "today I am scheduled to meet with the World Council of Rabbis, it says here. Do you have any idea how many? What is their agenda?"

The cardinal frowned, not sure of the number. "Head Rabbi Koburn from Jerusalem called me last week. It seems he needed to contact some rabbis from countries across the world. Laughingly, he also stated that like everyone else, they were startled by our election of a layman and wanted to wait to see what would be going on here. We estimate about sixty to seventy of them will be present."

"I talked to Ed Kirby yesterday," the pope said. "He's close to the leadership of the American Jewish community due to his helping the president develop diplomatic relations between Israel and the Vatican under you and John Paul II. He thinks the Jewish leaders are bound to raise the Holocaust apology issue."

"No doubt," replied Robitelli. "Even though this is a get-acquainted meeting, expect a serious discussion on several controversial issues. And you can be sure they will bring up the ten thousand hidden Jews," he added. "Children who were saved from Hitler by adoption into Catholic families and then baptized."

The cardinal sighed deeply. "A Mr. Gabe Wolfson of the Jewish Anti-Defamation League in New York, a friend of Kirby's, was urging us—especially Church officials in eastern Europe—to turn over baptismal records to international Jewish agencies, for determining every child's religious lineage. Those records are not kept here, they were in the churches where the children were baptized. Most were destroyed during the war. In fact many records were not kept to protect the children from the Nazis."

"I suppose that when Secretary of State Madeleine Albright discovered she was Jewish, not Catholic, it revived the issue," the pope said. "Although John Paul II's visit to Israel healed some wounds, many apparently still remain."

"I have arranged for Father Remi, who is our secretary for the Religious Relations Commission with Jews, to drop in this morning and brief you and answer any questions that you may have."

"Thank you, Gino." He held up his folder of notes. "I'll be ready."

"The meeting itself will be in the Vatican Picture Gallery, a beautiful and quite historic setting. The group has asked for a private tour of the museums and the Sistine Chapel, and a group photo with you in front of a famous painting by Pinturicchio and Perugino called *Moses Journeying to Egypt*."

The pope scribbled notes of his conversation with Robitelli. "Gino, have a papal chair placed at the head of that large Italian marble table. We can all sit around it and be comfortable. Find out what rabbis like and have some of our special wine there and light snacks, OK? And make sure it's kosher." Although the requests were unusual for a papal audience, the cardinal recognized what the pope was thinking and rose to attend to the details.

"Deference to the roots of Jesse...I must admit, that is a nice touch, Bill."

"Thanks, Gino. And oh, would you ask Sister Miriam to attend as well? Her family background—you know, coming from Brooklyn—and her education and religious training would make her prepared and qualified to be there. I may also have to dictate things if they make any requests. Be prepared for anything, eh?"

At twelve noon the gathering of eighty-three Jewish rabbis, scholars, and a few other representatives from Jewish groups from throughout the world were seated around the marble table in the magnificent Vatican Picture Gallery. They noticed that a painting of a German-born Jew, Edith Stein, killed by the Nazis at the Auschwitz concentration camp, was hanging there. Stein, the first Jewish-born canonized saint, had converted to Catholicism and had been a Carmelite nun.

Bottles of kosher wine, mineral water, juice, and crackers and cheese were in ample supply. At the far end on a slightly raised platform sat a gilded, cushioned papal chair that elicited negative comments from among the rabbis, bothered by the noticeable sign of authority. "What to expect from this new pope?"

A door at the front of the room opened and the pope entered in his simple white cassock and skullcap, accompanied by a tall thin nun but no other aides. The rabbis rose to show their respect. The pope stopped just short of the main chair and raised his hands.

"Shalom aleichem and good Shabbat. Dear brothers, I am honored to have you at the Vatican." He ventured further welcoming comments in Hebrew or Yiddish. Then, "May I ask which of you is Rabbi Koburn?"

An elderly and bearded rabbi near the front of the room raised his hand. The pope walked over and grasped it. "I'm happy to meet you, Rabbi." He turned to the group. "Please be seated and feel at home." Then, still holding the hand of the rabbi, "Now, Rabbi, ever since I knew I would be meeting you, I've had one burning desire. Would you do me a favor?"

The rabbi seemed nonplussed at being singled out, but fumbled a reply. "Why, yes, if I can. What may I do for you, Your Holiness?"

The pope turned and pointed to the gilded chair. "It would delight me to no end if you would sit in that big chair there with the papal seal. As you well know, it has been centuries since we had a Jewish pope. I'd love to have for my desk a picture of you in that papal chair."

Tension was lifted in a flash. Laughter rang out, nervous yet relieved, along with the clapping of hands. Rabbi Koburn, blushing, met the challenge. He walked up and seated himself, looked down from the dais, and waved a papal blessing as Sister Miriam snapped photos with a small camera. The rabbi stood up and returned to his seat. Kelly settled down in a chair directly across from Koburn in the middle of the group. No visible sign of superiority or subservience was to be evident at this historic meeting. Full attention was focused on Bill Kelly as he pushed himself out of his chair and stood behind it to be better seen. He made an effort to maintain eye contact with each of his visitors.

"Thank you for coming here." Bill paused for effect. "I hope to put you more at ease by first saying that the wine and food are kosher and are prepared to be taken. Feel free to indulge while we talk. I'll have some myself. I see we have no formal agenda per se, except we were all asked to comment generally on Jewish-Catholic relations. I was given a great deal of information, too much perhaps, before your coming. Some members of our college of cardinals offered me suggestions about what I might say, others on what I ought not to say." More laughter, greater relaxation.

"I thanked them for their concern, but after much thought, and prayer, I decided that I must do this my own way and explain my feelings to you about what we Christians would call the 'Jewish question.' Has the Church done enough through the years? During the war years? That's the debate that has driven us to a position of division and mistrust. I know my predecessor tried to begin the healing with his historic visit to Israel shortly before his death."

After a moment of silence he met the stares, some curious, some on the verge of hostility. Pope Peter continued. "I want to close those wounds, once and for all. Not by finger-pointing or accusations, but through mutual understanding. If I may, I would like to back up a bit and refer to the New Testament, specifically the Acts of the Apostles, chapter five, verse thirty-four, which I'm sure most of you know. Then it was hardly the 'Jewish question' but rather the 'Christian question.' You recall it says, 'A Pharisee named Gamaliel, a teacher of the law, who was honored by all the people, stood up at the Sanhedrin and ordered the Apostles to be put outside while he addressed the assembly.'"

The pope fixed one after another of the rabbis with his bright blue eyes. "Now, may I say that the next part of this speech has both bothered and delighted me ever since I was a young man studying for the priesthood at my seminary. Here we have this famous honored man reminding his brothers that if the Christian movement were merely human it would die out, but if from God, it could not. Thus we Christians through the centuries have boasted that since the Church has not died out, it must therefore—*eo ipso,* ipso facto, and ergo—be divine."

Once again the pope looked from one rabbi to the next before continuing. "The sad point I wish to make to you is that the story pointed out also the sincerity of those gathered with Gamaliel, for they agreed with him. How then did it happen that this persecution of Jews by Christians burgeoned for two millennia? I was appalled at this history. Edward Cardinal Casey of New Zealand, who has worked with religious and political leaders throughout the world, gave me a thorough review of the issue. The slaughter of Jews in western Europe during the first three of our Crusades. The extermination of Jews in Palestine. Jews expelled from England in

1290. Three hundred Jewish communities destroyed under the Holy Roman Empire in 1349. Jews expelled from France in 1494, Spain in 1492, and Portugal in 1497. I know you are painfully aware of these things and that they comprise but a small part of your Diaspora history. I state these few to let you know I am aware of them. Dear God, when will it ever end?

"Several cardinals have asked that I try to do what I can to help heal this original breach between Christians and Jews. I know that to ask the Jewish people to accept Jesus as the Messiah, however, would be as difficult as your asking me to give up my faith in Jesus as the Christ. We Christians, again as you know, have endured centuries-long struggles trying to come to some agreement amongst ourselves! But I would say, in that regard, there is a major difference in the several factions. I mentioned this to my cardinal secretary of state and he concurred. I said that other Christian communities, were they a part of the Roman Church, would then swell our number. But this cannot be said of Jews. If Jews recognized Jesus as the Messiah, as a few of you do, they would not be by extension Roman Catholics."

The audience gasped audibly at this near insult, but Pope Peter continued. "The Vatican, sacred as it is, would cease to be. Jerusalem would once more become the focus of Christianity. You cannot have a branch supporting the tree."

Pope Peter glanced about at the intent faces staring at him. "Jews, as St. Paul said, are 'the root of Jesse.' We are but the wild olive branch that has been engrafted. And I think it would take an enormous dispensation of grace from our own Jews—Jesus of Nazareth in particular—to cover that change. So perhaps we can begin to make our way, by common effort, first to study and then to measure the way to bring the Old and New Testaments together."

Again, after making eye contact at several points about the room, Pope Peter continued. "May I suggest first a Jewish chair of study in our Vatican Library, held by scholars of your choice, with complete access to our ancient and modern records. Also, a Christian chair of study at your Hebrew University or at a comparable venue, for Catholic scholars in Israel. Thus, when both Jews and Catholics make statements, they will be more and more the product of collaboration and love, and not political posturing."

There was a long and deliberate pause as the pope reached for a glass of water and some of the rabbis, for the first time, partook of the kosher wine before them.

"I do not make this request as an offer to appease the Jewish people. Let the chips fall where they may! I request it from a sincere Church burdened by guilt after centuries of persecution. And my own feeling goes beyond mere apologizing. In conclusion, just as the New Testament records Jesus as saying, 'Saul, Saul, why are you persecuting me?' he meant also, 'Rome, Rome, Christians, Christians, why are you persecuting my people?' "

The pope's voice had quivered as he spoke, touching the amazed and confused, not to say acutely embarrassed, gathering. Those who had begun to drink wine lowered their glasses, listening to this Roman pontiff, the successor of St. Peter, and an American at that, apologizing and admitting to something that had been buried in the minds of all of them. Rabbi Koburn rose from his seat, walked around the table, and warmly and with sincere emotion embraced the deeply moved pope. Light applause rose from the still-skeptical gathering as he returned to his seat.

A second rabbi stood in his place to face the pontiff. "I'm told you prefer to be called 'Pope Peter' rather than 'Your Holiness,' or, if people wish to be friendly, you even prefer 'Bill.' Well, Bill, I am Victor Weiss. I would like to here and now, in this great Vatican Gallery, volunteer as a contender for that chair of study that you have offered us."

The pontiff had regained his composure, vigorously wiped his eyes, and turned to Sister Miriam, seated nervously on the edge of her chair. "Sister Miriam, please note that Rabbi Victor Weiss has been named for consideration to the new office of Jewish chair at the Vatican and, if elected by his peers, will begin work as soon as he is available to us. We, in turn, will submit names to Rabbi Koburn. And since we are on the subject of names, record this, Sister. This gallery, being the place where important papal meetings have been held for centuries, I suggest will signify that all of us are sons of Abraham, and it is fitting that this hall should officially be known henceforth as the Gallery of Abraham."

Those gathered were collectively agape at this incredible announcement, but most were deeply touched by the historic gesture. Symbolism maybe, but meaningful, without doubt.

The pope turned his attention back to the rabbis, most of whom were moved, some of whom were still doubtful. A hand was raised at the far end of the table. The pope motioned in recognition.

"Bill, I'm Joshua Horvitz, Israeli ambassador to Washington. Although I am pleased to see you trying to bring the religious differences between our great histories together, I, a layman, have to face more practical issues that are important to my government. I am wondering if you might have some insights as to how our governments and religious faiths might handle issues like the West Bank, the Arabs, and the Palestinians. Those are my burdens daily and my country's major problems."

The pope noticed the rabbis were looking straight at the ambassador as though he had tried to change the subject or was putting the pope on the spot. Bill indicated it was all right, smiling and directing his attention back to the ambassador. "Joshua, your question is like asking me to explain God in five sentences or less. The legislative scene has always been hard for me to follow. I am not a bureaucrat. For now, though, I know the American ambassador to the Holy See, Edward Kirby, believes that John Paul II's historic visit to the Holy Land has generated so much positive publicity for all sides. With that, peace in the Middle East must be seized upon. But if you don't mind listening to the ravings of a crazy fisherman, when this meeting has concluded I invite you and anyone else interested to come up to my library and have a short political discussion."

The ambassador bowed his head slightly. "It will be an honor, Bill." The limited invitation brought a round of appreciative applause from the rest of the group and reestablished the earlier calm. The remaining hour was spent in small talk, wine imbibing, and the shaking of hands (and heads) as the members came forward to greet this strangest of popes. At one-thirty the chief rabbi of Rome, Elio Toaff, thanked the pope on behalf of the audience. The rabbi reminded the pope that the group was looking forward to seeing him at the synagogue located in the Jewish quarter, known as "the Ghetto," for prayer and reflection preceding dinner. It would be only the second time in history that a pontiff had set foot inside the most historic Roman synagogue.

The ambassador and a few other rabbis followed the pope and Monsignor Cippolini back to the private papal library next to the apartment. Once they were seated on the sofa and chairs in the library alcove and a bottle of wine had been opened and placed with glasses on the table, Pope Peter opened the discussion.

"Joshua, I would like to relate your concerns to some of my thoughts on Judaism over the years. Naturally my ideas are biased by the New Testament, particularly the writings of St. Paul."

The Israeli ambassador smiled and gestured at the pope, encouraging him to hold forth. "Bill, I will probably understand what you say, since I have read St. Paul—Rabbi Saul, we call him—with some interest myself."

The pope smiled but shook his head. "No, Joshua, I don't think you know what I will say. I'm not a biblical scholar. My thoughts on St. Paul are my own. But I believe they are true. I am absolutely sure, for a start, that the Jewish race was chosen by God as his special instrument in his plan for the world. You are the chosen people. We Gentiles, let me use the word, are part of God's universal salvation, but only through the chosen people. What bothers me so much, in all due respect, is that you are missing your calling. Struggling so hard to form a Promised Land, you have lowered your calling to the level of the rest of us. Arabs, Germans, Americans...no matter who you pick. Looking for a special piece of Near Eastern real estate, you are less different, indeed no longer different. Trying to reclaim a special place, you have lost the concept of that 'special people.' The Promised Land is in God himself. We all hope to be part of that. If you feel a need for a place of your own, why not just join with the other eastern groups and call the whole area not Zion but, in a common federation, the Promised Land, like the United States of America? People could then come and go inside any area they please. Boundaries only have meaning in relation to history and to the elections of local politicians. In pushing that idea you would truly be chosen...chosen to bring peace to lands that have not experienced genuine peace for thousands of years.

"Perhaps the ideal path, in my mind, that is, would be to build all those extra houses in the West Bank, every other house occupied by separate nationalities—one Jew, one Palestinian, and so forth. Build synagogues and mosques side by side, as in Jerusalem." Bill grinned slyly. "Throw in a Christian Church for good measure. Nothing like a good bingo game on a quiet Monday night."

Joshua and the rabbis who had accompanied him smiled, as if in pain, however. One guffawed outright.

"And lastly, only one police force, composed of equal numbers of Jews and Palestinians, or, if that proved impossible, ask the United Nations to send in a security force temporarily. They would be the only ones legally permitted to bear arms until things settled down. Well, there you have it, Joshua. What about those apples?"

Although there was no sign of outright anger in the faces before him, there was little indication of agreement either. The ambassador took a sip of his wine and rubbed his chin as he cleared his throat. "Well, now, Bill, I can agree with at least one of your pronouncements: The ideas are all a bit odd." Laughter rose from the small gathering.

The Israeli statesman continued. "I confess that I never pictured our concept of being 'chosen' quite your way. I also can see that if, by some miracle, we were the first nation in the world to lay down our arms and trust in God, it might exert an astonishing effect for a short time. Witness Gandhi in India. I also realize your own history would suggest that placing your trust and interests in others would not be in the best interests of Americans. By the same token, when we have left our fate to others to decide, it has often not been in the Jewish people's best interests. But I promise you this at least, Bill. I will sincerely convey what you have said to our leaders in Israel. Who knows…perhaps after they have recovered from the shock, there might be a microscopic seed planted for future action. It won't come close to anything you envision. But perhaps they could use an idea to make a new beginning for the never-ending peace talks."

"I quite understand your concern." The pope smiled. "Yet I think with the world news constantly before our eyes for all to see, your desire to disarm and bring in a NATO- or UN-type peacekeeping group would force your adversaries to give honest answers when you suggest they could also disarm." On that thoughtful note the meeting ended.

Several hours later, thousands of curious spectators who wanted to witness the historic event lined up beside the Tiber River and along the streets inside the Ghetto. The setting and pageantry were incredible as Jewish leaders throughout the world pulled up in their automobiles into an area that not too long ago had been the brutal and inhumane scene of Fascist and Nazi oppression. They heard the beautiful music of London's Royal Philharmonic Orchestra conducted by the talented Gilbert Levine. The flags of all the nations hung from the utility poles. Street musicians played Jewish festival music with an occasional "Santa Lucia" thrown in.

The pope, in his brief comments, once again condemned anti-Semitism and reminded all present that on the morning of October 16, 1943, Nazi SS officers had stormed these very streets and arrested more than twelve hundred people. They were taken to jails in Rome and a few days later sent by train to Auschwitz in Poland. Many suffered a cruel death at the hands of the Nazis. He reminded everyone of Winston Churchill's words that the Holocaust was "probably the greatest and most terrible crime ever committed in the entire history of the world."

A young college exchange student, Ellen Parks of New York's St. John's University, was with her class listening and watching the ceremonies from behind the roped-off area. She was heard telling her friends that her grandfather was a "liberator" of the Jews from a Nazi concentration camp in Poland while serving in the U.S. Army. "Who knows?" she said. "Maybe some of those liberated were from this very place."

The headlines in leading Italian newspapers the next day read, "A Night Made in Heaven" with a large color photo of Pope Peter II and Rabbi Koburn with his wife, Rachel, toasting one another in the most visibly friendly way. The respected *Jewish Advocate* and the archdiocese newspaper *The Pilot,* both based in Boston, perhaps best captured the events of the day in Rome with unprecedented dual lead editorials titled, "No Empty Gesture—We Remember."

AFRICA 35

Now the real work was starting for Bill Kelly in his improbable but, as he was more than ever convinced, divinely inspired role as Peter II. Colleen, still consumed by interests incompatible with the Church her father now led, had nonetheless decided to stay on and would enroll at Loyola University. Ryan was safely back in Buzzards Bay tending to business there. Monsignor Shanahan and Cardinal Motupu had persuaded the pope that Africa represented the single biggest struggle the Catholic Church faced now that a temporary peace, at least, had been reached in the Balkans. Not only was the "Dark Continent" experiencing the possible extermination of its population from the AIDS virus, civil wars, and starvation, but also extreme Islamic fundamentalism was literally pronouncing a death sentence on its African nonconformists. Many of the warnings laid out by John Paul II in his *avviso* pertained directly to Africa.

Furthermore, the Eastern Orthodox Church, having legislatively banned Catholicism in Russia, was now attempting to undermine the Catholic faith in sub-Saharan Christian Africa. The patriarch in Moscow had long led frequent forays into Catholic African states.

Tim Shanahan read Pope Peter II the comments of Pope John Paul II, written in September 1995, two days after his plane had touched down in Africa. Standing before a mosaic designed by a murdered priest in Cameroon, wearing his new green and gold vestments, the pope asked his African clerics to strike back at their continent's corruption, hopelessness, and "unspeakable suffering."

He likened Africa to a man left beaten and near death, and said the Church must come urgently to its aid. "This very sad situation...also has internal causes such as tribalism, nepotism, racism, religious intolerance, and a thirst for power to the extreme by totalitarian local governments."

"That was more than six years ago," Tim pointed out. "Since then almost a million members of the Tutsi tribes in central Africa have been massacred, slashed to pieces with machetes, or, if lucky, merely shot to death by the armies of provincial despots. Cardinal Motupu will tell you of Catholic missionaries and African priests found murdered by those Africans who supported the leadership of the highly visible Russian

Orthodox bishop, Yussotov. He was known formerly as the Mad Monk of Odessa," Tim chuckled. "His acolytes preach a combination of Communist doctrine peppered generously with a perverted Christian myth that has swept through so many sub-Saharan states and led to those totalitarian dictators whose 'one man, one vote' slogan had become 'one man, one vote, one time.' This is particularly noticeable in Zimbabwe, where the dictator, Robert Mugabe, has held power for twenty-one years and shows no signs of relinquishing his grip on the once-prosperous state of Rhodesia." Shanahan's reading of the former pope's 1995 letter, coupled with Bill's reading of the *avviso,* illuminated the overwhelming chaos that would be in store for the world if this pope and his successors stood idly by.

✢ ✢ ✢

Moputu had arrived at the Vatican, and the pope was now well briefed on his reasons for being there. Cardinal Robitelli was strongly against Pope Peter's intention to make a visit to Africa as Moputu urged. The health and safety risks were a serious enough factor. The entire Vatican senior staff was convinced that the Turk who had tried to assassinate Pope John Paul II in 1981 had been hired by the Soviet KGB with the knowledge and concurrence of the Russian patriarch. The latter felt that the pope was the single greatest threat to his world at that time. There was no reason why this American pope, Peter II, wouldn't constitute an even greater threat to Russian hopes for renewed totalitarianism at home or throughout the world. As secretary of state, Robitelli was au courant with all formal discussions of "the African problem." "The Forgotten Continent," as Bill Kelly referred to the land so full of potential, constituted the most pressing dark cloud looming on the papal horizon.

Motupu begged Pope Peter to visit Africa and carry on where his predecessor had left off. He even lobbied the pope's inner circle about the importance of the trip. Bill's kitchen cabinet consisted of Cardinal Comiskey (when he could fly in from Ireland), Tim Shanahan, U.S. ambassador Ed Kirby, and Cardinal Motupu himself, burning up frequent-flyer miles between central Africa and Rome.

Motupu laid out the situation at his first meeting with the inner circle during this mid-January visit. True, African priests and bishops had asked John Paul II to encourage the Church to tolerate more African traditions such as ancestor worship and typical African ceremonial customs including tom-toms and dancing in Church. Many Catholic clerics with experience in Africa believed the Church should rethink its opposition to passing out birth control information to help curb AIDS.

But, Motupu stressed, Pope John Paul II had only promised to consider studying African rites like spirit worship, insisting that the Catholic Church must remain "universal" in its tenets. He had urged his clergy to give "all possible material, moral, and spiritual comfort" to AIDS suffers, yet never permitted condom use to prevent its spread in the first place.

Kirby laid out the unexpressed but fervent attitude of the United States toward further involvement in Africa, fingering Sudan, Libya, and Ethiopia, all terrorist-dominated countries. The ambassador had access to all CIA and State Department cables, but was beginning to worry that his enemies in Washington knew he was sharing delicate information with the pope on African internal politics. Still, Kirby believed it was in U.S. national security interests that Africa become stable.

The ambassador had been present when the Muslim leader who had greeted Pope John Paul II in Cameroon called for yearly meetings between the two faiths "to block the way of all fanatics." Pope John Paul II had responded by urging better ties with moderate Muslims who shared the conviction that it was unacceptable "to kill another person in the name of religion."

Tim Shanahan pointed out that it was the religious fanatics who had infiltrated this mainstream religion who were causing trouble and instability throughout the world. They were using the United States' and Britain's favorable relationship with Israel as a tool to whip up anger among Arabs and Muslims. The real threat to the world would come from countries that owned or were developing chemical, biological, and nuclear weapons. "We cannot allow the Islamic world to feel that they need to acquire weapons of mass destruction in order to protect themselves," Tim summed up. Pope Peter now understood better than his predecessor had those heartrending scenes seen less frequently on TV that once awakened pity for the fly-covered babies with distended bellies and twig-skinny arms and legs. Americans, he realized, believed that to send food and aid merely filled the coffers of the warlords. They appropriated the bounty and sold it for profit or used it as leverage for political purposes, ignoring their dying people.

Americans had short memories, but with the help of a best-selling account they would never forget the fate of U.S. troops sent in to guard the food in Somalia and ensure that it was distributed fairly. The bodies of brave U.S. Marines dragged through the streets by Somalian warlords and desecrated by armed hoodlums reverberated in American minds whenever it was suggested the United States give financial and military aid to Africa. And the AIDS epidemic in Africa, into the third millennium, frightened Americans when it came to allowing Africans to enter America. The recent revelation of a 50 percent drop in life expectancy in many parts of the continent added to this fear.

"In other words," Kirby counseled, "do not depend upon help from America."

Motupu deplored what he was hearing, but he was a realist and knew what the ambassador said was the bottom line of American sentiment.

Cardinal Comiskey reported that even Ireland, despite its very special relationship with Africa, was slowly becoming disillusioned with the deaths from disease and the brutal violence against courageous nuns and priests who were trying to help. The families of the dead Irish nuns in particular were outraged at the lack of protection for their loved ones.

Tim Shanahan was hard put to come up with a solution for Motupu to an unsolvable problem. Famine and overpopulation were an unending crisis in most parts of Africa. The White House, influential and well-connected feminists, and pro-choice groups were pressuring the UN to adopt a population control policy via abortion and sterilization, which the Church flatly opposed. They ran TV spots on prime time and threatened to cut off economic aid if these developing countries did not support U.S. policy. There was even considerable debate in the Church coming from nuns about birth control and condoms to prevent disease spreading among the educated African minority and thence downward to the masses.

Monsignor Shanahan took the group back a year, telling of a crucial meeting he had attended in this very library with Pope John Paul II.

"If the Church would allow condoms and birth control in Africa," a leading African bishop had declared to some of the pope's intimate advisers, "we could do something meaningful to slow down the spread of disease and overpopulation in our countries. We have brought millions to the Church by injecting tribal customs and music into the Mass, so we could save millions from this virus that threatens to kill us by half. We need only advocate using condoms to control it."

"For an official of the Church to express this sentiment was virtual heresy," Shanahan pointed out. "Not a sound was uttered. It seemed nobody wanted to be critical of him. Finally the pope had his enigmatic say, and I quote him precisely. 'We must feed people and create a safe environment. But we always choose life over death.' That basically ended the debate," Tim recounted. "The bishop politely nodded to his pope in obedience."

Tim shifted the emphasis. "So, let's go on to your other problems a moment, Your Holiness." Bill Kelly breathed a sigh of relief at not having to opine on this most delicate Vatican subject.

"*Our* other problems, I should say," Tim amended. "Those concerning the Eastern Orthodox Church and extreme Islamic fundamentalism."

"I'm listening, Tim," Bill Kelly said as his mind drifted to the *avviso*.

"The patriarch and his man in Africa, Bishop Yussotov, take a less moral view of the African problem. They want to do whatever is necessary to convert Africans to their church and away from ours. They are on the cutting edge of doing to the Church what they were doing until 1991 and the fall of Communism. Emulating their KGB agents, they will create armies of national liberationists and take countries over using terror tactics, covertly, in the name of Communism."

"And the Muslim fundamentalists?" the pope asked.

"In sections of Africa they will spread the Prophet's word through terrorism as much as the Communists did, cutting the throats of any who do not accept 'true belief.'"

"I think," the pope offered, "Gus here is suggesting a papal visit to Africa to observe these problems firsthand. Then return here and develop solutions. The Church is gravely threatened in Africa. We must take a definite stand if it is going to survive."

"That is correct, Your Holiness," Motupu confirmed. "If you can see it firsthand and then report what you see and know to be true, you may convince the world community to accept those fundamental changes, bringing us up to date on famine, poverty, and disease, especially among my kind."

Ed Kirby conveyed an unexpected request from the Russian ambassador to arrange an informal meeting between the Russian patriarch and the pope as quickly as possible. Alexis II would fly to Rome from Moscow and the pontiff would receive him.

"It seems bold of the Russians to try to meet with us after the Duma banned Catholicism from their country," Monsignor Cippolini commented.

"To say nothing of the Orthodox Church's refusal to join Pope John Paul II in his plea for peace in the Balkans," Bill added.

"They have profound designs on Africa," Motupu answered. "A

meeting would be useful. We're still way ahead of them, but with U.S. foreign policy turning isolationist, Orthodoxy and Islam are gaining new footholds around me in the continent. I think we must hear them out."

"If time permits," the cardinal added, "we'll have a look at southern Sudan, where Christian Africans are still starving in their never-ending civil war against the extremist fundamental Islamic Arabs to the north. The Sudanese Government bombed more civilian hospitals last week."

"Gus, I agree," Pope Peter II affirmed. "If I am to make this trip to Africa, I'd like to know what our opposition has in mind."

"Would it be wise for Tim to have a preliminary meeting with the patriarch and his 'Mad Monk'?" Motupu grinned at the phrase. "He could get some idea of what they want from us."

"You've met this latter-day Rasputin, Gus?" the pope asked.

"Yussotov? I met him twice during claims on territorial disputes. Quite frankly I have taken pains to keep Russians from proselytizing in traditional Catholic areas. Zimbabwe is a good example. We have always been the undisputed leaders in Mozambique and the former British colonies bordering it, the two Rhodesias, now Zambia and Zimbabwe. Robert Mugabe, dictator of Zimbabwe, was brought up and educated at Catholic missions. Even though Soviet Communists armed and trained his so-called 'Freedom Fighters,' terrorists are what they are. Then, with the help of African-Americans like Andrew Young, the British were persuaded to give Rhodesia to Mugabe. He then chose to ignore the Orthodox establishment. So we won that one over the patriarch. That was in 1979. Since then the Russians have given their Orthodox Church far greater freedom to proselytize the world. And with the fall of Communism, the Orthodox Church has been the main catalyst for Russian territorial expansion in parts of Africa."

Tim Shanahan listened patiently to Motupu and then, succinctly as always, presented his own estimate of the situation. "It is important for me to find out exactly what the Russians want. Remember what John Paul II warned in his letter!"

Moputu breathed deeply. "Just how the *avviso* affects Africa I am unsure. But Tim, by all means, see what the Russians want, what sort of compromises they want to make. They made none to us in Russia when they shut Catholicism down five or six years back."

"I'll tell the Russian ambassador that a preliminary conference between the pope's intermediary and his representative should be arranged at once," Kirby, the only politician present, suggested. "Then let's move up a notch and have Cardinal Motupu here meet the patriarch prior to any private audience between him and the pope."

"Excellent, Ed," the pope enthused. Then to Tim he went on, "I doubt that the patriarch has any fear of, or for that matter belief in, the thoughts given to us in the *avviso*. But Gus has convinced me that we should smoke out his intentions as soon as possible before we get ourselves into some kind of religious war."

"I'll talk to the ambassador this afternoon," Ed declared.

"Strange...they outlaw us in Russia, yet send a top man here as ambassador," Al Cippolini mused aloud.

"He was Yeltsin's press secretary, but wrote a laudatory biography about his boss and critical of other government officials, which upset the ex-Communist party leaders, so Yeltsin appointed him to the Vatican as ambassador." Kirby grinned. "He's a fun guy, but don't meet him in the morning. Instead of cappuccino, you'll get a water glass of Stolichnaya."

The others chuckled and Ed dryly went on. "Perhaps you are unaware of this, but the Vatican may be the world's best diplomatic listening post once you learn how to hear things. The Russians are also hard to beat at intelligence gathering, especially in spots like Africa. Of course, with Vladimir Putin as President of Russia, my friend may not be in his job here much longer. It will be interesting to see what Putin's attitude toward following the Orthodox Church back into Africa will be."

✠ ✠ ✠

Ed Kirby had set up the Russian connection by evening that same day. Pleased he had been able to organize the meeting between Tim Shanahan and Bishop Yussotov so promptly, and in Rome, not Moscow, the ambassador sensed that he was playing into the hands of the Russians. He had never fallen for détente and for the softening of the historically hostile relationship between the former USSR dictators who now would have cozied up to the West. "Stalin, Khrushchev, Brezhnev, even Gorby—I wouldn't trust any of them," Kirby said openly. "They are all a bunch of butchers."

Bishop Yussotov was flown into Rome the next day, and that night he and Tim Shanahan had their first private meeting. The Russian ambassador provided his ornate library for the meeting, complete with a large political wall map of Africa covering one end of the room from the floor to the ceiling. Both the Russian and American clerics were dressed similarly, in black suits with the white collar above black silk vests.

The Russian was tall and swarthy, with black hair hanging down to his shoulders and parted in the middle. Tim, with his neatly trimmed, graying, reddish-blond locks and slightly rotund figure, stood in contrast to the lean and taller bishop. Decanters of vodka and brandy stood on the table in the middle of the room, and two stuffed armchairs faced one another in front of the map. Before each chair was a small table with pads, pencils, and pens laid out, and a carafe of water.

Ed Kirby had taken his leave of this meeting, explaining that it was policy for an American official not to get involved in such discussions without State Department permission. The Russian ambassador made light conversation with the two clerics, each of whom had been given a biographical sketch of the other to read. Tim was armed already with basic knowledge about the bishop's background, lurid details of which had been collected by Motupu in Africa.

Bishop Yussotov and Tim bowed to each other like adversaries, and the former monk poured a glass of cold vodka for himself and offered Tim either vodka, scotch, or brandy. Tim chose water, citing Vatican policy, and the bishop disdainfully poured him a glass as the two ecclesiastical emissaries settled down to hopefully productive negotiations.

The bishop first asked about Cardinal Motupu. Would he be renewing their acquaintanceship during this visit to Rome? Tim assured the Russian that Motupu would attend all subsequent meetings.

Gesturing toward the large hanging map of Africa, the Orthodox bishop moved closer to it, his finger tracing the new Republic of the Congo, formerly Zaire and before that Belgian Congo. "This is very interesting country." Despite Yussotov's thick accent Tim had to score one for the bishop who, at least, could negotiate in English. Few Americans could negotiate in Russian.

Seeing the dialogue getting under way, the Russian ambassador excused himself, leaving the two clerics to work out their own agenda. The former monk of Odessa poured himself another drink, filled Tim's glass again with water, and they started talking in earnest.

•‡• •‡• •‡•

The following morning Tim Shanahan reported to Motupu and the pope in the pontiff's library. "Would you believe it? After our meeting, Yussotov went out to some disco clubs to meet Italian girls!"

"So much for the sanctity of our Orthodox bishop," Motupu growled. "What was the upshot?"

"The bishop and his patriarch want to divide up your continent between us on religious lines," Tim replied. "He wants the Republic of the Congo. He'll give us Nigeria and Angola and the rest is up to us to negotiate after we meet in Africa, and as soon as possible."

"Absurd," the pope choked. "This isn't some Treaty of Versailles or Malta conference where you divide up continents politically. We're contemplating the fate of the very souls of a continent's people."

"Correct, Your Holiness," Tim agreed fervently.

There was a long silence, since the outcome of the meeting to come was a foregone conclusion and only the pope could express it. "How soon can we make the necessary travel and security arrangements?" Pope Peter asked. Motupu was hard-pressed to keep from clapping his hands in glee.

Tim answered the question. "It all depends who handles this trip. You can call in Robitelli and he will assign the Jesuit, Father Roberto Tucci, head of Vatican Radio and overall director of papal visits. He is a wise and thorough man. It will take six months. Or you can allow us to find a new, more expedient way to do things."

"The latter, Tim. And so for Yussotov, let's expedite this visit. I have a feeling that time is of the essence. I can sense, particularly after talking with Ed Kirby, that the Russians have discovered some new way of subjugating land areas. Give their Church establishment maximum backing, including military when needed, and let them propagandize for hearts and souls."

Pope Peter let out a guffaw. "If you'll excuse a crudity that came out of the Vietnam War, let me quote an American politician. The Russians believe that 'if you have the people by the balls, their hearts and minds will surely follow.'"

✜ ✜ ✜

To nobody's surprise, Cardinal Robitelli had deep misgivings about the pope's trip to Africa. He was openly critical of Cardinal Motupu, who had met with the Russian bishop the day after the nighttime conference between Shanahan and Yussotov. They had agreed to a meeting between the pope and the patriarch in Africa. No agenda was set for the encounter. It would be informal, although it was understood that spheres of influence in Africa would be the main topic of discussion. The actual venue was to be decided later. The secretary of state probed the pope's intentions, trying to read what he had in mind, and the replies he heard did little to alleviate his concerns about the African situation.

"To tell you the truth, *Eminenza*," the pope chuckled, "I haven't a clue about what is really going on down there. And I can't mount my agenda if I know nothing about the place. But I can promise you that the Church will still be here long after you and I are dead and gone, the prophecy of Nostradamus not withstanding."

The trip to Africa, while hardly clandestine, was not a Vatican high-profile publicity extravaganza, only a mission by the leader of the Roman Catholic Church to study saving millions of souls for Christ and millions of lives as well.

It was important that the trip not be understood as a power struggle between Russian Orthodoxy and the Catholic Church, or for that matter between Patriarch Alexis and Pope Peter II. Equally the dispute must not drag the Russian government into a struggle which could then draw in the United Nations and the United States. Much was riding on this African summit, even though a new, modern pope ostensibly planned it as only another spiritual pilgrimage.

Even without the benefit of Father Tucci's usual painstaking preparations and guidance, the flight to the Dark Continent went off almost as if it were a planned spy mission. The pope had quietly left the Vatican dressed in a long black overcoat and cap. It was not a highly publicized visit, although in Angola, the first stop, it was heralded as a major event in African history. This event, of course, was at the behest of Cardinal Motupu, who would greet the pope upon his arrival.

Flying south from the Mediterranean coast over Algeria, Monsignor Tim Shanahan described to the pope the many reports of brutality and oppression directed at Catholics. A very serious threat was developing in that region of the world, and no pope or patriarch would go anywhere near there, or Sudan or Libya or some of the other fundamentalist countries, for that matter.

It took the pope's jet plane over an hour to cross the Sahara before they came to green jungle foliage below. "Now, here is where black Africa begins and stretches all the way down to Cape Town, South Africa."

In another hour they were flying over Nigeria. "We'll stop there on the way back. Motupu has contacted the bishop, and you'll visit the most active seminary in Africa. There is no shortage of priests and seminarians studying to become priests in this country. I would say that the patriarch would find it tough to proselytize there. Despite the round of rapacious military dictators that have run Nigeria and its large Islamic population in the south, the country has the largest share of properly ordained priests in Africa."

For the next two hours, as they flew south over Cameroon and the Republic of the Congo, Tim pointed out other items of interest below. "Down there used to be Belgian Congo, then Zaire, and now the Republic of the Congo. It is potentially Africa's richest nation. Minerals, diamonds, and oil. This is where the patriarch and Bishop Yussotov, with the full backing of Moscow, are launching their biggest efforts to win Russian Orthodox converts."

The pope stared down thoughtfully. "Looks like tough terrain for missionaries."

"It's even worse in many other parts of the country," Tim said. "But Cardinal Motupu, operating out of Angola, is doing his best to get the Congo natives into the fold."

Finally the jet began losing altitude as it approached Luanda, the capital of Angola.

"Gus Motupu told me to tell you not to be surprised at anything you may see when we land. He will be heading the reception committee. Extensive TV coverage will be carried out to the natives in the far reaches of this part of Africa. Many villages still have only one TV set for the entire population to watch. That's why we arranged to land here at dusk, so the people can get to their sets and see a clear picture in at least partial darkness."

The plane circled out over the Atlantic and came in for landing at the coastal capital city. "When the Communists engineered their revolution in Portugal, they turned over Angola to a native population which was ready to follow Communist leaders. The only vestige of capitalism left was the Catholic Church. If the atheist leaders in Moscow had backed the patriarch as staunchly up to the fall of Communism in 1991 as they do now, we would have a hard time surviving a new onslaught of Communism here. Today it is getting more difficult to hang on to the majority of Christians still here, to say nothing of creating new Roman Catholics."

After landing, the Alitalia charter plane taxied up to the huge crowd of people waiting to greet the pope and came to a stop with its boarding door facing the crowd. Tim Shanahan led the papal entourage from the rear entrance of the plane, followed by several Church dignitaries, including Cardinal Bellotti, whom Robitelli had insisted be included on the trip. They walked through the door of the plane into a restful twilight, which was immediately punctured by TV lights.

Pope Peter II appeared at the front door. The first thing he noticed, waiting at the foot of the steps below, was what appeared to be a native chief, carrying a long spear and dressed in native loincloth, a mantle of feathers around his shoulders and a Roman collar around his neck. As the strange figure approached the steps up to the plane's door, Bill Kelly, in a sudden shock wave of recognition, realized that the native apparition was none other than Augustine Cardinal Motupu. It was he who now walked up the steps to the doorway and greeted the pope.

"Your humble spear chucker welcomes you to Africa, Bill!"

The pope could not contain his tears of laughter as he slowly recovered from his surprise. They walked down the steps together to greet other religious and political figures and then strode across the tarmac.

Monsignor Cippolini and Cardinal Bellotti, with Tim Shanahan along-side them, followed the pope and Motupu into the glare of the camera lights.

"I'm sorry to startle you, Bill," Moputu chuckled. "But this scene on TV shown around this part of Africa will get the Church perhaps a hun-dred thousand new parishioners. Oh, the president will be furious, but he doesn't have to worry about losing his flock as I do." Several dignitaries in formal diplomatic attire approached the pope. "Go with them, Bill. By the time you've been introduced and made your speech I'll be in my Vat-ican gold and reds again and up there with you. But wait until you see what this little charade does for my Church attendance."

Monsignor Cippolini and Cardinal Bellotti stared in awe as they watched the pope and Motupu greet each other. The cardinal turned to the smirking monsignor. "Forget it, Cippolini. I'll die before I walk around in a jockstrap. Let's go see what else this nut has in store for us." Almost instantly he found out.

A large group of young women, perhaps two dozen, danced to a throbbing drumbeat of tom-toms, enthusiastically, suggestively gyrating as they bent supple bodies back and forth, waving horsehair pompoms at the Vatican entourage in a show of hospitality.

A mischievous grin split Cippolini's face. "Your Eminence, I think these young ladies are indeed planning to offer you a kind of hospitality we of the Vatican are not permitted to dream of. But, of course, it is part of our mission to effect some compromises between Rome and Africa."

"Your confessor will assign you ten Hail Marys and ten Our Fathers as penance for what you are thinking!" Bellotti growled, unamused.

The pope and his entourage were escorted onto a raised platform and introduced to the new president of Angola, a plump black man who rep-resented the masses now that Portugal had totally relinquished the colony. The pope accepted his welcome and delivered a speech in Portuguese, which was vigorously applauded. He told the people of his experience giv-ing religious instruction to Portuguese children as well as children from the Azores. Pope Peter seemed off to a great start. He even told one TV reporter that he was looking forward to eating some good Portuguese home cooking, *bacalhau cozido com grão e batata*, once again.

✠ ✠ ✠

So far everything that had been quickly though efficiently planned by Tim Shanahan was on schedule. The trip was far from the carefully laid-out expeditions entailing six months of research required by the meticulous Jesuit Roberto Tucci. There just hadn't been time.

Somewhere a few hundred miles to the north of where the pope's plane had landed, Russian Patriarch Alexis and Bishop Yussotov were consolidating the gains the Orthodox Church had made in the Republic of the Congo after the bloody revolt of 1998 when the Hutu and Tutsi massacred each other.

In the Sudan, famine perennially raged in the wake of battles between the Islamic fundamentalists in the north and the somewhat Christianized tribesmen in the south, the latter seeking autonomy if not independence from Islam. Already half the population had starved to death since troops from both sides stole all the people's food they could get at gunpoint.

And in Angola, Jonas Savimbi, the old antigovernment revolutionary, was still alive, lurking in the jungles to the south with an army of boys. These children stole food from their homes and families and were willing to die fighting the ruling government forces. At one time, Savimbi had been well regarded by the Church and the Western nations as a force against the Communists, mostly Cubans, who had taken over when Portugal relinquished control, but now he was nothing but another rebel trying to gain control.

◆❙◆ ◆❙◆ ◆❙◆

The journey from the airport in the convoy of cars organized by Motupu took two hours to reach its destination, paved roads turning to dust at the outskirts of the city. Cardinal Bellotti registered his dismay and shock as the convoy pulled up before a large, thatched, circular hut, very neatly kept, with a lawn surrounding it. Crowds of ragged natives singing and chattering away peered from a distance at the pope's party.

"These are local tribesmen, all good Catholics, who are swelling the population out here, away from the two warring factions fighting to control the country. Jonas Savimbi's UNITA party, out in the jungles, is constantly attempting to surge into the main cities, like the capital, Luanda, where you landed. For a time we had peace here after the Communists so suddenly fell in 1991."

Motupu led the way into the large, primitive structure. Even the dirt floor seemed to have been polished for the occasion. As they entered what seemed to be the reception room, the pope, trying to appear casual, found his curiosity getting the better of him. "Is this your usual residence, Gus? Or are you pulling my leg just a bit?"

Motupu was obviously enjoying the moment as he watched the pope's immediate entourage staring at these unusual surroundings with undisguised apprehension. Only Monsignor Shanahan seemed to understand and approve of this first African stop.

A wide grin cracked Motupu's face. "To tell the truth, I do have a rather large and nice residence in the city, Pope Bill. But after I was made a cardinal, and wore the only red hat in this part of Africa, I served three countries—Angola, the Congo Republic, and Namibia, which is mostly Protestant." Motupu winked. "So wherever I could spread God's word as taught to us by Jesus, I began to feel a bit guilty in my high estate. I started inviting a few poor street people in to share my evening meal. Then, somehow, they showed up for lunch, and finally for breakfast. The next thing I knew, there were those who had no place to sleep and I ended up with a dormitory. As my family increased, I made acolytes of them and sent them out to bring more into our Catholic fold. Meanwhile I was traveling constantly to see the three bishops I am allowed in Congo, Namibia, and here in Angola." He gave Bellotti a furtive glance. "And I was creating numerous lay ministers to take care of my growing flock. I had so many they took over my house and left me little room to work, live, and even sleep. My family seemed to increase until I found I had no place left to do any work without ten people looking over my shoulder."

Motupu smiled ruefully and shrugged. "So I decided to come back here. This was my rectory when I was a priest. I sent the new pastor to live in my comparatively sumptuous place in the capital and had my things sent back here where I feel comfortable. I do all my paperwork here and only go to the city for solemn occasions or for meetings with visiting bishops and priests."

"And do you appear at these meetings in the habit in which you greeted us?" Cardinal Bellotti asked.

"No, Your Eminence. That was for the cameras. It does wonders for my priests and deacons out in the villages to see their cardinal appear sometimes as one of them as well as in his grand Italianate robes."

Monsignor Cippolini looked around the spacious thatched building, a dubious expression on his face. Motupu chuckled. "I thought you would prefer the quiet surroundings out here where we are closer to the outlying parishes. I want you to visit some of them before we go on to the Republic of Congo and its restless neighboring states where the serious problems lie."

"As you know, we have over twenty people with us, Gus," Al said. "I thought we were all staying on a floor of the new hotel in Luanda."

"Oh a floor of the new hotel is reserved for all of you," Motupu assured the papal housekeeper. "I just wanted everyone to see the real Africa, where we have the bulk of our work to do."

"Good thinking, Gus," the pope complimented him. "I, for one, will stay out here with you and work the territory."

A worried look came over Tim Shanahan's wide, usually cheerful features. "Your Eminence," he addressed the African cardinal, "while we know that for the moment this area is safe, between power struggles for a time, at least, do you think it safe or even dignified for His Holiness to be 'camping out,' so to speak?"

"Ninety-nine percent of the African population would consider this luxurious beyond compare." Motupu swept the round structure with a gesture. "I am trying to give you a feel for what the Church faces on this continent."

"Gus, you're right," the pope agreed. Then to Shanahan and a shocked Bellotti he avowed, "I'll stay out here with our cardinal and start trying to comprehend the problems we have to contend with. I'm just sorry Ed Kirby isn't with us."

"The U.S. State Department would finally have managed to fire him if he had come along," Tim said. "The situation is so volatile here, with one dictator overturning the next and competition among the great powers so intense for a piece of the mineral wealth here that the U.S. does not want to officially support this expedition."

Several servants came into the reception hall bearing bowls of tiny, tender-looking morsels and wine. "Try some of these good things," Motupu said.

The pope approached a bowl on the table full of roasted delicacies and smelling somewhat nutty. He delicately pinched a few from the bowl and nibbled cautiously. Then with a grunt of pleasure he plunged a hand into the bowl and came up with his fingers full of the nutlike morsels and chewed on them. The others followed the pope's lead and as they munched were each handed glasses of wine by the crisply clothed servants.

"This is really a sophisticated household." Cippolini gratefully sipped his wine.

"You must all be hungry after seven hours in the air," Motupu said. "We shall have a meal after Mass for the people out there and then we can decide last-minute scheduling. There are a few changes and additions I would like to make to the final schedule Monsignor Shanahan sent me by satellite last night. And let me say at the outset that only to this unique pope whom we are fortunate enough to have on the throne of St. Peter would I even attempt to make such a presentation as I have planned for his Holiness Pope Peter II." Motupu lifted his glass. "For his Holiness Pope Peter II."

"We will be attentive, Gus," Al Cippolini assured their host.

"I hope Your Eminence has not veered too far from the schedule Father Tucci and I worked out with Secretary of State Robitelli," Cardinal Bellotti intoned. The black pupils of his eyes gleamed in the lean face, a peak of black hair protruding almost between his eyes. "Never in the recorded history of the papacy has so"—he paused, considering his words—"impetuous a foreign tour been embarked upon."

"As I said, Your Eminence," Motupu replied, "the uniqueness of this pope to recognize and help to overcome these vast problems is indeed heaven sent. 'God's joke' turned out to be 'God's call' for sure!" He gestured toward the table set for the meal. "Shall we sit down? Your Holiness, please sit at the head of the table. I'll sit at the foot and everyone else can take any seat they wish."

When all of Motupu's guests were seated and the wine poured, they continued to reach into the bowls before them and chew on the tasty morsels while they sipped wine, waiting for the first course.

Cardinal Bellotti, seated to Motupu's right, reached for the bowl and popped a few more morsels into his mouth, drinking from his wineglass. He looked at Monsignor Cippolini, who was swallowing a long draft from his glass. A servant immediately filled it. Bellotti gave Cippolini an avuncular smile. "You better have some of these nuts to fill your belly, Alonso, if you are going to drink more of this Portuguese wine."

The monsignor looked from Motupu to the pope, and then with a grin answered Bellotti's rebuke. "I would have some if they were nuts, Your Eminence, but they're not."

The cardinal's eyes shifted to Motupu from Cippolini, and then to the morsels he was holding. "What...what are they?"

Motupu was enjoying the whole scene. He reached for the bowl and popped a few more into his mouth. "Why, Your Eminence, I thought that I should put only the best for the pope's visit. These are our favorite... roasted red ants."

Cardinal Bellotti stared at his smiling host, looked down at his hand, and watched the tiny gems fall to the table. His thick torso shook noticeably.

The pope gazed at Cippolini with a hint of a grin and then back at Motupu. "I suspected I was eating an unknown entity when Al didn't avail himself. He usually cleans out my nut bowl every time he comes to my office. I just had to trust you weren't trying to poison me." He held one of the morsels between thumb and forefinger, examining it closely. "Wow, you grow them big down here. I'm afraid to ask what the main course is going to be."

"After our Mass we'll enjoy roast pork and yams. Very 'civilized' and fresh, I might add. I wanted chicken but my cook caught the pig on the way over yesterday. But now, before we start, I would like to take us out to the parish where we will say Mass for our people."

"Gus, we are quite close to the Republic of Congo border here, are we not?" the pope asked.

"That we are," Motupu replied. "I tend to several parishes and dioceses inside that border."

"What do you do when one of these rulers starts lethal disputes with his counterpart on the other side?" the pope asked. "It seems to happen regularly. I mean, here we are just a short distance from the Congo. For three years the rulers here in Angola and in the Congo, then across into Rwanda, Sudan, and Uganda, have been fighting each other. There's constant unrest between rival tribes and leaders. What is it they're fighting over?"

"It all comes down to something that is unfortunately endemic among Africans. I call it the 'Me da boss—no, me da boss' syndrome. Everyone wants to be da boss man."

"You said it, Gus," the pope said. "But it's hard not to agree."

"As a Catholic cleric first and anything else second, my job is to look after these people's souls and their physical well-being as much as possible. We have had four bosses in the past five years in the Congo as we find ourselves in the third millennium. Each one has raped her natural resources until another one comes along who wants his turn on Congo's nipple. In Rwanda and here in Angola the situation has been almost the same. Rival tribes want their share of the loot while they're washing their spears in each other's blood. Just imagine what we could do—food, water, jobs, housing, education, and health care. So much," Motupu mourned.

"Why are we here, Gus?" the pope asked. "What can we do?"

"I try to believe that if we could make them all Christians, Catholics, it would help," Motupu said. "That's why, Bill, I felt that it was important to have the pope himself make an appearance, to help my priests and lay teachers and me preserve the faith."

"We will do our best, Gus. Unify the Africans. Has it ever happened?"

Moputu sighed deeply. "The closest we came to keeping this continent stable was during colonial rule. No boss thought he could take over another's land without running into European might. White man's rule, even though it is black heresy to admit it, kept artificial famines, caused by rivalry between tribes or religions, from occurring. What keeps happening in Sudan, where the Arab Islamic north is in constant war with the south, never happened when the British were there. Colonialism kept small despots from torturing their enemies. And it went a long way toward abolishing the washing of the spears among the tribes. Islam versus infidel, hacking each other to death wholesale, is more prevalent in the past decade than in the recorded history of this continent."

"What good can we do now"—the pope's eyes swept his rustic surroundings—"now that we are actually in Africa?"

"Being seen by great crowds on TV helps a lot. And of course we haven't discussed the Russian patriarch's plans since we met in Rome."

"What is the latest on that front?" the pope asked.

"Right now the 'Mad Monk' is in Congo—oh, I shouldn't be so disrespectful—Bishop Yussotov, that is. He is trying to persuade the latest tinhorn dictator up there to make Orthodoxy the state religion. What the Russians were unable to accomplish using the old Communist terror tactics they are now attempting through religion. They take all the work we have done and pervert our teaching to suit the African temperament, far more obtrusively than we do it. Before you know it they will get the people, and thus the political leaders, on their side."

Motupu glanced around the table meaningfully. "Where are they making real strides in converting the populace? In the diamond- and oil-producing areas. The Russians have diamonds in great quantity, but they are not the gemstones that come from here. So it's a three-way battle for black African souls between Islam, our Church, and Russian Orthodoxy."

The pope stared down the table at his host. "Let me tell you what Ed Kirby said, just before we left, of what I might expect from this Kremlin crowd. Based on everything he's read and heard, Kirby believes that Pope John Paul II was shot by Mehmet Ali Agca, who was a paid killer employed by the KGB in Russia. Foggy Bottom called Ed on the carpet for reopening this closed case. He told them, and I quote him, 'A moron could see that this assassination attempt was a carefully orchestrated plot led by Yuri Andropov,' who was at that time directing the KGB."

After a pause the pope continued, "And my predecessor, John Paul II, was also convinced of this even though he never publicly said as much. The Vatican is no different than any other government. If we don't want the story out, we just ignore or deny it. Kirby told me the Vatican wanted to protect Pope John Paul II's reputation as a man of peace, and it didn't help his image for people to suspect that other religions and other countries were out there trying to assassinate him."

Motupu took a long sip of wine, and the others followed his example as he stood up and stepped out of his thatched rectory for a stroll through the area in which his diocese was located. "I just can't find doctors, nurses, engineers, or educators to assist these people," he said sadly. "In Africa, the patriarch allows Bishop Yussotov or any other Russian Orthodox representative to personally ordain any man into the Orthodox priesthood and send him out to gather in more parishioners. They also train men and women in health care."

As they picked their way through the heavy bush, a loud chatter of voices rose in volume, coming from somewhere beyond the jungle outgrowth. Suddenly Bill, Gus, and the others emerged upon a large clearing in the center of which was another circular, thatched-over area. Well over two hundred Africans, dressed in what had to be the best clothing they owned, had filled the benches and were standing patiently, waiting for some sort of momentous event.

"Our local Church, Your Holiness," Motupu explained. "I promised the parishioners that just after sunset they would see the Holy Father himself, who came all the way from Rome to say Mass for them."

"I'm glad you prepared me for this, Gus," the pope said dryly.

"I wasn't sure of two things, Bill," Gus replied. "One, whether or not we would get a turnout; it depends upon political problems which I will explain. Second, I wasn't sure that if I asked you ahead of time, you would be allowed by the planners in Rome to say Mass out here. I'm sure that Cardinal Robitelli or Farther Tucci, who disapproves the haste with which you agreed to this visit, would not have permitted an evening Mass in the jungle your first day in Africa."

The pope looked around at the expectant crowd, reverently hushed as he appeared before them. "Will the congregation understand my broken Portuguese, Gus?"

"Certainly."

"Now, let us get started! The others will need to get back to the comforts of the hotel before it gets too late for a safe trip."

"Thank you, Bill. The word will go out all over Africa that the Holy Father from Rome himself appeared before these parishioners."

The pope and Cardinal Motupu, along with a local priest, walked to the front of the Church and sat down beside the altar, two large candles burning behind them. The rest of the pope's entourage sat down off to the right of the altar. At a signal from Motupu a group of drummers began rhythmically pounding their tom-toms. The "people in the pews" swayed and chanted. The Catholic Mass, African style, was under way.

Bill looked out over the throng of black parishioners and was pleased to see so many young people there, men and boys particularly. Slowly the drums came to a stop and a foot pump organ swelled as the parishioners stood up and sang a familiar hymn in Portuguese. They sat down and Motupu addressed them in their native African tongue for some moments. He then turned to the pope, who greeted the people in fluent if accented Portuguese, his New Bedford fisherman's fluency refined for the occasion.

The hushed crowd was astonished to be addressed in a language they understood. As the pope commenced the Mass, two bright, ebony-faced altar boys served him, each wearing the proper white smock over his shirt and pants.

Suddenly, in the middle of the Mass, shouts were heard from outside the makeshift African Church. The pope saw fear etched on the faces of the altar boys and the young men in the benches and those standing at the rear. All gave beseeching looks to the cardinal, who, with a gesture of upraised arms, dismissed them. The young men and older boys ran helter-skelter from the service and silently disappeared into the jungle.

Looking after them, perplexed a few moments, the pope turned to Motupu. The cardinal shook his head sadly. "Your Holiness, I'm sorry. I never thought the president would allow this to happen while you were here, in the middle of Mass. But that's Africa," he sighed.

The pope noticed that the old men and women who had been standing now quickly filled the empty seats as though nothing out of the ordinary had occurred. "What has happened?" the pope asked.

"Please go on. I'll explain later."

Cippolini, Tim Shanahan, Cardinal Bellotti, and the other visitors from Rome watched in trepidation as Pope Peter pressed on. As he and Moputu were about to give Communion, the open thatched Church was surrounded suddenly by uniformed troops, although it was done as respectfully as possible. Officers and government officials watched quietly as the majority of the parishioners walked down the aisle to take Communion from the pope himself. Then the service was cordoned off. The faithful came up to hear the pope say "Corpus Christi" to each one as he held up the wafer. Not a single person at the Mass took the symbolic body of Christ in their hand, as had become standard procedure in Catholic Churches in America. Each opened his or her mouth and received the wafer from the pope's hand directly on the tongue. This was a moment that would go down in each family's history—receiving full Communion directly from the Holy Father himself.

When the last communicant had received the Body of Christ and returned to his bench, kneeling directly on the ground in front of his seat, Cardinal Motupu said the benediction and led the procession up the aisle, the Vatican visitors following. The soldiers and officers surrounding the congregation stood aside respectfully, bowing their heads as the pope and his entourage walked by.

Then the troops ordered the congregation to walk through them in a line, inspecting each man as he walked by, the other soldiers spreading out through the surrounding terrain, probing and searching. For what, the pope did not understand, until Motupu led them back to his thatched and rustic rectory.

"The government has suffered a defeat by the rebels to the southeast and is in need of fresh troops," the cardinal explained. "This never-ending rebellion has been waged by Jonas Savimbi's UNITA guerrillas for fifteen years. He says he will take over the government or die. Both sides need fresh fighters. Where we stand, the government is the culprit. The president, that evil fat man who met you after you landed today, knew you'd attract this crowd, and he sent this gang out to scoop up a bunch of youngsters to draft into his army."

"How did the boys know that the troops were on the way?" the pope asked.

"They have quite a spy network out on the roads. When they see government vehicles and buses coming this way, they beat their drums. Other drummers relay the signals. By the time the government gets here, the boys are long gone." Motupu chuckled mirthlessly. "I guess the draft gang thought you would keep the attention of the youngsters here until they could grab a dozen or so and take them back, teach them to shoot, put them in uniform."

Inside Motupu's residence an officer approached the assembly. First he bowed to the pope. "Your Holiness," he said in Portuguese, "I apologize if we in any way disrupted your saying of Mass. It happened we had a duty to perform."

Then to Motupu he said deferentially, "*Eminenza,* I know of course that there were many young men here earlier. It is my duty to find them and give them the singular opportunity of serving their government in our army. As you know, we need every able-bodied man we can find to fight for our great and still-free nation of Angola."

"I am a man of God, Colonel," Motupu replied. "At this auspicious moment in our country's history when the Holy Father deigns to visit us, would you insult him with matters of state? Have you any idea what it means to Angola, to Africa, for the pope to come to us here in this place?"

"Yes, yes, of course," the colonel mumbled. "But our president himself has given me orders to strengthen our army."

"Colonel, His Holiness has not eaten all day. Now that he has conducted Mass, he and his group from the Vatican deserve a quiet dinner before returning to their hotel in Luanda."

Motupu winked at the pope making Bill understand that the less people who knew he was staying out here, the better.

"Of course," the colonel agreed. "I and my men will wait until your meal is over and then provide the proper escort back to the capital. After dark, godless UNITA rebels strike anywhere. Even the pope is not safe in these times."

"Colonel, thank you," Pope Peter said in Portuguese. "We appreciate your consideration."

"It is a supreme honor, Your Holiness," the colonel replied. "We shall be at your service when you are ready to return."

True to his promise, Motupu's dinner of roast pig and yams was hearty and tasty, and the Portuguese red wine pronounced "excellent" by the meticulous Monsignor Cippolini. After dinner the group discussed the next day's schedule.

"This trip was never designed to be ceremonial," the pope remarked. "I want to see what I can firsthand. Do what we came here to do and get back to the Vatican, where I shall report to the world on my Internet site, and perhaps to the UN, on what I have seen and the actions I intend to take."

"Tomorrow we have arranged to fly to Kigali, the capital of Rwanda," Motupu announced. "The dominant tribe, the Tutsi, has control of the military and mercantile pursuits. But the rival Hutu tribe has reestablished itself as the dominant party of laborers. They are short and bulky; the Tutsis tend to be taller, more ascetic looking. They hate each other from centuries past, and although both are Catholic they have traditionally massacred each other. Only in this year of the third millennium have they stopped the gratuitous slaughter.

"Next," the cardinal said, "we will visit Uganda and, if time permits, have a look at southern Sudan, where Christian Africans are still starving in their never-ending civil war against the Islamic extremists to the north. Pope John Paul II himself told Kirby and the U.S. president that the situation in Sudan is the worst he has ever seen or experienced."

"Quite an eye-opening statement coming from a man who, when he was young, lived under Nazi oppression and then under Communism in his native Poland," Tim Shanahan observed.

Despite the untoward haste in planning and executing the trip to Africa, the Vatican had chartered the newest and fastest jet designed and built for the twenty-first century. Because of the size of the area to be covered in the few days allowed for the pope's African survey, speed was a necessity.

This latest-model supersonic jet took off from Luanda the next morning after the pope and Motupu arrived at the airport from the cardinal's "country estate." En route everyone was handed a bottle of water to carry. "Don't drink or eat anything on the ground," Cippolini cautioned them. "The water is polluted everywhere."

Less than two hours later they were landing at the airport in Kigali. They were met by a nondescript collection of vehicles and one five-year-old black sedan for the pope and Motupu to ride in with Cardinal Bellotti and Monsignor Shanahan. Each man carried a full water bottle, Monsignor Cippolini carrying his and the pope's.

"Now, Bill, you will see firsthand what we have been able to do around here despite the tribal strife and"—Motupu paused and smiled slyly—"the lack of sufficient funds."

The first stop was a wooden building that looked like a military barracks. The motorcade came to a halt and Motupu led the pope out of the car and into the structure. "Yes, it is our hospital, Bill, run by Concern, the international humanitarian organization out of Dublin. Brian Comiskey can tell you about it. This Irish Catholic group of dedicated people reaches out to the desperate people of Africa. The nursing nuns who work here are saints, as you will soon see."

A sister welcomed Motupu, kneeling before the pope and reaching for his hand to kiss the ring. "Your Holiness, it means everything to this mission to have you visit us."

"Sister Winnie O'Brien here is superintendent of our nursing staff, Your Holiness." Motupu reached for the nun's hand and helped her to her feet. "Tell me, Sister, how are our sick sisters doing?"

"Oh, poor dears. Sister Martha...we fear she may go the way of the others who served in Rakai."

Motupu turned to the pope. "That's Uganda, just north of us here, where we have another mission hospital. Remember Ed Kirby telling us about his visit here? Over seventy-five percent of the young people studying at our mission school have lost one or both parents to a virus. If it isn't HIV, then it's something we can't diagnose. But people are dying so fast from disease that in this part of Africa, at least, half the population will die in the next two years." Then, to Sister Winnie, "Is she able to see His Holiness?"

"Oh, bless you, Your Eminence. She can leave us, if she must, in happiness."

"How many people are being treated here?" the pope asked.

"About fifty to seventy-five any given day. As fast as they die, or in some few cases, walk out cured or in remission, others are waiting to take their place."

"Lead me through, Gus."

The nun opened a door into a long ward lined with cotlike beds on both sides of the room. Many types of sanitizing fluids and floor washers failed to override the stench of infectious disease. Men, women, and children lay passively in the beds, eyes shut or rolled back in their heads so only the whites showed between fluttering lids.

"What do most of them suffer from?" the pope asked.

"The HIV virus, which develops into full-blown AIDS, is the biggest killer in Africa today. Half our babies are born with it," Motupu replied somberly. "While there was still time to prevent what you are seeing a thousand times over, I begged everyone to let us distribute birth control information and give some counseling on prevention of disease and, frankly, bringing diseased children into the world. We believe in the dignity and respect of everyone and we are pro-life from conception to natural death, but what do we do for these people? You have to be part of this tragedy every day and see it all around you to realize that God wants us to help alleviate this scourge. But the real issue is that there is nowhere near enough food or medicine. What you see in here is the most desperately sick. For every patient here there are two more who should be, but there is no room until one dies and is replaced by the next one. Of course condoms are not the only solution, but rather clean water, food, and medicine."

"Do any ever get cured?" the pope asked.

"Sometimes. More likely they go into remission. Here in Rwanda things aren't as bad as elsewhere. Of course that is partly because of the massacres which have wiped out many of the disease-carrying tribesmen."

They reached the end of the ward and stood a minute looking back over the dying patients. The pope sighed. "How much of this disease is sexually transmitted?"

"Much of it is STD, although many people get sick through skin breaks, cuts, puncture wounds, work accidents," Sister Winnie replied. "And then there are other diseases with symptoms similar to those of the deadly Ebola fever and the Nile Virus. And just this month in Kenya over two hundred died from an unknown disease in flooded villages on the Somalia border."

In reflective silence the pope followed Motupu and the sister down the aisle between the beds of shriveled, desperately sick patients. Cardinal Bellotti and the rest of the Vatican group turned around and left the ward through the door they had entered. The pope, followed by a silent Tim Shanahan, walked through a second door into a much smaller, cleaner ward.

Sister Winnie turned to face them. "In here are our own people, white volunteers who became infected while treating patients in hospitals run by Concern." She led them to a partitioned-off bed. "This is Sister Martha. Let me see if she is awake." The pope and Motupu waited while Sister Winnie slipped into the space between the side of the bed and the screen. "Martha, the Holy Father himself is here to see you. All the way from the Vatican he's come to help us."

They heard a faint response, and then Sister Winnie slipped away from the bed and came around to the pope. "For the first time she smiled. Please, come see her."

Bill Kelly felt humble and inadequate as he followed the sister back into the partitioned space and saw the wizened little face and the sticks of arms as Sister Martha reached upward. The pope took her hands in his and felt the last resurgence of strength within the nun as she pulled his hand down to her lips and kissed the ring on his finger.

"We are praying for you, Sister Martha."

"Thank you, Holy Father," she said faintly. "And please pray for all who do so much, but especially for the African souls here. They don't have a chance. Without God, they have nothing. You must witness what's happening here."

"I will go out to Rakai myself and see."

A look of alarm crossed her face. "Be careful, Holy Father!" With that her eyes closed and she sank back into a comalike sleep.

The pope and his group visited several other sick nuns and volunteers and then gathered outside the hospital facility near another roughly constructed wooden building. "This is an office building of International Concern," Motupu explained when they had all seated themselves in wooden chairs, thirstily taking long gulps from their water bottles. "This is just a rear-echelon view of the battle we are fighting against disease out here. But making it more difficult is the constant conflict between rival tribal groups, most frequently Hutu or Tutsi. Still, we are the dominant religious organization helping to curb disease and tribal infighting."

"What is the patriarch doing to get the Russian Church into this struggle?" the pope asked.

"No medical efforts like Concern or Doctors without Borders or the Red Cross. They have credibility with tribal leaders because of military and business interests, but they are doing nothing to help salve the wounds from the ravages of AIDS and other diseases. In the Congo, Russian Orthodox priests act as middlemen between arms dealers and buyers and sellers of diamonds. The African leaders get their share of guns and put their money in Swiss banks. In return the people are harangued by such as Bishop Yussotov without interference. The Russians also assure African countries there will be no terrorist activities sponsored in the states they control. The Islamic fundamentalists use terror to force their religion on victim nations. All we do is excel in humanitarian relief. It doesn't mean much to these African dictators." Motupu shrugged helplessly. "They simply don't care about their own people. They control them and they are 'da boss.' If the Russian Church can help them run the people and Russian traders can give them guns and money for diamonds and oil, that's what they want. They do not see the AIDS explosion happening before their eyes."

"I'd like to take a look at our people in Uganda, specifically Rakai, which I see as a typical breeding ground of disease," the pope said.

"I do not advise it, Your Holiness," Shanahan said quickly. "You can't imagine how bad it is. I'm told that one hundred percent of the population has an immediate member of the family dead or infected with HIV or some other virus that hasn't even got a name."

The pope looked at Motupu. "How many of our people, missionaries and medical workers, do we have there?"

"Maybe a dozen nuns and laypeople from Concern and Trocare," Motupu replied.

"Well, get transportation. I want to be there and see for myself. It just may be that certain Catholic prohibitions will have to be changed."

"We can make Entebbe in an hour. Rakai in another hour." As though shocked to expose the pope to all the vicissitudes Africa offered, Motupu quickly added a caveat, "But Your Holiness, it is too dangerous for you to go there."

"I am obviously not going to contract an STD!"

"Sister Martha and others of the mission contracted whatever it is," Shanahan argued.

"Make the arrangements," the pope commanded without thought of the *avviso*'s warnings.

"If you are certain, Your Holiness..." Motupu's voice trailed off.

"I'm certain, Gus."

Motupu's white-toothed smile cracked across his face. "Okay, Pope Bill. I had it arranged before we left this morning—just in case."

A shocked expression came across the face of Tim Shanahan, standing next to the pope. "You are a rascal, Eminence. Playing with the pope's life."

Cardinal Bellotti and the others were not close enough to hear the repartee.

Innocently, Motupu stared back at the man who had become the pope's closest adviser. "I only wanted to be ready to respond to the wishes of His Holiness."

"You were right, Gus." The pope's tone was vehement. "This entire trip was carried out against any and all Vatican protocol. If it is to mean anything it will have to proceed that way. No one need go with me."

Cardinal Bellotti, meanwhile, was horrified when he heard about the sudden apparent change in plans. With Monsignor Cippolini and the others he declined the opportunity to visit Rakai.

"Well, Gus," the pope boomed, "it looks like we'll only need one vehicle waiting at Entebbe."

"We'll be bringing a Concern nun and a medical missionary with us," Motupu replied grimly.

The pope stood firm against Cardinal Bellotti's remonstrances as he tried to get Cardinal Robitelli on his satellite phone. Finally, before taking off for Entebbe, Pope Peter came up with a suggestion that quieted Bellotti. "The worst thing that can happen, *Eminenza,* is that you or Robitelli will be *carmelengo* at another conclave sooner than expected."

Bellotti couldn't hide his sly smile of sudden cognizance as the pope clapped him on a shoulder cheerfully. With Tim Shanahan and Motupu flanking him, Bill Kelly turned away from the makeshift hospital toward the vehicles that had transported them from Kigali.

"We'll be back in a few hours, probably midafternoon," Motupu called to the others cheerfully. "While we're away you can visit with the people that keep this mission going. Sister Winnie will show you around and introduce you to the rest."

With that Motupu, Pope Peter, and Monsignor Shanahan took seats in the old mission sedan and were driven to the airport.

VIRUS 37

The sleek aircraft was waiting and the pilot greeted them with the news that, as requested, they were cleared into Ugandan airspace for a landing at Entebbe.

Sitting with Motupu and Shanahan in the front compartment, Bill Kelly could not stifle a broad, victorious smile. "Now I feel as though I am accomplishing something important for the first time since I took on this job. We're going to do whatever it takes to change things here."

"Bill, you haven't seen the worst," Motupu replied. "But I'm feeling vindicated in getting you here by the way you are moving in on the situation. All I can say is that God answered my position at the conclave. I knew we had to make a big change in Church procedure. Sometimes, like now, I really believe in divine intervention."

Once airborne, Bill Kelly stared out the window at the countryside below. The ground cover ranged from green jungle to sere brown, and when the plane reached a cruising altitude of twenty thousand feet and leveled off, central Africa in all its contrasts and hues stretched out below them. Half an hour after takeoff the pilot announced that directly ahead of them lay the western shore of Lake Victoria. They could see its waters below them as they proceeded north toward Entebbe.

"You know," Bill mused, "up here, soaring above God's beautiful earth, getting ready to put down in the middle of a starving, sick, and quarreling humanity, I can sympathize with God. He answers our selfish idiotic prayers, descending from his beautiful domain high above to straighten out the mess we humans make of the astonishing earth he gave us."

"An apt observation, Your Holiness," Motupu agreed. "I was thinking the same thing myself. And wait till you see the contrast between what we look down on from up here and what we find when we touch down into the real world."

The words came down from the cockpit. "We are starting our approach to Entebbe Airport. Seat belts please. We should be on the ground in twenty minutes."

"I have an arrangement with customs here," Motupu said. "Whenever someone from our mission comes in they are escorted with their medical supplies through official barriers and on to our transportation, such as it is."

"Do they know the pope is on this plane?" Shanahan asked.

"I told the pilot to so notify ground control," Motupu replied. "We'll soon find out how much, and if, our missionary work is appreciated in Uganda."

The squeal of tires on tarmac signaled they had landed. The airplane drew up to the terminal and the engines shut down. The copilot came out of the flight deck, walked past the pope to the door, which he opened, and pushed down the steps reaching to the ramp. Motupu led the way, followed by Monsignor Shanahan and finally Pope Peter. The few ground attendants waited, staring up at the door for a popelike figure to emerge. Bill Kelly was wearing black slacks and a white shirt with a silver cross around his neck. An official greeted Moputu and was introduced to Shanahan and then to His Holiness, who shook his hand.

"I'm sorry to arrive in your country in informal dress, but this trip is apparently going to require some agility on my part," the pope apologized.

"Your Holiness." The airport attendant was apparently a Catholic. "Welcome to Uganda. Had we known you were coming there would be a crowd to greet you."

"We weren't certain ourselves."

"Will you permit our Land Rover to pick us up out here?" Motupu asked.

"Certainly, Your Eminence." He muttered to a man behind him, who immediately ran toward the terminal.

"You are going out to Rakai, Your Eminence?"

"His Holiness wants to see for himself what our mission is doing."

The official shot a dubious look at the pope. "Maybe it is best not to go out to Rakai, Your Holiness. Many people are sick out here. Even I don't go."

"I'll advise you about it when I get back," the pope replied with a grin.

"Dr. Mainovic is out there now," the airport officer added.

The pope cast a questioning look at Motupu, who quickly replied, "Dr. Marija Mainovic is a Serb woman, a doctor from Yugoslavia. She is part of a group of medical professionals and a strong Eastern Orthodox Church member, personally close to the patriarch. When the Serb president began his ethnic cleansing policy, she left her nation and has been active out here ever since. Two American Catholic Relief medical personnel trying to help our effort have died recently."

The Land Rover came around the corner of the terminal building and stopped in front of Motupu. "In we go." He opened the back door for the pope, who climbed in, followed by Tim Shanahan and finally Motupu, pulling the door shut behind him. They all looked more like neatly attired tourists than high-ranking clerics.

For twenty minutes the Land Rover proceeded along a wide paved highway with the bush cut back on either side over a hundred meters. In some places the view from the road was half a mile of flatland. As they turned west off the main road, Lake Victoria, to the east, quickly faded from view to their rear. Now the bush closed in on the secondary road. They pushed northeast away from the main highway and the lake.

"Between the airport and the capital city of Kampala, whoever ran the government made sure there was no place for ambush sites along the main road," Motupu explained.

"But now, out in the bush?" Tim asked.

"No important traffic. Only us missionaries," Motupu answered wryly.

It was over an hour from the airport to Rakai, and when they arrived in the middle of a dirt square they heard the sound of children singing. "We'll visit the school after we've checked in with Sister Kaitlin," Motupu said as they stepped out of the Land Rover.

Moments later a tired-looking young woman wearing a scarf over her head and a nondescript shirt and long skirt appeared, carrying a radio telephone. She came up to the three visitors. "Your Eminence," she greeted Motupu and then stared at the pope for a few moments. Suddenly, "Your Holiness!" She started to kneel. "I didn't believe Dr. Mainovic when she said you would be here." The pope reached out for her hand and held her up.

"Sister Kaitlin, please. If anybody should be bowing it is I. What you and International Concern are doing here is indeed saintly. I will tell my dearest and oldest friend, Cardinal Comiskey, that I had the privilege of seeing your work firsthand."

"The cardinal is indeed a great man, Your Holiness. He keeps us going here."

"I will now see it all and personally report to him."

A worried Cardinal Motupu interrupted. "Sister Kaitlin, what's this about Dr. Marija Mainovic saying the Holy Father himself was on the way out here?"

"About an hour ago she got a call on her radio phone that he was on the way. None of us believed her."

Recognizing Motupu's concern, the pope and Tim Shanahan asked almost as one, "Who is this doctor with such a good intelligence net?"

"She's close to the patriarch," Sister Kaitlin explained. "She's one of his persuasion, of course, a rabid Serb Russian Orthodox. I wouldn't put it past her to kill an American as her president has urged and her patriarch has tacitly endorsed by saying nothing. Even down here we know what the Serbs did to the Muslim Kosovars, but this doctor only says it is all American propaganda. She is a doctor and it is good to have one here for a few days every month, but she is...possessed." The nun crossed herself nervously. "You can hear it in her voice and see it in her eyes." Sister Kaitlin shuddered. "It is a good thing we are not American or even NATO European. Dr. Mainovic blames the bomb destruction in her country on them. But she has given us some good medical help, not that there is much that anyone can do," the sister concluded helplessly.

"The *avviso* warned that the patriarch and his Serb and Russian followers would tacitly advocate a terror campaign against Americans to repay Western military action in the Balkans," the pope murmured to Tim. Then, to Sister Kaitlin, "May I visit your school and then the early medical treatment center?"

The nun looked fearfully at Motupu. "Your Eminence, surely we can't let the Holy Father expose himself to the virus." She turned to the pope. "Your Holiness, every one of the hundred children in the school has at least one parent dead of the virus, and more than a few are orphaned. They themselves die almost as fast as they are replaced by refugees coming in from the famine outside."

"Is there some way we can slow this thing down?" the pope asked.

The sister looked at Motupu, who shrugged. "Despite our teachings we cannot get the concept of abstinence across to them. They have endless children. Perhaps we could still have slowed the outbreak back in the late 1990s if we could have said, 'Go ahead and fulfill your natural functions, but if you want to avoid dying of the virus and having infected children, at least learn some good birth control information.' Needless to say, when I suggest such a thing, the notion is summarily rejected in Rome. And the UN people agree that things are terrible but they don't give us food or medicine. NGOs are not much help either."

"Nongovernmental organizations," Shanahan explained.

"Yes," the sister sniffed. "They are trying to help, but they think giving everyone a year's supply of condoms is the only answer."

"Let's go into the school," the pope suggested.

He intercepted the worried glance from Sister Kaitlin to Motupu. The cardinal stood firm. "Sister Kaitlin, unless the Holy Father sees for himself what is happening here, he will not understand our danger. We are, after all, a microcosm of the African macrocosm." Then, to the pope, "Come on into the school, Bill." Moputu led him and Shanahan into a rough wood-and-thatch building, with children playing in the yard outside.

Inside the "school" the pope caught his breath at the ravages of the viruses in the children. It was obvious they had not caught the virus from sexual contact but had inherited it from their parents. All suffered from malnutrition because of the food shortages. And a combination of virus and starvation diets had turned them into bug-eyed stick people with swollen bellies.

"These are the innocents, victims of the several viruses afflicting us. We get enough food to provide a minimum daily survival ration. If it wasn't for the virus we could probably keep most of them alive until the food situation improves."

"Do you mean to say that every one of these pathetic specimens is . . . has AIDS?"

"Or other viruses we haven't isolated yet, Your Holiness," Sister Kaitlin replied.

The pope walked among the listless children and reached another nun at a table facing the class. "Sister, how long have you been here?"

"Your Holiness, I flew in from Dublin three weeks ago to replace Sister Martha."

"Aren't you afraid of becoming infected?"

"I am careful not to suffer superficial cuts."

The pope let out a sigh and walked among the apathetic children. They stared at him with wide eyes from sallow faces. At the back of the room he watched as a sister went on teaching lessons.

"Gus, aren't there any Africans beside yourself to help these children?"

"They are orphans or have only one parent—sick, of course."

"And is it like this in many parts of Africa?"

"I could also arrange for you to see the starvation and brutality against Christians by the Islamic extremists in southern Sudan, where for several years international rescue agencies have tried to help, but the civil war keeps going on and food distributed goes only to the soldiers or those who are willing or forced to renounce Christianity."

The pope shook his head in disbelief. "Regarding this AIDS crisis," the pope said. "Why is it? What can be done?"

"We are doing what we can. In the case of these exposed children and those down with the virus, we simply cannot get the medicine that relieves the symptoms. AZT and the other ingredients of the AIDS cocktails help a little. But we don't always know which virus to treat. Some new and more powerful strain of virus, one we have never seen before, turns up every month."

"Well, we can't blame this on the Russian Orthodox Church," the pope declared. "It cannot be the fault of their church that AIDS is killing this continent."

"No. But while we are doing our best to help, the patriarch is spending his resources building up followers in the diamond mining areas and oil locations. He is backed by his civil government, Bill—secretly, of course—but making use of resources we do not have, like Russian government incentives to influence a pro-tem national leader."

"How does that work?" the pope asked.

"You will see it in the areas where the diamonds are found. Our people in the early part of this new millennium are being converted to the Russian Church. And the Church preaches birth control and safe sex, not abstinence, which is beyond an African's comprehension. It's not the people that they are concerned about, but the land and our rich minerals." Gus hit the palm of his left hand with his right fist.

At that moment a severe-looking middle-aged woman, her blond hair pulled back tightly and clasped behind her head, dressed in a denim skirt, dark cotton blouse, and bootlike shoes, entered the schoolroom. In one hand she carried a black satchel. She gave the pope an irreverent glance.

Motupu said a few words to her. "I am Cardinal Motupu." He gestured toward the pope. "This is—"

"Yes," the woman interrupted harshly. "Mr. Kelly of America and the Vatican. The so-called spiritual force behind the destruction of my country. What wreckage do you plan for Africa?"

Astounded, the pope was at a loss for words. Motupu, though equally surprised, quickly formed a rebuttal. "We appreciate any medical help you can offer us, Dr. Mainovic, but this is a Catholic mission and in no way affiliated with the Orthodox Church."

"Our purpose here is constructive, Doctor," the pope replied. "I am sorry you see fit to attach the blame for your government's ethnic genocide of the Muslim minority in your country to people other than your own."

In the intensity of her diatribe she virtually spit her words out in heavily accented English. "I worked hard to save the lives of my people badly injured by your bombs. Only the patriarch and his Russian Church come to our defense against your lies. It was you who killed and dispersed the Muslims of Kosovo when we tried to protect them from your air attacks."

Such blatant distortion of the truth shook Bill Kelly. He was reminded of the Serbian officials on television who had ranted and raved, eyes wild and flashing, mouths drawn, displaying the front teeth of their lower jaws, denying their depredations upon a defenseless population in Kosovo. This invective invariably flowed immediately after positive proof had just appeared on TV screens throughout the world showing refugees in the thousands escaping Serbian genocide. Now here in Africa, a year later, was the living proof of the warning John Paul II had left for the next pope, whose reign would indeed be short if these maniacal zealots had their way.

The pope watched, dumbstruck, as the Serbian doctor approached a boy of indeterminate age squirming on a chair directly in front of him. The doctor, wearing rubber gloves, pulled the child from a crumpled fetal sprawl to an upright position, momentarily halting a coughing fit. The doctor flashed a challenging stare at the pope. Bill Kelly immediately gave way to his natural instinct and knelt beside the pitifully thin boy, cradling his head in his arms. The child, gasping for air, mouth open, teeth chattering, turned into the strong, comforting hands holding him.

In horror, the nuns and Motupu snatched the boy away from the pope, and two African attendants, closely followed by the Serbian doctor, carried him out of the room.

"Where are you taking him?" Bill asked.

"To the ward for observation," the sister replied. Then she noticed that the skin on the back of the pope's hand was broken where the child had bitten him.

"Your Holiness," a worried Sister Kaitlin said hoarsely, "come into the dispensary with me and let me cauterize the spot where your skin is broken."

The pope and Shanahan, with Motupu worriedly following, walked across the dusty square of ground between the schoolroom and the building that served as an office and residence for the nuns and the medical technicians.

"Your Holiness, this will be uncomfortable for a minute, but the skin on the back of your hand was broken by the boy's teeth and we must try to kill any possibility of infection." As the Serbian doctor watched, the pope held his right hand out, and the sister took a bottle from the medicine cabinet and with a piece of cotton swabbed disinfectant acid over the broken skin, where a few drops of blood had appeared.

"There, that should do it."

"I am sorry I pulled the boy to his feet, but I had to stop his cough," the doctor said insincerely. Motupu and Kaitlin stared after her with ill-concealed hostility as she left the sick boy in the care of an African assistant.

"I want to see the town, talk to the people a little," the pope said. "Do they understand how viruses are transmitted?"

"We try to explain STD, but it is taking their basic human rights away to suggest continence. By now most men in this part of Africa are carriers. Sometimes they pass it on, sometimes not. We don't possess much medicine. There isn't much we can do."

"And," a second nun added, "if the international community had been more concerned about Africa even a year ago, and we had halfway decent medical supplies, we might have prevented the worst of this scourge. The world closed its eyes to our crisis even though reports have recently been widespread."

"Not, apparently, a fanatical Serb doctor," the pope replied. "Anyway, let me walk around this town and talk to the people."

"Your Holiness," Shanahan interjected, "we don't have much time. Besides, the longer you stay here, the greater the possibility of any of us picking up a virus."

This gave the pope pause. "If I can learn from these people, it is worth it to take that chance. But I don't want to subject you to it, Tim. Let me visit one or two homes alone and then we will go. I need to see for myself, so I can try and convince the world about the AIDS crisis," said Pope Bill.

"We must all stick together," Motupu said decisively. "Come, Your Holiness, let's call on one family together." He turned to Sister Kaitlin. "Whom can His Holiness talk to?"

"The headman lives nearby. He is a good Catholic who knows what we're doing and comes to the service every Sunday when the priest from Kampala says Mass."

"Yes, a good man, Father Umtali," Motupu said. "He does the best he can. He has several young priests to assist him but he needs resources as well." He gave the pope a speculative glance. "It would shock the curia to see what we have to do here to keep the people's faith. But we manage in our own way."

"Many changes will be made when I return to the Vatican," the pope said grimly. "So let's visit the headman. He speaks English?"

"Indeed. The British did a fine job here and in Kenya and Tanzania.

The natives have English first names. The school system still works, and it is the one thing the independent governments have tried to maintain. Project Concern has taken on some of the teaching burden. The government was so fractured, first with Idi Amin and then his imitators, that without us the schools would have collapsed."

The nun led them down the dusty pathway between thatched houses to a wooden structure.

"Like everyone here he has AIDS, or one of the mystery viruses," Sister Kaitlin said. "But he still functions well, and keeps order inside the village."

At the half-open door Motupu knocked, and a man's frail voice called out "Come." Motupu pushed the door open, and the others followed him into a dark room with one window in the board walls. A spare black man pulled himself out of a chair, his height emphasizing his emaciation. He was wearing a shirt and long pants held up by a thick pair of black leather suspenders that looked as though they had once been part of a uniform.

"Your Eminence." The voice shook as he greeted Motupu, maintaining a respectful distance.

"Andrew, I have brought a visitor to see you." Motupu stood aside and the pope approached the old man, who squinted in the dim light within the fragile structure. "Andrew, this is the Holy Father himself, come from Rome to try to help us better help ourselves."

Andrew tried to kneel and reach out for the pope's hand. "Your Holiness" he said hoarsely, "my home, our village, is forever blessed because you came." The pope caught his hand and held him upright before the old African could actually bend his frail limbs.

"Andrew, we will be here henceforward in every way. A cure for your ills will be discovered and we will get it to all of you."

"Thank you, Holiness. I wish God had found a way to help us stay healthy to begin with. Our land is beautiful, but usually now we have no clean water or any way to produce food." The old man's eyes were fixed on the two partially filled bottles of water Monsignor Shanahan was carrying. "When I was a boy none of this happened to us," Andrew wheezed through his dry throat.

The pope reached for the bottle Shanahan was carrying for him and, taking it out of his hand, thrust it toward the village headman.

"Here, Andrew. Drink."

Andrew gratefully reached out for the bottle, immediately swallowing from it.

"Keep it," the pope said. "We will leave what water we brought with us for the children. We pray to God the affliction will soon be gone." He was stung by the subtle reminder that there was something that might have been done, could still be done, to diminish the spread of the virus threatening an entire population.

Later Motupu wished Andrew well and assured him that Concern and its doctors, when called, would continue to care for Rakai. Then he led the pope away after a last blessing. The sisters had chosen half a dozen of the virus-infected children, those who might be saved with the advanced drugs available at Concern in Kigali, to return with Motupu and the pope.

The drive to the Entebbe airport was fraught with silent contemplation of what each had seen. And once aboard the plane there was little conversation on the flight.

By midafternoon they had landed once again in the capital of Rwanda and left the sick children with the sisters. After a blessing by the pope they picked up Cardinal Bellotti, Monsignor Shanahan, and the other Vatican group members who had started out that morning from Luanda.

Later that night in the hotel the pope met with Motupu and his delegation to discuss the next day's itinerary. There was considerable disagreement between Bellotti and Motupu regarding the big event planned for the visit to Kinshasa, capital of the Congo Republic. It was here that the Russian Church was making its steadiest gains, picking up where Orthodoxy had left off in 1991 with the fall of Soviet Communism.

"We are committed to a meeting with the patriarch and Bishop Yussotov in Kinshasa before the pope leaves Africa," Motupu reminded the Vatican group gathered in the Luanda hotel suite.

"Not necessarily," Tim Shanahan reminded them. "It was left open to us to decide and notify them."

"We are finding it difficult to operate in Congo," Motupu complained, "ever since our bishop and the Europeans, including all Catholic Relief organizations, were forced to leave in late 1998. That was the third time the rebels attacked key cities in the Congo and put in a new ruler. We have been unable to reconsolidate our infrastructure in that state."

"Why is it we can be the dominant influence everywhere else?" Bellotti asked.

"*Eminenza,*" Shanahan began to explain again, "when the third replacement in the power structure in the Congo started in late summer 1998, the foreign ministers of the African countries in the central region were invited in to help shape the new leadership. Almost every one of these ministers represented African countries that had been 'liberated' by Communist terrorists and were ruled by Communist-empowered dictatorships.

"The most powerful influences exerted on the third Congo government came from Zimbabwe, still ruled by Communist dictator Robert Mugabe. With Russian backing and a warped and emotional view in America of black democracy, Mugabe overthrew the moderate black African Rhodesian leadership, replacing it with a dictatorship which has lasted twenty-one years. The same, to a greater or lesser extent, is true of the other African states, which sent their representatives to the Congo. In short, a third new dictatorship is now established in Congo and the whites who fled will not be warmly accepted back. It was then that the patriarch and his Orthodox Church were made welcome. After all—bear this in mind—Alexis II had proved his loyalty to Communism by refusing to attend the funeral ceremonies in 1998, sponsored by Boris Yeltsin and his new government, for the czar and his family, executed by the Communists eighty years before."

Motupu nodded agreement with Shanahan's historical account. "So, with all these Communist-oriented ministers influencing the Congo of late 1998, the old Russian Bolsheviks turned crypto-capitalist themselves—brought their church in with them. Now we find it almost impossible to reestablish what had been the Roman Catholic Church of the old Belgian Congo. You will see for yourself. The Russians are gaining a new foothold in Africa, their church growing dominant. The areas of the diamond mines and the oil reserves are fast changing to a Russian Orthodox orientation."

"Do we really have the resources and people willing to devote their lifetimes to the struggle for Africa?" Bellotti questioned. "From what I've seen in these two days, I have to ask if this continent is going to be worth it." The Vatican cardinal shook his head in disgust. "It appears to be one big disease center, which gets worse because the people procreate out of wedlock and spread their deadly viruses. Why not leave it to the Russian Orthodox? Africa will keep them tied down for generations."

"Unfortunately, your argument, on the surface, has merit. I'm sure Robitelli would agree," Motupu replied. "However, this continent is too large and important to be written off by the world's largest religious sector. I believe we should meet with the patriarch as proposed by both sides in Rome. We, after all, are the only force between him and eventual religious control south of the Sahara. And nothing short of a nuclear holy war will shake off the Islamic fundamentalism of the Arab world. Do you agree, Bill?"

All eyes turned to the pope, who was the authoritative figure that ultimately decided all questions one way or the other. "We must not allow the Orthodox Church to destroy our work here in Africa. John Paul II has warned that the Orthodox pose one of the greatest dangers to the future of the Roman Catholic Church. If we lay down in Africa, where will we not lay down? Let us meet with the patriarch and his bishop," Bill Kelly answered decisively. Then to Motupu, "Confirm the arrangements, Gus."

+‡+ +‡+ +‡+

Upon landing at the large modern airport in Kinshasa, it was difficult for the pope and his cardinals and advisers to visualize the strife that had plagued Congo's last five years. Three dictators had been ousted by military alliances between the rebels and the leaders of neighboring and nearby countries, most notably Rwanda and Zimbabwe.

The pope and his advisers realized that United States influence had waned seriously. The diamond cartel, led by former smugglers now known as "New York financiers," could no longer count on American or South African power to back up their regulating the flow of diamonds to world markets from the Congo.

The Russian diamond merchants, on the other hand, had the backing of their government and the newly empowered Russian Orthodox Church. In the Congo countryside this extended down to the level of actual mining and collection. A different brand of Communism was flourishing this time under a directorate of profit-minded leaders advancing behind their Church among the people. Had Soviet Communists followed this concept instead of atheism, their influence around the world might have prevailed.

+‡+ +‡+ +‡+

There was the usual crowd of news media meeting the pope's entourage, their cameras rolling and flashing. Bill was greeted in French by the minister of the interior.

"Your Holiness, welcome to the Democratic Republic of Congo. Anything we can do to make your visit a pleasant one, please call me. Cardinal Moputu knows how to reach me." However, each member of the

delegation was asked to produce a passport, which was closely scruti-
nized before being handed back.

"We understand that you wish to visit Kindu in the countryside,
where there was once a large Catholic diocese and which is, incidentally,
a center for diamond mining and export," the minister murmured.

Motupu now took the lead. "We are not interested in commerce, Minister. But we would like to see what has happened at some of our larger
parishes. During the last two revolutions most of our priests were forced
to leave by the rebels. Many disappeared, maybe killed. His Holiness
hopes we can restore the Church to its former preeminence here in
Congo."

"I understand you are going to visit with the patriarch of the Russian
Orthodox Church." A mocking ivory smile cracked the minister's dark
face. "Perhaps he will offer some suggestions on how you can restore the
Church here."

At that moment Tim Shanahan recognized the tall, black-maned figure
of Bishop Yussotov coming toward them from behind the group of Con-
golese functionaries watching the pope's arrival.

"Ah, Timothy," the Russian bishop greeted him pleasantly. "I have
been looking forward to renewing our acquaintanceship. The patriarch
has asked me to bring His Holiness and all of you to his residence here.
Everybody can have a good discussion about the future."

Cardinal Bellotti pushed forward. "We have not yet made up our
minds that a meeting with the patriarch would be productive." Then,
looking at Motupu, "This excursion has been poorly planned."

Still smiling and genial, Bishop Yussotov put forth a hand. "Cardinal
Bellotti, we are particularly pleased to have you here representing Vatican
traditions."

In spite of himself, Bellotti was pleased. "Bishop Yussotov, I presume?
You see we have not decided whether a meeting with the patriarch is in
order just yet. We planned to see something of the Congo today, visit one
of our remaining parishes..." He paused as a black cleric in the tropical
attire of a monsignor came up to them.

Motupu took a step forward and embraced him. "I was worried for a
moment there, Monsignor Nabila. I expected you to be out front with the
minister when we deplaned." To the others Motupu explained, "Monsignor Francois Nabila is protecting our faith here in Kinshasa."

"And fine work he is doing," Yussotov said heartily, "against great
odds."

At that point Bill Kelly moved forward to take charge. "Monsignor

Nabila, may I call you Frank? It's good to meet you." Then, turning to the Russian, "Bishop, I am pleased to meet you also. I was unable to meet you in Rome, though Monsignor Shanahan gave me an account of what happened."

"Your Holiness, now that we are all here in this foreign land—neutral territory, you might say—I hope you and the patriarch will come to some agreement on a religious plan for this huge continent which dwarfs even Mother Russia."

Pope Peter looked about him, saw the array of power lined up, and made a fast decision on his own. "This appears to be the propitious time, Bishop Yussotov. Our agenda didn't quite read this way, but there is no time like the present. I believe Monsignor Nabila has transportation available? If you will lead the way we will follow you to the patriarch."

Kinshasa seemed calm and well ordered. There was new construction along almost every block as they entered the city from the airport. Motupu, the pope, and Monsignor Nabila sat in the back of an old but serviceable sedan. In the front Tim Shanahan was seated beside the driver; the rest of the Vatican group were in the following car.

"I'll ask Francois to tell you more about our problems," Motupu suggested.

"Yes. A former Belgian, French-speaking Catholic country. How did we lose it, Frank?" the pope asked.

"Corruption was always considerable, but over the past four or five years, with three dictators in a row, it became so pervasive that only Russians could adapt, and then thrive in the atmosphere." Nabila laughed dryly. "Cardinal Monassari—'Patsy,' as he became known to us all— alone understood how to get along with the second and third dictator and with the Russians. He kept our foothold in place. He could, how do you say, 'operate.'"

The pope turned to Motupu. "Maybe we can use Patsy to help us get reestablished."

Tim Shanahan laughed. "Old Patsy met with the Mad Monk in Rome."

"Well, let's see what we can learn from the patriarch."

"We're almost at his rectory, or whatever they call their quarters," Nabila said. "I know it only from the outside. Never been inside. I can tell you that there are a large number of people around here that have nothing to do with Church matters."

Yussotov was waiting outside the large, heavy wooden door of a residence that could have come directly out of nineteenth-century Brussels or Paris. It swung open, and two young men in white suits and clerical collars were standing inside. Yussotov led the pope, Shanahan, Motupu, and Bellotti into the cool, dark wooden interior and to the back of the structure and then paused outside another heavy door. "I will introduce you first, Your Holiness, and then the others."

They were led into what Bill Kelly characterized as the throne room. When the patriarch stood up from the ornate seat to greet his callers, he looked somehow frail beside the towering Pope Peter II. Beside the patriarch stood a handsome young blond woman dressed in a dark business suit with a thin black cravat circling a lace collar. The patriarch said a few words in Russian, which the young woman translated into a welcome speech in flawless English.

The patriarch did not hold out his hand but rather bowed to the pope, who returned the gesture. The patriarch was well known for his anti-Semitic, anti-Catholic, and anti-American rhetoric from his days as bishop of Leningrad in the old USSR. Even the Russian Synod of Bishops deferred to him for fear of reprisal. The fact that the pope was an American caused the patriarch to be doubly suspicious. The other visitors from Rome were introduced and bowed to the Russian primate, then took seats offered to them by Yussotov. They formed a semicircle around Alexis, who sat down, his comely interpreter standing by his side.

"I am glad we could meet here, in a place foreign to all of us. It is strange that this once Roman Catholic stronghold has passed over to our faith," Alexis began, pausing for the translation. "Constant civil wars over the past five years leave this country in political strife even now," he continued. "As it happened, we found a religious void which we have been trying to fill with some help from our Russian government."

"You have been lucky in that respect," the pope replied.

"Yes, the old hard-line Communists in our government took too long to realize what we could do to advance our national influence. They thought in terms of revolutionary terror tactics. But atheism cannot win in the long run." The patriarch sighed as his words were translated.

"We are aware how you established your stronghold after the last Congo revolution," the pope interjected. "All governments in the area which owe their existence, in part at least, to Communist terror helped the newest regime in Congo. Do you think, as happened in Russia itself five years ago, that all other religions but the Orthodox will be banned?" He paused and fixed the patriarch with a steady stare directly into the eyes. "While it may well be that throwing Protestantism out was a healthy move, you should never have banned Catholicism. After all, you allow Islam its place in Russia."

"We couldn't afford a holy war in Russia. There are too many Muslims in our country. And when you count the Muslim countries in Africa, well, we would be overrun right here by Islamic fundamentalist fanatics if we banished Islam from Russia."

"But you have no such fear—here that is—of Christians, Catholic or Protestant, overrunning your establishment?"

After listening to the translation the patriarch smiled smugly and nodded toward his bishop. "As Yussotov negotiated with your people in Rome, why don't we simply agree on territorial imperatives. Leave the Congo to us. Keep your missionaries and clergy from proselytizing the people here. They have already forgotten all their catechisms in the past five years. We will see to the souls of the Congo people as we are doing now. We will keep any creeping Islamic culture out. You fight it in your own way elsewhere in Africa. I understand you want to visit the Congo diamond-producing areas. Why? Why not leave the Congo to us, and we will leave the rest to you? There is no point in a three-way religious war here between Islam, you, and us. Africa is big enough for the three of us if we leave each other alone."

As the serious young woman made the translation, the pope smiled indulgently at his staff.

"What do you think, Gus?" the pope asked when the translation was complete. "I think we should leave the Congo for the time being. Further exploration of reestablishing ourselves at this moment is useless and may be dangerous." Pope Peter II was fond of playing the political game after his talk with Ed Kirby.

The interpreter whispered the words in the patriarch's ear. He nodded and his smile broadened. "Good advice, Your Holiness."

"So we leave Congo's diamonds and oil to the Russian sphere of influence?" Pope Peter half stated, half asked.

"Their state is behind their religion, and at last the state has learned how to fuse both advantages together," Tim Shanahan declared. "I do not believe that there are many practical Russians who are avowed atheists today."

"I see you are also practical men." The patriarch nodded approvingly on hearing the translation. "Tempting though it might be, I would advise our state to go no further than this in Africa. At least not without careful planning. I hope you will do likewise."

As the interpreter completed her translation, the patriarch's body language signaled that the conference was over except for one more matter. "We have members of our Church who are medical practitioners, doctors even, who work throughout Africa when there are medical emergencies. I understand you met one of our doctors yesterday. Dr. Marija Mainovic?"

Bill Kelly nodded warily, sensing that this was more than a casual question.

"She informed us of your slight accident," Bishop Yussotov murmured. "We keep in touch several times a day with our people in the field. If you decide to cooperate, you can ask our good doctor not to practice in your areas."

"We need all the medical help we can get," the pope replied, glancing down at the red splotch on the back of his right hand where the boy in Rakai had bitten him the day before.

"I can assure you that there will be no more hostility on the part of any of our medical people when they may be working in your areas. I am deeply sorry if in any way our loyal Serbian doctor contributed to your possible exposure to the virus."

Even before the translation the pope could not fail to notice the irony in the patriarch's tone of voice.

"I regret having contributed to Orthodox distrust of Americans and Europeans of the NATO countries." The patriarch waited for the translation to be completed. "But the war in Yugoslavia, Serbia, Kosovo, and Albania was a religious and ethnic conflict going back many centuries, and I would be remiss if I did not remind my Eastern Orthodox parishioners of the horrifying atrocities the Muslims, the Turks, committed against us. For instance, impalement, a horrible slow death. These atrocities will always live in our history. The evil monster in your literature, Dracula, is based on a Balkan Christian, Vlad the Impaler, who used to place a hundred Turks at a time on the greasy poles. I am surprised that your American press chose not to inform the American people of the religious divide in the world today and in the past. Much of the division has been religious, not just political or geographic."

Once again Alexis II waited for the translation and then continued. "No, there is little we can do to remove or neutralize the hatred. I am sorry if we knowingly sent a Serbian doctor with intense grievances against Americans and Europeans, Catholics, who she believes have all but destroyed her country, which, of course"—the patriarch clucked his tongue, waiting for the interpretation of his words "they you—have."

He stood up from his seat, bowing somberly to the pope, who bowed back, no handshake. Bishop Yussotov led the pope's delegation out of the room and through the hallways to the front door. "You seem to be pretty well ensconced here, Bishop," Shanahan observed.

"So it would seem."

"A most attractive interpreter the patriarch has on his staff," Monsignor Cippolini said, his first observation of the meeting.

Bishop Yussotov grinned crookedly. "Our church does not always believe in celibacy. Which makes it far more pleasant for your African Christian churchmen to join us." The concept was not lost on the pope, who nodded grudging agreement. He stepped out of the patriarch's rectory and onto the sidewalk of this strangely African and colonial European mixture of a city.

"Is there more you want us to know here in Congo, Gus?" the pope asked as they walked toward their cars.

"There isn't much use going to Kindu if we are not going to challenge the patriarch," Motupu replied.

"Will your people out there feel betrayed if we do not go?"

"Of course. But it is a tender little parish, barely existing in the wake of the revolutions and terrorism of the past few years. I have a very active priest out there, brought up in the colony when it was Belgian administrated. He would be greatly energized if the pope actually visited his diocese."

"He is expecting us?"

"Yes, but he will understand if we do not go out there. He knows the problems the Church faces here."

"I think we should go. Notify the pilot and your priest. What is his name?"

"Father Gregory Muzerowa. He went to the Belgian seminary in Brussels."

"Then let us keep our engagement with him. I'll tell our pilots myself."

The pope's brave little two-car motorcade proceeded to the airport, coming to a halt outside the crumbling administrative building. Orthodox Russian influence, fast spreading, still had not wiped out the last vestiges of Roman Catholic upbringing among certain older Congo citizens. Great deference was shown the pope at the airport, and his group's exit papers were quickly and respectfully processed. It was not until they were in their plane that the cold fingers of the patriarch's influence touched them. Their flight plan to any airport within Congo was negated by flight control. Permission to land at Kindu was specifically refused, and they were advised to return to Luanda.

The pope and Motupu looked at each other resignedly as the copilot came out of the flight deck and delivered the destination ban.

"The *avviso* warned me of Orthodoxy's far-reaching grasp," Bill remarked to Tim. "When Pope John Paul II went to see the Eastern Orthodox patriarch of Romania in Bucharest in the spring of 1999, he was blocked from visiting any other Catholic parish in the country. Most hypocritical of the Orthodox leader, but that's how they operate."

"Tell the pilot to return to Luanda," Motupu directed. Then to the pope he remarked, "This is an example of how quickly a neo-Communist alliance with the patriarch has developed. I am thankful that you saw it yourself."

The pope stared through the window as the plane's engines whined outside and the aircraft lumbered onto the nearly deserted runway to take off. His eyes fell to the back of his hand and the red splotch caused by the acid used to cauterize the child's bite. In silence he sat contemplating the implications of his brief visit.

Once airborne and headed south, the pope, Motupu, Shanahan, and Cardinal Bellotti sat on opposite sides of a table between the facing banks of seats. Monsignor Cippolini busied himself supervising the flight attendant's preparations for lunch. No one spoke until Bill broke the silence. "I guess," he began hesitantly, "that in Africa religion must be state-sponsored to succeed."

"It comes down to that, Your Holiness," Shanahan observed. "Islam prevails not only in the mosques but in the state governments to the north. Indeed, they are one and the same. We would have as much chance of bringing religion to the perpetually starving south of Sudan as a Jew during the Spanish Inquisition or the Holocaust. The true Muslim faith is so perverted by the extremists that even Mohammed himself would be ostracized by these fanatics."

"But we can't just give it all up," the pope said resolutely. "We've got to rebuild."

"I am thankful you see for yourself what's happening here," Motupu said. "First we had religious-sponsored state governments; now we've slipped into state-sponsored religions. And it isn't our Roman brand of Catholicism which these warlords' leaders sponsor. Like the mullahs in the north"—he gazed balefully out the window at the ground below—"who overthrow one another by arms and terror, in these central African countries so their religion conforms to their 'me da boss' objectives."

"We need a few strong nations behind us," Tim Shanahan declared. "How about the U.S.A.? Could Ed Kirby help?"

"He might have some ideas, but the *avviso* also warns us about the apathy of the American Church hurting our efforts here and elsewhere," the pope offered nevertheless. "God knows these extremist Islamic countries shaped up when we, America, that is, went after their terrorists with cruise missiles."

"Just the threat of something like that can keep our petty dictators in line," Motupu agreed.

"Well, Gus, what do we do now? Where do you want me to go?"

"I could have taken you up to Nigeria. That country, despite the pervasive corruption, has more dedicated Catholic priests doing their job than any other. And it has a large Muslim population as well."

"Should we have gone there?" the pope questioned.

"Why?" Motupu asked. "It is here the international community needs to know about the suffering and death. Reforms are essential if we are to do our work in this primitive climate that nobody in Rome cares to understand."

Cardinal Bellotti raised his eyebrows. "What are you suggesting, Eminence?"

"I think the Holy Father hears me perfectly. In terms of time this has been a short visit, but the Holy Spirit was with us, showing Pope Peter II that new policies must be instituted. We need an entirely new course of action, a comprehensive African policy for the Catholic Church. Besides AIDS and other viruses, there are many forces at work here ready and willing to destroy my continent."

"New course?" Bellotti questioned sharply.

"Yes, *Eminenza*. And for us. I don't need to go further into the matter at this time," Motupu enunciated. Bellotti sat back in his seat, noticeably disturbed but silent.

For several minutes Pope Peter seemed preoccupied, as though he had absented himself. Then, stroking his chin thoughtfully, he rejoined the conversation.

"*Eminenza*," he addressed Cardinal Bellotti, "I would appreciate it greatly if you would fly back to Rome tomorrow on a commercial flight and brief Cardinal Robitelli and the Office on Justice and Peace on everything you have seen and heard here. This will save me time when I return and we discuss the situation."

Bellotti smiled broadly. The opportunity of briefing the cardinal secretary of state with the pope absent was appealing.

"I want to visit Gus's parish again, talk more openly with the nuns and nurses, and absorb the spiritual significance of the place."

✦✦ ✦✦ ✦✦

Thus, two days later, on his last evening in Africa, Bill Kelly sat quietly listening and praying in the small Church that had been Motupu's parish before he was made a bishop. Luxurious beyond belief to the Africans, though crude in the sight of the party from Rome it was where the pope chose to return.

As he sat down in a chair on the dirt floor the pope sighed deeply. "Dear God, Augustine, how can we conquer such poverty and disease?"

The cardinal shook his head and wiped the tiredness from his eyes. "I have struggled with these problems all my life. We can only try to ease the pain by providing spiritual support...to offer hope for the future, whether it be here or the hereafter. We don't have the resources, not enough doctors, teachers, or priests to go around. Some of them cover such large areas that it may be six months before the people talk to a doctor, never mind their children attending school. Do you have any ex-priests who are medically trained, or teachers who want to teach in the jungles of Africa that you can spare?"

The pope smiled knowingly at his friend, whose frustration was palpable. Bill tried to lighten the situation by reaching into his pockets and turning them inside out. "Nobody in here, Gus. Sorry about that."

Then came a magic moment of mystery. The sense of an unknown force present suddenly prompted the pope to brighten. The cardinal was caught up in the same mood. The pope pointed to a Bible lying on the cardinal's desk. "There's our answer, Gus. What did the early Church do? It certainly couldn't send people off to the seminary for seven or eight years to study. No. The first Christians just appointed worthy believers to be its priests in the Churches. We must consider some major changes here. We all have good laypeople giving religious instruction in parishes throughout the world. I'm sure you have them in most of the parishes scattered throughout Africa. We will...no, you could ordain them as deacons immediately and we will train them in health care, education, and agriculture. Like the Peace Corps—perhaps a Catholic-sponsored, multinational, ecumenical Peace Corps. Former priests can return to the Church and perform most, maybe even all of their other functions, like burying the dead, dispensing Communion, sanctifying marriages, even saying Mass. We will establish within the Church itself a world ministry office and use several of our shut-down seminaries to train newcomers and former Churchmen and priests in important areas of need."

The cardinal jumped from his seat and began pacing back and forth, rubbing his hands together. He stopped and looked at the pope. "Yes, I can see that. But...dear God, what will they say in Rome? I mean...can you do this?" He blushed. "Of course you can. You're the pope. But what will it do? You'll create enormous problems. What will the faithful think in the rest of the world?" Then, a sheepish grin on his face, the cardinal confessed, "To tell the truth I've often thought of it before but considered it beyond my wildest dreams."

The pope stood up and looked his friend squarely in the eyes. "Gus, it has to be done sometime. Let it begin here. Have the Church help save these people and itself."

Bill reached for the Bible and leafed through the Scriptures. Then, triumphantly, "Here! Paul's epistle to Titus." He glanced down the page for a moment, and then looked up. "You see, all I have to do is change one word. Rather than 'Crete,' I will say 'Africa.' So now it can read like this." He coughed slightly to mimic clearing his throat for a speech. Then he began to read. "Titus, chapter one, verses five to seven. 'The reason I left you in'"—he winked and emphasized the next word—"'*Africa* was that you might straighten out what was left unfinished and ordain elders in every town as I directed you. An elder'"—he looked up at Motupu significantly—"read *bishop*, 'must be blameless, the husband of but one wife, a man whose children believe and are not open to the charge of being wild and disobedient.'"

The pope looked up from the Scriptures in triumph. "There you have it, old boy! We'll make Africa the test case. Like they used to have 'model cities' programs in places like Detroit, Watts, and the South Bronx. Africa is our model continent. This effort must be everyone's responsibility, not just that of the Church, but everyone."

Bill enthusiastically pulled a leather pouch from his briefcase on the desk and opened it. "I'll draw up the decree...get the ball rolling. I just happen to have my official seal with me. I am appointing you, my dear friend, to gather your present bishops together as best you can and commence discussing this with your instructors in the villages. If you have priests who have left to marry, invite them back and let them once again serve their God. I already have a fine ex-priest named Milton Drapeaux working on that project as a researcher. Select all your laypeople who are worthy and willing."

The pope's excitement at what he was about to do rose as he took a seal from the bag and put it beside him on the table. "Give them the training and instruction if necessary. If you have some who are more educated and capable of understanding the role of the Church, give them more authority and responsibility. We should even recruit professional people of importance in fields like finance and administration and give them special status."

Bill paused thoughtfully a moment and then in a more restrained manner continued. "But I would say that in some areas, the people and the Church are still best served by those of your present priests who have years of study behind them. We must maintain our loyalty to all those good and dedicated ones who remained celibate and loyal to tradition, rewarding them for their many years of service." Then his exuberance bubbled over again. "But don't get stuck on formal education if you find some layperson who you think might do a good job."

The cardinal found himself caught up in the excitement of the moment. "Your Holiness, start writing that memo. Then pack your bags and go home. You have observed what I wanted you to see and have responded more positively than I dared hope."

The pope pulled a sheaf of writing paper to him and placed the seal on top of it. "The seal, Your Eminence." He smiled broadly. "I thought it might come in handy."

"Bill, I'd like to add…when we accepted you as pope, many of us thought we could use you to get some new ideas and reforms accomplished. I realize you will take some flak because of this. I just want you to know we, the non-Vatican Church leaders, will provide you with as much support as you need."

"I already knew that, Gus. I learned much about you from Cardinal Comiskey. I think you are the perfect man to begin making the changes. Just wait until I get back and tell Robitelli what I've done personally before you begin the process of instituting these drastic but necessary reforms."

"You can trust me on that account, Pope Bill. I promise." Motupu turned on a speculative smile. "Oh, Bill, one more thing—"

The pope suppressed a shudder, sensing what might be coming. "Let her rip, Gus," he invited.

"I don't have to tell you now about the epidemic proportions this part of Africa is experiencing in famine and disease," he went on at the pope's questioning glance. "The UN and the U.S. government have been nothing short of hypocritical in giving our people only condoms when what really is needed are clean water and food."

"Maybe that's why the Irish can identify with you folks, Gus—the British did the same sort of thing to them during the Great Famine."

Motupu laughed. "The very concept of sexual abstinence is lost on

Africans." He bestowed an owlish look on the pope. "However, the people know the pain and suffering they are experiencing and are willing to consider almost anything else." He paused significantly.

"Oh my God, Gus. If you mean what I think you do, this trip is going to result in Vatican Three—before we've even totally implemented Vatican Two!"

"Of course, population and disease control must be maintained, indeed enhanced, here in Africa. There are a number of humanitarian relief agencies throughout the world, including International Concern, Doctors without Borders, Catholic Relief Services, Concern World Wide, Catholic Charities, and World Vision, that will join us in this fight. And of course, there's the Red Cross."

The pope interrupted his enthusiastic cardinal. "We've got to bring this to the attention of the international community, to the UN. Perhaps a conference that Ed Kirby talked about to be held at the Eleanor Roosevelt Center in Hyde Park, New York, where human rights and humanitarian leaders from around the world assemble from time to time to focus attention on this crisis in an international seminar setting. What Mrs. Roosevelt once said describes what happened to me on this visit."

"What's that, Bill?"

"As she put it, 'My interest or sympathy or indignation is not aroused by an abstract cause but by the plight of a single person...Out of my response to an individual develops an awareness of a problem to the community, then to the country, and finally to the world. In each case my feeling of obligation to do something stemmed from one individual and then widened and became applied to a broader area.'"

The cardinal felt almost guilty as he watched his friend pull the writing paper toward him and, fountain pen in hand, wrestling with his pains and prayers, distilled in his clear and legible handwriting the conclusions arrived at on this last night of the African visit. Finally, he turned to the cardinal as he took the seal from the desk and prepared to stamp his imprimatur on the words over which he had so conscientiously struggled. "Dear God, Augustine, I pray that St. Paul will send me some sign that he approves of my change of venue from Crete to Africa."

The cardinal could only try to wipe the tiredness from his eyes. "Who knows, Bill? But the real sin is in not trying. Right now, the world community could look itself in the mirror and say, we've met the enemy and he is us."

"The enemy, dear Gus, is world apathy and lack of concern. That is what I, we, must overcome."

The chills, fever, and stomach pains hit Pope Peter even before he boarded the charted plane in Luanda and continued until his return from Africa. He went straight to the Vatican's Gimelli Hospital. The doctors, although unable to diagnose his illness, were at least finding ways to make him comfortable and for the moment to relieve his symptoms.

Despite intermittent bouts of fever, Pope Peter was at work on the important reforms that he had envisioned in Africa. A Catholic-sponsored ecumenical Peace Corps, proclaiming central and eastern Africa a humanitarian disaster area, and including an expanded role for women, ex-priests, and laypeople were high on his list of priorities. But he also felt a deep obligation to those dedicated priests who had remained loyal and faithful to the teachings of the Church. They had played by the rules of the game, but the problem now was that the rules of the game had to be changed, or it would be more than a game that was lost—along with millions more souls.

At the Gimelli Hospital the doctors were baffled by his illness. Discreetly, Mayor Martin O'Malley and the cardinal from Baltimore had arranged for medical specialists to be brought in from the Johns Hopkins Hospital in Baltimore, but had no more success than did the doctors in Rome. It was a perplexing medical problem. It went away for a week or two and then recurred. At times Bill felt as fit as ever, and it was on one of these days that he summoned Ambassador Ed Kirby to a private meeting in his apartment to talk about his recent trip.

"Ed, now that I have seen for myself the tragic problems in Africa, I am almost totally lost on how to deal with it all from a Christian religious point of view."

The ambassador nodded sympathetically and waited for the pope to continue.

"It has crossed my mind that perhaps our religious training has put blinders on the eyes of us priests. We see only the prayerful 'hope to God' way and we may overlook the fact that the laity needs to be a major factor from now on. I don't mean just the 'people in the pews' thing. I think the first Peter had the same problem. You may recall in Acts, chapter six, verses one to five, that the Grecian Jewish widows were complaining against Hebrew Jewish widows that they were not given their fair share of the food collected for the poor. The apostles, probably urged by Peter, said, 'It would not be right for us to neglect the ministry of the word of God to wait on tables.' So seven of the laity or nonapostles were chosen to deal with this and undoubtedly other unjust situations while the priests or apostles minded the word of God."

Pope Peter chuckled at the look of puzzlement on the ambassador's face. "What I'm saying, Ed, is that priests, bishops, cardinals are really poorly equipped to understand politics, governmental structures, and economics. Indeed that is not their place. You laypeople must take command and leave the religious to do the praying and preaching of the love of God for all his people."

"I could not agree more, Bill. Why, maybe you could appoint a few laypeople to do your bookkeeping and even"—he shot a quizzical glance at the pope—"appoint qualified, honest accountants to run your bank! You know, Arthur Andersen is headquartered in my lovely Windy City."

Bill smiled and nodded. "Good advice, Ed. How about a touch of Irish Mist before you dash off?"

The pope felt he was on the verge of accomplishing his goals even though Robitelli was putting up as many slow-down signs, if not roadblocks, as possible. However, the bold venture into Africa moved Bill to give deep thought to other reforms he had been envisioning. From the input he received from both bishops and laity in various parts of the Catholic world, he felt he was on the proper course to steer the Church deep into the third millennium.

At a moment when he felt physically fit and perhaps even cured of his illness, he made arrangements to meet with his secretary of state and key members of the curia to discuss reform platforms. It was late in the morning, a time when he felt at his best physically, that the cardinal and prominent representatives of the Holy See arrived.

Robitelli was anxious to know what had really happened in Africa, although Cardinal Bellotti had given him a briefing. The coverage and the farewell at the airport only indicated that the pope had seen Motupu, visited some hamlets, and hoped things would someday get better. Robitelli was too wise in the ways of men to be taken in by the pope's initial, soothing words. But Bill Kelly had gained enough confidence in his new position now to be open with the cardinal.

"Well, Your Eminence—and members of the curia! There are some things I should let you know immediately. The cardinal secretary of state and curia members should not have to learn anything secondhand. So here it is from the horse's mouth, so to speak."

He went on to give them a detailed explanation of his findings and the proposals he had written out for Gus, presenting them copies.

"I have also instructed Cardinal Motupu to contact all priests who left active priesthood to marry. We must call them back to service...and if they are willing to retrain as teachers, spread the word of God, help to provide medical care, and participate in other projects such as developing land for food or drilling for clean water in Third World countries, then they are worthy of reinstatement.

"Certain parts of Africa, Nigeria in particular, have many wonderful young priests, but the entire continent is desperately in need of doctors, nurses, and educators. We certainly need priests in the U.S. and other parts of the world, so why not have the priests go to where they are needed, and send the former priests to where they can do the most good as teachers and medical people? They are all serving God.

"Africa, central and east, would be the best place to begin, since many American ex-priests already live in remote areas, on farms, and many have gone into teaching. More shepherds to care for the sheep. Why not use those men who have been thus well educated? It is a crime to waste all those years of preparation and study. I'm convinced it won't have an earthshaking effect on the celibate-priesthood controversy. As you know, I've assigned Father Drapeaux to meet with the members of Corpus in various countries to discuss ways in which ex-priests can become active in the Church again. I would like you to discuss this far-reaching innovation with whatever congregations in the Vatican you feel can provide some positive input."

The pope paused, unable to gauge his reception by the curia members, who could make it extremely difficult for him to promote his ideas or heed the direction in which he was trying to steer St. Peter's bark. "Perhaps you would compose a letter for me, maybe an encyclical, a decree, to be read in all churches. Of course, stress the dignity of the call to the celibate life with special admiration and praise for those who dedicate their lives totally to God. But also add that, due to the needs of the Church at this time, particularly in certain crisis areas like education, agriculture, and medical service, we need to welcome back any who may have left to marry. Stress the point that their services are needed and are requested."

The cardinal secretary of state and the curia followed this cursory outline carefully and took copious notes.

"Think also of the resources we will save not having to pay for a housekeeper...maybe the children could even take over janitorial jobs." His joking was not appreciated, and he hastened back to business.

"If there are members of the clergy who now feel they want to join the married clergy, let them apply to their bishops for permission and we'll see if they can be trained in an area critical to the needs of the people of God's Church. We don't want priests serving God as celibates unless they choose to do so freely. Perhaps a little historical review on how we moved from a married to a celibate clergy would be in order. No more secrets! Especially public secrets! The world knows we have had our share of failures keeping the vow of chastity. We must not let a few tear down the reputation of so many that are good. I was appalled last year when, as a layman, never expecting to serve the Church again, I read about the number of priests dying of AIDS. A spokesman for this disgraced portion of our clergy complained that no seminary gave young men studying for the priesthood any guidance in dealing with their sexuality. Now let's see how things go if we let them choose the role in which they wish to function. This will take months to organize, I know that. But let us start now. Are you with me so far?" He could see that the traditional hard-line cardinals were "with him" in the room, but not in attitude.

Predictably, Robitelli made the first objection. "Slow down, please. You are moving too fast, Your Holiness. We need to discuss these things with our theologians and bishops in all the dioceses. We must have a response from the priests who have remained faithful to their vows. Some may feel slighted, even betrayed, if Rome welcomes back those who have left it and married. After all, we have allowed them to continue as part of the faithful. They can take the sacraments like the rest of us. Shouldn't that be enough?"

The pope politely shook his head and tapped his finger on the Bible. "According to this book, Your Eminence, we are to seek the lost sheep. If Jesus took time to tell us of the prodigal son welcomed back by his father, let us remind the faithful sons they are going to inherit everything belonging to that same father. It doesn't say much for the faithful sons if they hold themselves slighted. The problem has been discussed to death for the past twenty years. I expect a good, organized plan of attack from your office within two weeks. I know you can do it. You see all the possible problems, better than I ever could. Just solve them! But, Gino, do it in a loving way so that we may better serve our constituents. The laity needs us now. The world is losing its reason. Show them that Rome is still the shepherd that leads its flock."

The cardinal became more and more exasperated as, in his opinion, the pope rambled on. Finally he could hold back his vexation no longer. He rose from his chair and leaned on the desk. "Please stop this, Your Holiness! This needs to be thought out. You could hurt the Church, and I know you don't want that. You even told the conclave that. The faithful will never adjust to this either, with all due respect."

Other members of the curia just sat motionless as Kelly and Robitelli squared off. "It was like the first *Rocky* fight," said the rotund Patsy Monassari of the Vatican Bank to others later. No other members spoke a word throughout the meeting. It was the Bill versus Gino show.

Robitelli paused. "Let us call a meeting of the various offices here to discuss the possible consequences of this approach. You state that you don't know everything about Church law, so you must please listen to the advice the Church gives you."

The pope slowly rose from his chair, leaned his own hands on the desk, and looked directly at the cardinal, face-to-face.

"Let's use your own words, Your Eminence. You want the Church to give me advice. Fine! Then why not send letters to all the faithful, all of them. We'll ask them to vote on the issue. A giant council. Two-thirds-plus-one wins! I'll agree with whatever 'the Church' says." A cunning smile crossed the pope's lips. "Or do you mean the magisterium when you speak of the Church? I think Vatican Two would disagree with you if you say that, Your Eminence. I think tradition has blinded you, my friend. Our people in the pews are more educated now. They have studied and have the same degrees as we. They must play a role far beyond what they are doing now. This was clearly expressed in the Vatican Two decrees, but never put into effect. The people, the laity, build our churches, support them, and care for our ministers who serve them there. But somehow the clergy displays a bizarre view of its being the sole authority for temporal work."

The pope paused and took in the others with a glance. "Maybe it was because I was on the outside and could look at the Church I love in a more objective light," he continued. "I could see, hear, and understand what Catholics were saying about it. Not only about the ordination of women or about married priests, but about those critical issues like birth control, capital punishment, abortion, gays and lesbians, and the annulment of marriages. I realize that these matters cannot be determined by what is termed 'politically correct' or what the elite media and the polls have to say. No. God's teaching and what is best for the Church must determine our future."

The pope was silent, uninterrupted for a moment. Then he spoke up again. "And another area of deep concern to me is, what are we going to do about reforming the Vatican Bank?"

Patsy's head sank, and a drained feeling seemed to weaken his entire body.

"This has become a matter of deep embarrassment to the Church," the pope said sternly, looking at Patsy. "In the past we have had certain officials who many believe did not act in our Church's interests, but in their own financial interests. Has this changed? That area also needs investigation and reform." The pope nodded at his declaration. "At least the windows need to be open and some fresh air let in. The same goes for the opening of our Vatican archives for scholars."

"Those are very big and powerful toes you want to step on, Your Holiness." After a pause Robitelli added dryly, "It has been tried before but without much success."

"No success in allowing the laity to be more involved in their Church? To decide what is to be done with their funds the Church collects?" Bill exclaimed. "We have experts in the pews who are not permitted to use the particular talents God gave them on behalf of the Church. Should engineers, carpenters, accountants, lawyers, and doctors remain mute? A sad thought, because such specialists could become more 'active' and help us. We need priests and bishops to celebrate the Holy Sacrifice of the Mass and perform other priestly duties."

The pope stopped suddenly, an affronted look coming across his features. Then, "But should we not open the Church up and expand the role of women? Allow them to serve us in meaningful positions of authority? After all, aren't they also God's children? Has anyone here served God and Church better than Mother Teresa? Are we more important in God's eyes than she is just because we are men?"

The pope paused, but the question remained unanswered. "We don't need to apologize for the past," he continued, "but rather to build on it. The laity at one time were poor, uneducated immigrants who could hope for nothing more than the mere necessities of life. Their one breath of fresh air was the faith that when they passed on, they would secure a better life under God. Now that they are educated they should not seem a threat but rather a strong right arm. We must become servants as Christ was, or turn into an empty shell. Based on what I've experienced from both sides of the altar, I know that the Holy Spirit will direct us through these adjustments that cry out to be made. We respect sacred Scripture, but must seek ways within Church law to effect change, reform, and inclusion. I know that God will guide us in this important matter, Your Eminence."

The pope's lecture to the key members of the curia was interrupted suddenly by a loud knock on the door. Cardinal Robitelli, astonished, turned to see who could be possibly interrupting them.

"Come in!" The pope called out, also surprised by the interruption. The door slowly opened to reveal a flushed workman and a very disheveled Meghan standing with her head down, covered with dust and dirt from head to toe.

"Sorry, Your Holiness," the man began. "May we speak with you?"

The pope was already on his feet and moving toward his daughter. Robitelli and the four other key members along with Patsy stood with a look of horror at a sight they had probably never seen before, certainly not in the Vatican.

"Dear God, child! What happened to you?"

She looked up sheepishly at her father. "I...I fell into a hole, Dad."

"It was an accident," the worker cut in before she could finish. "Please, Your Holiness, I am to blame. I should have been watching more closely. I was told you wanted Meghan to watch us work as we were excavating beneath the basilica. We got busy and I did not watch her closely. She went into the area we had not yet secured or even explored. I am sorry I did not watch her closer, Your Holiness."

The pope watched as the curia members hastily left the pope and Robitelli in the private meeting room, the nervous worker mangling his cap in his hands. Bill also caught the expression on his daughter's face. It was all he needed, and parenthood took over. "Go back to your work, friend. Meghan will be fine."

The pope closed the door as the embarrassed man hurried off.

"OK, baby, Dad knows that guilty look. What really happened?"

Meghan's red face told him he was on the right track. "It wasn't Antonio's fault at all. I got a little bored watching them clean stuff. I thought I would scout around a bit...I went into the restricted area when they were not looking and the ground dropped out from under me."

The pope grabbed his daughter's shoulders with both hands, shaking his head in disbelief and anger. "You could have been buried alive. I told you to stay in the assigned area with the other students. You kids will be the death of me yet!" He stepped back to examine her more closely. "Are you hurt or cut?"

"Just a few bruises. I only fell about six feet and landed on my feet."

"Well, you'll have to stop going down there."

"No, Dad, please, not now. It's a big find. Everyone is excited."

"What do you mean...'big find'?"

"Dad, I found what they have been digging for for the last three months. They were wrong in their calculations on which way the tunnel ran. I found the burial entrance site they were looking for!"

"Found? It sounds more like you just fell into it." He smiled at Cardinal Robitelli. "Gino, would you go check on this whole thing and let me know what is going on down there? Also, tell that Antonio guy that it's not his fault. The culprit has confessed."

The cardinal stared in disbelief. Evidently the Holy Family came before the Holy See. "Very well, Bill. We'll finish our conversation later if you wish." He was out the door before the pope could frame a reply.

"And you, young lady, go get cleaned up." He looked down at his own soiled white cassock. "I will, too." She reached out to hug her father, but his hand stopped her. "I'll take a hug later when you're clean. Get going."

He gathered his papers into a neat pile on his desk and glanced at the empty chairs where Cardinal Robitelli and the others had been in session. He felt distinctly ashamed as he realized that right in the middle of a heated debate, he had sent his secretary of state out to check on a hole in the ground. *Well,* he thought, *even laypeople have an effect on the magisterium.* He made his way to Meghan's bedroom. She had showered and dressed in clean clothes and was putting a Band-Aid on her leg to cover a minor cut.

"Well, baby, you had better take a few days off, away from the catacombs, and you'll stay in one piece." He leaned over to kiss her on the head.

"Dad, I know I was wrong. Am I to be punished?"

He smiled at the question, then decided it might be a good idea. "Why, yes, maybe we should punish you. Now, let's see...how does a pope punish his child? It can't be a spanking...no, the pope's daughter must have a truly papal punishment. Let's say that you have to read one of the four Gospels of Matthew, Mark, Luke, or John...completely. How's that?"

"Dad, you're off the wall!"

"True. But that's it. Let me know the one you read and I'll test you on it."

"Dad...you really mean it?" His stern look answered the question. "OK, give me a week," she said.

Bill Kelly, satisfied, left his archeology-minded daughter to finish cleaning up from her explorations.

The pope returned to his office and started reviewing his notes when the phone rang. It was Cardinal Robitelli. "Your Holiness, do you think we spoke long enough? Perhaps I should begin organizing certain things. And with your permission, I'll talk to Church scholars and theologians from the Angelicum and the Gregorian University."

"I appreciate your willingness to go where you are opposed to exploring, Gino," Bill said gratefully.

"Yes. The Jesuits and Dominicans can have much fun playing with this 'hot potato,' as you Americans say." Robitelli chuckled mirthlessly. Then, after a pause, "In regard to the accident, I checked into it personally. It seems that your daughter has become the outstanding archeologist of the year. That hole—or perhaps we should say tomb—she uncovered is a site that has eluded the Church for centuries. It appears Meghan has discovered the actual burial crypt of St. Paul!"

The cardinal was silent a moment, contemplating this revelation. Then, "It was thought by some that St. Paul was buried in a vineyard where San Paolo fuori le Mura, St. Paul's Church outside the walls, is presently located, but other historians say his remains had never been found. The remains of many saints and Church heroes were buried in secret locations in Rome and elsewhere in pagan times so the emperors could not exhume and desecrate them. It is possible, even likely, that Meghan has found St. Paul." The excitement in the voice of the cardinal secretary of state reverberated over the line.

For Bill Kelly it was a revelation similar to the moment he saw Brian on the dock during the conclave and cried out, "Oh, my God! So it's true!"

"Thank you, Gino. My course is now clear, crystal clear. I know exactly what to do so long as the Holy Spirit allows me to live. Saul of Tarsus, the Apostle Paul, St. Paul has given Pope Peter II the sign I was looking for. It is so bright, so clear, and so unmistakable. Crete becomes Africa today! I am where I should be."

Shaken at the sudden resolve, the unchallengeable self-confidence so suddenly taking over the pope's total psyche, Cardinal Robitelli beat a mental retreat from further confrontation with Bill Kelly, hanging up the phone.

The pope leaned back peacefully in his chair, now certain he was on the correct path for at least the start of his ambitious African program. If only his usual good health could be reestablished, he now felt confident that he would accomplish all the reforms the Holy Spirit had helped him envision when it had worked the miracle of Bill Kelly and the bark of St. Peter.

The enigmatic virus Bill had contracted was reminiscent of the one that had stricken the famous White House lawyer, Charles Ruff, on a visit to Africa as a young man, Ed Kirby had pointed out. It had put him in a wheelchair for life. But he had managed the vigorous defense of President Clinton in 1999, and Bill Kelly prayed that, whatever happened, he too could remain equally effective.

Nevertheless, it was impossible for the pope not to reflect on the *avviso* left to him by his predecessor. If he seemed to be accomplishing his mission, his life would indeed be endangered, as had the life of John Paul II when he set out to destroy European Communism. The former pontiff's warning that the Orthodox Church would be a powerful adversary to Catholicism had been reinforced by the meeting with the patriarch. But now his spirit rejoiced at the clear sign from St. Paul telling him the course he had set in Africa was right and to keep on following it, undeterred by distractions and the disapproval of others.

The pope decided to pause and say a bit of his Rosary to refocus his spirits. He caressed the silver beads, miraculously burnished to a bright new luster on his fishing boat that last morning, and his finger touched the sharp nick in the joiner inflicted thirty-five years before when he had tightened the screw on Brian's doorknob at the seminary. Bill was just heading into the third decade of his prayer when there was a knock at his library door.

Since only the highest-ranking members of the Vatican family could even approach this entrance, the pope called out to come in. His calm dissipated when Cardinal Bellotti entered. This visit meant a further attempt to dissuade the pope from his Africa program.

"Sorry to disturb you, Your Holiness, but I thought you might be interested in some news I have."

Bill Kelly was really confused as he watched the cardinal pause by the small serving table and glance down.

"Tell me, Bill, are those real peanuts or treated red ants?"

This was not the usual Bellotti. The pope regained his composure. "Help yourself to the real thing, Eminence." Bill Kelly had never been drawn to calling this cardinal by his first name, the majestic "Leonardo." "The coffee there is still hot."

The cardinal indulged himself and sat down in front of the pope's desk.

"Well, now, Bellotti, what is this interesting news you have?"

The cardinal gulped another mouthful of coffee to clear the nuts and smiled omnisciently. "Bill, I have been involved in a most absorbing situation here."

"I'm listening."

The cardinal's black eyes gleamed hypnotically. "It seems that my outstanding charm has motivated a nonreligious personage within the Vatican family to approach me to learn a bit more about the Church. As you know, we cardinals do not often get involved in proselytizing, but since it was you who specifically asked that some non-Catholics be welcomed here, I thought I would accept the challenge."

Bellotti paused, gauging the pope's interest in the point he was trying to make, and thought he caught a sympathetic gleam in the pontiff's eye. "And so, with my usual brilliance"—he smiled at his own self-mockery—"I was able to show how sweet the gentle Jesus really is, despite some idiots who try to serve him. In short, Your Holiness, I have made a convert. So I thought it would be appropriate if I offered a private Mass in the pope's chapel—with his permission, of course. Then my convert could have a private breakfast with the pope and me. To use your vernacular, what do you think of those apples?"

The pope hazarded a cautious chuckle at the evident joy in the cardinal's face. This man had proved a subtle impediment in Bill's papal planning toward the unorthodox and the forward thinking. But Bill expected roadblocks from the traditional-minded Robitelli and Bellotti.

"I think that's amazing, Bellotti." He still couldn't use the cardinal's first name, or a suitable diminutive. "Imagine, a genuine missionary right here in the Vatican. When do you want this joyous event to take place?"

The cardinal rubbed his hands together in expectation. "I say we strike while the iron is hot. What about tomorrow morning at your seven o'clock Mass? You can just sit in your place to watch or join me in a concelebration. What's your choice?"

The pope could see that Bellotti had something else on his mind, something missing from the conversation. "Well, I don't want your convert to think that I'm trying to steal the show. I'll just sit in my seat and be a simple attendant tomorrow, if that meets with your approval."

The cardinal stood up and stretched out his hand. "Magnificent. Thank you so much." He turned toward the door, pausing to grab another handful of nuts. "See you in the chapel."

❖❖ ❖❖ ❖❖

Just before seven the next morning Pope Peter finished his morning mediation and took his seat at the front of the private chapel. Waiting for the Mass to begin, he glanced to one side to see if he could identify the new convert but soon realized that his knowledge of the laypeople who came to his Mass was still limited. He did not want to turn around and stare at those filling the small chapel. He gave himself completely to the celebration and was lost in the peace of Christ until Communion.

Cardinal Bellotti paused, smiling at the pope before continuing. "At this time, dear friends, I would like to announce that we have a convert who has been moved by Christ's grace to join us wholeheartedly in His Church. I would like her to come forward first to receive Communion."

The cardinal walked around the altar and held the chalice and host to await his convert. The pope felt a knot tighten in his throat as he turned and watched his daughter, Colleen, advance to receive the Body and Blood of Christ. His two younger children followed her. He reached for his handkerchief to wipe away his tears of joy. It was going to be a beautiful day, he thought. Perhaps the happiest he had known in Rome since the day he had gone to Leonardo da Vinci airport to meet his family when they first arrived. If Mary Kelly had been there, she would have been filled with pride for the growth her oldest daughter had accomplished.

After Communion the pope stood up and walked to the back of the chapel, where he hugged and kissed Colleen and shook hands with Cardinal Bellotti. "Well, Leo, or would it be Lenny? What a marvelous and happy surprise."

"Try 'Leo.'" The cardinal paused. "Bill."

Fortunately, when Cardinal Comiskey arrived in Rome on only a day's notice, Bill was feeling his old rugged self. He had almost daily visited the tunnel in the catacombs where Meghan had fallen down into the now virtually confirmed burial place of St. Paul. The pope had accompanied Meghan to the site of her discovery and actually laid his hands on the uncovered stone sarcophagus in which the Vatican archeologists had pronounced the interred human bones almost surely those of St. Paul. There was no question in Bill Kelly's mind that Paul had come to him in his hour of self-doubt and was now showing him the way. Paul's Crete was indeed his own Africa.

Cardinal Robitelli noticed the marked change in Bill Kelly's demeanor and self-confidence. It was as though overnight he had quietly become the self-assured pontiff, unshakable in his beliefs, and undisputed ruler of the Holy See.

The secretary of state was annoyed by the short notice the cardinal of Ireland gave when he requested a meeting with the pope on the day of his arrival. "He's got too much access and is slighting our protocol," Robitelli complained to the curia.

Bill Kelly was pleased to hear Brian was on the way, short notice notwithstanding. He planned a family dinner that evening for his friend, to be followed by a quiet meeting afterward with Tim Shanahan.

Roger, Colleen, and Meghan were happy to see "Uncle Brian" again and asked during dinner when they might visit Ireland. With his omniscient smile Brian replied, "That's what I came to talk to your dad about."

"Is it, now, Brian?" Bill cut into the cries of joy from his two youngest children. "And just when does the pope amend his schedule to accommodate this visit?"

"How about St. Patrick's Day and a few days around it?" Brian asked.

Roger let out a whoop of joy.

"Doesn't His Holiness have anything to say about it?" Bill asked.

"Well, it's three weeks to St. Patrick's Day. Can we cart you over to Ireland for the occasion?"

"Yes!" Roger cried joyously.

Later, after dinner, Brian, Tim, and Bill met as usual in the library. "Now, Brian, how do we handle this?" the pope asked. "Robitelli and

Father Tucci will have fits if I even suggest it to them. They weren't happy with the planning of the Africa trip."

Cardinal Comiskey turned his sad eyes to the pope. "In case you missed it while you were away, there's been a deepening of the mistrust among the people and political parties in Northern Ireland. Even a resurgence of the "troubles." Certainly nothing like Omagh in '98. But new threats. I try to keep the Catholic side steady, but it doesn't take much to get the latest IRA faction all riled up. Paisley is always going to be his same nasty, hateful self. Let a Protestant fire a Catholic from his job, a Catholic complain about discrimination in Belfast, or a Protestant girl go out for a drink in a bar with a Catholic boy and we have the makings of violence all over again. We need some sort of ecumenical peacemaking gesture right now. The "troubles" are not in the news, but they're on the minds of Protestants and Catholics alike."

"Well," the pope said cheerfully, "it is close to St. Patrick's Day. What better place for the Kelly family to celebrate the feast day of the patron saint of Ireland than the Emerald Isle itself? What do I tell my cardinal secretary of state? Not that his objections carry much weight anymore."

"I'll tell Robitelli that we need the pope to make the visit," Brian agreed. "And when would that be more appropriate than St. Patrick's Day?"

"I'll tell him from me that the family wants to go. So to you, Brian," Bill smiled sympathetically, "I leave the explanations of how the presence of the Holy Father can help calm things down and fend off disaster."

The pope turned to Tim Shanahan. "Tim, maybe you can help explain to these last-century clerics around me that things move faster now. Planes arrive in less time and problems mount faster. A week or even a day for the old-fashioned planning, as important as it is, can lose us the reason for going in the first place." He turned back to Brian. "I take it things are urgent in Ireland?"

"I'm afraid so. The six counties in the North still see sporadic violence and threats from both the Catholic and Protestant sides. I have pretty good relations with both the Unionists and Nationalists. They consider me an honest broker. I have worked very closely with both Protestant and Catholic children on a number of projects, which have created good relations. We now have an Irish-American pope, and Pope Peter II is in an unparalleled position to help heal deep wounds. Much as the Polish pope brought the Communists into reconciliation with the population, I believe that Pope Peter can accomplish the same in Ireland. But our problems, despite the peace process, frayed by the bombing at Omagh and subsequent outbreaks and the long-standing tensions during the marching season, are likely to erupt. Time is essential if we are to get them behind us once and for all as we take on the third millennium. We hear dire warnings in the Fatima prophecies that the twenty-first century will unleash some sort of apocalyptic conflagration. Let it not start in Ireland." Brian gave his old friend a beseeching look.

Bill Kelly stood in the middle of the small library where he held these most intimate meetings. "The Vatican must also adjust to this new era of advanced communications. We have to be able to move as fast as any modern government if we are to make the Holy See as viable as any other world nation. If I have to be perceived as impetuous and antitraditionalist so be it." He clapped a hand on the cardinal's shoulder and smiled broadly. "So the Kellys will be in Ireland for St. Patrick's Day. Like it or not at the curia."

"Bill," Brian said, "thank you. As the Polish pope ended by personal diplomacy the blight of Communism on his people, Bill Kelly has that same opportunity. I need a power behind my efforts as the honest broker to end, once and for all, the Irish troubles."

•╂• •╂• •╂•

Brian Comiskey spent a day of preliminary planning for the Irish visit with Tim Shanahan, and visited again a second time with the pope. They met this time in his small personal study, and, it being six o'clock, Bill Kelly brought out a bottle of Jameson Irish whiskey and poured them each a drink, placing the bottle on the table.

"I'm glad you came, Brian, very glad. I probably would have sent for you. I have a list of reforms I want to see addressed. They have been ignored or swept under the rug by the previous cardinal secretaries of state, but the necessity for them can't go away. A few of them are even now being activated in Africa under Gus Motupu's authority, signed and sealed by me personally. I don't have to tell you what he is trying to do there: the disease, starvation, and genocidal tribal wars. We face a covert challenge from Russian Orthodoxy, which is no more than an attempt to gain political control in the new millennium. Islamic fundamentalism, the extremist movement which resorts to murder, war, and bombings in the names of Mohammed and of Allah, is different and has a better God than ours, they say." Bill raised his glass, and he and Brian sipped the fine Irish whiskey.

"Bill, you look worn out," Brian said. "What's the matter?"

"I don't know! I picked up something in Africa, some kind of virus. God, when I think of those poor nuns out there with the diseased and starving, trying to live up to their vows. I wish I could do more."

A worried look came over Brian's countenance. "Are you getting the right medical attention?"

"Yes, I believe so. You are the only person outside the medical staff that knows now. I pray I'll accomplish all I want to do. Use me every way you can."

"Robitelli has no idea you may have a really serious medical problem?"

"I don't believe so, Brian." His eyes searched his friend's face. "When I first came here I thought that was the miracle and I wondered if I was up to the job. But I placed my trust and confidence in God, worked hard, and now I feel good about the Church being on the right course. It doesn't seem a miracle at all. People's faith has kept my dream alive. That's an easy concept if you see it as a Church of martyrs fed to the lions. But when the pain, confusion, and disagreement come from inside, it is hard to comprehend. Yet here we have Cardinal Robitelli, opposed to my way of doing things, against my even being here in the first place, nevertheless willing to obey my commands. And that is what holds the Church together from top to bottom. You can call it 'loyalty to God.' That is why the Church has survived all these centuries. We have disagreements with one another within it, but as a Church we are 'serious.' Persecutions, wars, or dictators cannot silence the word of God."

"I expect that we will hold both the Church and Ireland together, and your coming will ensure that. I have built up considerable Catholic and Protestant cooperation and even a certain amount of mutual respect and understanding. But your presence in the country...that's the key."

✛ ✛ ✛

As the days before the trip to Ireland passed and planning intensified, general excitement also built. Colleen was delighted that Jan Christensen would be part of the pope's retinue. Roger was happy that Michael Degulis, the big affable Swiss guardsman and the other victim of the skateboard accident who had since become his best friend, was the second guardsman sent along for special security. Bill Kelly realized once again that his commander of the Guard was not only practical, but also knowing.

Before Brian flew back to Ireland, he explained to Robitelli the extreme importance of the pope making the trip at this time. Brian was prepared for a long, drawn-out battle over the timing and the rushed planning, but he was such a clever negotiator that even the skeptical Robitelli shortly realized he was no match for the witty and convincing Irishman. He was also in no hurry to test the pope's mettle again. Robitelli almost offhandedly agreed and told Brian to work with Father Tucci.

The morning following his meeting with Comiskey, the secretary of state arranged to meet with the pope to discuss the Irish trip. Bill Kelly felt like popping a few Tums pills before the cardinal arrived, figuring he was in for a battle.

As the cardinal seated himself, the pope was somewhat surprised to see a wide smile on the cardinal's angular face. Robitelli laughed softly. "I can see by your expression that you are expecting our usual confrontation, Bill. Well, as you no doubt are already aware, your friend Comiskey is hard to slow up. He did all the arguing for you. And after we had both calmed down he was able to convince me of the value a papal visit to Ireland could bring to the Church overall. That's not to say I'm delighted, but..." He spread his hands in front of him. "But I think perhaps—"

His words were suddenly broken off by a bang on the door, which flew open as Meghan came rushing into the office. "Dad! Dad!" she exclaimed, holding up her Bible. "I've been reading this like you told me to. Listen to this!"

The pope was shocked by the interruption. "Meghan, what is the matter with you? Don't you know enough to knock before you enter a room? Especially this office?"

"But, Dad, this is important. Listen!"

"Meghan, I'm happy you are reading your Bible, but can't you see we are busy here?" He glanced at the cardinal. "Sorry for the interruption, Gino. She should know better."

The cardinal smiled benevolently and waved his hand. "Take a moment, Bill. Let's see what Scripture is inspiring her. After all, she discovered St. Paul."

The reply caught the pope off guard. He suddenly realized he was making too much effort to listen to the cardinal and not to his own daughter. "All right, little dirt digger, what is it that's so important that you have to interrupt us?"

As if on cue, Meghan flopped to the floor, crossed her legs, and opened her New Testament. "Okay, now listen to this: 'And the devils seeing the herd of swine begged Jesus to allow them to enter them and he allowed them to do so. Then the herd, about two thousand in number, rushed down the side of the hill and were drowned.' Isn't that great, Dad?"

The pope looked at the cardinal, both of them with blank expressions. Meghan immediately sensed their confusion.

"Don't you guys see? Don't you know what this means? We could prove that Jesus did miracles. We could go dig up the bones and show everyone that it really happened! You could organize a dig right there, Dad!"

The cardinal and the pope broke into laughter, almost to tears. The pained expression on Meghan's face caused the pope to regain his composure. He rose from his chair and reached for his daughter's hand.

"Dad, don't you believe it? You said the Bible was God's word. Isn't that true?"

He recognized her anxiety and pulled her to her feet, giving her a warm hug. "Yes, baby. We do believe it. We were just too lost in other matters to see what you were saying. Now, tell you what. Cardinal Robitelli here is in charge of overseeing any digs that go on here beneath St. Peter's. I'll ask him to discuss this with our archeologists and we'll see what they think."

Meghan's hurt expression quickly disappeared as she beamed her smile.

The cardinal hastily assessed the situation and nodded at her triumphantly twitching lips.

"Why, yes, yes, Meghan, I'll certainly be glad to discuss this with our archeologists and see what they think of this most interesting idea. I'll get on it as soon as possible." He winked at the pope as he jotted it down on his notepad.

"Wow! Thanks, Gino." She dashed from her father to kiss the now blushing cardinal on his face. Then she went toward the door, stopped, and turned, planted a kiss of her father's cheek, and skipped to the door, heading out with all the gusto with which she had entered. The pope sat down again, and the two men paused to review the new idea.

"Well, Gino, there you have it 'out of the mouths of babes.'" Bill chuckled. "I've read that Scripture many times, but Meghan's idea never crossed my mind. What do you think?"

Robitelli leaned back in his chair thoughtfully. Then, after a few moments' rumination, "Let's say we went and dug up some bones in the Sea of Galilee. What would it mean? To some it would merely confirm the faith they already have in Jesus. To others it would just mean that we found some pigs' bones. All they need to say is 'So what?' Sometimes animals do drown in a lake. Perhaps the Christians heard of some swine drowning and they used that fact to develop a story to tell Jesus' power over evil. It seems to me that God has left us wide open to act as we please but he always sends his messengers to show us how much nicer life could be if we just try harder to care for each other." Suddenly he sat up straight. "Here I am rambling along like a preacher instead of discussing our present concern, the trip to Ireland."

"Gino, I appreciate your being so understanding of my daughter's extraordinary ideas."

"Glad to be of some help." The cardinal stood. "And we must never forget Meghan's contribution at the beginning of this millennium. The discovery of St. Paul's sarcophagus."

As he walked toward the door, the pope could not resist a final comment. "Gino, wouldn't it be amazing if we did find those old pig bones there?"

The cardinal could only smile wanly and shake his head as he passed through the door, left open by the budding archeologist.

Robitelli, having been convinced by Brian of the wisdom of the ordinary-tourist approach to the Irish visit, had taken pains to push the private trip concept heavily with the media. This was mostly to be a family affair, no special media arrangements except for the two ecumenical events, one in Dublin's Phoenix Park, the other in Belfast in the North. The pope would also celebrate Mass at Mary Kelly's family home in Galway for relatives and friends, and a farewell Mass during a short visit to Our Lady of Knock Chapel in Mayo. The pope's new car would be utilized.

Brian Comiskey had quietly arranged affairs that would be politically salubrious to all the Irish factions. Thus, on March 15 the pope, his family, Ambassador Kirby, Monsignor Shanahan, and a small contingent of Vatican officials landed at Shannon International Airport. Cardinal Comiskey, the president of the Republic, and the prime minister met them, informally. Officials from Counties Cork and Galway, where Kelly's grandparents were from, and a large media detail were also on hand. Although it had been made clear that this was a family trip to visit friends and relatives and not an official state function, the press turnout was equal to that for President Bill Clinton a few years before. The crowd, many among it carrying welcome signs, appeared and sounded overwhelmingly joyous. The Ancient Order of Hibernians and the Ladies A.O.H. in America were asked by Cardinal Comiskey to help in the details of the visit, because of their effective work in promoting Irish-Catholic values in the United States.

After an hour of speeches, handshaking, and photos, the three children with the pope proceeded by car to Oughterard, Connemara, Galway. Just about the entire hotel was taken up by the Vatican delegation and members of the press who had been fortunate enough to reserve rooms for the pope's first visit to Ireland.

The group was checked in by early afternoon, and, after visiting two popular tourist sites, Bill, along with Brian, Ed, and Tim met Father Jim Lane, formerly of South Boston, Massachusetts, and now living in Galway. They drove to Jim Regan's Pub in Moycullen around six o'clock in the evening. Men finishing work were stopping by on their way home. Brian had arranged everything carefully to give the pope a "regular guy with his family on holiday" ambience. Father Jim was beside Bill and Brian as they walked in for a pint of Guinness stout. Photos going back many years decorated the wood-paneled walls. In one photo, General Michael Collins was shown standing at the bar with a pint, and another was a more recent one of American tourists from Scranton and Wilkes-Barre, Pennsylvania, holding a sign reading FRIENDLY SONS OF ST. PATRICK.

Standing beside Bill, Kirby gave him an important tip on procedure. "The owner, the man with the pipe, will invite you to pull a few pints of Guinness. Don't make the mistake the United States president made with me at J. J. Foley's Café back home. You've got to have a nice touch on the pump when you pull a pint of beer. Tilt the glass; let the beer go in against the glass, not on top of itself. The more slowly you pull the beer the less foam and the more beer. The president pulled a glass which was one part beer and five parts foam and held it up to the TV cameras. The millions who saw it on TV half joked they wouldn't vote for a man who pulled so much foam and so little beer."

"Thank you, Ed," Bill said. "I'll remember that."

"And one other thing, Bill." Kirbys voice lowered. "For the sake of your mission here, I won't be seen with you in the North. I made some remarks a year or so ago in Belfast that were thought by some to be anti-Unionist. Particularly Ian Paisley. I called for a united Ireland, which got me in trouble both here and at Foggy Bottom. I don't need to sic my enemies on you."

"I appreciate it, Ed."

The pope and the cardinal, in plain black suits and Roman collars, bellied up to the bar, savoring the cheers of the overflowing pub crowd. "Set the place up," Billy announced. "The drinks are on His Eminence."

The patrons roared with delight. The owner, Jim Regan, standing behind the bar himself, called out, "Your Holiness, come back and pull a few pints of stout for the lads. Holy water it will be, and giving the boys and girls something to boast about the rest of their lives." He winked at the crowd, who cheered the pope on as he sidled along to the hinged section that Regan pulled up. Bill found himself facing a boisterous crowd of thirsty people. The owner proceeded to tie a white apron around the pope, emulating the other bartenders. "We want you to look like the handsome Irishman you are standing next to that Protestant, Dr. Clark, on St. Patrick's Day in Dublin," bellowed out the affable Martin Hanley, a pub regular.

Bill was handed a pint glass, which he carefully placed under the pump, tilted so the beer would flow along the side, and pulled the pump toward him, gently filling it with the dark liquid and a very small cap of foam on top. He handed it to Frank Noonan, the oldest customer. Cheers went up and cries of "Jim, keep His Holiness behind the bar. He gives the first fair pull we ever had in here."

The owner laughed, merrily shouting, "Your Holiness, you'll bankrupt the house!" TV cameras caught the generous beer the pope had pulled. Bill Kelly, enjoying himself immensely, continued to hand out liberal pulls to Ed Kirby, Brian Comiskey, Father Jim, and the rest of the papal party as well as to the pub patrons, who clamored for more of "the most generous Guinness ever drawn at Jim Regan's Pub." Bill Kelly had left the perfect half-inch head on his pours.

Finally, Bill pulled one last Guinness for himself, this time deliberately making it half foam. "I hope this one will make up for the maybe overgenerous ones I pulled," he laughed, and worked his way out to where Brian and Ed Kirby were standing. He took a long swallow of Guinness, wiped the foam from his nose, and enjoyed himself conversing with the patrons who crowded round, cameras flicking away.

"Well, that was one great photo op," Tim Shanahan laughed.

"Give us a song!" shouted Mike Foley to Father Jim, who topped the "grand" evening off by singing the traditional Irish ballad, "The Isle of Innisfree," featured in the movie *The Quiet Man* starring John Wayne, to whom Bill Kelly bore a striking resemblance.

"Are you ready for some dinner?" Ed Kirby asked. "You're looking kind of tired. We don't want to exhaust you on your first day."

Gratefully, Bill allowed himself to be led through the cheering throng and driven back to the hotel where his family was waiting.

"We're going to have dinner served upstairs, just the two of us, Bill.

Your kids are going to an arcade in Salthill and after to a movie in Galway City," Comiskey announced imperiously. "Tomorrow is soon enough for you to meet more people."

"Thanks, Brian. I am a bit tired. See what's on the television."

✠ ✠ ✠

All evening, as Bill and Brian dined in the suite, they switched television news stations. There was the pope at the pub drawing Guinness stouts and being cheered by patrons. CNN had Pope Peter drawing beers for the crowd every five minutes in its "Headline News."

"I just hope the Guinness people remember this when they make their contributions next Sunday," Bill joked wearily before heading off to sleep.

The next morning, the day before St. Patrick's, Bill Kelly felt considerably better, and he and the family did some sightseeing and shopping in Galway City. They bought Waterford crystal and Claddagh rings at Faller's Jewelers. After having tea and scones with a delegation of Galwegians, including civic officials and area residents at the Great Southern Hotel in Eire Square, they drove to his deceased wife's family home in Clifden, County Galway, where they spent the afternoon and early evening with Mary's parents, John and Lil Dorion, and the rest of the family. Bill celebrated Mass for the family at the residence.

None of the three Kelly children had ever met their Irish cousins before, so this was an exciting visit. Bill presented Mary's father, John, with a bottle of Paddy Irish whiskey and gave Mary's mother, Lil, a large replica made of Italian marble of Michelangelo's *Pietà*. No allusion was made to the bitterness that had once enshrouded the family when their daughter had married a "fallen priest." That was how the curmudgeonly old priest, brother of Mary's mother, for whom Father Bill Kelly had served as assistant, referred to the man who married his niece. But that was all behind them now. This was the first family dinner ever, and it was a time of great pride and celebration. The smoked shoulder, boiled potatoes, cabbage, and turnips were cooked to perfection. John broke out the bottle of Paddy for a couple of good nightcaps. At eight-thirty, with an hour's drive ahead of them, Colleen explained, "Dad hasn't been feeling well lately. He seems to have picked up some kind of stomach virus in Africa."

They drove back via Clifden Road, to Connemara, where they retired for the evening. Bill spent some time reviewing his ecumenical speech for the service at Phoenix Park the next day.

✠⊷   ✠⊷   ✠⊷

Everybody in Ireland had read the morning papers and seen the pictures of Pope Peter pulling a magnanimous pint of Guinness and handing it to their popular cardinal, Brian Comiskey. Suddenly the Irish felt they had their own pope after two thousand years, never mind that Bill had only been to Ireland once before, to claim his bride from a reluctant family.

Brian Comiskey and Tim Shanahan rode in one limousine with Bill; the children and guards followed in a second. Other members of the delegation trailed them in Church-supplied vehicles. As they proceeded from village to village, thousands of people cheered along the road waving signs: WELCOME HOME BILL KELLY! and GOD BLESS THE POPE. The visitors stopped for a few minutes outside St. Joseph's Church in Athenry, Galway, to bless the famine memorial built in memory of the millions who had perished in the great starvation in the 1840s.

In Dublin City they proceeded to the residence of Cardinal Comiskey's newly appointed bishop. They had tea and Irish bread with him, and then the pope changed into his long white cassock and a green cape with a gold Celtic cross especially woven by Irish nuns for this occasion. With a white skullcap on his head he was ready to ride with Brian in the glass-enclosed "popemobile" brought over for this day.

They drove up Grafton Street. Many thousands were waving at him. The Vatican vehicle proceeded past Trinity College and thence into Phoenix Park, where many thousands had been waiting since morning.

Catholics and Protestants alike welcomed the pope as he was driven to the back of the outdoor altar specially set up for the event. There the leader of the Anglican Church of Ireland, Dr. Wilson Clark, and leaders of several other religious faiths, including the chief rabbi, greeted him. A Muslim leader and even a Buddhist monk in saffron robes briefly addressed the pope.

Thunderous applause resounded as the group walked onto the stage and came fully into view. Minister Elisabeth Craddock, an ordained Episcopalian, recited the opening prayer and introduced all the religious leaders on the stage and the civic leaders in the audience. The "Our Father" hymn, (sacred equally to Protestants and Catholics,) was played and sung by the Dublin Philharmonic Orchestra and a choir from all the churches in the city.

When Dr. Clark concluded a moving ecumenical message of peace to the audience, Pope Bill walked over to him and gave him a warm embrace, at which the huge crowd erupted into a ten-minute standing ovation. Observers and historians said they had never witnessed or even read of such a dramatic moment in the annals of Irish history. Press photographers and TV cameras captured the inspiring event in pictures destined to make Irish history—the pope with the head of the Anglican Church. More than a few had lumps in their throats and tears in their eyes.

The pope concluded the ecumenical service with a message directed to the children of Ireland in this and the next generation. "May all the children in Ireland live in peace and justice all their lives, and may their children's children know God's harmony forever."

The pope also announced, "At this moment Vatican sculptors are carving in Italian marble a statue dedicated to all the children of Ireland and the harmony to surround them from now on. I will put this monument in the hands of the Lord Mayor of Dublin. All will be reminded of our pledge for peace and our prayer today for all the children of Ireland."

After this formal ceremony, which ran from noon to a little after one o'clock, the pope was escorted to the car with Bishop Clark. A family picnic and concert featuring the infinitely famous Irish rock group U2 was to follow in the festive Phoenix Park. The pope and the bishop drove to the Church of Ireland Cathedral and went inside together, the first time in history that a pope had set foot in this monument to Irish Protestantism.

Soon after, when the pope and Dr. Clark reached the bishop's residence, Mrs. Clark had a tea service prepared. The three sat down for a lunch of Irish salmon. Then Dr. Clark invited Bill to the bishop's study. "Mind if I light up my pipe, Bill?"

"Not at all, Wilson," the pope replied.

Puffing his pipe into life, the Anglican prelate smiled and held up three fingers parallel to the floor. "Would you like a taste of an aged single-malt Scotch?"

Three fingers signified a solid two ounces at least. "Fine thought," Bill agreed. The bishop poured from the bottle on the table into two crystal glasses three fingers neat of the well-aged Scotch whisky and handed one to Bill. Each man lifted the glass, nodded to the other, took the glass to his lips, and embarked on a long, satisfying swallow before reminiscing about the day's event.

The pope was escorted out of the bishop's residence. His limousine had just arrived and Brian was waiting in the front seat. Brian opened the back door and let Bill in. "The kids are taken care of by their two Swiss guards. We'll meet them in Belfast," Brian announced as he reached for Dr. Clark's hand. The two primates obviously had a cordial relationship.

"Well, Wilson," Brian said, "I arranged for you to have the distinction of escorting the first pope in history into your Anglican cathedral, the symbol of the Protestant Church of Ireland. I hope you didn't give His Holiness any of that special Irish that you save for my visits?"

"No, Brian, I gave His Holiness a touch of a rare liquor left over from some of the weddings of Henry VIII after he turned the country Protestant, remember? Your pope had banned the king's divorce and Henry took over the Church, marrying and divorcing to his heart's content."

"With odd head-choppings mixed in," Brian added dryly, not to be bested in any sectarian game of wit.

The smiling pope lifted himself into the car with a warm wave back to his newfound friend, Bishop Clark. "Come to Rome and I'll return the favor, Wilson."

Outside Dublin City, driving past the ubiquitous crowds, the pope headed north to Belfast, stopping at Drogheda to visit and pray over the remains of the martyred saint Oliver Plunkett. It was a must stop and an opportunity to meet his other Irish friend from seminary days, Monsignor James O'Brien, and wave to the crowd on hand and greet them. Plunkett was a symbol of centuries of British oppression of Irish Catholics. Pope John Paul II had also stopped here while in Ireland in September 1979.

Driving into Belfast, they couldn't miss the symbols painted on the sides of buildings: graffiti picturing IRA guerrillas in black berets holding Uzi machine guns and the words IRELAND DIVIDED WILL NEVER BE AT PEACE. Close by, another wall with graffiti of the queen in her robes and the Union Jack behind her featured the words GOD SAVE THE QUEEN, UNIONISTS FOREVER. Some new graffiti could be seen on many other buildings. Much of it had been removed by city authorities, but YANKEE POPE GO HOME remained visible.

They proceeded to the five-star Europa Hotel in downtown Belfast. It had recently undergone extensive renovation following violent bombings in the area. Many Unionist dignitaries had stayed there and conducted meetings and other functions in the main ballroom. People were gathered outside, mostly Catholic, waiting to glimpse the pope as his car turned up the driveway, which once had boasted heavy steel lifts because of all the car bombings and nearby terrorist activities.

They checked in at seven P.M. Cardinal Comiskey knocked on the parlor door of the pope's suite, and Bill asked him in.

"You're looking in fine fettle this evening, Bill. Do you remember how to throw darts?"

Despite the long day the pope felt quite buoyed up and accepted with alacrity Cardinal Comiskey's challenge to a game of darts. "I still can beat you, like I always did at the seminary and in that Portuguese place in Fall River. Remember?"

"Well, a dollar and the first pint of Harp says you won't beat me tonight."

"Oh?" Bill questioned. "Practicing when you should have been with your people in the pews, eh?"

"The ones needing spiritual guidance most are out there where the dartboards hang," Brian laughed. "We'll go down to the pub where the shipyard shift will be gathered, about equally divided between Protestants and Catholics, and decide right there who the best thrower really is."

Even during the height of the troubles, the one place in all Belfast where workingmen and -women could go after work and have a "jar or two" without fearing the political tensions tearing the city apart was the Landsdown Road Pub. Both Catholics and Protestants from Victoria Hospital and Belfast Shipyard could relax there and nobody gave them any "political cow dung," as Vinny McCormack (a Protestant human rights and union leader in Belfast) used to say. For most people, the answer to the troubles was fair employment and well-paying jobs.

Brian felt that taking the pope quietly and unannounced to the Landsdown Road Pub to meet the workers with no fanfare, TV cameras, or political agenda would go a long way toward sending the right message to the entire nation.

"Good," Bill laughed. "I get it. Nobody will recognize me up here in Belfast. Just a poor parish priest I'll be."

The limousine, at the pope's direction, dropped them off around the corner from the pub. Even at a distance, they could hear the festive crowd laughing and singing. They walked through the double doors with frosted glass panels, and the interior was indeed filled with workmen from the shipyards three deep at the bar. Both clerics were wearing the uniform of the day: work clothes, including a baseball cap worn by Bill with *LRP*—Landsdown Road Pub—embroidered on it. The men nearest the door observed the entrance of the cardinal, a popular figure to all.

"Your Eminence," the cries went up. Men turned from the bar to see Comiskey enter. There was respectful applause and some cheers for the well-liked and respected cleric. At first his companion went unnoticed until a patron at the bar held up a page from the previous day's newspaper. It pictured the pope handing a pint of Guinness to the cardinal at Regan's Pub in Connemara.

"Glory be to God, it's the pope himself," the bar customer cried out.

A profound silence fell over the bar. Finally, the owner of the pub, John Stinson, shouted even louder, "It's His Holiness. Well, sir, you've come to the right place. You're probably dying for a good pint," John loudly said to the pope, for all to hear. "Not that black mud they served you down south!" That broke the ice. The pub resounded in laughter and jubilation.

There was a sudden outpouring of universal respect and reverence for a pope joining this mixed group of Catholic and Protestant workingmen and the -women at their own place. The crowd, cheering, rushed up to shake his hand. Ann Castle reached for her accordion and Danny Gill his tin whistle, and soon singing broke out in honor of such distinguished visitors and friends.

Before the pub's bartender could get the pope to pull a few pints, he and the cardinal walked over to one of the dartboards as the men made them a path through the throng. The pub resounded with cheering as the pope and cardinal squared off in a serious contest of darts. Photographers and a TV crew showed up from nowhere, and every dart that scored a double became a public event. The pope threw one into the triple ring and the cardinal was unable to match it as the score rose. Newspapers with pictures taken in the Galway pub had circulated throughout Ireland. Neighbors began surrounding the pub as word flashed through Belfast streets that the pope himself was inside. Catholics and Protestants vied to see and exchange a word with this "man's man," which was the way regular customer Dermot Doyne described him.

While the dart game was in progress, a well-dressed, distinguished gentleman in his sixties, wearing an orange sash across his chest, came close to Bill Kelly and introduced himself. "Bill Martin. My friends call me 'Digger.' Head of the Orange Order up here. Welcome to Belfast, Mr. Kelly. I trust you will enjoy your visit. If our order can assist you in any way, please never hesitate to ask."

Even Brian did not realize what had just happened. The significance of Mr. Martin's handshake would vibrate through the entire North. It was to have more impact on Catholic-Protestant relations than any treaty or accord.

"If I may call you 'Bill,' would you like to join me, when you're through playing your game, at the bar for a taste of heaven?" Mr. Martin invited. The crowd watched in amazement. Martin, who prided himself as an after-dinner storyteller, said to Pope Peter, "As I said, my name is Bill Martin and I'm in the funeral business—"

But before he could finish his introduction to Bill Kelly he was interrupted by Tim Murphy, who finished the rest of the line by saying, "But my friends call me 'Digger' because I'm the last guy to let you down!" Martin never missed an opportunity to promote his funeral business and the line never failed to generate a good laugh, no matter how many times one heard it. The bar atmosphere was suddenly as friendly as anyone could ever remember.

Bill Kelly went back to his dart game with Brian after a brief sojourn at the bar with Digger Martin. The TV cameras followed every shot as though this was the finale of the national championship tournament.

Finally, Pope Peter won two out of three hard-fought dart games, and with much show, Cardinal Comiskey pulled out a pound coin and solemnly handed it to Bill.

"Now I see why it takes so long for me to get a new bishop appointed. The pope is practicing darts in his den all day."

For luck, some of the men took out their personal darts and handed them to the pope to throw at the board. "Sure I'll never lose a game again to a mick with this dart after the pope's blessing it." The crowd laughed and drank as the pope scored another triple ringer. Brian watched the pope closely. He was enjoying the evening immensely, but when he seemed to be tiring the cardinal insisted on taking him back to the Europa Hotel.

They had hardly returned to their suite when Bill turned on the television, to find his celebrated dart game with the cardinal as big as life on all three stations. He laughed uproariously at the close-up of Brian paying off his wager as they each sipped a Harp.

"Ah, Brian, it all makes me forget the *avviso*," he murmured.

•┼• •┼• •┼•

The next day, in Belfast's downtown business area, the pope and the cardinal met again at the site of a concert scheduled for noon. The Belfast Children's Choir had been founded by Cardinal Comiskey to bring children together to help heal the wounds of division and violence. Catholics and Protestants fondly regarded Brian because of his success in forming this bond through building schools and creating youth recreation programs.

The children's outdoor concert was held on what was once the scene of bombed-out buildings from the time of the worst of the troubles. The rubble had been cleared to build a park dedicated to peaceful communion among all children.

Both the pope and the cardinal were surprised at the empathetic accolades of Belfast's bisectarian populace upon seeing the TV and newspaper pictures of their dart game. As the crowds arrived at the park in Belfast, half the people were brandishing the morning newspapers featuring the pope aiming a dart. "Direct Hit on Heart of Belfast," the papers proclaimed.

✦⫶ ✦⫶ ✦⫶

With the concert behind them an invigorated Cardinal Comiskey joined the pope's venture across the North. Tim Shanahan, Brian, and the pope rode in the lead limousine, the children and two guards following in two vehicles and the Vatican observers bringing up the rear. At every village crowds turned out to wave to the pope, the limousine slowing down so the people could see him smiling and waving back.

"It's hard to imagine real trouble breaking out again," Bill remarked to Brian. "People seem so in accord today."

"The real political fact of life is that in four hundred years, Bill, Catholics and Protestants have been unable to reconcile their differences. There is always an Ian Paisley trying to stir up trouble on the Unionist side and our hotheaded lads causing it on the Nationalist side."

Bill chuckled. "The Lady Lord Mayor pointed Paisley out to me standing on the edge of the crowd with a bullhorn and his own bully boys around him."

"It is a tribute to you, Bill, and the moderate Protestants that the Unionists kept their protests under wraps today," Brian observed. "The best thing that happened in the park was when Mrs. Dawn Richarson, Lord Mayor of Belfast and the city's leading Protestant woman, couldn't bring herself to introduce the pope himself so she introduced the pope's children." Brian laughed. "Ah, that's a clever Protestant woman. How gracefully she avoided personally introducing the pope, leaving his children to do those honors. It was a charming moment indeed! And, of course, the Protestant Lord Mayor pointed out to everyone at the gathering that Catholics were seeing the mystical power of a clerical celibacy challenged at the highest level for the first time in the Church's history." He chuckled dryly. "At least as far as they have been allowed to learn it."

Bill changed the subject. "The kids must be getting hungry."

"We'll stop in Derry for supper." Brian glanced at his watch. "Say, half an hour. Then push across to Donegal to stay the night."

✦⫶ ✦⫶ ✦⫶

Ed and Kathy Kirby did not accompany the pope's party beyond Dublin. Ed had apprised Bill of his all-too-controversial status in the North of

Ireland. Even before he was first elected mayor of Chicago he had openly sided with the Catholic peace and justice movement. After his election, he had never hesitated to lend his prestige to Irish Nationalist causes. He had made his share of enemies, especially Ian Paisley of the extreme Unionist wing, who was Northern Ireland's most virulent anti-Catholic demagogue.

The U.S. Department of State was anxious to keep Kirby out of the North, and Ed knew he would harm the pope's trip in Protestant Belfast by appearing close to the American pontiff. Irish-American groups in the U.S. were always suspected, not without cause, of giving material aid to the families of imprisoned members of the violent Irish Republican Army.

Instead of the North, Ed and Kathy traveled south to County Cork to see their own families, the Collinses and Kirbys. They attended a rollicking family reunion in Clonakilty and stayed overnight with Gerry Collins on his Buttlerstown farm. The following morning they visited cemeteries where many Kirby and Collins family members were buried, including the grave of the "big guy himself," third cousin Michael Collins, the great Irish patriot who had been killed in nearby Bael Na Mblath.

Kirby also touched the grave of one of his personal heroes, Terence MacSwiney, once Lord Mayor of Cork. His death in 1920 after a hunger strike in London's Brixton Prison had drawn international attention. People like MacSwiney and Gandhi of India had inspired Kirby's personal drive for social justice and commitment to civil and human rights.

Ed and Kathy Kirby traveled in company with International Concern founder Father Aengus Finucume of the Holy Ghost Fathers in Dublin. Together Kirby and Finucume had visited the ravaged parts of east and central Africa with the previous pope and had worked together on world humanitarian issues. Stopping at a Kerry pub on their way to Mayo, where they would meet the pope, the two ordered a beer while Kathy went shopping.

"I would have thought you'd be with the pope, but I'm happy to have this time with you," the weathered old priest said.

"That old son of a bitch Paisley, a throwback to Trevelyan and Cromwell, would have made the pope's life impossible if I'd been along."

Aengus wanted to talk about human rights in various parts of the world and after a long swallow started in on the more depressing aspects of his findings. "Look, Ed, we don't get involved in politics. Who the president, prime minister, or dictator is doesn't matter to me. I only care how God's children are treated, and it's not very good from what I see." Grumpily Father Aengus swallowed another long draft of bitter. "Your president and Congress are playing footsie with dictators in countries like

China, Vietnam, Indonesia. Special trade deals and White House dinners with bums who are putting the screws to their people." Fiercely he gulped another measure of the amber drink.

Ed couldn't let the priest blame it all on a White House that had appointed him. "The queen of England entertained some pretty nasty African dictators recently."

"Pay no heed for the queen," Aengus muttered. "America's human rights record is a bunch of you-know-what-makes-the-grass-grow-green. I have priests and nuns being beaten and killed, and nurses raped by these government-sponsored puppets. And then we are told that nothing can be done about it! My priests can't celebrate Mass in Beijing unless they clear the text with the government. They can't wear the Roman collar. You heard Father Leo Shea of the Maryknoll Order tell us in Rome about China, that most of the food and medicine sent into the provinces for peasants on the verge of starvation is stolen by the officials and never reaches the sick and hungry. Yet when I look at the TV news I see these U.S. businessmen and politicians kissing that Chinese Communist chairman's fat rear end at lavish parties. It makes me sick. I've brought this to your attention before, Ed. You have seen it yourself, yet nothing changes."

Father Aengus took another swallow of his beer as though to calm himself down. "Ed, I know you discussed this business with your president and secretary of state. But the letter you got back laying out the official U.S. position is a joke. I hate to say this, but your country is more concerned with trade than with humanity. Or, as we settle into the third millennium, your country is concerned about human rights if, and only if, it does not conflict with big trade deals." Again a long pull on his jar quieted the priest for a moment.

Uneasily Ed noticed a bespectacled intellectual type down the bar listening to every word the exercised old priest was saying. As Aengus continued to air his grievances, Ed had the distinct impression that the young man, definitely a journalist type, recognized him as the ambassador to the Vatican.

"I'm sorry to put this on you, Ed, but I know how strongly you feel about it. The pope and the president will meet sometime soon. Could this be a topic of concern between 'em?"

Kirby was sipping his beer, listening to his friend, and watching the TV coverage of the pope's visit up north. He was also following what the bartender and customers were saying about the pope's trip, what it meant to both the republic and Northern Ireland. A photo of the pope playing darts in a Belfast pub had been ripped from the front page of the *Cork Examiner* and hung behind the bar for all to see.

After Aengus got his grievances off his chest they left the pub and caught up with Kathy. "Find anything interesting at the shops?" the straightforward but likable priest asked in his deep Irish brogue.

"I did," Kathy snapped. "I found that no matter where you two go, whether in the jungles of Africa, the poverty-ravaged streets of Calcutta, or even visiting the dead in an Irish cemetery, you'll ultimately manage to find a pub."

Their chauffeur, Tom, a retired bus driver, was waiting in the parking lot reading the paper when Kathy, Aengus, and Ed got in the car. "How long will it take to get to Mayo?" asked Kathy.

"Without stopping, about four hours, but the way these two lads are going"—nodding to the ambassador and Father Aengus—"we won't be there till after the pope concludes his High Mass in Knock."

As if to ignore any response Tom turned up the car radio, playing music as he drove along the main highway until they came to Charlestown in County Mayo.

Ed's party and the papal delegation all arrived at Our Lady of Knock at the same time. Knock is revered because it is where the Blessed Virgin Mary, queen of Ireland, appeared to the Irish people with a message of peace and love. Following the service, presided over by Pope Peter II and Brian Cardinal Comiskey, primate of all Ireland and successor to St. Patrick, the entire group drove the short distance to Monsignor Horan Airport in Mayo and boarded the pope's chartered Aer Lingus flagship, *St. Brendan,* back to Rome.

But before leaving Knock for the airport, Ed Kirby asked Monsignor Tim Shanahan if Father Aengus might ride with the pope to the airport. "As someone who heads a large organization of humanitarian workers in central and east Africa, he wants to give His Holiness some impressions on what needs to be done for the poor of the area."

"I'm sure that will be OK," Tim said. "But let me get approval."

Once in the car, Father Aengus told Bill in a torrent of words how important it was for the Church to get a handle on the situation. "The U.S. and Russians don't give a damn about the people. Both are concerned only about oil and minerals, especially the silver and diamonds. They treat the people like dirt. I predict that more famine and tribal war will break out soon. Not even to mention the threat of Islamic fundamentalists and the Russian Orthodox jockeying for power. They see the enormous economic potential and have to control the land in order to exploit it."

Aengus talked about the deep divisions in Africa and the hardships on the horizon for the people in the pews. "Famine, plague—you mark my words. Every kind of fatal virus infection is even now sweeping rampant through Africa."

Suddenly the priest was caught by a thought, and he stared at the pope. "I heard from my nuns that you were exposed to some of the worst strains of virus there that we have seen. One sister said that a Russian Orthodox Serbian woman doctor deliberately did it. Are you all right, Your Holiness?"

"I hope so, Aengus." After an unsurpassable sigh and a long reflective pause, "I found your observations sobering and helpful. Thanks." Not that the priest had told him anything he didn't know, but it obviously made him feel better.

On the plane winging its way back to Rome, Ed Kirby filled Bill in on how well the visit up north had played in the republic. "This whole trip was very positive. The people thought you were wonderful at the pub in Belfast. Be very happy with it," Ed declared.

✦⫶✦ ✦⫶✦ ✦⫶✦

It was only a few days later that Kirby found out how much additional trouble he had fallen into with the State Department. He was hosting an important diplomatic lunch when Seri, the Sri Lankan waiter at Villa Richardson, interrupted him at lunch and handed him a note.

> Call DCM ASAP, important. State Department called this morning—concerned.

Reading the note, Kirby murmured under his breath, "What the hell are they up to now? They are always looking for a way to bust my chops!"

After lunch, Ed went down to his office at the embassy, but Cal Seedworth, he was told by the DCM's secretary, Evelyn, was out playing tennis for a couple of hours. Ed asked her what time the State Department call had come in.

Evelyn looked at her call list. "We received no call this morning, nor did we call Washington."

"Are you sure?" asked Ed.

"Positive," said the always competent secretary. "Here is the log. All the calls received or made."

While looking for State Department calls, Ed noticed two calls from the *London Star,* a tabloid newspaper. "What the hell is that rag calling us for?"

"A reporter by the name of Randolph Bradlee called yesterday afternoon asking to talk to you. The DCM told me to refer all media calls to him," said Evelyn. "Let's see. They talked for about twenty minutes, and Mr. Bradlee called back again this morning and spoke to the DCM." Evelyn picked up a note on her desk. "Oh, the State Department did call the DCM at his residence early this morning."

"It seems that the *London Star* and State Department calls are connected," Kirby muttered. "But I don't know what it is all about. Tell Seedworth I want to talk to him."—Ed could not restrain the sneer in his tone—"whenever he gets back from his tennis. OK?"

Later that afternoon, Seedworth returned to the embassy and immediately went up to Kirby's office. "Ambassador, the State Department did call me. They received a call from the *London Star,* which has a story going that is very negative about you. It concerns an incident that took place in a bar in Kerry, Ireland, when you were drinking with a Catholic priest. They say the conversation got very loud and unruly, and your conversation was overheard by many. Your comments were critical of the queen of England. You were quoted as calling Paisley, Cromwell, and Trevelyan 'sons of bitches.' Eyewitness sources also said you and the priest were pub-crawling throughout southern Ireland. The story further reported that you could not go north with the pope because of your less than past civility toward Reverend Ian Paisley. The reporter followed the incident up with a quote from the British government, who were outraged by the comments of the U.S. ambassador and a certain Catholic priest."

Seedworth flashed his maddeningly owlish look through heavy glasses. "It seems your comments took place just before you were going to meet the pope in Mayo. SD wants to talk to you. They are embarrassed. The British government demands an apology."

Kirby was stunned but not surprised. Typical of the State Department.

"Shall I get SD on the phone?" Seedworth prompted.

"No, I'll talk to them in a little while," Kirby replied. He went to his residence, where his phone call couldn't be immediately monitored, and called up Father Aengus, explaining the situation.

"That's a lot of garbage," the priest shot back. "I'm assuming that the story is referring to the stop we made coming up from visiting the graves in Clonakilty. We stopped in Kerry for no more than thirty minutes, watched the pope on TV. Maybe you called Trevelyan and Cromwell sons of bitches, but that is mild compared to what historians could call them for all they did to Catholics. You did mention Paisley and we also talked about U.S. foreign policy. The newspaper story is nonsense," Aengus said emphatically.

"You better put it all down in a letter, Aengus, as accurately as possible. Check with the bartender too. He seemed like a pretty nice man. What about the postman who was delivering the mail? We talked to him for about five minutes. As best as I can remember, there were no more than ten people in the entire bar and everyone was looking up at the TV, watching the pope in Belfast," Ed recalled.

"Is this all your State Department has got to do?" Finucume carped. "No problems to solve? The rest of the world wants to know why the U.S. walked away from the genocide in Africa and your State Department is worrying about what you called Trevelyan? You should have called him much worse. A British official who said that starvation was actually good for Ireland. A man responsible for exporting tons of food out of the country while more than a million people starved to death. What are you supposed to call him? Sir Charles? I can only imagine what John Morrison from the An Gorta Mor committee in Chicago and Dave Burke with the A.O.H. in Lawrence, Massachusetts, would have called Trevelyan."

An hour or so later, the State Department called back and, before Kirby could say a word, told him how embarrassed the secretary was with his behavior in that bar in Kerry. "The British press is all over the story," an assistant desk officer recited, "and the U.S. press is picking it up big-time. It has made the talk shows and CNN. State has ordered the inspector general to Ireland to get the details from the people at the bar and then is coming to Rome to interview you. A report will be filed with the secretary of state, and Senator Delms has already asked for a copy. He will probably hold a public hearing on the matter."

Ten days later, two men and a young woman from the inspector general's office came to Rome from Ireland to interview Kirby. They checked into the Excelsior Hotel for four days and sampled Sabitino's and other luxury restaurants. They concluded that after interviewing several people in the bar in Kerry, including the bartender, postman, a reporter for the local weekly newspaper, and the cook who was preparing the lunch, as well as Father Aengus Finucume, nobody had any idea what the story was all about. The report cleared Kirby, but it wasn't the only inaccurate and made-up negative story that found its way into the press.

LOST AT SEA 40

Shortly after returning from his successful journey to Ireland, Pope Bill was more than ever determined to help the desperate people of east and central Africa. The trip there had had a profound and moving effect on him. Now he was expending considerable time and much of his waning energy on the project. The pope did not underestimate the massive international aid necessary to lift that part of the continent out of its morass of disease and famine. Nevertheless Pope Peter II was determined to somehow arrange for the cultivation of available land for food, provide cleaner water, build schools and hospitals, and establish an international medical research center.

He realized that neither he nor the Church could do it alone. The project needed the active support of the United Nations and other international humanitarian, medical, and business organizations, as well as not-for-profit foundations. What he had going for him was the considerable goodwill of many sincere believers and supporters both within and outside the Church. As pope, he could reach them all. In this context his nuncio to the United Nations was busy scheduling the speech the pope would deliver reporting on his visit to Africa.

Meanwhile, the Kelly children were occupied with unexpected plans for the wedding of their brother Ryan and Paula Novak. It was a stressful time for Colleen and Meghan, who were dedicated to easing their father's self-imposed burden and his obviously failing health.

The pope's family was just beginning to realize the extent of the intrusions and lack of privacy that they were in for and to understand why popes, in fact all dedicated priests, took on a vow of celibacy. That was a reason why Ryan and Paula wanted a very brief engagement. The pope's son was fast becoming a tabloid item, with reporters and photographers covering his New Bedford fish marketing after he came in from a week at sea to deliver his catch.

Late one afternoon, Al Cippolini hurried into the pope's small family room at the Vatican and, finding Colleen, told her that she needed to talk to Fall River Bishop Sean Patrick immediately. "He is on the phone right now from Cape Cod," said the monsignor.

"Yes, Uncle Sean," she said, picking up the telephone. Listening, she became increasingly distressed. "Oh, my God! Oh, please, God help him!

Yes, I understand. How long? Is the Coast Guard involved? Yes, Senator Lane is a family friend."

She reflected on her statement a moment, thinking of young Lane's annulment problem, soon to come up at the Vatican. "Yes, we know the senator," she amended. "I understand. I'll be there as soon as possible. Call me with any news. Thank you, Uncle Sean. Yes, I will. Good-bye."

Colleen turned to Monsignor Cippolini. "This is terrible, Al. Ryan and his crew are missing at sea. I've got to tell Dad right away." As Colleen briskly walked down the long marble corridor and into her father's office, she heard Monsignor Tim running down the corridor behind her.

"You've heard, Colleen? I just spoke to Senator Lane in Washington. He is on his way to the Cape. He will call you when he gets an assessment of the situation."

They both hurried into the pope's office. He was on the phone being briefed by the Coast Guard from Cape Cod. "There is no contact at all?" they heard him ask.

The pope concluded his conversation with the Coast Guard commander. Colleen hugged her father, holding back her tears.

"He'll be all right, Colleen. God will protect them, and besides, all of them are good seamen. We must pray now to Our Lady of Fatima for their safety." The pope smiled mistily at his daughter. "We can all be thankful that you have learned to pray again." He reached into his pocket, took out the shining rosary beads, and handed them to his daughter. "Keep them with you all the time the search is going on and say a decade now and then. Your prayers will be heard. I know that."

Solemnly Colleen took them. The group held hands and Tim led them in prayer.

After informing Roger and Meghan, Colleen called Paula at her Loyola hostel. A distraught Paula begged to accompany her back to New England. They made arrangements to take an Alitalia flight that night to Boston and be driven by car to the Cape. They would arrive at the Coast Guard air terminal near Buzzards Bay in the early morning to help join in the search by helicopter. Senator Lane called two hours later and gave the pope an update on what was happening. It was obvious he was using all his power as a U.S. senator to keep the search going.

Upon arriving in Boston early the next morning, Colleen and Paula were met by a young priest and taken immediately by car to Buzzards Bay. Ryan and his crew had sent out a distress signal but had now been missing somewhere on the outer edge of Georges Bank for about thirty-six hours.

After a restless night with no encouraging news, Coast Guard authorities started to question whether continued search could prove fruitful. Colleen pleaded with Senator Lane to keep the effort going. Senator Lane was able to convince the commander to continue searching for the lost fishermen. Colleen asked Lane if she could go on the Coast Guard helicopter search of the lost fishing boat. Bishop McCarrick, who was at the scene the whole time, also wanted to go. Senator Lane obtained grudging permission from the base commander for Sean and Colleen to accompany the Coast Guard pilot and crew on the search out over the ocean. Paula stayed in the communication center.

They remained in the air for several hours, stopping twice to refuel. Colleen held the rosary that her father had given her tightly in her hands as she stared out first through the side windows, then out the front windshield between the two pilots sitting in front of her.

All this time, prayers and novenas were being said for the pope's son and crew in homes and Churches all over the world. Hundreds of fishermen based on the Cape and the islands joined the search.

In the meantime, the pope was conducting an all-day and all-night vigil at the Chapel of Our Lady of Fatima in the Vatican. His devotion and love for her were endless, and at no time was that special relationship ever needed more than now. *She has always been there for me, especially in a time of great crisis,* Bill thought to himself.

Back on the Cape, the sun was setting, and just before it turned dark and the mission would have to be discontinued for the day, Colleen spotted a small but remarkable bright orange and blue light about ten miles away. "What's that over there? What is it?" she cried, pointing in the direction of a seemingly pulsating glow in the sky, the silver beads of her rosary shining in her hands.

The pilot turned to the southeast and proceeded toward the gleam. The flickering light blossomed larger as they closed on it. The pilot could not discern what the light in the sky had to do with the missing boat, but he followed Colleen's importunings. As they came closer to the light they could now see that it was some sort of break in the cloud formation through which a golden beam flickered and reflected on the waters below.

Colleen looked down at the ocean and cried out, "Look, look, there is something down there." She pointed out the side window. "Oh, my God, it looks like a small raft."

The pilot could not see what it was some two or three thousand feet below him. The mysterious ray of light was fading as the helicopter descended closer to the surface of sea. As the object on which the dimming light was focused became increasingly visible, it was now clear that there was an orange life raft directly below them. They could see that the crew was frantically waving a white sheet back and forth. The pilot radioed his base, giving them the small craft's exact location.

"Coast Guard cutter on the way," crackled the return message.

The helicopter continued to circle the boat, and the pilot counted the number of crew members. "I make out five men. That's how many I was told were reported to have left the dock. Five put out on Monday, and there are five down there."

"Thank God," Colleen and the bishop kept saying.

An air crewman dropped a long rope from which was suspended a first aid survival kit, flares, and a radio signal transmitter. Colleen kept trying to see Ryan, but it was now too dark to recognize anyone's face. The helicopter dropped a flare just as the shimmering light disappeared in the dark sky above them. Colleen imagined she could distinguish Ryan's tall figure.

The helicopter turned back to base and landed just as the fuel tanks were registering empty. But the search had been successful. Continuing it had paid off.

Colleen and Bishop Sean stepped out of the helicopter and walked into the base command office, where Paula and Senator Lane were waiting together. They entered just in time to hear, "We have control of the situation, all accounted for," crackle over the radio from the Coast Guard cutter.

The next voice said, "Hello, sis. It's me, Ryan. I'm OK, and everyone else is, but we were scared to hell."

"Ryan, the bishop is with me. Thank God you and everyone are OK."

"Thank God is right. Hey, I heard you got religion. That's great."

Colleen smiled and pressed the rosary beads in her hand. "Everyone had been worried sick. Paula wants to talk with you."

"I love you, Ryan. Are you OK?" Paula called over the radio.

"I'm fine—now. I love you, Paula."

"Can we call the Vatican from here?" Colleen asked the commandant, who had just entered the base communications center.

"Certainly, I think so. I'll ask the base operator to notify the Vatican."

A few minutes later, the pope was on the radio.

"Your Holiness, this is Senator Lane. We established contact with

Ryan, who had just been picked up with all hands by a Coast Guard cutter. I'll put Colleen on."

"Oh, Dad," Colleen cried. "It was amazing how we found the boat. I saw a bright orange and blue light in the sky, and as we headed toward it, just before the sky turned dark, we saw Ryan's lifeboat just below in the light."

"I know," was all the pope said.

"It was weird, the beam from the sky and all," Colleen went on. Then, reflecting a moment on her father's comment, "What did you mean when you said, 'I know'?"

"Faith, darling."

•⊹• •⊹• •⊹•

Later that night the cutter churned into the base. TV klieg lights were trained on the debarking fishermen as they were greeted by a small crowd of happy and cheering family members. That evening Ryan, Paula, and Colleen were eating sandwiches and vegetable soup sent over to the Kelly home from the town deli.

Colleen asked Ryan, "What do you think Dad meant when I told him about the bright orange and blue light in the sky over the spot in the ocean where we found you? What do you think he meant when he said, 'I know'?"

Ryan just shrugged and finished devouring his ham and cheese sandwich.

"He answered that question with one word. That word was 'faith.'"

Ryan pushed his food aside and gave his sister a long, adoring look. "They really got to you at the Vatican, didn't they. I mean you really do believe in God once more."

"If I had any doubts they are gone now."

"What are your plans now, Col?" he asked.

"Dad needs me. He's sicker than anyone knows. I'll fly back tomorrow evening."

"Tell him he was right about those giant combers that creep out of the Bermuda Triangle and side-whack a lone boat. Luckily it was daylight so we saw it coming and we were in the second trawler. The *Mary One* is in dry dock for extensive repairs. I'll write up a report tomorrow before you have to go to Dad." He paused, his eyes dropping. "And tell Dad I myself and the crew are all believers. Someone up there was looking out for us." Ryan grinned at Paula. "And you, sweetheart?"

"I'm staying. For a while, anyway. Until you go to sea again."

✦╎✦ ✦╎✦ ✦╎✦

Back at the Vatican, praying in his private chapel, the pope kept saying to himself, "Ryan is no longer lost at sea, but safe in Our Lady's hands."

He spent the entire night ruminating over the majesty of Our Lady of Fatima, who had appeared to three children in Portugal in 1917. While praying, he relived that morning on the fishing banks when he had sensed the message from Our Lady. Then Brian came with a message from the college of cardinals, calling him back to God's service.

Bill Kelly thought of the previous pope, how he had been shot at the edge of St. Peter's Square on May 13, feast of Our Lady of Fatima. Later in Rome, the Polish pope told a special convergence of the college of cardinals that it was Our Lady who had saved his life from the assassin's bullets and Our Lady who had freed his native Poland from Communist shackles at the end of the 1980s. "If you follow and believe her word, she will help you," the pope told them.

Bill's mind returned to that early morning on his boat off Cape Cod when he had heard Our Lady calling him back into service. His role now, as long as God gave him strength, was to serve Him, helping His people, His Church—not only as his responsibility but also as his calling from Our Lady. He not only lived for Christ, but also was ready to die for Christ.

At five o'clock the next morning Bill showered and dressed and went to celebrate Mass for some five hundred men at the maximum security prison just outside Rome. He presented each of the men rosary beads, a small prayer book, and a story of the life of Christ and his suffering and death on the cross for the sins of everyone. Following the Mass, Bill breakfasted with the men and talked separately with several of them for two more hours.

One prisoner asked the pope why people sinned and committed crime. "If you say, 'God loves me,' why would he let me commit crimes?" asked the swarthy inmate.

As Bill was struggling, trying to answer the question, he suddenly realized that this was where Mehmet Ali Agca, the man who had tried to kill

Pope John Paul II had been imprisoned until John Paul II pardoned him and he was returned to a Turkish prison for his other crimes.

Bill remembered Ed Kirby telling him that after reading CIA cables, talking with Italian intelligence officials, and most important in discussions with certain highest-ranking Vatican officials, he had became convinced that Agca had not acted alone in the assassination plot. Knowledgeable officials believed, and Ed Kirby concurred, that responsibility for his attempt went all the way up to the highest minister at the KGB. Bill Casey, the former CIA director, once had told Kirby that Agca was a professionally trained assassin paid and instructed to carry out this mission by the Russian Communists through Bulgarian intermediaries.

"God gives us all a free will," the new pope told the prisoner. "He does not force us to do or act in this or that way. You make your own choices. That's why we need God's grace to lead us in the right direction. To do what is right can be difficult and require sacrifice, but if you place your trust and confidence in him, you can find peace with yourself."

For a moment in his mind's eye Bill saw the middle-aged blond Serbian woman who had somehow maneuvered the virus-struck African boy to a position where, either accidentally or purposefully, he bit the back of Bill's hand. And the words of his predecessor in the *avviso* came back to him. If he did what was right, what had to be done, his reign would not be a long one unless some miracle intervened.

Just then, Father Salvatore, the prison chaplain, stepped in. He requested that the pope meet other inmates. Later, when Bill was leaving the prison, walking out the portal with Father Sal, he asked, "Padre, how long have you been a chaplain here?"

"About forty years," the old priest replied.

"Wouldn't you like to do something else? Have your own parish in some beautiful suburban Italian community with your own house and school?" asked Bill.

"Of course, Holy Father, but this is what God wanted me to do."

"Well, then," said Bill, "you knew Agca during his time here. Agca had once asked if trying to kill Pope John Paul II was something that God wanted him to do."

"Certainly not," Father Sal snapped. "He did what the Bulgarian Communists and the Soviets paid him to do. One Italian defense attorney told me that just after talking with Agca, his client, about a possible parole, Agca told him, 'You must not wish too much because sometimes your wish may come true.' Our little Agca may be safer in his new Turkish prison than out on the street."

THE UNITED NATIONS TRIP 41

When Colleen walked into the papal office immediately upon her return from Cape Cod, she found Bill quietly slumped in his chair. The quick bounce he had once had was noticeably absent as he slowly stood up to greet her. He mustered a forced smile, extending his open arms to his daughter. He thought to himself as he affectionately held her of his life with Mary, Colleen's mother, since he had first met her twenty-five years earlier in a small town on Cape Cod. It seemed like a hundred years since the young priest had turned rugged fisherman in order to become one with Mary, had taken on the powerful lobby of international corporations in an emotional congressional hearing. Backed by the present Senator Lane's father, he had fought back the seafood cartel when they wanted to end all trade protections for small American fishermen, most of whom were poor immigrant Portuguese with large families and no political clout.

They talked for an hour or so, until Colleen's eyes started to close.

"Well, our prayers were answered, Colleen. I hope that the experience wasn't too much for you. You must be exhausted. Are Ryan and the crew getting some rest?"

"Yes, Dad. All's well."

"I'm grateful for the help and support we received. It was so kind of everybody." He kissed her forehead. "You must get some rest now, Colleen."

"We both must," said Colleen.

"I'll say amen to that."

With the stress of the fishing boat near-disaster behind them, Bill went back to work preparing for his upcoming presentation to the United Nations in New York City, and for the briefings and cajoling ahead. He must get the necessary support and financing for the international medical research center and hospital he dreamed of building in central Africa.

❖❖ ❖❖ ❖❖

Accompanied by Ed Kirby and Tim Shanahan as well as Cardinal Robitelli's small cadre of Vatican specialists, Pope Peter II left Rome in a chartered Alitalia luxury jet. This visit to New York was to be of short duration. The pope had allotted a day at the Johns Hopkins Hospital outside Washington for further testing. He and his handlers were trying to downplay his mysterious affliction. His doctors in Rome and the specialists flown in from the States all agreed on only one thing; if he were not receiving expert medical attention, he could not have survived as long as he had. People with similar infections invariably succumbed quickly, in a week or so at the most, in Africa. The fact that he had survived and to an extent remained able to function normally attested to the fact that someday a cure for the mysterious African virus he had contracted would be discovered.

The president of the United States was anxious to meet with the pope during the pontiff's first visit as leader of the nearly one billion Catholics worldwide and about more than 62 million Catholics in the U.S. The pope was now extremely popular stateside, and all the top political leaders there were hoping for a handshake and photo opportunity with him. Any photograph with the pope would certainly appear in their next campaign brochure and on their TV ads. Pro-choice politicians, like the president, particularly wanted to be identified with the Catholic vote even if only by such a photo.

When the pope's Alitalia jet arrived at Kennedy Airport, a huge crowd turned out to welcome it. Press from all over the world was on hand, and most national media affiliates were giving live coverage to the entire visit. The tone in New York City was very upbeat since the voters had just elected a new popular mayor, the Rangers had won the Stanley Cup, and the economy was very strong. The mayor and the governor were engaged in playful talk with the new New York archbishop before the pope's plane set down. The archbishop of New York, Ed Egan, was playing a key role in civic life, so a positive relationship with him was important in the life of any politician. A new spirit of excitement existed in the Big Apple.

"Welcome to the capital city of the world," the mayor greeted the pope.

"Oh, my God, did the pilot take me to Boston by mistake?" the pope quipped while shaking hands with the mayor.

When the dynamic president of the International Longshoremen's Association was introduced, he said, "Holy Father, we are very proud in the ILA to have you as one of our members!"

The pope responded to the union boss by whispering in his ear, "I'm sorry to be behind in my monthly dues."

After greeting the usual delegation of civic and religious officials, Pope

Peter walked over to an area reserved for handicapped children and was greeted with a beautiful rendition of the song "New York, New York."

Just as the pope and the archbishop were stepping into the waiting limousine that would take them to the cardinal's residence behind St. Patrick's Cathedral, he noticed a line of police officers and a uniformed patrolman sitting in a wheelchair with a young woman and a boy standing next to him. The archbishop, a new friend to most of the NYC police and firefighters, noticed that the pope was looking in the direction of the officer. "That's Steve McDonald, a highly decorated NYC police officer, with his wife Patty Ann and young son. He was paralyzed after getting shot in the line of duty. He even visited the man in prison who shot him. He forgave him, and it touched the entire city in a profound way."

"I remember reading about that," said the pope as he walked over to Officer McDonald and put both hands on the officer's shoulders. The pope talked with the McDonalds a few minutes before getting in his car. McDonald, a devout Catholic, hugged his wife and son with joy in a moving embrace.

Crowds were lined up along the route through Manhattan. Pope Peter II was a tremendously popular figure in the United States, and his popularity extended to the most unlikely circles for a Catholic Church leader. He was particularly well received in the black and minority communities for standing up for the poor and needy, and of course among the Portuguese.

After Mass and a novena in honor of Our Lady of Fatima at St. Patrick's, assisted by seminarians from Dunwoodie in Yonkers, Pope Peter adjourned to the archbishop's residence and had dinner with the archbishop and other prominent Catholic bishops. Also included was the pope's son, Ryan. After dinner, the pope retired early to prepare for his address to the UN the next morning, but not before he had coffee in the kitchen with the members of his fishing crew, who had driven up from New Bedford to spend a few minutes with their former skipper.

The next morning, after a private Mass at St. Patrick's, the pope and the papal nuncio to the UN left by car for the UN building, where the pope was introduced by the secretary-general as "the conscience of the world."

The pope spoke for forty-five minutes and was interrupted fifteen times, three times with a standing ovation. He not only reported on his recent trip to Africa but also called on the world community to "nourish and protect the children of Africa, like a mother would her own." He referred to the children of Africa as "God's special children" and to Africa as "God's home away from home."

After leaving the UN, the pope was taken by helicopter to Seton Hall University in South Orange, New Jersey, where he spoke before the entire student body and faculty. President Father Peterson presented him with the school's highest honor. "Seton Hall University is proud to welcome you into our family, and pray that you have the strength and good health to accomplish your humanitarian, life-caring goals." Little did people realize how his strength and health were fading each and every day.

The pope departed Newark Airport feeling he had achieved his mission in alerting the world community to the suffering and plight of millions of suffering people in Africa. The flight to Baltimore was a short one, and the staff of Johns Hopkins was waiting for him. He spent the night and most of the next day undergoing intensive tests and examinations, and late in the afternoon a police escort whisked him to Dulles Airport, where his chartered TWA jet was waiting to take him back home to the Vatican; but not before he stopped at the Shrine to St. Jude in Baltimore and prayed briefly and spoke to the Italian priests.

Just after the plane took off, the flight attendants started to serve before-dinner drinks. Bill, who was in the first-class section with Motupu, decided to take a walk through the plane to thank his staff and say hello to the press. This was a very brief visit. Because of the importance of the mission, almost one hundred members of the world press made the trip. Tim Shanahan handed everyone on the plane a memento of the trip, a gold coin with the imprint of the UN on one side and a map of the continent of Africa on the other and an inscription under it reading, "*Reaching Out in Christ's Name.*"

The pope shook hands with everyone, including the cynical and always-critical Communist reporter Francisco Ortolani, who saw a conspiracy in just about everything the Vatican ever did. He was the reporter who had brought a great deal of negative publicity to the Catholic Church with his constant exposés on the alleged murder plot of Pope John Paul I and the Vatican Bank controversy. He ridiculed each and every pope as a matter of routine. Now he pushed for an answer to his question, "Why did it take the Church this long to address the concerns of the Africans?"

Pope Peter II smiled almost fondly at the brash Italian. "Seven years ago my predecessor, Pope John Paul II, described Africa as the biblical character who was robbed and beaten to near death, and then was aided by the Good Samaritan. The pope's exact quote was 'Africa is a continent where countless human beings are lying, as it were, on the edge of the road, sick, injured, disabled, marginalized, and abandoned.' So you see, I am not the first to recognize the African problem. Please, look up the strong efforts and statements from the Vatican in its efforts to point out and materially aid Africa."

Only slightly chastised, the reporter's sarcastic rejoinder was, "Don't you think that you have taken on a problem that is too big to be solved by one person? Aren't you unrealistic?"

The pope smiled at Francisco, saying, "Maybe this pope is too stupid to know better. But maybe he sees the image and likeness of God in each and every suffering child."

When the pope returned to the front section of the plane, Motupu asked him how he felt. "I'm still functioning," Bill declared.

"Don't try to fool me, Bill. Brian called before we left and told me to keep my eye on you. He told me the virus I let you pick up in Africa was getting to you." Motupu shook his head. "No, he did not blame me directly."

"Gus, Gus, nobody let me get whatever bug is in my system. I wanted to be part of things. At that moment, that second, that I reached out for the dying boy, I was part of the overall scene. And this affliction is proof I know what I'm talking about."

"You made a great speech at the UN, Bill, but you don't look good, and you're losing a lot of weight, too. You have to get strong again for the important things God still has for you to do. The future of my black children rests on your shoulders."

"Not on mine alone, Gus. On ours. And not just your black children, but ours."

The pope sank back in his seat. "Gus, maybe I'll have one good taste of Jameson. And if you'll do the Rosary with me, I'll close my eyes and think of all the wonderful people I've met like you, and of beautiful, magnificent Africa."

WEDDING 42

It was now mid-June and Pope Bill, his travel plans at an end, sat down to compose his first encyclical. It would, he knew, also be his last work. He planned to single out the conditions of children and of families, especially in Third World countries, concentrating on Africa, where he had been given a personal look at the prevailing conditions. He realized that things were getting worse. He kept thinking about all the beautiful people reporting the news on TV and of those handsome U.S. millionaire senators in Washington. They sounded and looked so important. Yet in this robust economy so many people were starving on the one hand and others had been making so much money that they hardly knew what to do with it.

Monsignor Tim had arranged to bring together a group of economists, sociologists, doctors, academics, and practicing theologians who had proved themselves as committed to social and economic justice as was the Vatican of Peter II. The pope himself would moderate this in-depth three-day conference and discussion. Some twenty people from throughout the world were invited to participate in the conference, to be held at Castel Gandolfo, the pope's villa outside of Rome.

The media were not allowed access, nor were phone calls permitted, except in an emergency situation. Everyone invited knew the rules in advance, yet surprisingly no one declined the invitation. Even the former surgeon general of the United States as well as a recent Nobel Peace Prize winner canceled other engagements to be present.

Following an eight A.M. Mass and breakfast, the group met in a large reception room around a long wooden refectory table. The pope gave the experts his draft encyclical and a written statement, which he then proceeded to discuss with them. He apologized that his research and comments were not fully in print. "I still do everything by hand," he explained.

Jesuit scholar and historian Pierre LaMonte was amazed by how clear and concise the thirty-page draft document was. "You have developed a great talent, Bill. Maybe you ought to start a memoir."

"Not a bad idea," the pope replied. "But it will have to be a short story, I'm afraid." Nobody laughed. The group had all heard the frequent rumors of the pope's declining health. By nine-fifteen, however, the group was fast at work. Bill had asked everyone to introduce themselves because "it's important we get to know one another and work as a team." He went on to explain the goals and objectives he was looking for.

One hour later, after the pope finished reading his encyclical, the group applauded his clarity of thought. "He wants another *Rerum Novarum* with a Dorothy Day flair," said one of the astonished scholars after hearing the pope's dissertation. *Rerum Novarum,* of course, was the famous 1891 encyclical of Pope Leo XIII on social and economic justice, and Dorothy Day had been one of the most important social activists in the history of the American Church.

The three Dominican priest-scholars from the Angelicum and three from the Gregorian University recorded every word on tape and in voluminous notes. The brilliant Father Tom O'Hara of Kings College in Wilkes-Barre, Pennsylvania, was asked to chair the prestigious committee. The group stopped only briefly for lunch, and again in the evening for a tasty Italian dinner. This went on for three days and the pope stayed with the group the entire time, with only a few brief absences. They were racing against the clock and they knew it. Everyone realized that they had to put their professional egos aside and work as a team if this definitive encyclical was to have a meaningful and lasting impact. They were working for Peter II's place in history.

When Professor Fred Weiderhold of Munich left Castel Gandolfo, he gave a German reporter who had been camped outside the first official quote from inside. "I was, of course, not present when they drafted the Magna Carta, the U.S. Constitution, or Deuteronomy, but this encyclical made me feel I was in that league."

Bill Kelly wanted his legacy, reflected through this encyclical, to exert a profound impact on the world's poor and needy. Also, he hoped to set a new moral tone for children and family. The drafters of the document recognized the intent of their work and knew it would get the right media attention. The pope had told the group that he wanted them to feel themselves part of the encyclical. Like the apostles they would be expected to explain and defend it as their own.

"I read *Beyond the Melting Pot* by Nathan Glazer and Daniel Patrick Moynihan and it had a lasting impact on me," Bill told the gathering. "I hope to raise the consciousness of everyone who reads this document of ours. I'll sign it, but it is a joint effort."

From the beginning everyone at the conference table knew that the encyclical would dominate the debate and even the news for the next several years. They were anxious to make sure that all the points made were soundly researched and documented. "What an opportunity!" said one of the scholars. "We're probably the only ones to have open and clear access to all the Vatican files and records. The Inquisition, World War II, annulments, excommunications—they're all laid out before us. It's amazing! An interesting strategy Bill here has devised. Even when he is not around to debate the proposal himself, he will have twenty multilingual scholars from around the planet carrying his message, Catholics and non-Catholics alike, who are obviously invested in its success."

The pope had summoned enormous strength and resiliency in focusing his attention on this three-day meeting and in overseeing drafting the document. Even after the original twenty left Castel Gandolfo, a six-member drafting committee had achieved a sound first draft, ready for review, in just fifteen days. The remarkable thing was that no portion of the draft was leaked to the press. Every participant in the work accomplished behind the walls of Castel Gandolfo respected the pope's plea for confidentiality.

Members of the original committee returned intermittently to meet with the drafters. The closest thing to a news leak was the report that all fifty-three books at the Vatican Library on marriage and annulment had been removed and taken somewhere. The media, always on watch, also observed that two Church historians and scholars of theology and sacred Scriptures from the University of Portugal had spent a few days at the papal villa. They were regarded as the foremost authorities on the appearance of Our Lady of Fatima in 1917. The pope discussed some of the *avviso*'s warnings with them.

"At first I read it to mean that aggressor nations will emerge, inflicting great pain on the children and families of the world," the pope explained. "The language can been interpreted differently by historians and scholars. Some may say the aggressor will emerge along with the rise of religious extremists. Others could interpret it to be countries like North Korea and Iraq, with their developing nuclear power. Others might say the ugly hand of Satan will wreak havoc from within our society in a complete breakdown of values and morals."

Eyes were opened when the retired Cardinal Casserole, cardinal secretary of state when Pope John Paul II was shot, visited the drafting committee at Castel Gandolfo. He had believed, as did many of the knowledgeable, that Mehmet Ali Agca did not act alone but was directed by the Russian KGB.

Casserole repeated to the pope, in the presence of the framers, the extraordinary story about how the fifteen-year-old daughter of a Vatican employee was kidnapped by KGB agents and offered as ransom for Agca's release from Rebibbia Prison. "William Casey, director of the Central Intelligence Agency, told Pope John Paul II directly, and I heard it with my own ears, that Agca, a professionally trained terrorist and hit man, was paid by Moscow to kill the pope. John Paul II felt it was not in his interest to create a second international situation. It might result in further pain and the killing of thousands of people. He wanted the issue to go away. How would it sound if this universal man of peace had become himself a victim of violence?" the cardinal asked rhetorically.

Vatican observers also believed that there was considerable manipulation of letters of credit and raw currency going on without the pope's knowledge or approval. John Paul II cleaned up much of the mess, but there was a lot more to do before the case was closed. With no public disclosure of its finances, Vatican Bank methods were prone to considerable adverse speculating. This frustrated Bill Kelly, and when he tried to seek out the real answers even he could not get the kind of information he needed.

On one occasion, after waiting five weeks for a list of depositors and how much they had in their accounts, he finally received from Patsy Monassari an eighteenth-century tome about administrative affairs of the worldwide Catholic Church, printed in Italian. Bill was still trying to gather as much information as possible, but the control of Church administrative matters had fallen to this Italian bishop who was closely connected to Secretary of State Robitelli. Bill had never forgotten Ed Kirby's advice when he had returned from Africa: "Let the priests take care of God's business and let lay businessmen and politicians take care of business and political matters." Good advice, but hard to follow in the convoluted world of the Vatican.

The pope spent most of his time working on the encyclical until July 1, when he left for the United States to attend Ryan's wedding on the Cape.

Colleen had gone back to the U.S. on June 24 to help Paula and Ryan with their wedding preparations. The pope, meanwhile, met with his doctors nearly every day while working on the document that had virtually become his last will and testament. His health continued to deteriorate as he lost weight and appetite. When Bill asked his doctors how much time he had left, Dr. Luigi Biaggio gently answered, "Between one day and one year."

On the morning of July 1, Bill, Gus Motupu, Tim Shanahan, and Dr. Biaggio arrived at Rome Airport, where they had booked a private commercial plane and headed out over the Alps and the Atlantic to the States.

Bill, Tim, and Gus copyedited the third draft of the encyclical virtually the entire time they were airborne. The plane landed at Otis Air Force Base on the Cape, where Bishop Sean Patrick and State Police Trooper Collins met the group and escorted them to the Kellys' home on Buzzards Bay. The press had not been informed, so there were no reporters were at the airport when the plane arrived. There had been some reports that, due to ill health, the pope might not attend his son's wedding.

The *Cape Cod Times* did have an alert photographer staked out at the Kellys' home who was able to shoot a picture of the pope getting out of Bishop Sean Patrick's car and entering the house. After news of the pope's arrival surfaced, the entire area was cordoned off for security reasons. The public could see only cars going along the dirt road to and from the Kelly home.

Gus, Tim, and Dr. Biaggio stayed at a cottage directly beside the Kellys' home that had been rented for the week. U.S. Secret Service agents headed up security in collaboration with the Massachusetts commissioner of public safety.

The entire family warmly greeted Bill and assured him that plans for the wedding were working out perfectly.

"We have more relatives than we ever thought," said Colleen. "Your so-called cousin from Boston, an Al 'Chico' Goldofsky, came by and said he needed an invitation to the reception. I told him I never heard Dad mention him before. He said, 'Unbelievable, we go way back.' I asked him if he had been in the seminary with Bill. 'Hell no,' he said, 'I'm Jewish.'" Colleen chuckled. "I didn't know what to do. He was so insistent, so I gave him an invitation. He said something about going up to Boston to get his hairpiece set. He left in a car that looked very official. He scared the daylights out of me when he backed his car out of the driveway with his siren and blue panel lights flashing."

"I remember him," Bill laughed. "Your Uncle Brian and I worked in his father's fish market in Newton when we were in the seminary."

Colleen nodded. "By the way, that phone over there connects directly to the Vatican should you need to use it."

"Good idea. I need to talk to the Castel Gandolfo team about some changes in the encyclical we made on the plane." He sighed and sat down. "I'm exhausted from the plane ride. I'm going to get some rest. Call me when the other kids are all back."

The following day was not a good one for Bill, although he managed to conceal his sickness from the family. But he enjoyed all the family news.

"Tonight is the wedding rehearsal and a dinner party, Dad, if you are up to it. If not, Bishop Sean Patrick said he'll take care of everything," Ryan assured his father.

"I'm feeling fine and I'll be there. Wouldn't miss it for the world. I'm so happy for you, my boy. Paula is lovely. I'm looking forward to meeting her family tonight. Poles from Milwaukee, huh? The only reason they sent their daughter to Rome in the first place to study was they thought she would meet the Polish pope. So what happens? Their daughter marries the son of an American fisherman pope."

The events and arrangements leading up to the wedding went without a hitch. Colleen served as Paula's maid of honor. Jan stood by to serve as Ryan's best man. Maureen Kirby, with her father and mother, represented the United States at the pope's son's wedding, an important political affair. Ever mindful of the Catholic vote, the president of the United States sent a personal message to be read at the reception. Brian arrived on schedule from Ireland to perform the ceremony the next morning with Bishop Sean Patrick. The pope stood up well at the rehearsal with Paula's parents. All was well until after he retired for the night and the younger men and women decided to go into Hyannisport for a few drinks with Senator Lane. Some of the Lane family were at their compound nearby for the weekend and were looking forward to the wedding next day.

At a favorite bar Ryan and his fishing crew once again expressed their thanks to Senator Lane for his perseverance during the hunt that had saved their lives. Ryan was about to say he hoped he'd have the opportunity to do something for the young senator from an old political family. Then he cut himself off, remembering in a flash that Lane was mixed up in a flap over the annulment he had been granted by a Virginia bishop from his first wife. Lane's new, pretty, staunchly Catholic bride was devastated at the idea that she and her husband could not take Communion together if the annulment was reversed by Rome. And Lane's first wife, mother of their three children, was vigorously pursuing her appeal against it. A thorny problem was raising its head. If, in fact, an annulment was obtained, decreeing that a marriage had never taken place, then what was the status of the children?

Much as he would like to, Ryan knew he would be dissuaded by the senator of asking his father to intervene on the senator's behalf. As he drank a beer, Ryan believed that Lane would not appeal to the pope for special treatment. It was something Ryan would have to face later, but he wished it would not be necessary to disturb his thoughts just now. Then, putting his mug on the table, an off-duty Swiss guard inadvertently came to rescue him from his daydreaming.

One of Jan's guard friends had put five dollars' worth of quarters in the jukebox at the 19th Hole Irish Pub. As he sipped Irish whiskey, the guardsman played the only two rap songs in the jukebox over and over, which fascinated the Europeans. A fight broke out with two locals who wanted to hear either Irish or country music.

Ryan, summoned by Jan, ran next door to stop the fight. When the police came, the owner, Chris Doherty, who just happened to come in, told them it was only a misunderstanding. The police looked at the Swiss guard with blood coming from his nose and a cut above his eye. "He looks more like Swiss cheese than a Swiss guard," said Officer Ed McGuillan. But the interruption took Ryan's mind off the annulment issue, for which Ryan was grateful, especially so close to his wedding day.

✛✛　✛✛　✛✛

Saturday, July 7, was a big day for the Kelly family. At the beginning of the wedding ceremony, Pope Peter stood next to his son at the altar, looking out over the rustic Church. In the front row on the groom's side sat Roger and Meghan. Beside them were Senator Lane and his wife. The row directly behind them was filled with the Kirby family—Ed, Kathy, Maureen, and the rest of the children.

"I haven't had a chance yet to personally thank the senator for his part in saving you, son," Bill said quietly.

"You know he admires you, Dad," Ryan replied.

"I know, son."

"It was his clout that saved me and the crew," Ryan said.

"The senator and both his wives are in quite a bind."

"I know, Dad. It's too bad, seeing what he's done for you."

Bill glanced up the aisle. "Look now. No bride was ever as beautiful as your Paula."

Ryan looked up and smiled at Paula, on her father's arm, sweeping majestically toward them. All was well. His mind was immediately cleared of Lane's problem upon the vision of his bride.

The crowds of sightseers surrounding St. Margaret's Church were backed up all the way to the Cape bridge. Police and traffic control guards had been sent in from Plymouth.

✛✛　✛✛　✛✛

The crusty, outspoken society editor of the *Boston Herald,* Susan Downs, muttered comments on the wedding scene as she elbowed her way through the crowd. "A beautiful Saturday, July fourth weekend afternoon down here is crowded enough already, but now you have the biggest event on the Cape since JFK's election or, for that matter, his wedding in Newport." She fought her way forward and finally captured a close-up photograph of the pope, his son, and his new daughter-in-law.

The reception was held near the dock of the Kelly home in a big tent. The music was a combination of Polish, Irish, Swiss, Italian, and American songs. Noel Henry's Band provided it, and Paddy Reilly made a special appearance, singing "Ave Maria" and "Our Lady of Knock," in homage to the late Frank Patterson, a favorite of the Kellys. He later sang "My Son" and "Wind Beneath My Wings" at the reception while Bill Kelly danced with his daughters. Few guests could help inadvertently thinking to themselves that, given the way he looked, this might well be their last dance together.

Later Brian Comiskey and Bill relaxed on the porch in the same rocking chairs they had sat in the previous October 4. They looked out at the sea and listened to the laughter and music coming from the tent near the foot of the dock. Bill asked Meghan to collect Bishop Sean Patrick, Ed Kirby, Gus, and Tim to join them on the porch. They talked about the encyclical, the pope's health, and his happy family. Bill did not want to upset anyone on this special and joyful day, but Brian had to leave that night for an important service in Glasgow. Bill wanted to talk more openly with this special group of trusted advisers and friends about the future.

❖❖ ❖❖ ❖❖

The following day Bill and his family, along with Gus, Tim, Ed and Kathy Kirby, and Dr. Biaggio left by the same chartered commercial plane for Rome. They had great fun reminiscing about the wedding and the fireworks display over Cape Cod Canal, which they had witnessed from their front lawn. No serious palaver broke the spell.

The plane landed in Rome, and the pope was transported directly to Gemelli Hospital, where he stayed overnight for a complete checkup. At some point, he realized, he would have to be up front with the public about his health. *The wedding is over. I should level with my friends and the Church,* he resolved.

HOME IS THE CAPTAIN, HOME FROM THE SEA 43

✠ It was a stiflingly hot morning on August 13 in Rome when Brian Cardinal Comiskey disembarked after his Aer Lingus flight from Dublin, Ireland. Rome in August is usually the last place in the world that clergy would go. Everyone at the Vatican leaves around July 10, and if they can help it, they are not seen again until early September.

The pope himself travels to the mountains in northern Italy for a ten-day retreat, then goes to Castel Gandolfo, his villa in the hills some thirty miles outside Rome. Generally he would travel to the castle by helicopter, especially when so many tourists escape by car to the popular and beautiful Lake Albano region, which surrounds the papal summer home.

When Brian picked up his bags, the rector of the Pontifical Irish College, Monsignor John Fleming, met him. They went first to the college for a meeting to discuss future construction plans. Brian was obviously distracted. He was constantly thinking of his friend, the pope, Billy Kelly.

Brian did, however, present John with a beautiful leather-bound photo album of the pope's recent visit to Ireland for the college library. Cardinal Comiskey, himself a graduate of the college, told John that the pope was going to give the city of Dublin a marble sculpture of Irish children to be permanently placed in Phoenix Park. Dublin was going to present a large color painting of the pope and his entire family at Knock, with Our Lady of Knock looking down at them and St. Patrick himself behind her. "It will be beautiful, and after I spoke with the Holy Father on the phone yesterday, he indicated that he would like to donate it to the Pontifical Irish College. Isn't that great!"

"Oh, glory to God," said John. "It will look wonderful in the main lobby right alongside Oliver Plunkett. How is the pope, by the way? We hear all kinds of rumors. You don't know what to believe."

"I am heading up to Castel Gandolfo for a couple of days to visit him. I guess we all hear the same things. No secrets anymore, God knows, with all the media attention his health is getting," Brian sighed.

"Would you like me to drive you there?" John offered.

"No, no, thank you. I'll take the train. It's my favorite ride and I can grab a taxi when I get to the station. I'm told that there is a lot of press at

Liberty Square, so nobody will recognize me if I duck in the side entrance rather than enter through the main door," the cardinal replied.

"I can at least drive you to the Stazione Terminali, but call me if you need anything. It's quiet around here, so I'm available, Eminence."

Off Brian went with an overnight bag and another photo album that he had proudly carried with him all the way from Ireland. He was going to give the second one to the Kelly children. When he got to the town, the square was crowded with tourists and TV trucks and the traffic couldn't have been worse. But it was cooler in the hills.

Thank God I went by train, Brian thought to himself. He avoided press recognition by walking around the main street leading up to the front door, then slipping into the side entrance. Inside the villa Brian knocked on the door of the study and found Bill sitting in a big leather chair looking out at the beautiful lake below. His son Roger was standing at the window watching something through a large telescope. As Brian gazed at Bill, countless memories of happy days raced through his head. He remembered Bill teaching him how to hit a curve ball when they were at the seminary. Fishing trips on the Cape and the day he married Bill and Mary came rushing back to him with memories of the rugged, handsome fisherman he once knew, now a tired and frail man half himself.

They looked at each other, realizing what they both were thinking, and before they could say anything, Roger cried out, "Hey, Uncle Brian, look at this! You can see everything going on with this telescope. Kids water-skiing and even the mountainside villas and villages."

Brian walked over to Bill and held his two hands, smiling warmly, looking into his eyes. "Hey, buddy, how are you doing?"

"I'm doing just great now that you're here. How was your trip? Is it as hot in Eire as it is in Rome?"

They chattered a few minutes, and then Colleen came in and gave Brian a big hug. "Oh, Brian, it's so good to see you again. We're so happy that you can spend some time with us. It's really peaceful and beautiful, isn't it?"

"I used to come up this way years ago when I was down at the Pontifical Irish College. The British College had a summer place on the other side of the lake, and they would invite us up for picnics on Sundays after Mass. It was the first time I ever had a gin and tonic with one small ice cube."

"You're always great for stories," said Bill. "Pull over a chair or get into something more comfortable. Your room is just down the corridor. I told them to leave the air conditioner on for you, but it's not very cool. Not much electric power up here, you know, what with the girls' hair dryers going all the time and Roger's computer games. We hardly get enough power to see the hand in front of you."

"What do you hear from the married couple?"

"They're grand. So happy that everything turned out well at the wedding. You were great to come, Brian, all the way from Ireland, then back again and travel to Scotland."

They talked for hours, Brian with gin and tonics, Bill sipping hot tea, stopping only when the nurse came in. She gave Bill a shot and left. The nurse made soup and sandwiches, but Bill only took a few sips of his soup. Colleen joined in the conversation and blushingly told them how fond she was of her Swiss guard, Jan. They ended the night with Brian leading them in the Rosary.

⁀ *⁀* *⁀*

Next morning, after Mass in the chapel and breakfast, Brian said he was going to take Meghan and Roger water-skiing on the lake.

"Now, Roger, don't go out very far," Colleen entreated.

"You can see us if you look out the telescope over there by Dad's window," Roger suggested.

Colleen announced that she and Jan Christensen were going to drive around the lake and have lunch at a restaurant on the other side.

That evening there was a concert in the next town, so a couple of the nuns took the kids to it, but they were back in less than two hours.

"The kids have been great," Bill said to Brian. "Not much doing around here for them; mostly older tourists." He grinned broadly. "Colleen is happy, of course, with her Swiss guard on duty at her side." He was silent a moment, then, "Tomorrow I have an appointment at the Gemelli with the doctors, at eleven. If you want to go with me, Brian, on the helicopter, you are welcome. There's plenty of room."

"Sure. I'd love to. Ed Kirby once told me how beautiful flying over Rome is in a helicopter, looking down at the ruins, the Appian Way, and the Colosseum."

"I'm told that when you're on the chopper, if you look closely, you can even see Molly Malone's Pub in Trastevere, where you and other Irish lads used to sneak after study hours," Colleen teased Brian.

"Who told you that? That's a big fib!" Brian mocked shock at the accusation. "Sure you'd never see Molly's from the sky. Our rector couldn't find us from the ground."

Marveling at his friend's broad wit, Bill smiled with delight.

The helicopter landed on the grounds of the Gemelli Hospital, and Bill and Brian proceeded to the examination room, where two doctors from Johns Hopkins in Baltimore and two Italian medical specialists took blood tests and once again examined Bill. About two hours later Bill was wheeled into the doctors' conference room, where Brian and Tim were waiting.

"Not much to tell you. No change. Yes, the pope is still losing weight, so get as much chicken soup and bread in him as you can. That will give him strength," one of the doctors told Tim and Brian. "I would advise you to stay the night at the Vatican. It's close and you don't have to take the helicopter. I'll drop by later. Are you sure you don't want to stay here with us at the hospital, Bill?"

"No, I'd much rather be in my own bed," Bill replied. "Besides, tomorrow is a big day, the feast of Our Lady of the Assumption. I'd like to tape a little message to all the pilgrims who will attend Mass at St. Peter's and be at St. Peter's Square at noontime. Let me tape it tonight, Tim, and have it ready for tomorrow, OK?" Bill seemed to light up as he gave Monsignor Shanahan instructions.

After dinner that evening, at the apostolic apartment, Bill sat in his old comfortable reclining armchair, and Colleen, who with Jan had driven back to the Vatican, sat next to him holding his hand. Meghan and Roger were watching TV. Brian was in the next room reading his prayers, and Tim was on the phone telling the doctor what Bill had eaten for dinner. Brian had been in and out of the room, but decided Bill would rather rest now and talk to Colleen.

Around nine o'clock, as Bill sat thinking and staring at the bookcase in his bedroom, he asked Colleen to get Brian.

"What's up, Bill?" Brian asked as he entered the room.

"Please go over there to the bookcase and lift up the replica of Our Lady of Fatima with the three children. You'll find a key. Take the key and go into my office. In my big desk, open the bottom right-hand drawer. There is a wooden box. I want you to open it and take out a folder that is marked 'Avviso.' Please bring it to me."

Brian did exactly as Bill said. Colleen gave her father his glasses and he began to read. "When I'm finished rereading this, I want you to give it to the next pope, but don't let anyone else see or read it. Capito? Understand?"

"Yes, Bill, I understand." Brian walked over to the window and looked out over St. Peter's Square. He could see several TV trucks at Via della Conciliazione getting ready to do the eleven o'clock news live. Brian thought how his life had intertwined with Bill's. Bill and Brian had always been there for each other.

"When I first came to Boston, I didn't know anybody." Brian had told the story often. "A greenhorn from Ireland with no money. Bill got me a part-time job cleaning fish at a Jewish market in Newton."

"Did you see the son at the wedding?" Colleen asked.

"Yes, I hardly recognized him." Brian continued his reprise. "His father got his work out of your dad and me, and then we would hitchhike to your grandparents' house down on the Cape and your grandmother would make fish chowder and crab cakes. I even had my own bed there. I remember the night we graduated from St. John's and I was flying back to Ireland that same night. I'll never forget the look on Bill's face as he said good-bye to me at the airport. I felt so empty, like I'd lost everything. Then I pulled the rosary your dad gave me from my pocket and pressed my hand around it. Here it was the happiest day of my life, just graduated from St. John's, and I'm on my way back home to see my family, get ordained, and celebrate my first Mass. Yet I couldn't get your father's face out of my mind. I remember not eating on the plane, just recalling all the days at school together. We were such close friends. I remember clearly the day your dad called to tell me he wanted to leave the priesthood and marry your mother."

"Brian, Brian," he heard the pope's soft voice call.

"Oh, sorry, Bill, I was just reminiscing with Colleen. What is it?"

"Pull up that chair over there and sit down next to me. I'm a little tired, so if I doze off, I'll finish the story tomorrow, OK?" After a moment Bill continue. "Brian, think back to the day you left the conclave and came to Buzzards Bay to tell me what had happened. Do you remember what I said when I first looked at you?"

"I'll never forget it, and the look on your face." The sense of awe Brian had felt at that moment last October was still pervasive. "You stared up at me while you were kneeling on the dock mending the nets and you said, 'Oh, my God. So it's true.' You had this strange expression on your face. You were not very clear with me, Bill," Brian went on. "But you made me understand that while you were out fishing, just before the sun came up, you had a vision. We thought it might have been something you ate. Fish not cooked enough, or whatever."

"Well, Brian." Bill reached out to take his hand while still holding on to

Colleen's. "I'm sure Our Lady of Fatima appeared to me that early morning out at sea. I know it was she. I wasn't afraid at all. I almost knew what she wanted me to do. The world and the family are divided, she said. She said more, but that was the main point. Her eyes held me for maybe a couple of minutes, and then the vision disappeared and the rosary which I had dropped onto the floor below my bunk was in my hand and it was beautiful and shiny, like the day you gave it to me. The blanket had slipped off me and even though I was sleeping with the porthole open I felt so warm. That was early October and it gets real cool out on Georges Bank."

Bill was silent for a moment. Then, "When I later walked into the conclave, I could feel her standing next to me. Giving me strength to carry on.

"Now, Brian, I never felt like a saint or anything, just an average guy who had loved his wife, was gladdened by his children, and wanted to serve his Christ with all his heart and soul. Every day I would pray to Our Lady of Fatima, asking her how I could help my Church. I would ask her to please give me the grace to best serve Jesus Christ.

"Brian, I will always thank the Lord for all he has done for me. I've tried to live and spread his message of faith."

Both Brian's and Colleen's eyes filled with tears as Bill seemed to be passing on to them a fateful message. It was noticeable to both Colleen and Brian that an intense enthusiasm resounded in Bill's voice when he was talking about Our Lady. He would often look at the folder resting on his lap marked *Avviso*.

"This is the letter Pope John Paul II gave me, but its contents have never been publicly released. I have read it carefully."

Bill did not divulge the specific contents of the *avviso* as he continued. "John Paul II is expressing his concern to all of us that we must stop the abuse of the spirit and the body. Yes, you are your brother's keeper. You must not bypass the word of God in all that you do. At work, school, at home."

Bill continued to talk openly without referring specifically to the *avviso*, but obviously with its words still very much on his mind. "The true meaning of justice must be practiced. The laborers in the field must be justly compensated. The father must be the pillar of the family as Christ is the pillar of the Church."

Bill's eyes started to grow heavy, and then, as though mustering a final, resolute decision, he spoke categorically. "Pope John Paul II was sending a clear message to the world through this *avviso*. We are facing a crisis that is far more devastating than floods, fires, or even wars.

"Brian, please give this folder to the next pope. My encyclical is done. It's a specific follow-up to the pope's message and what he wanted me to do. I have tried to do all that he asked. I spoke about some of those things at the UN. The deterioration of the body, such as we have seen in Africa, and the decline of the spirit that we are seeing in so many young people in the U.S. today. They've no family foundation to fall back on. The breakup of the family is a far greater threat to young people than any military or nuclear power in the world." As though pausing to catch his breath or muster the strength to proceed, Bill was quiet for perhaps as long as a minute. Neither Brian nor Colleen interrupted.

"That sealed envelope"—Bill pointed to an envelope lying on the folder marked *Avviso*—"contains my encyclical with a final few notes. Please release that letter on the day I die. I will date it August 15, feast day of Our Lady of the Assumption, because much of what is in the encyclical pertains to Our Lady and, specifically, her prophecies at Fatima."

After a few moments' silence Bill went on. "I think I've covered everything. The problem of thousands of Catholics who seek annulments. The Church will deny no one Communion who has lived within the law of the land, even if until now we in Rome pronounced the curia the final arbiter. But no longer."

Cardinal Comiskey's face showed his shock, but he only said, "Yours is the last word, Bill."

"Christ has given me the personal gift of his love and compassion. I am grateful for his friendship. You know, allowing me to serve the poor, the needy, the weak. I thank God for his giving me my Mary and our four wonderful children. Always there for me, good times and bad."

Just then the private phone rang. Colleen answered, her voice rising in excitement. "Ryan, it's so good to hear from you. And how is Paula, that lovely sister-in-law of mine? Oh, that's nice. Here's Dad." Colleen handed the telephone to Bill.

"Ryan, I'm so proud and thankful for you being so strong in keeping the business together and never causing us any pain. We were so happy at your wedding. I love you son, always will. You have made me happy. God bless. Yeah, I'm okay. I just wanted to say hello and tell you how much I love you, my boy. And that thing we talked about at the altar a moment before Paula came down the aisle to you? I fixed it. You'll see. Tell our friend no one need worry. We'll be together again soon. Maybe at Christmas, all of us. That would be great. Maybe some Christmas soon we'll see some toys under the pope's Christmas tree for his grandchildren."

Colleen and Brian were fighting back the tears as Bill said "So long" to his oldest son on the phone.

"I'm a little tired," Bill murmured. "Think I'll catch some shut-eye."

Climbing into his bed, Bill asked Brian and Colleen to say a decade of the Rosary with him. Then he took his rosary back from Brian. He rubbed the shiny beads a moment and then handed the rosary to his daughter. "This will remind you never to lose faith again. Look at them glow. Brian will tell you about them." Then he closed his eyes and fell asleep.

✛ ✛ ✛

The next morning, Cardinal Comiskey walked down the long marble corridor of the apostolic apartment, looking straight ahead, not saying a word. He took the elevator down to the main level of St. Peter's Basilica, led the procession of cardinals and bishops, and celebrated Mass on the feast of Our Lady of the Assumption.

It was a beautiful, warm, August 15 morning, and pilgrims from all over the world came to honor the Virgin Mother of God on her feast day, an event celebrated by Catholics everywhere. Cardinal Comiskey had been chosen by Pope Peter II himself to lead the procession down the center aisle and celebrate the Mass. The great Church was filled to capacity. Before Mass started, Brian briefly said to the assembled, "Welcome to St. Peter's Basilica, the center of the worldwide Roman Catholic Church. Today we honor Our Lady. We thank her for the love she has for all of us and for the devotion we all have for her."

At the end of Mass and before the procession out of the basilica, Brian walked over to the podium. He stopped, cleared his throat, swallowed as if he was trying to catch his breath, and said, "Nobody loved and honored Our Lady more than Pope Peter II. Last night the Holy Father taped a message for all of you." Cardinal Comiskey gave the signal for the tape to play.

The pope, in his recorded message, spoke movingly about Our Lady and what she had meant to the world. He thanked God for sharing his mother with everybody. "She has been our own mother who loves us, as she does her own son," Pope Peter avowed. "She saw him born and she saw him die."

When the brief recorded message ended, Brian looked out at the vast audience. "And now I have some sad news. Our beloved Pope Peter II, or

'Billy Kelly, the fisherman from the Cape,' as he often referred to himself, has passed on."

The audience gasped and was stunned.

"As a fellow priest said, he taught us how to live and he wasn't afraid to die. On this feast of Our Lady of the Assumption, there is one more good fisherman with Our Lord in Heaven."

The people broke into tears, but it quickly turned to song as the large organ played "Ave Maria." Cardinal Comiskey walked down the main aisle of St. Peter's, singing as the tears flowed down his cheeks.

Immediately after Mass, Brian went back up to the apostolic apartment to be with the children. He spent the next few hours helping to console the grief-stricken family. He also called in Tim Shanahan and Father Tucci to discuss funeral arrangements. Cardinal Robitelli and several of the other cardinals also paid their respects to the bereaved family.

"When you feel up to it, Miss Kelly, Cardinal Bellotti and I will stop by to discuss the funeral and all other arrangements," said Robitelli.

"Thank you, Your Eminence, but Uncle Brian and I are planning them now," Colleen replied softly but clearly.

A startled Cardinal Robitelli could only respond, "But, but..." Then, resignation in his tone, "Just as you say." And he walked out.

Brian took out the envelope and the encyclical predated August 15, the feast day of Our Lady of Assumption.

"Are you going to release Bill's encyclical today, Uncle Brian?" Colleen asked.

"Just as the Holy Father said. He wanted it released today, and it will be released later on today. I'll get it faxed to all the members of the special drafting team so they can release it and explain it in their various languages and countries. I'll also get it to all the members of the curia and the college of cardinals," Brian declared.

Maureen Kirby was on her way to classes at Marymount with her school friends, walking through Piazza Venezia, when they heard the bells ringing at St. Peter's Basilica. Maureen looked at her watch—ten-thirty. The bells didn't normally ring till noontime, when the Angelus was prayed.

Just as they were ready to go into the school building, the bells at St. Mark's started to ring. "What's going on? Why are all the bells ringing?" the people cried out as they started to emerge onto St. Peter's Square.

"The pope is dead," was broadcast in Italian, English, and the other languages of the people gathered for the feast day of Our Lady of Assumption.

"*Mio Dio!*" The great square was filling up with celebrants turned mourners. Even though the pope's poor health was well known, the actual news of his death stupefied everyone. In such a short time, Bill Kelly had become an icon throughout Italy and most of the world. Within an hour the people were looking up at the window of the pope's apartment, praying, almost expecting him to look out and wave as every pope had done for centuries.

Businesses closed down for the day, and the president of Italy proclaimed the following Friday, the day of the funeral, a national day of mourning.

Within three hours, the crowds were backed up all the way to Viadella Conciliazione to Castel Sant'Angelo. Within twenty-four hours, TV trucks and hundreds of camera crews filled the city. Tel Pace, RAI, CNN, Sky News, BBC, ABC, NBC, CBS, and Fox announced that on Friday they were going to cover the funeral live.

Cardinal Robitelli met with his loyalists, planning aspects of the funeral despite Colleen Kelly's wishes that she and Brian Comiskey should make all the arrangements. To Comiskey and a few other cardinals on the spot, it seemed more as if he was conducting a political meeting, planning the coming conclave, than a funeral. The next few days would be spent preparing for the funeral and the customary period for *Novemdiales,* the days of mourning, which could run to fifteen or more days.

This was a time usually spent praising the accomplishments of the deceased pope and discussing what the priorities of the Church should be. But for some members of the college of cardinals, their major objective was to line up the votes for the next pope, before the next conclave even began.

Meghan Kelly called her brother, Ryan, to give him the sad but not unexpected news.

"Dad knew as I was speaking to him that it was his last night," Ryan grieved. "I could hear it in his voice. I love and respect him so much. Yes, I'll miss him deeply, but what better father could anyone ask for?"

Tim Shanahan called Kathy Kirby and asked if she and Maureen could come up to the papal apartment to help console the children. Tim was also making arrangements for Ryan and Paula to fly to Rome that afternoon from Boston.

Calls and telegrams of sympathy poured in from all over the world. From the president of the United States, the prime minister of the United Kingdom, and the king of Spain to the Japanese diet, which recessed in honor of Pope Peter II. The crown prince of Saudi Arabia shocked the

Islamic world by flying the Vatican flag at half-staff over the government buildings, a scene never imaginable in that or any other Muslim country.

But probably the most spontaneous outpouring of love came from the little village of Rakai in Uganda, where the pope had visited with Cardinal Motupu. It was the village where every one of the children in the school had lost at least one member of their immediate family to AIDS or another, still unidentifiable, virus. They loved the pope and he had loved them, and they knew it.

When these forgotten children heard the news of Bill's death, they worked all night painting a sign over the school door reading POPE BILL KELLY SCHOOL and sent out invitations to every one in the village and surrounding towns to attend a Mass and pay special tribute to their deceased friend. As one of the sixth graders told a Reuters reporter, "The pope saw goodness in each one of us, when nobody even wanted to look at us." Reuters photographer Gail Oskin took a photo that captured the feeling of these African children as they held up a small sign reading THANK GOD FOR THE POPE.

In Northern Ireland, Catholic political leader John Hume and Protestant leader David Trimble introduced a measure to build a memorial to Pope Bill Kelly in downtown Belfast, the main square. This square had once been the center of the violence and the one main area connecting the Protestant community to the Catholic. It was the same square that Pope Bill Kelly had visited.

✛ ✛ ✛

While the world mourned for this regular guy, Bill, there was one person on the verge of severe depression over his death, and that was Augustine Cardinal Motupu, in Africa. When Shahahan told Comiskey that Motupu wouldn't come to the phone to talk to anyone, they became deeply concerned. Repeated calls got the same response from the African cardinal's secretary: "I'm sorry, Cardinal Comiskey, but His Eminence is not taking any calls."

Gus blamed himself for the pope's death. *I was too selfish. I coaxed him to come to Africa. He'd be alive today if he hadn't come and caught that virus. It was my fault. Why did I do it?* he kept castigating himself.

After two days of Gus refusing to come out of his room and not taking calls from the Vatican or from anyone else, Brian explained the situation to Meghan, whom Gus used to call "little princess." Tim had the Vatican switchboard operator put a call through to Cardinal Motupu's personal and private phone number from "your little princess," Meghan Kelly.

"Hello," answered a man who seemed to be trying to disguise his voice. "Sorry, wrong number."

But Meghan was prepared for that. "Uncle Gus, my father loved you very much. You can't imagine how happy and proud he was in talking about how he was going to help the poor children of Africa. That's all he talked about. He even said that maybe next summer we could all go there and work in the health clinic. He really believed in what he was doing. He believed he was doing what Our Lady wanted him to do. He was so happy. My family and I need you here. Please come."

An hour later a message came into the Vatican switchboard that Cardinal Motupu was on his way to Rome, and he was bringing four young children with him to represent the continent of Africa.

By six o'clock on the morning of the funeral, St. Peter's Square was nearly full with people who had come from all over the world. They carried flags from Japan, Mexico, Canada, the United States, Kenya, and Germany. Old people arrived four hours before the funeral Mass would begin. Many people had to stand the whole time, as the limited chairs were given to the elderly. In each section of the square, someone would lead a group in song or prayer. Hawkers were out in force selling Pope Billy Kelly souvenirs: hats, photos, and even miniature fishing rods with *Pope Bill the Fisherman* printed on them. The U.S. president and First Lady, with thirty members of the U.S. House and Senate, were joined by heads of state or other high-ranking representatives from nearly every other country in the world.

At Colleen Kelly's request, Brian Comiskey, Gus Motupu, and American cardinal William Baum, who had also been Kelly's personal confessor, celebrated the High Mass. At the end of the Mass, the deceased pope's son, Ryan Kelly, was invited to speak for the family. His remarks moved the audience to tears and laughter. In his eulogy, Ryan talked about his father's loyalty to God and family, and about the inner conflicts that this dual loyalty sometimes entailed.

"Whenever anything bothered him and this tension developed, he would go down to the fishing dock to do some work around the boats. Every once in a while, it would appear obvious that something else was disturbing him. He often rhetorically asked the question whether he had done enough for Jesus. We later realized that his problem wasn't that he chose family over God or that he loved one less than the other. His dilemma was how he could love both God and family more. In his heart he had made the right decision to become a priest. He also made the right decision, when he fell in love, to get married. But leaving the priesthood made him feel guilty. He kept thinking, Had he let God down? Could he have done more? Is that all there is to my relationship with Christ? Leading a good life and going to Mass on Sunday when I'm not out at sea?'

"When Our Lady of Fatima, to whom he used to privately pray all the time when he was working out at sea, called him once again to serve God and Church, it was all that he could have hoped for. For this way he was able to love God and family more. It was a short but remarkable life. So, while our family has lost a wonderful father, the Church its pope, and society a compassionate friend, all of us won. I know exactly what my dad would say if he were here with us today. He'd say thank you to all the people for their kindness and patience in helping him lead a Church and a religion he loved and passionately believed in. He'd say thank you to all those he worked with, from the docks of New Bedford and Buzzards Bay to the ancient palatial buildings of the Vatican. And as even now he is saying thank you to his partner in life, his wife, Mary, our mom, he would say, 'I love you, kids,' because he really did, and he constantly tried to prove it. He'd certainly say thank you to the Holy Mother for always being there with him, in good and difficult times. And lastly, he'd thank Almighty God, for giving him the opportunity to know, love, and serve him.

"We will leave my father's body here with another fisherman, St. Peter. When we go back to our home and boats, we will take with us a spirit and memory of not just another important man, but a special man—a man who was happy to achieve his life's goal. Good-bye to our pope, a widower, a dad, and a caring friend, a fisherman."

Walking over to his dad's casket and placing a red rose on it, Ryan said, "The journey's complete, O Captain. Home is the captain, home from the sea."

Following the burial service, limousines carrying the Kelly family, Brian, Gus, and Tim drove out of St. Peter's Square and headed to the Leonardo da Vinci Airport. Cardinal Robitelli, smarting because he'd had no serious role to play since the pope's death, immediately went to his private dining room to have lunch with the rest of the voting members of the college of cardinals, those under eighty, to try to lock up their votes at the conclave.

Bellotti already had a detailed game plan worked out for how to get the vote of each and every one of these cardinals.

"Eugenio is trying to lock this up early, tighter than a drum," Canadian cardinal Pegot was heard to say later that afternoon.

Over a million people, holding signs and waving U.S. and Vatican flags, lined the route from St. Peter's Square to Leonardo da Vinci Airport to say good-bye to the deceased pope's family. When the Kellys got there, they drove directly onto the tarmac, where the U.S. president and his delegation stood alongside the huge Air Force One jet, decorated with the seal of the United States of America on it.

Not much was said on Air Force One until an hour out of Rome. Ed Kirby invited the four children to join the president and First Lady in the forward cabin. Colleen Kelly, Ed, and the president talked about how moving the funeral was and how proud everyone was of Ryan.

"Colleen, would you like a drink?" Ed Kirby offered. "I know your dad liked Irish Mist."

She nodded.

"See what the others want too," said the president.

Ryan and Paula also accepted the offer of an Irish Mist. The steward took the orders and soon returned with the drinks.

"Ms. Kelly," the president went on, "your father made quite an impact on everyone, and all Americans are truly proud of you and your family. The Massachusetts congressional delegation and I would be honored to name, in his memory, a commercial and recreational fishing pier and park to be constructed next to the Massachusetts Maritime Academy in Buzzards Bay. I know your father loved the area very much. My staff has already talked to the officials in the town and at the academy. They say that they would be delighted."

"If you think it appropriate, Mr. President, our family would be honored," Colleen said.

"Then it's settled," said the president.

The Kellys regaled the president and First Lady with funny stories about their experiences at the Vatican together. It was a kind of wake now commencing. Meghan told the president and First Lady how her brother had had to get stitches over his eye when, skateboarding inside the Vatican, he crashed into one of the Swiss guards wearing armor and carrying a large steel ax. Roger told how his sister had fallen into the tomb of St. Paul. A wistful Colleen indicated she would miss her Swiss guardsman, but that he was going to come over to visit her on his next vacation. The entire flight home was taken up with enjoyable stories about the Kelly family's days at the Vatican.

As they neared their destination, flight commander Colonel Rossi said to Ambassador Kirby, "Air Force One has been called into the service of our country on many important and historic missions, but I can't recall one with the pride and the love that accompanied this one." The plane landed at Logan Airport in Boston, where many friends and public officials were waiting to greet it.

The First Lady and president exited by the main door, followed by the Kelly children close behind. As they stepped out onto the platform and stairs, the president held Colleen Kelly's arm and looked out at an enormous crowd as it came to attention as the National Guard military band played "God Bless America."

The Kellys bade farewell to the president and stepped into the cars waiting to take them back to their home on the Cape. Two state troopers on motorcycles escorted them for the hour-and-a-half drive.

When they came to the narrow dirt road approaching the house where the Kelly children had lived almost their entire lives, twenty-one years of happy memories flashed through Colleen's head. It was an overcast day. Just as her car pulled up to the modest house, recently painted for the wedding, Colleen saw Bishop Sean Patrick and Trooper Collins standing on the front steps. It was almost as if nothing had changed during the past eleven months.

When Colleen stepped out of the car she could immediately smell the ocean. She stared down at the fishing docks below and whispered under her breath, "You're home, Daddy. You're home."

Colleen Kelly and her sister Meghan were just pulling up to the driveway of their home on Buzzards Bay after doing a little shopping when they heard Roger shout, "Girls, come quick!"

Colleen and Meghan hastily ran into the living room and saw Roger's eyes riveted on the TV. "What is it, Roger? What's wrong?"

"I just saw all the cardinals." On the screen the members of the college of cardinals were walking majestically into St. Peter's Basilica to pray to the Holy Spirit for guidance as the conclave at the Sistine Chapel was about to start.

The procession was headed by Eugenio Cardinal Robitelli, a man of the Roman nobility and the odds-on favorite to become the next pope, according to TV commentator and Vatican Church expert Father Ron Farrell. He had been reporting all week on the event and authoritatively pretending to provide his viewers with inside information about the conversations and deals going on behind the Vatican walls.

"Look! There's Uncle Brian!" Meghan excitedly pointed to the TV. "And there's Uncle Gus!" When Cardinal Robitelli walked in front, of the TV camera, there was conspicuously no "There's Uncle Gino!" from the Kelly children.

Ordinarily, Cardinal Robitelli would have had the conclave wrapped up, but Pope Peter II's first and only encyclical was released on the very day of his death, which happened to be August 15, the feast of Our Lady of the Assumption. His death had completely taken the Church by surprise. The encyclical created a debate like nothing ever heard before. He had taken on issues that nobody wanted to touch: marriage annulments, the role of women in the Church, the poor, disease, birth control, and famine.

Senator Lane and his divorced wife were fortunate beneficiaries of the encyclical, as were many other divorced Catholic couples. The pope spelled out Church dogma that impinged upon civil law was no longer mandatory and divorced couples with or without annulments were still welcome communicants.

"What he said about Africa, the family, faith, and social and economic justice was profound and visionary," wrote the *Washington Post.* "Church to Lead U.S." is what the headline of several prominent newspapers read.

Bill Kelly's encyclical demanded attention all around the world. His thoughts, following those of his predecessor's *avviso,* would challenge the Church and its followers as both advanced into the third millennium.

Had the family structure permanently endangered society? Were decency and respect no longer important in today's world? Was this a what's-in-it-for-me society? The question asked more and more was, Were the people of the world experiencing a culture of death and violence? Since the release of the encyclical all these questions and others were open for discussion on street corners and in newsrooms, boardrooms, college campuses factories, and especially in Churches of all denominations, synagogues, and mosques. The *New York Times* had a lead editorial on the encyclical and printed a twenty-three-page supplement. Magazines had the encyclical featured prominently on their covers.

The pope's words on the life issue remained firm and unambiguous:

Good moral principles must create good civics and good policy. Everyone must exercise strong personal standards on the questions pro-life, pro-family, pro-poor, and other matters upon which the Church has clear views. However, Catholic politicians may be comforted that their Church will not desert them when they are abiding by the civil law of their land, but they must personally vote for those measures which are fundamental to the teachings of Jesus Christ.

"This was only the second occasion in our lifetime when a Church matter dominated the news. The first was Vatican II," declared the secretary-general of the United Nations.

Cardinal Robitelli might have had enough votes locked up at the upcoming conclave, but Billy Kelly's last message was building and beginning to have a powerful impact. "It will change the debate if not the direction of the Church and society forever," said religion editor Ken Woodward of *Newsweek. Time* magazine, in a cover story by Jay Carney, wrote under a picture of Billy Kelly, MESSAGE WON'T DIE!

People were talking about the message all over the world, and for the first time in the history of the Church, Catholics in America could feel that somebody really understood their concerns in the new millennium.

In talking about the conclave, TV analysts were trying to sound knowledgeable in predicting the winner. "It will be the Jesuit from Milan," said one.

"No, definitely Robitelli," said another. "Definitely another Italian noble."

"What about the cardinal from Africa?" queried the next. "Or maybe the cardinal from Munich? He is certainly a contender. Is a black pope possible?"

All these remarks and predictions were generating big news from the Vatican. "Who will be the next pope?" was the title of a one-hour special on ABC.

"The Catholic Church is at a crossroads," pronounced NBC. Comiskey and Motupu got prominent mention, but not as much as Robitelli.

Ed Kirby had just returned to his post in Rome from a private White House meeting with the president. After the Mass at St. Peter's as the conclave began, Ed and Kathy joined the ambassador to the Holy See from Slovenia, Steve Frietz, and his wife, Josephine, for lunch at Ignazio's Ristorante in Piazza Sant'Ignazio. Also along were the ambassadors from Brazil and Canada and their wives.

"We can hear on the television if there is any news from the conclave," said Josephine. Steve had been a personal friend to three popes.

"Nothing is going to happen for at least a few days. They're more concerned with the incredible impact of the encyclical than with electing the next pope. That was an unintentional master stroke by Kelly. He is the only pope who is more powerful in death than he was in life. *Salute!* God bless the pope," Steve toasted.

"Hear, hear!" the other ambassadors agreed.

The group talked affectionately about the Kelly encyclical over lunch and its effect in their respective countries. But they kept coming back to the conclave.

"But don't you think Robitelli has it locked up?" the Brazilian ambassador asked.

"Locked up?" Steve questioned. "The conclave? Let me tell you an old saying around here. You walk in the favorite, you walk out...a cardinal."

"A wiser voice in Rome doesn't exist," Kirby complimented his friend.

Mario, their waiter, had served food to some of the world's top academics, statesmen, clerics, and businessmen for thirty years. He never hesitated to converse as though he were seated at the table and asked the ambassadors what five things the college of cardinals should be looking for in the new pope. Kirby wrote his top five requirements on the menu, which, as it happened, would be framed and hung on the restaurant wall.

1. A humble man with a deep religious faith, but who sees the many challenges and threats to the Church ahead.
2. A consensus builder, especially with fallen-away Catholics and women. Very important.
3. A person who possesses administrative as well as diplomatic skills.
4. Able to rebuild the foundation of the Church in the new millennium.
5. An effective communicator who is multilingual.

The ambassador from Canada examined the menu adorned with Ed Kirby's words of wisdom and said, "I don't need five. There's only one question to answer. 'How are you going to get Catholics to come back to hear and learn the message of Christ?' That's the single biggest challenge."

In the Brazilian ambassador's opinion, "The most serious problems facing the Church and the next pope will be the spread of militant religious extremism, especially Islamic fundamentalists and the Eastern Orthodoxy."

All nodded wisely. It was known among Vatican diplomats that there was a strong possibility that the Russian Orthodox Church hierarchy, encouraged by certain neo-Communists in the government, might well have been behind the pope's mysterious exposure to the African virus that killed him. But no member of the international diplomatic community would ever be caught openly expressing the view that such a possibility was valid, now that Russia was part of the North Atlantic Treaty Organization and had helped settle the Balkan wars diplomatically.

"In any case," Kirby said to his peers, "Bill Kelly, whether or not intentionally, delivered a stroke of public relations genius in the content and timing of his encyclical. Perhaps the work truly is a case of divine intervention. It gives the world and media something healthy to focus on instead of treating the conclave and the election like an American political campaign with all its negativism."

In the back-and-forth banter among these expert Vatican watchers, each tried to extract something of value from his fellow ambassadors that he then could pass on to his head of state. Then Ed Kirby made a telling observation.

"After Pope John Paul II broke the four-hundred-and-fifty-year streak of Italian popes and Bill became the second to do so, we have acquired many new non-Italian cardinals. In some ways the leading princes of the Church have lately become traveling salesmen, visiting each other, helping out in national emergencies like hurricanes and revolutions, subtly promoting themselves. They also travel to Rome more often."

Ambassador Frietz leaned across the table. "That's right, my friend. Frequent travel to meet and assist other cardinals is apt to be a clear sign of papal ambition. Maybe we ought to start recording certain travel schedules."

"*Sì*, like Frequent Flyer Pope," said the ever-engaging Italian waiter.

The last word the gathered ambassadors heard was that the conclave had retired for the evening without electing a pope and would resume the following day. No surprise. Saying *buonasera* and *ciao* to their fellow ambassadors and their wives, Ed and Kathy headed back to the residence at the Gianicolo. His voice mail had a few messages from the State Department along with several press calls. Ed turned on the TV in his study and began to write his letter of resignation to the president of the United States. Five years as ambassador was enough. He loved the job, but without Billy Kelly around, he wanted to go back to Chicago.

At five A.M. the letter was finished, and with a few hours of sleep behind him, Ambassador Kirby went for his usual several-mile run through the Roman streets and paths. When he got to St. Peter's, he could see hundreds of people on an all-night vigil, looking up at the balcony as if expecting a pope to appear. That of course was not about to happen, at least not for a while.

After returning from his run, he showered, shaved, dressed, and went to his office across the street from Circo Massimo, where the famous chariot race took place in the movie *Ben Hur*. For a moment he visualized the early Christians being mauled by wild beasts here and in the Colosseum. Then the realities of the day set in. Several additional messages had around from the State Department wanting to know who was going to be pope and asking if Opus Dei still would be in power at the Vatican with the new one.

How stupid, Kirby thought. *The State Department thinks Opus Dei is some sort of militant anti-American group of right-wing extremists. They actually believe that.*

"It is amazing how out of touch State has become," Ed Kirby said to Kathy as he showed her his letter of resignation. "Even worse is how inept the White House is in evaluating the culture, tradition, and importance of religion in various countries. The Vatican is a valuable source of important information from all around the world. But sometimes Foggy Bottom seems more concerned about trade and how the new pope will get along with Opus Dei than about human rights and peace and stability in the world."

"It will be nice to go home again," Kathy mused.

"It suppose Maureen will miss Rome and the excitement here."

Kathy shook her head. "Maureen will be happy to go back to the States. She and Colleen became great friends, and I guess our daughter is thinking of going to a college in or near Boston."

"It's been a great experience, Kathy, for all of us. Who knows what's next? Hopefully we'll have some grandkids and we can tell them about Bill Kelly the pope fisherman."

✛ ✛ ✛

Meghan Kelly was putting Roger's new back-to-school clothes away and looking out of the corner of her eye at the TV. Roger was watching the events from Rome. She also noticed a photo of Bill and Mary Kelly's wedding on the fireplace. Just then the phone rang. "Hello. Colleen, we were wondering where you were. Still at the admissions office?"

Meghan listened a moment and let out a joyous cry. "How wonderful! A full scholarship? Books and everything?"

"That's right, Meg. Boston College said they recognized that popes do not have pensions or life insurance policies. I'll be home as soon as I can make it."

"We'll be waiting. We're watching the conclave. It's kind of strange. Being on the outside looking in on the Vatican again through TV."

Meghan hung up the phone and stared out the window, looking down to the fishing dock below. The beautiful, bright, late-August sunlight was glancing off the boats. She saw a tall, young, rugged, and handsome fisherman walking toward the house carrying a duffel bag over his shoulder. She froze for a few seconds. Then she heard Roger call out, "Meghan, it's Ryan. He's home from the sea!"

ACKNOWLEDGMENTS

I would like to dedicate this labor of love, *The Accidental Pope*, to my loyal and wonderful wife, Kathy, and our six children, Ray Jr., Edward, Julie, Nancy, Kate, and Maureen. And of course, our grandson, James Flynn Long, and his dad, Jamie Long.

Thanks to my brothers Dennis, Steve and wife Bridie, and Al for their loyalty and support throughout the years. In telling Dennis how much he means to me, I also want to thank his wife, Rosemary, and their four wonderful children—Sheila and Danny Kelly, Colleen, Dunnie, and John Mannion, Tara and Kaitlyn and their special grandson Brian, and also Jake for their love.

To our trusted friends the Foley Family—Jerry, Marianne, and son Michael—who is a real credit. A special thank-you to Matthew from Catholic University of America for his help and research, along with Patrick, Caitlyn, Meghan, Jeremiah, and Brendan. To Mike Degulis, a great friend, proofreader, and attorney, and his parents Janice and Dr. Joe. My deepest thanks to dear friend Kristen Hansen for her tireless effort in helping make this book a reality.

What a pleasure to get to know a genius, noted bestselling author Robin Moore, who taught me so much about writing and the ability to express my thoughts and experiences in words. My gratitude to his dear wife, Mary Olga, and his brother, Attorney John Moore, who suggested contacting St. Martin's Press with the draft manuscript. Richard J. Lynch and his wife, Sara, can indeed be given credit for the idea in the construction of this novel.

To John Kilcommons and Suzie and their children Jack, Meghan, and Maureen. John is special and has always been there for me. Laurie, Brian Wallace, and sons Cullen and Brendan, you can't get more loyal friends.

Thanks to State Representative Jim Hart and Professor Bob Evans.

There are so many other people who have touched my life and helped me with this book who I would like to acknowledge and say a special thank-you to: Jim and Kathy Long, a better family Julie could have never met. Laura and Garrath Conachy. Katie and Bob Hayden. Authors Doris and Dick Goodwin. Joe Fisher, Charlie, Mary Burke, Attorney Harry Grill and his wife, Betsy, who have always been there. Father Richard Shmaruk of St. Columbkille's Church for his advice and direction, and whose great writing skills should be encouraged. Monsignor Tom McDonnell, St. Augustine's Church. Roger Oliveira and parents Rogerio and Maria. John Hill, whose devotion to Our Lady of Fatima is unmatched and whose contributions to this book are deeply appreciated. Tom Coyne and his daughters.

The William Morris Agency, Jim Griffin and Mel Berger, better agents you could never have.

My pals Fran and Joan Coyne, their children and grandchildren. John and Carol and their children. Mary Downs, who will always be with us. Ted Downs and all his children and grandchildren. Brian and Kerry O'Hearn and their children. Frank and Maura Doyle and their children.

Friends at the U.S. Vatican Embassy. Mirella and Lou Giacolone, Evelyn McWade, Claudio Manno, Umberto Bernadini, Fabio Tombasi, Gerry Masaro, Giovanni, Marco Nasso, Piero Fratecceli, Stefano, Aida, Ofelia, Seri and Santiago and Livia Curzi.

Cardinal Law and the late Cardinal O'Connor of New York, true men of God! Boston labor leader Joe Quilty. Uncle Eddie and Mary Kirby and their children.

Lloyd MacDonald, Monsignor Tim Dolan (a priest's priest), Paul Quinn, Fran and Franny Duggan. Jack Barry, Will McDonough, Ronnie Perry, Vinnie Collins, Don Murray, Sis and Doc Tynan. A great man, John Dorion, and his dear wife, Lil. Bob and Kathy Walton. Mickey's at the Pantheon. Agusto at the Giancolo, Joe Callahan and Frank Fallon. Father Gerry Barry. Dan Horgan of the *South Boston Tribune*. Joe Mullaney and Dave Gavitt, and my Providence College teammates. Scoop Canavan, Father James Quigley, O.P., Jimmy Foley from J.J. Foley's. Dave Burke and Ned McGinley of the The Ancient Order of Hibernians. A real gentleman, Jeremiah Foley, and his wife, Eileen (gone, but not forgotten). Evelyn and Ken Lyons and all my good friends at N.A.G.E. My godchildren: Sheila Kelly, Jeremiah Foley, Ann Flynn, Jennifer Hurley, Matthew Doyle, Maura Coyne, Kevin Paul, Owen Costello, and Michael Coyne.

Marie Donovan, Gerry Dooley, John Nucci, John Martin. Neighbors Rosie and Bernie McCarthy, Jack Nee and Ellie Matulivich, Anne, Mickey, and Mary Burke. Ann and Kevin Phelan, Attorney Phil Fina.

To my great parish, Gate of Heaven, all my neighbors of South Boston, where I am so proud to have lived all my life.

Two outstanding physicians, Dr. Sheila MacDonnell and Dr. Kenneth MacDonnell, at St. Elizabeth's Hospital. Ray and Mary Teatum. Paul O'Dwyer. All at the Farragut House. New York City policeman Steve McDonald and wife, Patti Ann, who taught us how to forgive one another. Tricia and Frankie Murray, in memory of Eddie Sheehy. Attorney Phil Moran and wife Carol. Attorney Dennis Lynch of New York, a heroic pro-life leader of Catholic Alliance. Gerry and Anne Ridge. Father Jim Lane, Dr. Al Arcidi, a special friend, Betty Mahoney, Pat Morelli, Charlene Bizokas, Dottie Mahoney, Anne McDonnell, Janet Healey, and Geri O'Shea.

My great dad and mom, Steve and Lil Flynn, Kathy's dad and mom, Frank and Winnie Coyne. Four wonderful parents.

To the entire staff at St. Martin's Press and to respected editor Diane Higgins and Patricia Fernandez, with gratitude for their confidence.

Lastly, Ray Jr., for your passionate devotion to your Catholic faith. Your personal courage is an inspiration to all of us. We're proud of you, Ray.

And of course, my deepest respect and love for my friend Pope John Paul II.

Ray Flynn, October 2000